CHRISTMAS *Sweater* WEATHER

Also by Jaqueline Snowe

Snowed In for Christmas

CHRISTMAS
Sweater
WEATHER

Jaqueline Snowe

FOREVER
New York   Boston

Copyright © 2024 by Jaqueline Snowe

Cover design and illustration by Sarah Congdon
Cover copyright © 2024 by Hachette Book Group, Inc.

Forever
Hachette Book Group
1290 Avenue of the Americas, New York, NY 10104
read-forever.com
@readforeverpub

First Edition: October 2024

Forever is an imprint of Grand Central Publishing. The Forever name and logo are registered trademarks of Hachette Book Group, Inc.

The publisher is not responsible for websites (or their content) that are not owned by the publisher.

The Hachette Speakers Bureau provides a wide range of authors for speaking events. To find out more, go to hachettespeakersbureau.com or email HachetteSpeakers@hbgusa.com.

Forever books may be purchased in bulk for business, educational, or promotional use. For information, please contact your local bookseller or the Hachette Book Group Special Markets Department at special.markets@hbgusa.com.

Library of Congress Cataloging-in-Publication Data
Names: Snowe, Jaqueline, author.
Title: Christmas sweater weather / Jaqueline Snowe.
Description: First edition. | New York ; Boston : Forever, 2024.
Identifiers: LCCN 2024012025 | ISBN 9781538739839 (trade paperback) | ISBN 9781538739846 (ebook)
Subjects: LCGFT: Christmas fiction. | Romance fiction. | Novels.
Classification: LCC PS3619.N693 C57 2024 | DDC 813/.6—dc23/eng/20240322
LC record available at https://lccn.loc.gov/2024012025

ISBN: 9781538739839 (trade paperback), 9781538739846 (ebook)

Printed in the United States of America

CCD

10   9   8   7   6   5   4   3   2

To the family you create for yourself. Found families are one of my favorite things to read, and write, because surrounding yourself with a village of love is the best thing you can do for yourself.

CHAPTER ONE

CHARLOTTE

Midwestern weather was like a toddler who refused to nap or eat—out of control and untamable. Sixty degrees one day, twenty the next—it was like it was trying to win a competition of how many seasons can we fit within seventy hours. Well, you won, Illinois. Congrats. Hats off to you, you temperamental toddler.

My fingers ached from gripping the steering wheel so damn hard. My knuckles were white and my palms sweaty as I held on for dear life. Snow covered the road, secret patches of ice underneath it threatening to off me. My heart leaped into my throat as I skidded to the left, then right, and then straightened. *Breathe. Focus. Remain calm.*

Needing someone to blame for this, I gritted my teeth and cursed my brother. I would be at home, in sweats and preparing for my head coaching interview. This was my dream job, and even though the athletic director insisted I was *too young*, I was hell-bent on proving him wrong. But instead of preparing my pitch on how I would run the Prairie State

High School girls' softball team, I was driving to a ski resort for my brother and his stupid pre-wedding trip.

He refused to call it a bachelorette or bachelor party, but that's what it was. We all knew it. Yes, I loved him and his fiancée. They were my best friends. Yes, this was a fun idea in theory. Yes, I'd probably have a good time once I got up there—if I made it alive. Everyone else had headed up yesterday while I finished up the workweek because my students had a huge project due this morning, so carpooling hadn't been an option. Hence me driving alone in terrible weather, risking my life to go skiing. I also did it to appease the nagging feeling that my brother and his fiancée needed this trip.

Wedding planning was getting to them, and I worried that it was becoming too much. It wasn't my place to speak up, but driving in this blizzard of death to support them was my way of helping. If they wanted this weekend of fun, then they'd have it.

Gah! A drift at least five feet tall crept closer and closer, and I yanked the wheel to the left hoping to avoid it, but there was a semitruck coming in hot behind me. I didn't want to die. Not like this, on I-55 in the middle of nowhere. I had things I wanted to do! People to meet! Food to try! Wine to drink and ultimately regret! "Please, please stop," I cried, panic flaring in my chest to the point it ached.

No one answered, not even the voice in the back of my head. I swore my soul left my body as the semi got closer in my rearview mirror. The drift grew closer ahead of me. The car couldn't slow down. There wasn't a way out. It was a snowdrift-semi sandwich with my car in the middle. I closed my eyes, praying it'd be quick, and *oof.*

My head jerked forward, smacking the wheel with the force of a tornado. Pain exploded throughout my forehead and neck. Something sputtered. A loud thud. *Please let me pass out.* The screeching of tires blurred while my own heart rate pounded in my ears. This was it. My parents would find me in a stained crewneck sweater and mismatched socks. They'd be so proud of me.

Wincing, I waited for darkness to take over, but after thirty seconds, nothing happened. Did I survive the sandwich? I blinked one eye open, and then the other. My face got to know my steering wheel very well, and I rubbed a finger over my nose. *Sonofa.* That hurt. Pain was good. That meant I was still among the living.

At least, for now. My car had wedged itself into the snowdrift so far that light only streamed from the back window. Did I live here now? In my Mazda Igloo?

Incoming call.

I jumped in my seat at the loud intrusion of my car stereo. The number danced across the dash, and my shoulders sagged in relief. My brother. My fingers trembled as I hit the answer button. "Christian, hi."

"Where the hell are you? I want to ski but Penny insists on waiting for you." Loud music blared in the background, and I squinted at the stereo. Eleven a.m. Only my party animal brother would be this energetic and probably intoxicated this early.

"Uh, no, go ahead without me." I cleared my throat, my eyes welling up as the adrenaline gripped me from head to toe. I almost died. I didn't. But almost. One didn't just get over that in two minutes. I used my left hand to rub the back of my neck and willed myself to take a deep breath. Christian didn't need to worry about me. He deserved fun. "Go skiing."

"What's wrong?" Just like that, his tone changed. "Turn that music off. Char, what's going on?"

No more loud music, only my brother's angry breathing.

"N-nothing, why?"

"You're a shit liar, and your voice is off. Are you okay?"

I pinched the bridge of my nose. "I got into a little accident."

"Are you hurt? Where are you?"

"What happened? Oh my, is Char okay?" Penny's voice carried over the phone, and I could picture her little pixie face and bright red hair. I loved my brother's fiancée, almost more than him. She was about the only human on the planet capable of being with my brother forever, and God bless her for that.

Hearing her concern caused my tears to spill over. There was no way to avoid the truth now. I sniffled. "I'm fine. Just skidded into a drift."

"You're crying. You *never* cry." Christian's voice softened. "What mile marker are you at? We can come help you."

Great question. I should've looked at my surroundings before becoming a permanent part of an igloo. Snow covered each door, and even though I knew what would happen, I tried opening my side. Nothing. Cool. I was stuck. "I don't know."

"Are you able to walk and look?"

I swallowed. "I can't... get out of the car."

He sucked in a breath, and I could almost hear his mind whirling. Christian might be a party boy, goofball, and general menace to society, but he was the most loyal and caring person I knew. We rarely fought and had remained close as we grew up, and now he was in full-blown fix-it mode. "Okay, you're snowed in your car, somewhere on the highway, without a way out or to tell me your location. Shit, Charmander, this is bad."

"I'm sorry." My voice broke again. The use of my nickname made the tears come harder.

"What? No, I'm not mad *at* you. I just want you to be okay."

Penny mumbled something in the background that I didn't quite catch. "Hey, great idea, babe," my brother said. "Send your location to Hayden."

"Hayden?" I repeated, my face growing red despite no one being able to actually see me. "Hayden Porter?"

"You hit your head that hard? Yes, *Hayden Porter*. He couldn't make it here last night because of Gwen, so he's on his way up now. I'll call him, give him a heads-up."

"Wait, no!" I shouted, unable to produce a single, rational reason why this was a terrible idea. My brother's best friend was my personal fantasy and single biggest regret combined into one broad-shouldered, giant, walking Greek God. *Okay, maybe I did bump my head.* I now pictured him as a Greek statue with his perfectly unperfect nose and dark gray eyes that paired with his suntanned skin from always being outdoors. He'd feed me grapes and flash that dangerous smile my way.

"Charlotte, send him a pin of your location now."

My brother ended the call, bringing me back to reality. *Breath in, out.* Unless I wanted to be the mayor and only resident of this car igloo, I should text him my location. Even if it meant having Hayden find me this way. Would he drive me the rest of the way too? In his car? Us alone?

My heart raced for an entirely different reason. I'd done my best to never be alone with him after *that night* three years ago. His beautiful baby girl Gwen was always there, or my brother, or their friends they had somehow kept since high school. Honestly, how? Making friends as an adult is hard. Unless you work with them, you had to actually leave your house to see other people, and frankly, I didn't want to do that most days.

Ever, okay? I never wanted to leave my house. Especially not in winter when the cold tried to eat my face. My phone pinged.

Christian: YOUR LOCATION. NOW.

Focus. Right. I sent my brother and Hayden a location pin and leaned back in my seat. I knew I'd have to see Hayden at the ski resort, but I had practiced my fake smile and pleasant talking points that would be needed around the group. Where five of us all sat around drinking and eating and skiing. Not…the two of us in a car alone. Not with him rescuing me from my igloo. Maybe I could live here forever? I had snacks and four pairs of socks. It'd be a short lifespan but filled with joy.

I rubbed my temples and wished I had brought pain meds. The throbbing at my skull had nothing to do with Hayden and our past, well, lack of a past, and more to do with the fact that my face became a steering wheel pancake five minutes ago.

Silver linings. I was that kinda person, always focusing on the bright side.

I was alive. That was great. I could still eat and drink to my heart's delight.

My car still had power, which meant I had heat.

I could move my limbs. Again, another huge win.

Incoming call.

"I sent the dang location, Christian," I answered, so annoyed that my irritation snuck out.

"Hello to you too."

"Hayden." I sucked in a breath and felt the color draining from my face. I must match the snow now. We were twinning in paleness. "Hello. Hi."

Could I be more of a dork? Shame danced along my neck and down my spine. I shouldn't care what he thought of me, not after that night, yet I still wanted him to view me as someone other than his best friend's kid sister.

"Are you alright?" His voice was deep and low with concern. "Christian said you were in an accident and I needed to rescue you?"

"Of course he did." I sighed.

"Were you not?"

"No, I'm stuck in a snowdrift, have no idea where I am, and can't get out of my car." Saying the situation aloud made me laugh. "This is a scene from a terrible movie. How is this my life? Why did I wear my knee-high orange and yellow socks today of all days?"

Hayden didn't answer but I swore I could *feel* him annoyed. He had a habit of breathing heavier whenever I was around. Great for the ego, knowing he could keep his calm demeanor around everyone except me.

"How do you not know where you're at?" he asked, his voice not kind.

"Because I didn't pay attention to the street signs when all I saw was the snowdrift and semi wanting to make a sandwich out of me," I snapped. A shiver cascaded down my body at the reminder. "It was terrifying. I thought... I thought I was gonna die so I'm sorry for not—"

"Hey, whoa," he said, his rough voice gentler than before. "Char, it's okay. I'll find you. I'll get you out."

I closed my eyes and rested my forehead against the steering wheel. Despite our history that I refused to think about, I felt safe with Hayden. Ever resourceful, reliable, and protective, he would do whatever it took to help me. He was an absolute teddy bear on the inside, total mush when it came to people he cared about. I'd seen how he treated my brother, his parents, his daughter, even me. Shame hit me hard, almost harder than the steering wheel to the face. Of course Hayden would make sure I was safe. He'd never let me remain hurt because he viewed me like a little sister, and if there was one thing Hayden cared most about? It was family.

"Okay. Okay," I repeated, my too-tight muscles relaxing at the thought of him saving me.

"What time did you leave this morning?"

"An hour ago."

"Perfect. I left forty-five minutes ago, so I shouldn't be too far behind. Now, do you remember passing the tractor store?"

I blinked. "Yes, because it reminded me of the time I tried to steal a tractor as a prank but didn't realize I couldn't drive one. Too many clutches."

"Ah, yes." Hayden laughed. The bastard had a rich, joyful laugh that made angel wings double in size and rainbows shoot out of flowers. "That was a fun summer."

It was also the summer I went from crushing on Hayden to falling head over heels, madly in love with him. I cleared my throat. That summer didn't contain the best memories for me. "Right, uh, the tractor store."

"I'm passing it now."

Neither of us said anything, but his breathing carried through the phone. It was enough for me. The dark confines of the car had started to make me nervous, claustrophobia creeping into my mind. What if I never got out? I could joke about being mayor, but my sense of humor had limits. Especially when it came to potential death. I must've whimpered or something, because he sucked in a breath. "Charlotte, are you hurt?"

"Not really. Bruised my face, but that's it. I'm... not loving the car right now. I don't want to be mayor anymore."

"Mayor?"

"Of the Mazda Igloo. I'm the only resident, so I'd be the de facto mayor," I said. "Obviously."

"Only you, Charlotte."

He said my name all grumbly and soft, and once upon a time, I fantasized about him saying my name as he declared his love for me. *Yes, Charlotte, I love you too and want a life with you and to be your best friend and have inside jokes and coach a team with you.* But I learned all too well that would never happen. I tried. He rejected me. Not even a little *no thank you* rejection. It was a *don't touch me ever again* rejection and a *you're like a sister to me* rejection, which, on a list of the worst ways to have your heart broken, was in the top five.

That was three years ago, and it still stung.

Had we ever talked about it? No.

Would we? I'd rather die mayor of the Mazda Igloo.

But neither of those facts kept my imagination in line when he said my name that way. It brought back all the memories—and unrequited feelings—that dominated my early twenties. Where I swore his gaze lingered on me a few seconds too long or he'd always put his hand on my lower back. I misread every interaction we had, and that was on me. It just sucked my heart never got the memo that we were *not* in love with Hayden Porter, single dad to the cutest baby girl ever.

"Wait, I think I see something up ahead. Shit."

"What?"

"There's a semi off to the right side of the road and skid marks into . . . oh, honey."

"Don't *oh, honey* me. What do you see?" My heart raced at all the scenarios in my head. Did he somehow read my mind thinking about our kiss that night? Did he know I still thought about him even though he made his feelings very clear?

"I think... I think your clothes fell out of your trunk, and well, you have a red bra and panties hanging on your exhaust pipe."

CHAPTER TWO

HAYDEN

Charlotte Calhoun had a unique talent for making me smile while simultaneously making me lose my shit. She'd lived under my skin for years due to her quick wit and sense of humor. That was her dark green Mazda alright, jam-packed into a monster of a snowdrift. The trunk had popped open, and sure enough, Charlotte's clothes were strewn about. She took what she needed and tossed them in the back like that was enough.

I'd seen her do that a hundred times before. Once when we went to the lake, once when we went to the beach with our families together, and hell, even on a road trip.

Maybe, after this trip, she'd learn her lesson and bring a fucking suitcase. There was no reason everyone had to see her red underwear in the wind. Especially with all the lace and strings...

Not her. Never her. I forced the blip of attraction away.

"I put it there! Yes. To be flagged down!" she said, her voice going an octave higher.

She almost made me laugh.

"Thought you were stuck and couldn't open the door." My lips curved up, but I was desperate not to smile. That was the thing with her. She was utterly ridiculous in the most charming way. The damn woman had no idea her personality pulled in people like a magnet. Even in high school, she never realized her charisma. It's why she was a hell of a teacher; she made everyone feel special for being authentically themselves. Her confidence and genuine heart were hard to find. She was one of the best humans, and you knew it after being around her for even three minutes.

"I can't. Couldn't. I crawled through the back seat and put it there."

"You found your way into the trunk, tied a pair of red panties and bra on the exhaust, and instead of waiting outside the car like a normal person, you crawled back inside?"

"Ew. Don't say *panties*. That's on my no list. But that's what I did. Yup."

I laughed. I couldn't help it. "We're revisiting your no list later, but, Char, we both know you're lying."

"Fine. Fine!"

I shook my head, my damn grin stretching across my face. Life was never boring with Charlotte around. The woman got herself into the most bizarre situations, the present one included, and each time, she acted surprised, like she had no idea what happened. I put on my signal and pulled over, making sure not to be a hazard on the road before backing up toward her car. My truck would easily pull her out if I had enough traction.

And to think my parents convinced me to get four-wheel drive. They were right, this time. I'd be sure to tell them it happened *once* in all my years. When I was a teenager, they had installed a chalkboard in our living room with two columns. One tally for every time they were right, and one tally for every time I was, and it annoyed me to no end that they ended up right more than me. They said it kept me humble, but it only made me more competitive.

The momentary joy formed a rock in my gut. I'd have to erase that board, which was another harsh reminder that they were moving away. The constant pressure in my chest flared, the absolute sadness fighting with understanding. I loved my parents. They were my rock and helped me take care of Gwen. After playing in some crappy bar bands on and off for two years, the perfect opportunity showed up. They were offered to play together in a rock band and tour retirement homes in Arizona for one year, for a crazy amount of money. It was a dream for both of them to do something like this, and I couldn't let Gwen be the reason they wouldn't chase it. I'd always support them, but Gwen went to their house three times a week, saw them more than I did, and with their move...I had no idea what the hell I was gonna do. They were watching her for this damn pre-wedding trip, and it was their final weekend here. A goodbye weekend with Gwen. And finding a nanny or babysitter was becoming a nightmare.

I coughed into my fist, pushing the ache away. I'd worry about that after this weekend. Right now? I wanted to help Charlotte.

"I'm going to hook your car to my truck and try to tow you out," I said, still on the phone.

"Am I safe . . . in here?"

My chest tightened at how small she sounded. Charlotte was bold with a big personality, and hearing her sound scared felt like someone reached inside my body and squeezed my heart. My circle of people was small, six people whom I'd do anything for, and she was one of them. She might not know that, which was how I intended it to remain, but I'd move mountains for her. "I'll make sure you're safe."

I put on my gloves and hat, zipped up my coat, and grabbed the chains I kept under the driver's seat. Gwen's car seat was covered in Goldfish, and for the second time in minutes, my pulse raced. I missed my baby girl. I hated leaving her. Not seeing her face and knowing she was safe every second of the day caused me enormous amounts of stress. Becoming her father was singlehandedly the best thing ever to happen to me.

I thought baseball was my sole purpose to walk this earth, and it had been, until Gwen, and leaving her with my parents—people I trusted more than anyone in the world—still gutted me. Was Gwen worried I wouldn't come back . . . like her mom? Or did she forget about me? Either option seemed worse than the other, and my jaw tensed. What was I gonna do without my parents to bail me out during emergencies? Shit.

I willed my emotions down and focused on getting Charlotte out safely. I connected the chain to the back of my trunk and then carried it to hers. Her damn clothes were everywhere.

Reds and pinks and yellows. Lace. Small. Silky. I swallowed, hard, and tried my best to not picture my best friend's younger sister in these things. There was a time, once, for a moment, that I let myself cross that line, and I still hated myself for it. So much had changed since then. Some good, some bad, but the biggest thing was Gwen.

Christian and Penny, and Charlotte even, were the aunts and uncle by choice, not by blood. Christian helped me raise Gwen since Simone dropped her off at my door three years ago with a letter. Not a text or a call. A fucking *letter* saying she couldn't be a mom and reverted all parental rights to me. Coaching baseball at a D1 college meant long nights, and who would take her whenever I needed? Christian or my parents.

Who helped me when I lost my mind? Christian or my parents. And when my parents were in another state?

Christian had always been my best friend, but he was also…my family. To even think about Charlotte in any sexual way would be a slap in the face to him. I'd seen him react to her dipshit boyfriends, and I damn well knew I wasn't good enough for her either. I owed Christian the moon, and that was the only reason I agreed to drive up to a ski resort for two nights.

And why I was in this fun situation rescuing his sister, the woman who never quite left my mind.

"Damn, Charlotte." I had to touch the garments and ensure they were tucked in a weird, oddly smelling sports bag? Thank the Lord I wore gloves. They gave me a layer of protection from touching her panties.

For one split second, my mind went back to that night in the bar. When Charlotte approached me with cherry-red lips and a sinful matching dress that nearly killed me. The music blared, and the drinks flowed, and her damn smile drew me to her and she tasted like… *No.*

We never speak of that night, and for good reason. It was locked and tucked deep, much like all the best memories I had of her.

"Put it in neutral and sit tight," I commanded her. I hid my annoyance, but she got under my skin. So while I thought of Charlotte in the *oh, she's my best friend's younger sister* way from time to time, I realized we hadn't been alone in… years.

Shit.

I hooked the chain to the rear of her car and jogged to my truck. It didn't take much horsepower to pull her out of the drift, and once her entire car came into view, I put my truck in park. A flurry of anxiety nestled in my chest thinking about seeing her face-to-face. Not only was I concerned for her about the accident, but our past… it was messy. I always avoided being around her when it was just the two of us. Even when she helped out with Gwen, my mom or her brother would be there. It was like I didn't trust myself alone with her, and now there were three years of awkwardness squished into my front seat, where it was gonna be the two of us for the rest of the drive.

I was two steps away from her door when she fell out of the car, headfirst.

"Oh hello, ground. I missed you." She kissed the snow with her lips. "I'll never take you for granted, you cold bastard."

Charlotte plastered herself to the snow-covered grass and sighed long and contentedly. Her jeans hugged her ass, and sure enough, her long socks went to her knees and clashed with her fuzzy black boots. Her curly brown hair sat in a mess on top of her head, and *damn*. There was something about her that made me smile. Her unabashed joy. Her quiet confidence. Her goofy spirit that never seemed to break.

Well, that wasn't true. I had seen her eyes dim and her face contort in shame after I pushed her away that night. Despite it happening years ago, guilt still ate at me. I had had to tell her no, no matter how much it killed me. I shook my head as I continued to watch her on the ground. Why the fuck did she not wear a coat? I hissed at her thin sweater being her only winter gear.

"I've seen you throw up in your hands, Porter, so not a word from you right now. I'm reacquainting myself with land," she fired my way, still not looking at me.

"I wouldn't dare laugh." My lips quirked though, and I couldn't stop staring at her. She looked okay and not injured. No bones were broken or shaped weird. No visible blood. Her neck seemed fine, long and covered with small tattoos I had no idea she had.

Why would you, dipshit?

God, I wanted to know what they were. Were they flowers? Shapes? Lines from her favorite book?

"I'm familiarized with land again. Thanks for waiting."

She pushed herself up onto her knees and stood, and only then did I see her face.

I sucked in a breath, alarm coursing through me. Blood dripped from her forehead, and there were two very large bruises around her eyes. "Charlotte."

"Oh no. My face is still…here, right?" She smacked her hands on her cheeks and then winced. "Blah, that hurt. Hey! I'm not numb. That's…good?"

"Let me see." I closed the distance, hating seeing blood. Her creamy skin held only two freckles, right in the middle of one cheek, and I knew that because I spent way too much time staring at her when I was at their house as a teenager. Those two little dots were so out of place yet fit her perfectly. Adorable, cute, sexy even. I didn't wait before cupping one side of her face with my left hand and using my other to assess the damage. "Does this hurt?"

She tensed, her entire body stiffer than a block of ice. "Uh, you're touching me."

"Yes." I pushed her forehead gently. She didn't wince. "I'm trying to see if I need to call an ambulance instead of taking you to the hospital."

"Oh, none of that. I'm…fine." Her voice sounded flustered and off, like she very well wasn't fine. "Great. Dandy. Ready to pretend I give a crap about skiing."

Our eyes met, and I laughed. "I hate skiing too."

"Christian is the worst," she said, but without real venom to her words.

Her brown eyes were dark. There wasn't a difference between the pupil and the iris. Her lashes were the same rich color, longer than they had any right being, and a guy could get lost in her gaze. There were reasons people wrote songs about brown-eyed girls.

Even my baby girl's eyes could make me do things I'd never imagine. Dancing to "Baby Shark"? Pretending I was a princess with her? Drinking imaginary tea? Yeah. Gwen only had to bat her big brown eyes at me, and I'd do it.

Women with brown eyes didn't realize their true power. If they did, our country would be led by them, and we wouldn't have nearly the issues we did.

"Y'all need any help?"

I jumped, annoyed that I let myself fall into Char's orbit. A very large man with a huge smile waved at us from outside a semitruck. I removed my hands from Charlotte and shoved them back into my pockets, where things were safer and warmer. "I think we're alright for now. You the one who skidded off the road?"

"Yeah. About hit this poor woman's car. Thankfully, I didn't."

I shuddered at the thought. *I thought I was gonna die.* I still hadn't digested Char's words and wasn't sure I could. "I'm thankful everyone is okay. You need anything from us?"

"Nah, might just camp here for the night and wait for the blizzard to settle."

"Take care," I said, waving as he got back into his cab. I returned my attention back to Char, who stood frozen, except for her trembling body. "Hey, you're safe now."

She nodded but her face was ghostly. Without overthinking it, I rubbed my hands up and down her arms until she looked up at me. Those gorgeous eyes gutted me, again.

"I-I think the a-adrenaline needs an o-out. T-that's all."

"Okay, honey." *Shit.* The name slipped out. I called Gwen *honey bear* all the time. "Sorry, girl-dad oops."

Charlotte smiled. The first real smile I'd seen from her in...a long time. Seeing her pale pink lips curve up and light entering her eyes had me shifting my weight left to right.

"You're a good dad, Hop. Gwen is lucky."

Hop, short for Hayden Orion Porter. It was the dumb nickname Christian gave me at fourteen when I thought I was cool as hell. But Charlotte stared at me and used my nickname...

My face heated, and I cleared my throat. "We'll leave your car here. Get your stuff, lock it, then I'll call a tow company to take it home."

Her eyes grew to saucers. "Home? I need to drive back—"

"I'll take you home too. It's fine." I waved my hand in the air, dismissing her.

"You and me?" she asked, the warmth leaving her voice. If anything, her tone matched the winter wind blowing around us.

"Yes. I'm driving you." *Damn.* That came out like a bossy growl. My coaching voice leaked through time to time, which often led me into trouble.

Char wet her bottom lip with her tongue and sighed. "Fine. *Fine.*"

"Don't look so grateful."

She shot me a glare that almost made me smile again. She was adorable. And cold. The tips of her ears had turned pink, and she shivered. "Come on," I said, quickly unhooking my truck from her car. "Get in the front and sit by the heater."

"What about my stuff?"

"You, warm up." I pointed at her and raised my brows. I used that look to stare down pissant coaches who made up rules and umpires who forgot how to use their own eye-balls. I'd made grown men cower with my stern look, but not Charlotte.

"I don't have to listen to you, *Coach*." She huffed before moving to her trunk and shoving all the bright things into the back of my car. The red lingerie was still hooked to her exhaust, and I fought the urge to remind her. Did I just grab them to not embarrass her more? Or would that be worse?

Definitely worse.

"Is there a reason you don't enjoy packing like a normal person?"

If she could shoot daggers out of her eyes, they'd stab me in the heart. "I was in a rush, and forgive me for not assum-ing I'd be stuck in a drift with *you*."

I held up my hands. "Whoa, I didn't do anything wrong here."

"Right. Of course not." Her answering fake smile seemed strange on her pretty face. Her lips twisted in a scowl, and the warmth I had sworn I observed in her eyes was long gone. If anything, I sensed a new tone. One I didn't care for.

"Char, hey, what's wrong?" I gently grabbed her elbow with two fingers and waited for her to look at me. It took a few seconds, but then she faced me, her big, brown doe eyes swirling with . . . *anger*?

"Nothing. I'm fine." She yanked her arm out of my reach. "Just rattled from almost dying. That's all."

Right. I was being an ass. I exhaled, a large plume of mist billowing around me from the frigid temperatures, and put my hand on her shoulder. That seemed like a nice, friendly, innocent gesture. Nothing unpleasant in a gentle arm touch between pals. "I'm really glad you're safe. I can't imagine how scary it was."

She swallowed hard and did that fake tight smile bullshit again. "I'll be alright."

"You have everything you need?"

She dropped the clothes, patted her pockets, and then her eyes went wide. "My phone! Shit. That could have been bad."

She went to the side of her car. I tried, albeit not very hard, to *not* stare at her ass, but the jeans were torture. They hugged her curves as she swayed her hips. Charlotte had been an athlete her entire life, something she and I had in common, and it was clear she kept in shape, because *Goddamn*. Her thick thighs and round ass were all muscle, and something like lust grew hot and deep in my gut.

Christian's sister. Off-limits.

She needs a partner, a guy who can give her the attention she deserves.

Don't do it. Close your fucking eyes.

The muscle in my cheek contracted as Charlotte jogged toward the passenger side of my truck, the reality of the situation hitting me. I'd have to talk to her on the drive up, something I had avoided since that night we kissed.

CHAPTER THREE

CHARLOTTE

I couldn't sit still. My left leg bounced and my right foot tingled and my heart raced faster than the time I challenged myself to sprint upstairs without breathing. I crossed my legs, then uncrossed, and then pulled my knees up to my chest.

Mr. Silent and Sexy wasn't helping either. He hadn't said a word since we'd gotten in the truck. My face flushed red, and my mouth seemed too dry. I wanted a huge sip of—

"Shit!"

Hayden jerked the truck to the right, his gaze slicing to me. "What? What is it?"

"I left my water bottle back in my car. What if someone steals it? It has my stickers on it, and that collection might be my pride and joy. You have a child, I have my stickers. You get it."

His jaw twitched. Typical Hayden. I'd seen that action a million and a half times since I'd known him. Call it a point of pride, getting under his skin.

"I thought I was gonna hit something. Just settle down.

Have some of my water." He picked up his large Hawk-eye Baseball water bottle and handed it to me. Our fingers brushed when I grabbed it, and my body temperature spiked like a fever.

I'd played softball my whole life. As a kid, in college, and now I was about to interview for the varsity head coach position at the high school where I'd taught for four years. I'd shared thousands of water bottles. So many that it was gross. Yet the thought of putting my mouth where his lips had touched made me giddy and silly and warm. "Can I crack a window?"

"Or we could turn the heat down. Char," he said, his deep voice all gravelly. "Are you alright? You're acting strange...r than normal."

"I don't know. I could've died, and now I'm stuck in a car with—" I clamped a hand over my mouth, the flames of embarrassment clawing up my throat. *Save the situation!* "With a wedgie. Yeah, that's it. I'm uncomfortable."

Hayden cleared his throat, clearly uncomfortable too. The nice thing about having him crush my fantasy three years ago was that I stopped caring what he thought. No more *Oh, will Hayden notice me in this?* or *Does this shirt make my boobs look like Hayden would check me out?*

He had made it real clear he'd never view me that way. How was a girl supposed to move on from the most embarrassing night of her life when he was always around?

"Ah, well, do what you need to do."

"I will, thanks." *Jeez.* That was close.

I pretended to adjust my pants, which was just the cherry on top of the morning from hell. First, my best friend at work texted me saying how she heard the coaches at school talking shit about me. They felt I was too young and inexperienced to run an entire program. She meant well, she really did, but that's not the crap I needed to hear before my interview. Secondly, I almost died in the Mazda Igloo. Third, I was stuck sitting next to Hayden Porter, the guy I have loved my whole life and who thinks of me as a foolish kid sister. His words, not mine.

My eye roll made my head pound, again.

"You really should see a doctor. I'm sure the resort will have one."

His voice broke through my trip down bad-memory lane. I didn't spare him a glance as I replied, "I have some medicine. That'll help."

"I'll feel better if you get checked for a concussion." He stared at me for a beat. "You already have a bruise forming and blood on your face."

I rubbed my forehead and winced at the small lump. "When I wanted an excuse to not ski, this wasn't on my list."

"Dare I ask what was on your list?"

"Lost a contact. Jammed a toe. Or a finger. Forgot how to walk. Have a weird rash. The usual."

He puffed out a breath that was almost like a laugh. God, why did the grumpy, silent ones have to be my type? When did that even become a thing for me?

Oh. Right.

When I was twelve and Hayden was sixteen. My brother was the chatterbox, the outgoing, annoying pain in the ass, while Hayden was strong, silent, and careful. Earning a smile from him felt like a million dollars. Even back then, when he was the hotshot shortstop for the Hawkeye baseball team, he led the team by example. By small gestures, not loud, shiny ones. It was how he never drank and was always the designated driver for the other players or how he cleaned up the dugout after every game. It's why he was such a good assistant college coach now.

What are you doing, ding-dong? I was supposed to not think of all the reasons why I used to have feelings for Hayden. Unreciprocated ones at that. My brain and my heart and my vagina had a team meeting and agreed, wholeheartedly, to passively ignore him. Or to do the casual small talk like *Oh, how's your daughter? You like the weather? What's your favorite Christmas movie?*

It was safer and less embarrassing to keep it shallow. Easy peasy, lemon squeezy. God, what a terrible phrase. My third-grade teacher repeated that every day, and now it was tattooed on my memory card no matter how much I wished it away. The phrase did not apply to my feelings about Hayden. Not even a little bit. I scooted closer to the door, like adding two extra inches between us would settle me down.

"So," he said, his grumbly voice hitting me right in the soul, "what are you going to do if everyone else skis?"

"Great question. I have ideas. There's a hot tub and a nail salon. Plus I have my e-reader. I never leave home without it, and I can read by the fire all day. I downloaded three new books, all with serial killers, obviously, and I can do that while you all frolic on your skis."

"Not sure I'd call it frolicking."

"Listen, Hop, who chooses to go down a big-ass hill on tiny, skinny sticks at the speed of light for fun?"

He did the grunt-snort thing and ran a hand over his jaw like maybe my question had merit. (It did. It was a great question.) "It's a sport, one could argue the same thing about basketball. Why shoot a ball into a basket?"

"People don't die playing basketball."

"I don't remember you being this scared when we were younger." His dark-gray eyes held a twinkle I didn't like. *Is he baiting me?*

My right eye twitched, and I recrossed my legs aggressively. "I'm fearless except when it comes to snow."

"Or the word *panties.*"

"Damn it, Hayden." I covered my ears with my hands, acting like the teenagers I taught and really showing my maturity. *He already thinks I'm foolish and a kid sister.* "Look, there are just some sounds I don't enjoy hearing. It's why I don't like country music. The twang. The *ang* sound or the *anti* or the first part of the word *ointment.* It makes my skin crawl like lizards are swimming in my veins."

"So definitely don't ask if you brought your *ointment?*"

"You are the worst." I crossed my arms, my skin crawling. "Let's just enjoy silence for the next seventy minutes. I could use this free time to prepare."

"For what?" he asked, his tone a little lighter. "Stuff at school?"

Like he was genuinely curious about my life.

Okay, that wasn't fair. He cared about me in the way you did a family friend.

"Kinda," I said, scrolling through my phone to my interview brainstorm doc. The fifteen most commonly used coaching interview questions sat there, along with my own notes about what I would do if I led the softball program. Goose bumps broke out head to toe, not from the cold but from excitement. The thought of creating and running a softball program for our hometown had been a dream of mine for years. Coaching the same teams I played on from junior high on? I wanted it so badly. I knew the odds were stacked against me and that the good ole boys' club would probably continue, but I had to give it my all.

Even if the athletics director didn't like me one bit.

"Is it finals?"

"No, those are in two weeks." I chewed my lip, my pulse racing at the possibility of achieving my goal. I knew I'd be young to run a softball program, but age didn't equate to passion or experience or drive. I'd be going against older men who'd coached for longer, but did they have the same life experience I did? No. Not at all. I exhaled, willing myself to stop comparing my journey to theirs.

"Prepare for what then?"

Oh shit. I'd forgotten about Hayden's question.

"My interview," I said, way too quickly.

"Are you changing jobs?"

A prickle of annoyance weaved its way down my back. I'd been talking about this head coaching spot for months, hell, years. Everyone in my circle knew. Even my parents' backyard neighbors, Curt and Mindy, knew about it. Was Hayden being obtuse on purpose? The thought angered me. "Didn't Christian mention it? The head coaching job?"

He sat taller, stiffer. Then he said, "We rarely talk about you."

Okay, did he have to say it with so much attitude? My chest tightened, and a gross, terrible weight sank in my gut. His response rattled me, and I hugged myself tighter. "Right. Of course. Why would you?"

I wasn't important to him.

The air shifted, and my dumb eyes prickled. The night I kissed him changed everything. It wasn't just that he turned me down; our entire friendship ended. We used to do all sorts of things together, sometimes with more friends or just him and my brother. It was fun and easy. But since that kiss, things changed. I wasn't part of their trio anymore. Penny was, which was great. I loved her! I did. She was my sister from another mister, but the divide between Hayden and me seemed to grow bigger and bigger.

"Wait, no, it's not—"

"Please, it's fine." I waved my hand in the air, dismissing his excuse.

It wasn't fine. *I* wasn't fine but that didn't matter. Confrontation so wasn't my thing. I hated it at school when students acted out and even more so when parents wanted to talk about their students' grades. I cowered, desperate to find the middle ground always. The only time I felt in my element and confident was on the diamond. An ump made the wrong call? I was right there demanding an answer. An opposing coach yelled at my girls? Bring it on.

But outside those chalked lines, I avoided confrontation at all costs.

"Charlotte," Hayden said, his voice hesitant, "that came out harsher than I intended. I'm sorry. Of course we talk about you."

I chewed the inside of my cheek, forcing myself to read the words on my phone instead of looking at him. His answer didn't feel genuine, and a part of me wanted to demand details, but it'd be more embarrassing because there would be none. No reaction was the best reaction. The path of least resistance. "Okay," I said, using the customer service voice I perfected when I made parent phone calls.

Yes, your child is the smartest in the world. No, they've never done a single thing wrong. Yes, they are a gem! I had the voice down.

"What's your—"

"Favorite holiday movie, go," I interrupted him. I had the pre-holiday blues, which was, frankly, unacceptable as a Calhoun. Thanksgiving to New Year's was our time to shine, our Super Bowl, our World Series. You get the idea. Christmas lived in our blood. I mean, come on, Christian and Penny were getting married on Christmas Day. They joked they would never forget their anniversary, but I knew why.

Calhouns adored the holidays. Ugly sweater parties, gift exchanges, volunteering at a soup kitchen, Toys for Tots, Angel Tree. Our family jam-packed every possible thing into the holidays. We also had movie marathons and eggnog competitions and decorated every possible surface in the house with green or red.

Hallmark movies had nothing on my parents.

Our family home had been in magazines when we were kids. We'd been featured in articles across the country and went viral on social media five times. You know those places that win awards and music playing where people who drove by had to tune in to a radio station to hear the music? That was us.

"Am I getting Calhouned?"

"Don't use my last name as a verb, Hop. You should know this comes with the territory. Now answer."

He sighed. "*The Grinch.*"

"Which one?"

"The original, obviously. Gwen is obsessed. I've been a little lazy in parenting, and we may have watched it every single morning all month. She does this thing where she wants me to watch her do her Grinch smile and she shows all her teeth and it's the cutest thing ever."

"I think Christian sent me a video of her doing that. Adorable."

"My mom got her a Grinch stuffed animal this year. She's my little weirdo."

Whenever he talked about his daughter, his entire face lit up. He smiled, and his eyes went all warm, and it made my insides turn into complete goo. Normal Hayden was hot, Dad Hayden was ridiculously sexy.

No. We don't like him like that.

Talking about Gwen was a safe topic. Nodding, mainly to myself, I cracked the knuckles on my hands as I hoped to sound super casual and not like I wanted to throw myself at him. "So, how is Gwen doing with you leaving for two nights?"

He grunted. "She's fine. My parents are her favorite people besides me, and they are all best friends. She'll be spoiled rotten with 'Baby Shark' videos, treats, and cuddles."

CHRISTMAS SWEATER WEATHER

"Why do you sound mad then?"

"Ah, well." He ran a hand through his hair, where I did not stare at the cords in his forearms. Baseball arms were also a weakness for me. Specifically, Hayden's, but really any of them.

I fanned myself with the hem of my sweater. It was toasty in here again. I needed to keep busy, so I found a tissue and wet it before wiping away the blood on my forehead.

"I'm not upset. I've left her overnight before for the team, but I dread it every time." A muscle contracted in his jaw, and he switched his left hand to right on the wheel. "I fucking hate skiing."

I snorted. "Want to use an excuse from my list?"

"I just might, Char."

Our eyes met for a moment, and his face softened. My stomach swooped, and my heart pitter-pattered. Why couldn't I get over this man? Why?

Incoming call.

I jumped at the intrusive sound, recognizing my brother's number on the dash. Phew. That was a dose of *pull it together*.

"Hey, Christian," Hayden said, no trace of the warm tone he had just used for me. "We're about an hour away due to the snow."

"How is she?"

"I'm fine," I answered, touched at the concern in Christian's voice.

"She needs to be checked for a concussion to be safe," Hayden replied, cutting me off. "No skiing for her today."

"Hell, that's okay. Shit, I'm so sorry, Charlotte. We should've waited to carpool with you today."

"No, it's alright. I know how excited you and Penny were to head up early. I don't think I have a concussion, but yeah, no skiing today for me. I'm bummed."

Hayden caught my gaze, and we shared a brief smile.

"I can stay back with you. They have games and shit, and we can sneak whiskey into the coffee." Penny's voice was muffled in the background.

"Yeah, Pen says she'll take you to the salon too."

"I'm not going to be a burden on your pre-wedding party. I refuse. You ski and snowboard and do mountainous adventures, I will be fine on my own."

"Garrett's down for the whiskey coffee too. We can do shifts."

"No," Hayden said, his aggressive coaching voice silencing my brother. "My shoulder is bothering me again, so I'll rest with Charlotte today."

"Dude, you told me it wasn't flaring up."

"I lied."

"What the fuck? You can't keep that shit from me. I would've changed plans or something. I certainly wouldn't have taken you skiing."

I rolled my eyes. Christian would change his dream pre-wedding plans for Hayden, but not for anyone else. Stupid bromance.

"No big deal, just gotta be careful. We'll be there soon."

"Thanks for helping her out, man, and, Charlotte, I'll be glad to see your face."

3535 35

CHRISTMAS SWEATER WEATHER 35

"Right back at you," I said, smiling.

Hayden hung up, and I swore my skin tingled as he stared at me. "What?" I said. His eyes sparkled, and his lips curved up in a smile, one that went right to my core. "Why are you looking at me like that?"

"My shoulder is fine. I lied, Charmander."

My face heated at the nickname, and his gaze dropped to my lips for one hot second.

"You little sneak." I grinned. "Well done."

"Fuck skiing."

I snorted, and while his smile still dazzled me and made my brain work twice as slow, the reality of the situation hit me again. Hayden and I would spend the day together, alone.

The one thing I really didn't want to do.

CHAPTER FOUR

HAYDEN

The resort looked like a Christmas-plosion. The parking lot left nothing undecorated. Green and red garland covered the streetlamps and hung from the pine trees lining the road. There were no less than ten blow-up figures ranging from Santa to reindeer to gifts to elves. And so many holiday lights.

Gwen would love this.

"Holy Christmas," Charlotte mumbled, pressing her face against the window. "Did my parents rent this place out? I bet they volunteered to do this for Christian and Penny. This place looks beautiful."

"It looks great." I fought the urge to laugh. The Calhouns would legit volunteer their time to drive three hours north to decorate for a weekend. Christopher and Claire were intense. Also the best chosen grandparents to Gwen.

Gratitude overwhelmed me when I thought about the village of people helping me raise Gwen alone. The Calhouns specifically treated her like one of their own, and I'd never forget it. I usually didn't have an issue with the fact that I never dated or slept around. It sucked, but my entire life was for Gwen now. Gwen and baseball. I had had a few friends with benefits going on, but the last time I saw them was...months ago. Half a year, probably.

This was a mistake, knowing I'd be seeing Charlotte all weekend. I should've taken preventative measures, because she made me have wild and inappropriate thoughts. Fantasies, really. A part of me regretted my coy excuse about my shoulder, but it was better than her drinking whiskey with Garrett.

My body tensed. With my parents moving, my main source of help was gone. No more babysitting, overnight stays, or help with appointments or sick days. My heart raced at all the things I'd have to do alone. The last four people I interviewed to help were all a bust too. I had a schedule, but it wasn't enough for a full-time nanny. I needed someone to stay overnight a few times a month and during baseball season...I winced. Who would help watch a toddler that often?

I wasn't resentful. I loved my daughter more than life, but between figuring out how I'd get support and balance my job, it was taking all my energy. Dating wasn't something I could afford. A one-night stand? Sure. No strings, no emotions. I eyed Charlotte, hating the way my body hummed around her. She was all strings, all emotions.

With how entangled our families were, I could never cross the line. The risk of losing all of them wasn't worth the feelings I had hidden all these years, especially when my life wasn't in order.

"Wow," Charlotte said, a little breathless. "This is a snow globe of a place."

"Despite your car being a hockey puck, the snow made this place perfect."

"It really did."

I could hear the smile in her voice, and my breath hitched. Charlotte's orbit pulled me in, where all I wanted was to earn more of her smiles. My gut tightened, thinking about her going for a head coaching job when I had no idea. Christian never told me, and it wasn't like I asked about her life when I saw her. I kept our convos simple and short, by choice. It was no wonder she didn't seek me out.

I found an empty spot to park near the main drive, and once I had shifted into park, I unclicked my seat belt, watching her.

She still stared out the window, her lips slightly parted and her large brown eyes wide. She looked happy and excited. Even with the dried blood and bruising, Charlotte was a knockout. I wanted to touch those two little freckles on her cheek and bite the spot on her neck where her shoulder met her collarbone.

Fuck. I needed distance, from her, and from my thoughts.

"Come on. Let's go check in and prepare to chat with your brother and his betrothed."

Her lips quirked, her warm gaze meeting mine before her expression cooled. It was almost as if she didn't want us to find a truce. Not that we had a war or a fight. But the gesture hurt. She shut me out the second things seemed nice.

Yeah, I had to fix this, somehow. I didn't realize how bad it was between us without the barrier of Gwen.

The wind whipped my face as I exited my side to help carry our stuff inside. Charlotte had the pile of clothes clutched to her chest. Some curls escaped her bun and damn, it was cute.

"You going to waltz in there with your clothes, just like that?" I indicated my chin toward her chest. "No judgment, but if you wanted to borrow a bag, you just need to ask."

She pursed her lips. The bruise on her forehead looked worse, and worry ate at me. The woman was stubborn as an ox, and I really wanted her to see a doctor.

"Hm, maybe I wanted to make a statement. I'm anti-bag." She arched her brow in defiance, the same look she had had her whole life.

I held up my hands. "I support your stance, Char, but do you want everyone seeing your red underwear?" I indicated her left hand, where a red garment stood out against the rest. I grabbed my suitcase and backpack, trying not to smile as she waged war with herself.

She didn't want to ask me for help but also knew she needed to. I leaned over the back, pushing away some of Gwen's things until I pulled out an old duffel. It smelled lightly of dust and leather, but it would work. "Still anti-bag?" I asked, teasing her.

She rolled her eyes before setting her clothes down in the back. The wind blew her shirts and socks to the ground, and I quickly scooped them up. I absolutely ignored the feel of her clothes on my hands. "Thank you," she mumbled as she nudged her shoulder against mine.

"Did it hurt saying that?"

"Slightly." She shoved the items into the bag, including her toothbrush and bra, before standing and hoisting it on to her shoulder. She rubbed her forehead with her other hand, and worry replaced the amusement.

"Headache?"

"A bit, yeah."

"Alright, let's get our rooms so you can rest before they all descend on you."

I quickly grabbed our coats. Locking the vehicle, I placed my hand on her lower back. While I led us into the main entrance, I let my mind wander for a few seconds.

What would it be like if we came up here alone for a weekend? What if I gave in to this attraction instead of fighting it? I eyed the largest Christmas tree I had ever seen and wished that our timing were different. In some universe, Charlotte and I could be together, but it wasn't the present one.

Even though the thick sweater separated my skin from hers, she was warm to touch. She smelled like cinnamon and vanilla, and I wanted to wrap myself up in her heat and scent. I didn't expect to spend hours with her in my truck or to foolishly volunteer to keep her company today either. That was the problem with being an adult with a small child—I just didn't think. Most days were complete survival mode. We ate, slept, were clean, and that was enough. Thinking ahead beyond Gwen's well-being or the team just didn't happen. And now not having a secure place for Gwen to go when I coached added another layer of stress I wasn't equipped to deal with.

The automatic doors to the resort whooshed open, and my first thought was *Gwen needs to visit here.* The scent of pine trees hung in the air, and I counted ten Christmas trees in sight. There were more, I'd bet Gwen's college fund on it. I kept moving and *oomph.*

"Shit, Char, are you alright?" I wrapped an arm around her middle, righting her posture. That pushed her even closer to me, her back to my chest, her curves underneath my forearm. She smelled even better in this position. I lingered for a second, and then another, before stepping back. "Why did you stop?"

Her lips parted, and her eyes filled with glee. She turned halfway and swatted me on the arm. "Do you see this place? I want to live here. I want my entire personality to become this place. Look at the decorations! The popcorn string! That took hours! Oh, and the tinsel and glass ornaments and two fireplaces. Not one, *two.* Pine cones!" she shouted.

"Good afternoon," a very tall man in a dark green tux said. His name tag read BERNARD.

"That can't be your real name," I said, without thinking. "My daughter is obsessed with *Santa Clause,* and you know, the elf's name is Bernard."

"Hayden, shh." Charlotte hit me again. "Hi, Bernard. Do people call you Bernie? Nard-dawg?"

His lips curved into a smile as his gaze swept over Charlotte. A flicker of interest flashed on his face. Oh, he was into her. He stepped closer, speaking only to her. "My real name is Brendon."

"I fucking knew it," I muttered, but neither of them paid attention to me.

"Hi, Brendon. This is the best place I've ever seen in my entire life."

"I saw your face light up. I'm so glad you like it. I'm head of decorations on top of managing the resort. It pleases me to see you so happy. Are you both here together or—"

"Oh, no. I'm here to meet my brother and his bachelor-bachelorette party." Charlotte moved closer to Bernard-slash-Brendon-slash–the guy who really annoyed me.

"Do we check in with you or at the counter?" I interrupted. They both looked at me with frowns. I was the resident Grinch, stealing joy and ruining Christmas. Put me in a green suit.

"I can help. This way, please." He winked at Charlotte, and she beamed up at him, her cheeks rosy. She eyed him up and down, and I clenched my fists.

If I had to watch her flirt with this dude, I'd rather eat yellow snow.

"Do you have a doctor here? She needs to see someone," I barked out, annoyed at their flirting. Then I annoyed myself. *I need a damn drink.*

Bernard-Brendon tilted his head and scanned her body again, lingering on her legs. "We do have an on-site triage. Are you okay? What happened?"

She sighed, slicing me a *shut up* look. "Ignore Grumpy Pants over there. He's basically like my overprotective brother. I'm okay, just got into a little fender bender."

Overprotective brother.

The thoughts I had about Charlotte were not *brotherly* in any way. Her comment stung like she had intended, using my own words against me from that night.

We had happened to be at the same bar on campus. I had signed my first coaching contract mere hours before and wanted a large whiskey to celebrate. The head coach, Nelson, the one who hired me, sat at the bar. We brainstormed all the pie-in-the-sky ideas we had, leaving no dream unmentioned, when I had to use the bathroom.

That's when I saw her.

Charlotte had just turned twenty-one, me twenty-five. I didn't know she'd be at the same bar even though I knew she went to the same university. She wore a skintight red dress that dipped low in the front and showed off every single one of her curves. Her arms waved in the air as she danced, her smile large enough for the entire place to see how happy she was. She shimmied and wiggled and stole the breath from my lungs.

She was beautiful. Inside and out, and her smoky eyes fell on me and lit up. "Hayden!" She ran to me and threw her arms around my neck, her vanilla perfume surrounding me. I held her against me, obsessed with the feel of her. I let my hand linger on her lower back and then her side.

"My birthday wish came true!"

"Oh yeah?" I tilted her head back, unable to stop my own grin at seeing her joy. I always had a little thing for my best friend's sister. I hid it, but every time she was around, my day just improved. "What was your wish?"

"You finally see me." She licked the corner of her lip, and the gesture sent a hot bolt of lust through me. I wanted to taste that lip, her mouth, feel her heat. She shouted, and her words were a little slurred, clearly from the drinking.

I'd never take advantage of anyone when they were drunk. That was a hard stop, and Charlotte had clearly had quite a few. Yet I couldn't stop myself from asking, "What do you mean see you?"

She dug her nails into my shoulder and stood on her tiptoes, pressing her lips against the base of my neck. Goose bumps exploded down my skin, lighting me on fire. She nipped my earlobe, and I forgot everything that made sense. I didn't know where we were, what year it was, who I even was as a person. I had to feel those pillow-soft lips against mine. "Charlotte," I said.

She ran her fingers through my hair and tugged until my mouth met hers, and she gave me possibly the messiest, sexiest kiss of my life. She tasted like champagne and cherries, and when she sucked my tongue into her mouth, I groaned, holding her tighter against me.

Charlotte Calhoun. My secret crush.

She's drunk.

She's a student. Where I work. Where I got my dream job so young.

Fuck.

I broke the kiss and put a hand on her chest. Her heart pounded against her ribs at the same rate mine did. "Char," I said, unsure what I wanted to tell her.

"I felt it too, Hayden." She smiled. "I've loved you my

entire life and knew it would be the best feeling ever to finally kiss you. God, what does this mean?"

"It means nothing." I pushed her farther away from me, the hair on the back of my neck standing on end. She'd been drinking! What if Nelson saw this? What if I got fired from my job before it even started? What the fuck was I thinking? Kissing *Charlotte Calhoun*?

"Wait, n-nothing?"

"Don't be foolish, Charlotte." I lost control, panic clawing up my throat, making me almost gag. "You're like a sister to me."

Yeah, that's right. Lie. That'll help.

She blinked, and in that exact moment, I crushed her. The nicest woman in the world.

I shook my head and ran my hand through my hair, forcing that memory away. We'd never spoken about it, and maybe it was time. Except now another man, the ridiculous elf, had his fingers on her forehead.

What kind of manager touched guests?

"We need to check in. Now," I said.

Charlotte scowled. The manager remained professional as he strutted to the counter. It was one thing to battle my own feelings for Charlotte, but watching other guys around her gutted me. Every time there had been an event in the last three years, I had had a date. It made me behave and not hyperfocus on whether Charlotte's date was treating her well or touching her or doing whatever the hell Bernie was doing.

"Calhoun and Porter," I said, jutting my chin toward his computer. "Check us in."

My phone buzzed in my pocket. A blip of anxiety had me grabbing for it. It could've been a player or Nelson. My instinct always went to Gwen though.

Mom.

My anxiety doubled in size, like a hot-air balloon. "Mom, is everything okay?"

CHAPTER FIVE

CHARLOTTE

Hayden walked out of earshot, leaving me to deal with checking in alone. He sounded worried, rattled even. It had to be about Gwen. He paced near the line of Christmas trees decorated in all reds and blues, and his shoulders were about up to his ears with tension. Exhaling, I tried to shake off the worry, and focus on the resort and getting our rooms.

"Everything alright?" Brendon asked.

"I'm sure. His parents are watching his daughter back home." I forced a smile and leaned my forearms onto the counter. Christmas music played, and there was a holiday candle lit. Each breath was a hug to my soul. "This is so festive. What do you do the other eleven months of the year?"

"Other themes." Brendon typed on the computer while maintaining eye contact with me. He was a bit much, but flirting was fun for me. Innocent enough. Plus it annoyed Hayden, and I didn't care if I was immature. I enjoyed poking and rattling him. I had no endgame, not really, but that muscle in his cheek would twitch, and I found it sexy.

Plus I never quite forgave him for making me feel our chemistry was one-sided. Maybe my personal mission was to remind him he was wrong for the rest of my life.

"Yeah, what's January?" I rested my chin on my wrist. Brendon's eyes sparkled, and honestly, he'd be a fun one-night stand. His playful energy and broad shoulders were kryptonite to me. Not that one-night stands were my thing. I wished they were.

"Ice. Lots of blues and whites." He reached into a drawer and pulled out magnetic cards. He swiped them on a machinelike thing and tucked them into a packet. "You are in room 100, Ms. Calhoun."

"What about June? Or May, or August? They don't have... well, shit. May has Memorial Day. What about the other two?"

Brendon adjusted his collar and seemed to stand taller. He took his decorating seriously, and I dug it. Anyone who loved something and was good at it was special in my book. The world was too harsh not to enjoy things. "June is summer, and August is back to school."

"Makes sense." I nodded, picturing rulers and notebooks and backpacks hanging everywhere.

"What was your friend's name? Portobello? Peter?"

"Porter, but I prefer Portobello. That would be a great nickname." I grinned, glancing over my shoulder at Hayden as he approached us. I tried to find evidence on his face to make sure Gwen was okay, but he remained stoic. Unreadable as usual. "All good?"

"Yeah. Gwen wanted to FaceTime." He flashed a quick smile before putting his excessively large hand on my shoulder and squeezing. "You get us checked in?"

He's touching me. Hayden is touching my shoulder. Alert the authorities.

"Uh," I said, unable to form words because the warmth from his palm sent SOS signals to my loins. He had huge hands, and I swore I could feel the callouses through my sweater. First with touching my lower back, now this. It was Too Much. Damn, he had asked me a question. Something important. One I should definitely know the answer to but all I could focus on was his hand on me...and was he moving his thumb?

Hayden grazed his thumb over my collarbone. The little brush of naughtiness had my brain malfunctioning. What were words, even, really? Just combinations of letters that made sense to some people. Weird sounds that were a code?

"Ms. Calhoun?"

"Hi. Yes, that's me." I spun around, my face fire-engine red, and I blinked a lot. Like that would restart my brain.

Brendon smiled, and Hayden released his hold on me. Finally. Breathing became easy again, and I adjusted the hair at the base of my neck. "Did you check in Portobello here too?"

"Portobello?" Hayden asked.

"Inside joke," I quipped, winking at Brendon. The handsome man laughed hard, and I felt kinda cool. "Anyhoodle, tell me he's on the highest floor."

"Ah, no. Mr. Porter is in room—" He paused, frowned even. "One oh two."

"First floor. Great." Hayden's clipped tone made me glance at him. Maybe Gwen was sick or something.

"Where are you, Char?"

"One hundred." I gulped, like having our rooms close together was dirty. Forbidden. Wrong. Did we have attaching doors? Oh my, what if we did? What if I sleepwalked naked into his room for him to turn me down, again? "They aren't connected, right?"

"No. They aren't." Brendon smiled. "Let me know if you need anything, please, and I'll let the on-site doctor know to expect you."

"Yes, thank you. You've been the best." I flashed my biggest grin at him before facing the hallway. A sign with an arrow showed rooms 70–150 to the right, along with the pool, and the bar. "How convenient for me."

"What's that?" Hayden asked. He hoisted the duffel bag onto his shoulder.

"The pool and the bar are near my room. It was a gift, really. With a little effort, I could never leave this wing of the resort, and wouldn't that be fantastic?"

He snorted. "Pretty sure Christian has an agenda for us."

"Don't let my brother boss you around. Be your own person. Stick it to the man." Even as I said the words, my stomach tightened with dread at the harsh reminder that it really was a man's world. I talked a great talk, but could I walk the walk? My athletic director certainly didn't think so. All the head coaches at our school were men, and they made it known they wanted to keep it that way. My shoulders slumped, and I lost a little bit of my bluster as we made our way down the hallway. I wasn't giving in to their bullshit, but the reality of it was something I had to acknowledge.

This place was a perfect holiday hideout where I had no business stressing about my sexist, ageist boss. Greens and reds covered every free inch of wall space. Green lights, red ornaments, and wrapping paper in picture frames greeted us. I inhaled, the delicious scent of pine and cinnamon creating an intoxicating combination.

We passed a mirror, and my breath caught in my throat. We looked like a couple. It wouldn't be a big deal, but seeing the reflection of us standing next to each other had my heart aching for something that would never happen. We weren't heading to a shared room where I could peel off his shirt and lick his muscles until he whimpered. We weren't going to fool around behind Christmas trees or make out in the hot tub. We definitely weren't about to strip naked and fall onto the bed. I cleared my throat, my face overheating. My breaths came out in shallow gasps, and Hayden touched my shoulder.

"Am I walking too fast? I'm sorry. We can slow down."

My face flushed even more. The guy of my daydreams thought I was winded from walking. "No, we could walk faster! Yes, let's do that."

I wanted space, a moment away from his gorgeous eyes and gentle demeanor. Hayden was so in control on the field and with his daughter. The one time he wasn't, he kissed me before crushing my soul. Before I did anything stupid, I picked up my pace until we arrived at our doors. "Ah, home. Yes. Mama wants to see."

Hayden shuffled next to me, but I refused to look at him. Call me a coward, but his nearness made my senses work overtime. That happened when you had secretly loved someone for ten years, told them one night after they kissed you, and then avoided them at all costs because of the humiliation.

When I let my deepest, most secret thoughts come out from the cave in the back of my mind, I always asked myself the same question. If I had the chance to be with Hayden, would I?

The answer was always the same: *Hell yes*.

Even if I knew it'd end in heartbreak, because despite trying to date other guys, no one came close to the spark I felt with Hayden. Without trying, he ruined me for other men. His kind soul, the way he loved his daughter and parents, the little things he did that made such a difference. He set the bar high, and I refused to lower my expectations. Even if it made me single as a Pringle forever, I was waiting for someone to be better than Hayden.

Sliding the card into the slot, I pushed open my door and was met with a roaring fireplace and the smell of gingerbread cookies. "This is heaven."

Hayden coughed before brushing past me. He dropped my bag on the floor, and without a glance at me, he marched out. "Let me put my stuff in my room before going to the on-site doctor."

I don't want to go to the doctor when I have this waiting for me. A cozy oasis! A comfy corner! A Christmas cuddle zone!

"Yeah, you need to get checked out. Pretty sure you have a concussion." Hayden faced me, his gorgeous smile on display. "What, pray tell, is a Christmas cuddle zone?"

"I didn't realize I'd said it out loud." I rubbed the center of my forehead. Sighing, I stood to my full height and plastered on my best fake smile. "Thanks for your help. I plan to remain in this snow globe room until Christian drags me out with cash bribes."

His jaw clenched before he stepped closer. "You're seeing a doctor."

"I feel fine, Hayden."

"Stop being an idiot," he bit out. The wrinkle had returned between his eyes, and he dragged a thumb over one of his eyebrows, something he did when stressed. "That came out harsher than I intended."

"Clearly." I placed my hands on my hips as a bout of dizziness hit me.

"Char—" Hayden reached out and gently gripped my elbow, his large fingers rubbing circles over my sweater. "You have two choices. Either I carry you to the doctor, or you walk with me."

Something about his statement reminded me of how he spoke to Gwen. The soft voice, the either/or option I'd witnessed him using. *You have two choices, Gwen, the red or the blue cup.* "Are you being a daddy to me right now?"

Something flashed in his eyes. "You're not leaving me a choice when you're acting this stubborn."

The grip on my elbow tightened as he pulled me gently toward him. Our chests were two inches apart, and I forgot how to use my lungs, even though their sole purpose was to breathe in oxygen. We were so close. *Oh my goodness.*

His breath hit my face, and the base of my neck throbbed with my pulse. *He's touching me.* He tilted my chin up, his gray gaze moving from my eyes to my mouth and then to my forehead. "You have a bruise, right here." His fingertips grazed my forehead, sending goose bumps down my spine.

"And a lump, Charlotte." He sighed, pressing his lips together as his gaze darkened. "When you got out of your car, with blood on your forehead and face, my heart stopped for a second. I need to make sure you're okay. I'll do whatever you want after, just...stop being so stubborn."

His voice was rougher, deeper than I was used to.

"You make me sound ridiculous. I was always going to go."

His lips quirked as he narrowed his eyes. "Mm, sure."

"I was." I poked him in his chest and immediately pulled back my finger. He was rock hard and warm.

"You choose the second option then?"

"The one where you walk me to the doctor?" I stepped out of his reach and felt the absence of his warmth. How annoying, my personal fantasy was also a furnace. Just yet another reason we'd be perfect together, because I was always cold. It was unfair. Maybe it was the accident, or the fact that he had touched my chin, but I decided, in that moment, that I wanted to play with fire, see if I could find any evidence that he viewed me as more than Christian's sister. "I actually want the first option." I put my arm to my forehead. "I'm feeling faint. Not sure I can walk. Please, be my daddy."

The second those words left my mouth, the temperature in the room skyrocketed. Hayden's gray eyes burned like charcoal, his breathing quickened, and his jaw tightened, but in a different way than I was used to. This wasn't an annoyed look, it was interest. Heat.

He remained a statue, unmoving, but his eyes told me enough.

We were in a stare down, a war where I wasn't sure what the winner won or the loser lost. I never thought I'd get a reaction, and now I didn't know what to do with it. Was it the use of *daddy* to rile him up? Words escaped me, which had happened three times in my entire life. This being the third.

I arched a brow, daring him to make the first move, to say anything. Ten, twenty seconds went by before he ran a finger over his eyebrow.

"Charlotte," he said, his voice deeper than I'd ever heard. He cleared his throat. "If you need me to carry you, I certainty can."

Before I could respond, a knock pounded at the door. I jumped, my heart bursting out of my chest at the interruption.

"Knock, knock! Let us in, Charmander!" Christian's voice boomed through the wood. "We have ice, medicine, and whiskey."

"I'm good at massages too," Garrett said.

Whatever moment, if one could even call it that, between Hayden and me evaporated like boiling water in a blizzard. Poof. Gone. Burst. His expression hardened and went back to indifference, like he didn't care if I was a goat or a pizza or me.

"Do you give forehead massages?" I asked, teasing Garrett as I opened the door.

"I'm a forehead virgin, but I can still make you feel good."

"Shut the fuck up, Garrett." Christian shoved his friend in the shoulder before coming into my hotel room. Penny and Garrett followed, and for the first time since I got in my car that morning, I relaxed and was happy to be here.

These were some of my favorite people in the world, and yes, they preferred a sport I hated, but this trip would be fun. A nice reprieve from my lack of love life and battle against the boys' club at work.

Christian pulled me into a hug, his grip harder than normal before he looked down at me. "Gross. I'm gonna have to photoshop this egg out of all the photos."

"Christian, don't be an asshole." Penny came up and pulled me from his arms. "Let me have a look." She frowned and clicked her tongue. "Come on, sis. Let's leave the guys and go check the doctor. We're not doing a damn thing until we make sure you're okay."

As Penny dragged me to the door, I spared a glance at Hayden over my shoulder. His gaze was on me, his eyes unreadable. No trace of the brief moment we had. No sign of a truce between us. But when Penny looped her arm in mine, a different feeling warmed me. I might never get a chance with Hayden, but I had an incredible friend group around me. My brother and his fiancée were more best friends than family, and Garrett would lend anyone the shirt off his back. Would he flex and show off his muscles? For sure, but he'd do anything for anyone he cared about. I would focus on those people and not the guy who broke my heart.

CHAPTER SIX

HAYDEN

Christian, Garrett, and I found a spot at the resort bar as we waited for the women to return. The leather booths were covered in Christmas lights, and an evergreen scent filled the air. If I were someone who cared about the holidays as much as the Calhouns, I'd say it was magical. Intoxicating, even, with how the cheery music in the background went with the classy decorations. Presents were everywhere. Probably fake, but they were expertly wrapped. Families and couples lined the bar, bright red and green mugs steaming in their hands. Was it hot chocolate or whiskey? Why did I want both?

My skin tightened with unease as Christian slid into a booth. It was rare that I had a moment like this, where I was responsible for only myself. I didn't know how to relax like Christian and Garrett. They were laughing, not giving a single shit about anything.

They were worried about Charlotte—that was clear—but besides that? They were so carefree. I stopped being that way when I learned about Gwen. I wouldn't trade her for the entire world, but it was tough to turn back into the old me. Even now, I tried not to stress about everything I needed to do with my parents moving, but failed. The pre-dad me was buried deep, hibernating, unwilling to come out.

Christian must've sensed my mood, and he nudged my knee with his. "My man, there are no frowns on my trip. You figure your shit out and be fun."

"Yes, that's how normal people operate, Chrissy." Garrett rolled his eyes. "He's worried about Charlotte. Once she's back, he'll cheer up. Am I right?"

My gaze slid to Garrett, his knowing smirk grating every single one of my nerves. Was he hinting at something? No, this was more than a hint. Did she tell him what happened all those years ago? No, there was no way. Unless they grew closer, and no one told me. The thought of them together caused a hurricane of emotions, all bad ones, to swirl under my skin. Garrett wasn't good enough for her. Not even a little bit.

"Okay, good." Christian sobered, his face tight. "Penny texted that Charlotte's doing fine. No concussion, just a bruise and a cut. They'll be back soon. No need to stress, okay? Charmander is tough."

"Yeah. She's all attitude and muscles." Garrett winked at me. "The second you realize she's my dream girl, I'm going after her."

Christian stilled, his eyes turning to slits. "No."

"She's grown up now, bro. She can make her own choices.

She doesn't need her older brother to make them for her."
Garrett played with fire. The group daredevil, he arched his
fingers so they were together like a villain as he leaned back
in his chair. "Hayden agrees with me."

Well, fuck.

I shrugged. "Char can make her own decisions, but I
agree, if she chose Garrett for any reason, she's not well."

"If I go to jail for beating his ass, can you bail me out?"
Christian held out his fist, and I hit it.

"Yup."

It was our continual joke. Since Gwen arrived, we knew
I'd never be the one to get arrested, but before fatherhood,
we had a back-and-forth thing going. It was all in fun, but I
had a feeling this time he wasn't kidding. The way Garrett
spoke about his women, how much of a bachelor he was,
there was no fucking way Christian would be cool with him
getting together with his sister.

I'm nothing like him. I shook the thought away. I might
not be a womanizer like Garrett, but I still couldn't offer
Charlotte what she deserved, no matter how much I
wanted her. Instead I'd find other ways to support her, any
way I could. Like this interview she never told me about.
"Hey, you never told me Char was going for a head coaching job."

"Oh yeah." Christian scoffed. "It's in two weeks—right
before our wedding!"

It still stung that she chose not to tell me—an assistant
coach of a D1 college baseball team. Guilt ate me up inside
out because I knew it was my fault. I had pushed her away
and made it impossible for us to be friends. I hated that.

Gripping a Christmas tree coaster left on the table, I tore the paper into pieces to keep my fingers busy.

"She sent me her résumé and vision for the team. She nailed it." Garrett sighed and rubbed his hands on top of the table. "Y'all like busting my balls, but one of my many talents is copyediting. I do freelance jobs, and Charlotte sends me stuff from time to time. She helps me out with things. We're friends. Why are you both staring at me like that?"

What things did she help him out with? I thought she disliked Garrett? When did they become closer? Did she move on from me and to her brother's other best friend?

Why did my chest ache? I scratched it, willing the dull pain to disappear.

"How long has this been going on?" Christian asked, his voice steady. "What things does she help you with?"

Great fucking question.

Garrett smirked. "Don't worry about it."

"I don't like this. Charlotte didn't tell me anything."

"Didn't tell you what?" Charlotte asked, appearing right behind the booth.

She had pulled her hair up into a bun, but some curls escaped around her temples. There was a bandage on her forehead, but other than that, she looked beautiful. Her jeans hugged her thick legs, and her holiday sweater pulled tight against her chest, but it was her smile that did me in. She was back to happy Charlotte, my favorite version.

"You and G have a thing?" Christian asked, his eyebrows disappearing into his hairline. "What is this?"

"Oh." She laughed, her gaze softening at the player. She moved to sit on Garrett's chair arm, like she had done it a million times before. She looked comfortable with him, and he with her. He grinned at me, almost like a taunt, and he rubbed her lower back. She smiled down at him, the two of them sharing an inside joke that made me see red, and not the fun Christmas kind.

"I'm volunteering in her journalism class to show I'm mature and giving back to the community."

"Yeah, and it has nothing to do with you hitting on my friend who happens to teach English across the hall." Charlotte rolled her eyes, the gesture so much like her brother.

"Hey, Christian, can I talk to you for a quick second?" Penny asked, her brows pulling together. Her voice sounded meek for her, like something was wrong.

Char frowned, her gaze seeking mine with the same concern.

"Sure, babe." Christian hit the table, and the two of them left the seating area. It was rare to see both of them without a smile, and judging by Charlotte's continual assault of her bottom lip, she was worried too.

"Is everything okay with them?" she asked, pulling the sleeves of her sweater over her hands. She always loved doing that. Gwen did too. It made me smile.

"Probably. Shit." Garrett stared down at his phone, sighing. "I have to take this. It won't be more than a few minutes. It's my boss. I took today off, damn it. Would one of you order me another coffee?"

I nodded, watching him walk away. That left Char and me, and her energy was almost tangible. "Penny for your thoughts."

She stared down the hallway, the worry leaving her face. "I'm thirsty. I'm fantasizing about a delicious holiday cocktail."

"You almost had to live in your car forever. I think you deserve a drink."

She slid her gaze to me, her lips quirking. "Look at you joking. Humor looks good on you, Hop."

Warmth spread through me at her compliment. "My treat. Let's get you a Candy Cane Sex on a Beach."

"That is so not a drink." She chuckled as she stood.

I followed her toward the bar. The only spot free was toward the right, near the hall Penny and Christian had escaped to. She leaned over the copper top, humming a holiday song as she read the drink names. "These are absolutely ridiculous."

"A gingerbread old-fashioned sounds divine." She licked her lips and wiggled her brows like a cartoon character. "I'll take one, please," she said to the bartender.

"I think you may be—"

"Shh!" She held a finger to my mouth, her head tilted to hear better. It took a second, but then I heard it too. Penny and Christian.

"I don't want to do this anymore," Penny said, her voice shaking.

"We have to. You know why."

"I don't anymore. It's...Christian, is this even what we want?"

"Fuck." Christian groaned. "Makes me want to cancel the entire thing."

Charlotte's body tensed. My stomach bottomed out. *Cancel the entire thing?*

The wedding?

Shit.

Their voices faded down the hall, the sounds inaudible. Charlotte gripped the edge of the bar, her face pale. "Hayden."

I blew a breath, working my jaw to relieve the tension that had built up. Overhearing them wasn't good. Not at all. "Maybe it's not what we think."

She laughed, a horrible, sad sound. "It sounds like they want to cancel the wedding."

I nodded, torn at what to do. There was no world where Penny and Christian didn't end up together, and it seemed crazy to me that this had even happened. The bartender returned with Charlotte's drink, and she took a large gulp before glancing at me with wild eyes. I knew that look. She had an idea.

"We can save this, somehow."

"How do you envision that happening?"

"They are Christmas fiends! I'm sure Penny has a plan, and we just... do whatever they ask."

"Honey." I eyed her, clearing my throat and correcting myself. "Charlotte, you can't ski after the accident. You going skiing won't save whatever it is they are working through."

She opened her mouth, but just then Penny and Christian returned. They looked relatively normal. Penny's eyes were a little red, and Christian's stance wasn't as relaxed as it usually was. I nodded at him, aware of Charlotte's gaping. "You good?"

"Yeah, just some wedding stuff."

Penny's smile was stiff. Then she blinked, and her usual joy was back. "Once you get your drinks, come to the table. Our agendas are officially ready to be announced!"

"The secret agenda you wouldn't share with any of us?" Charlotte asked, her voice a little strained. Besides that, no one would know she was stressed.

"Yup. I've been waiting years for this moment." The decorations had to reflect in her eyes because, for a moment, it spooked me. Penny's eyes almost glowed red and green. If anyone would be the embodiment of Christmas, it would be her.

I laid down some cash and motioned for everyone to return to the table. "Here, go ahead. You take the chair," I said softly to Charlotte.

"Thanks, Hayden," she said. I breathed in her vanilla perfume, my body going taut. She smelled the same as she always did, a delicious, intoxicating scent.

Garrett returned, sitting in the plush lounge chair, leaving the rocking chair open.

"Okay, Pen, what's the plan?" Charlotte asked.

Penny shared a look with Christian, her face pinching before she smiled. If I hadn't heard their argument earlier, I never would've seen the tension, but now it was worrying me.

She set a stack of papers on the center of the table. "I knew what it meant marrying into the Calhoun family. Christmas is a way of life, and instead of running to the South Pole, I embraced it."

"Yeah, you did, sexy Mrs. Claus," Garrett said, earning a smack from Christian.

"We have three days up here, two nights, to go Holiday Hog Wild."

"What does that even mean?" Charlotte asked.

I nodded, wanting to know the same damn thing.

"Here is your Calhoun-Nolan pre-wedding weekend agenda. We have activities every day, with the mornings for your skiing pleasure. Or if you're Char, then spa and rest."

"You're my favorite," Charlotte said.

"Now," Penny said, lowering her voice, "tonight is the scavenger hunt, the Lost Days of Christmas. We can enter as a team, and the winning team gets gift cards!"

"And a trophy. Don't forget the trophy, babe." Christian urged her on. "We need that trophy."

The same tight look returned to her face before she masked it. "Right, the trophy. Now, this might seem silly to some."

"You mean, to everyone but you two lovebirds," Garrett said.

"Well, fine. But I want to impress my future in-laws, okay? They are Mother and Father Christmas, and it'd be awesome to show them we won this competition."

"Pen, they love you. We all love you. With or without a ring, you're still a Calhoun." Charlotte reached over and patted her hand with a contemplative look entering her eyes. "We will win this thing, or we burn it down."

"That's my competitive sister." Christian's eyes flashed. "We win this for Penny."

Everyone put their hands in the middle, waiting for me to finish the team cheer. I did it, fighting a smile. This was utterly ridiculous. The wildest thing I'd done in years. My hand was on top of Charlotte's, her focus on me as she nodded. I understood her. We had to win this thing for Christian and Penny. I'd do anything for my best friend and anything for Charlotte. It was an easy decision to let myself go for the holiday extravaganza.

"Now that we know Char is okay, we can ski or board for the next few hours. I have a holiday drink happy hour scheduled for us at five. Then a quick dinner before the games start at seven. Any questions?" Penny looked like a tree right now, all lit up.

"No, ma'am, we're gonna have a hell of a time." I pounded the table. "Go, team!"

Charlotte burst out laughing, her eyes seeking mine. Her gaze warmed. "What's gotten into you?"

"Holiday spirit?"

"No, no way." She grinned, her dimples popping out. "It's more than that."

"Maybe it's the drink."

"Or maybe, it's the—" she said.

"You coming or what?" Garrett interrupted her, pointing at me.

"I'm not skiing this afternoon. I'll go in the morning with you. Take off, have fun, break one leg, but not two."

"Dick." He laughed and hit my shoulder. "Charlie baby, find me under a mistletoe later."

"We'll see how I'm feeling."

He blew her a kiss, making her laugh. Seeing her dimples, the way she tossed her head back, and the pure joy on her face punched me in the gut.

When was the last time I made her laugh like that? Made her chuckle with her whole body? I used to. When we were teenagers and hung out all the time, we'd laugh together often. I missed it. It was as if my body refused to remember how much I liked her when I wasn't around her, but the second I was? All restraint was forgotten.

"He's a goon. I should dislike everything about him, but I think, because I know his heart, I can't let him go." She sighed, shaking her head. Her eyes always gave her away, and she looked at Garrett with a softness I wasn't used to seeing. They had grown closer the last three years.

I rubbed my eyebrow and took a deep breath, steeling myself up for a big ask. "Can we talk, just you and me?"

CHAPTER SEVEN

CHARLOTTE

Some people lost their composure under pressure. I wasn't one of them. If chaos happened in the classroom, then I'd keep my game face on and stay calm. A kid having a seizure? No big deal. A fight? Cool cucumber over here.

My face might appear neutral, bored even at his words. But inside? It was the Hot Mess Express going off the rails at one hundred miles an hour. No conductor on this train.

I didn't know which emotion to follow first. Fear? Regret? Anger? Curiosity? Lust? What did he want to talk about? And why just the two of us? Was this about Garrett? I saw him studying us. Or was this about...before? The time we don't talk about, ever?

Shit. I was hot. Getting hotter by the second too. Was the fire getting bigger? I fanned my sweater over my chest, wondering if it would be weird to ask the bartender to lessen the flames. I was sure that was a thing. *Oh, sir, could you turn down the fire over here? Thanks so much.* Not weird at all.

"Char?" Hayden said, my name all soft and deep from his lips.

"Hm?" I squeaked. "Yes? A talk between us pals? Sure."

He studied my face, his intelligent gaze narrowing at whatever he found. Then he sighed and gently took my elbow in his fingers. "Let's go somewhere private."

"Private like my bedroom?" I blurted out, giving away my nerves.

He stilled, his entire six-foot-something body turning to cement. He was a living gargoyle. A sexy one, but still, unmoving. It only lasted three seconds, but they felt like a lifetime. "No. Not your bedroom. Just away from everyone."

"Of course. Bedroom was a silly guess."

He spun around, his cheek twitching as his grip on my elbow tightened. He stopped walking, and without meaning to, I glanced up and found a gorgeous, perfect little mistletoe hanging above us. Something inside me came to life.

Flustering him, pushing him to the edge, was a pastime of mine. Even before that night at the bar, I'd flirt with him to the point he blushed. Licking my lips, I nodded up. "If you wanted to kiss me again, all you had to do was ask. No need to pretend with mistletoe, Hayden."

I swore the heat from his fingers moved through my sweater, into my skin, and flowed through my veins, warming me inside out. Christmas music played in the background, with the sounds of people laughing carrying through the air like wind chimes. The fire crackled. I squeezed my toes in my fuzzy boots, waiting, breathing, hoping for Hayden to take the bait. My tummy felt like a firecracker had gone off, exploding inside me as I waited.

And waited.

Time stood still, like we had frozen in a movie. Our gazes met, his dark pupils expanding before cooling. His body leaned toward me, just an inch, his lips parted and wet, like he too couldn't wait for our mouths to meet again. But then he growled, "Charlotte."

He said my name like it was ten syllables long and a warning. All the maybes and hope-filled thoughts crashed and burned, just like they did three years ago. His angry eyes bored into me, telling me the things he wouldn't say.

Gulping my pride, I poked his trim side and flashed a fake smile. "Gotcha. Been there, done that, no repeats. I'd rate you five out of ten stars."

Something like a grunt or groan left his mouth, but I paid no attention. My adrenaline would get me through this. I was cool as a cloud. My heart wasn't racing and my skin itching with embarrassment. Nope. Not me.

Liar.

"Char," he said, the timbre of his voice back to normal, "there's a bench over there. Let's sit."

He jutted his chin to a cozy bench near a different fireplace. There was a small Christmas tree, covered in popcorn and only blue ornaments. I loved the look. It was like a sexy winter tree. Dark and light blues combined with grays, and wow, they were all snowflakes. I touched one shaped like a star. It had the names Maggie and Mark and the year on it.

Our family went bonkers on Christmas, but I'd be lying if I didn't fantasize about having what my parents had, what

Christian and Penny would have. *As long as they still have a wedding.*

Worry etched its way down my spine, swirling and gripping me. I knew what I had heard, and couldn't believe it. What could've happened to have them consider calling off the wedding? I chewed my nail as I took another sip of my old-fashioned.

Hayden slid into the other side of the booth, his eyes intense as he stared at me. "I can't drink whiskey and not think of you."

"I feel like that's a compliment," I said, nervously laughing.

"It is. Very much so." He sipped his Guinness, his attention all on me. He had a way of making me feel like the center of the universe when he looked at me that way. "So about us—"

"Penny and Christian," I blurted out, refusing to acknowledge whatever he wanted to say. I thought myself bold, and over him, but I was neither bold enough to have this conversation nor over all my feelings for him. I wanted to be friends with him again someday, but these pesky feelings remained. "Can you sense their tension?"

Hayden gripped the back of his neck, wincing. "Yeah. I see it now. I've been a little distracted, so I didn't pick up on it, but Christian has been acting weird the last week or so too."

"Right? Okay, I thought the same, but with my interview—wait, why are you distracted? Is everything alright?" My thoughts went to Gwen, but he wouldn't be up here if he was stressed about her.

"Work stuff." He shifted in his chair, his sweater pulling against his chest in a magnificent way. "I think you were right earlier."

I blinked. "I mean, I love hearing those words any time of day, but what are you specifically referring to?"

"Doing whatever Penny and Christian want, which are these games. Every time they are involved in a challenge, they bond, or maybe it's an aphrodisiac. I don't really know with them, but competition is romantic to them."

"That's true." I tapped my chin, focusing outside the window. A couple kissed next to a candy cane sculpture. "We could remind them of all the times they teamed up and won?"

"Yes, and we do everything in our power to win these stupid games." He lowered his voice, leaning closer to me. "If we win, they'll be so thrilled, they'll forget about whatever they were arguing about."

I sighed, a deep sadness seeping into my bones. I met his stare and poured my heart out. "That's our endgame. They have to get married. I can't fathom..." My voice shook, and I cleared my throat, taking a quick sip to settle. "Okay, we focus on winning these games for them, at all costs."

"I'll toast to that." He held up his glass, his lips quirked up on the side like he had an inside joke. "Win at all costs."

"For Penny and Christian." I clinked his glass and relaxed further into my chair.

Hayden sipped his Guinness before placing it on the table, his large fingers tapping on the top. The movement caused the table to shake. He ran a finger over his eyebrow before leaning on his elbows. "I have a question for you."

I braced myself as my stomach flipped. "What is it?"

His jaw twitched before he asked, "Why didn't you come to me to talk about this potential coaching job?"

It was my turn to raise my eyebrows. I wasn't expecting that question. "That's what you wanted to talk about?"

"Yes." He pursed his lips and stared out the window, his gorgeous gray eyes reflecting the icy landscape. "You sent your résumé to Garrett. He's never coached a day in his life."

"True." I traced the rim of my glass, studying his micro-expressions. His jaw was tense. His muscles were tight. He squinted his eyes. He wasn't pleased. "Garrett and I are friends, and he offered. It wasn't really a question of if I'd have him look it over."

My sweater stuck to my skin, and I took another long swig. It burned all the way down, but I welcomed it. It was better than this stare down. Hayden had asked to speak with me, not the other way around. I refused to do a thing about this silence.

"You could've come to me," he said, his tone gentle. "I would've helped you."

"And said what, Hayden?" I laughed, but it wasn't happy. "If you look at the last few years, we barely speak unless it involves Gwen. I love that baby girl more than life itself, and this isn't about her in the slightest, but when was the last time we spoke of anything besides her?"

His face paled. "You're right."

"It became easier to just ignore you, really." I shrugged, hating the ache in my chest and the prickle in my eyes. "I care about you and Gwen, obviously, but I didn't feel like going to you for help was an option."

"Charlotte, I would do anything—"

I waved a hand in the air. "I know, if I was in a dire situation, you'd drop everything. I truly know that. You'd do that for anyone you care about. But advice? Help preparing for an interview? That's what friends do. Not...whatever we are."

"You really feel this way, don't you?" he asked. His face crumpled, and he leaned back in his chair and stared at me.

"Yeah, I do." I ran a hand over my hair, adjusting the bun at the top, and I winced.

"Are you okay?" He frowned. "Your neck?"

"Whiplash got me." I rubbed the spot where my neck and shoulder met, closing my eyes as pain radiated throughout my body. "The doc said this would be normal, but wow, didn't expect that with a little movement."

"You should be resting."

"No, I'm fine, Hayden. I didn't come here to lie in a bed. I could've done that at home, in sweats, without crashing my car." I jumped up. "Wait, did you ever get my car towed? What do I owe you?"

Hayden lifted his hand. "Nothing. All taken care of."

"Um, no? I'll pay you back."

"It's fine, Char. We can worry about it once we get back home, okay? You need to focus on relaxing your muscles and winning this stupid competition. Not a few hundred bucks."

I fought the urge to argue with him and bit my tongue. Hayden was a man of actions, not words. He showed he cared by doing things, like the time in high school he drove a very drunk Christian home and hid it from my parents.

I'd figure out a way to get him the money back, so I smiled. "Thank you."

"You're welcome." He sighed and leaned his forearms onto his knees, a serious look crossing his face. "I'm sorry."

I desperately wanted him to clarify if it was for breaking my heart or not, but it wasn't the time. This moment was about the present, about our relationship now. An uncomfortable itch formed behind my chest, the familiar sign of guilt right behind it. "I am too. You can't bear the weight of everything."

A beat passed, and he nodded, almost like he wanted the conversation to end and move to the next topic. "We're here now, together, for Christian and Penny, doing all sorts of weird holiday shit."

"A perfect time to be friends again," I blurted.

"Okay then." He smiled. "Now, talk to me about this job."

I shrugged. Talking about this would be a great first step in reconnecting as friends. "My athletic director told me I'm too young to apply for the varsity position."

"That's bullshit and illegal." Hayden's jaw tensed. "He can't say that to you."

"I know, but it happened. That's the small-town world I work in. It's all a boys' network, where they have each other's backs, and it's all who you know." I pulled the edges of my sleeves up to cover the tips of my fingers. "The baseball, basketball, and football coaches are all buds with this new guy, Chad Rogers. He's the front-runner for the position."

"I don't give a damn about Chad Rogers." Hayden placed both of his large hands on top of the table, spreading his fingers out like he was pushing it away from him.

"You talk like I have a shot at this," I whispered.

"Of course you do." He frowned. "When have you ever accepted defeat, Char?"

When it came to you, I almost said. Somehow, I found superhero strength and kept my mouth shut against that little comment. Besides my emotional business with him, I never accepted defeat. I went after what I wanted. Always. I lived with moxie and a kind heart.

"Okay, okay, okay," I said. My pulse raced. "All this talk has me desperate to get this job. I want it so badly, and if I don't get it, it'll crush me."

"What's your other option then? Giving up before you have a chance?" He shook his head, his voice getting deeper, more passionate. "You can't control the outcome of a game, or an interview, because there are so many external factors. But what can you control? You. How much you try. How you leave everything on the field and walk away knowing you gave it your all. You play your heart out. You interview with everything you've got."

"You're being awfully nice." I laughed nervously. "I'm not used to this."

"That's what you get when we're friends. The truth." He sighed, leaned back against his bench, and took another long drink. "One thing we have in common that none of our friends have is our experience being D1 athletes. That's a lifestyle that is hard to compare unless you've lived it. And we have. So I know, from that experience alone, you got this."

"I might need to call you every day until the interview to boost up my confidence." I smiled, but it was shaky. "I feel bolder now, but when I head into work Monday, the guys will snicker or say something rude."

"You call me anytime you need, alright? I'm sorry you didn't know that before." His face was set in serious lines as his voice hardened. "Now, did you bring your laptop? I want to see what you have."

"Garrett sent me some feedback that—"

"He doesn't know shit." He stared me down, daring me to argue.

Garrett didn't have as much coaching experience as Hayden. Garrett was a wizard at editing and wordsmithing, not the content though. It was practical to have Hayden help me too. I nodded. "Operation Kick Chad's Ass is underway, OKCA, if you will."

Hayden barked out a laugh, the sound like a warm hug to my soul. His eyes sparkled with amusement, and for one final second, I let myself imagine what it'd be like to laugh with him all the time. Then I focused on the fact that he was helping me. I gave him two thumbs-up. "Let me get my laptop and then we can get to work."

CHAPTER EIGHT

HAYDEN

Two hours later, it was clear as hell to me why I stayed away from Charlotte. Everything she did captivated me. Her intelligence and passion, the way she laughed at herself but refused to back down from her strengths. She had the confidence I wanted Gwen to have in this world.

A memory of Charlotte holding Gwen came to mind, the two of them sitting together and singing a song. Charlotte had volunteered to watch her so I could coach an away game, and when I walked in the next morning and found them all cuddled up, my knees almost gave out. My baby girl loved Charlotte, and seeing them like that made me think about what life could be like with her in it. That fantasy barged in unwarranted from time to time, but being around Charlotte brought it back to the top of my mind.

"Hop, hey, I rambled too much, didn't I?" Charlotte scrunched her nose, shaking her head at herself. "I guess I didn't need to get too into the details about the new scoreboard."

"No, you're fine." I scrubbed my face with my free hand. "Thinking about Gwen."

"You miss her." Her face softened. "You're such a good dad, Hayden. It's one of my favorite things about you." She nudged her knee against mine under the table. "I don't have a lot of friends with children, but every time you speak about her, your face lights up."

"She's the best part of my life."

"And she knows it. That's wonderful." She beamed at me, like my love for my daughter made her happy. When Charlotte looked at me like I personally hung the stars for her, it made my stomach ache with want, with the need to kiss her.

"Back to your idea," I said, my voice scratchy. We were here to talk about the interview. I would do whatever I could to make sure Charlotte had the best chance of earning this. I lived and breathed the boys' club circle. I hated it while knowing I benefited from the politics. One of my professional goals was to acknowledge the unfair practices and call them out when possible.

It was one of the many reasons I had hired a female assistant coach. Silvia Reyes was my second-in-command, someone I trusted implicitly and the person I'd risk my career for. Hiring her made shock waves in our small-town college community. But she was the best. End of story. She worked harder than anyone I had ever met and was game to weather the storm.

The best part about all of this? The guys on the team didn't give a shit. They respected her knowledge of the game, how she spoke to them, and how she pushed them to be better athletes on and off the field. Respect is earned, not given.

Fuck, this got me fired up. I hired Silvia two years ago, and things have finally started to calm down, but hashing this out with Char reminded me of the shitstorm it had caused.

"Why do you want this?" I asked Charlotte.

She chewed inside her cheek as she stared at me. Her large doe eyes and long lashes were her best feature. They were windows to her soul, and when she looked at me like this, open and vulnerable, it made me want to move mountains for her.

"I want to cultivate a program for student athletes where they feel safe and where they grow and learn the value of friendship and sisterhood and teamwork. I want them to develop skills that'll help them their entire lives. I want them to be proud to play and love coming to school. I want depth from middle school to senior year. I want to bring a championship to the community. I had so many coaches who made my life better, and I want to give back, do that for others. Mentor those who need it. Be a family for those who lack one. Plus I want to elevate female athletes because they matter just as much." Her chest heaved, and red splotched her cheeks. "Wow, that was a messy answer."

"It was passionate." I fought the urge to grab her hand. "That was a great fucking answer, Char. It was unfiltered, sure, but that answer? We can work with it and make it into professional-speak."

She furrowed her brows. "What do you mean?"

"If you're going against this Chad Douche, you need to polish this so they can't say you're too young. Again, it's bullshit and illegal, but it's reality. If Chad is the chosen one and the bro, you need to be better than him in every way."

Charlotte nodded. "Okay, I like this plan. Let's do it right now. Do I do a PowerPoint? Write this all out? I'd love—"

"Hey," I said, smiling at her. "First, take a breath and another drink."

She blinked fast, her face lighting up with energy. Charlotte was like a bolt of lightning when she put her mind to something, and I always admired that about her. She learned to drive a stick shift out of pure determination. She earned a scholarship because she spent every waking second improving herself. Honestly, I don't know how I didn't even think to have Charlotte and Silvia talk. She'd be an incredible resource for her too.

Charlotte breathed in and out, long and slow, her lips forming a little O shape. They seemed redder, plumper. *Shit.* I cleared my throat, sipping my beer to cool down my thoughts. This was game time, nothing more.

"First lesson for you: perception is reality."

"Um, okay? Are you a philosopher? What does that even mean?" She frowned. Tight lines formed around her eyes and mouth, and they looked so out of place.

Charlotte was one of the happiest people I knew, and even her face seemed to repel the thought of not smiling. The little line between her eyebrows was adorable. My finger twitched, the urge to trace the little indent overwhelmingly strong.

"The athletic director clearly has an agenda already. His perception of the role, of who should have it, is his reality. So in his mind, you're too young. Chad is better, older."

"Um, I hate this."

"I know, but hold on. There's a purpose to this." I fought a smile.

"Are you sure? I thought this might be punishment for calling you *daddy* earlier, so you want to make me sweat." She chuckled.

A flash of heat pounded through me. *No. Not now.*

"No. I'm trying to prepare you for how to win. Much like coaching, you have to scout the competition. If the AD has this notion already, how can you pick it apart? How can you change his perception of you? Is it experience? Is it familiarity with the parent groups? Is it contacts in the community? We figure out the root of his opinion, and then we exploit it."

"Wow." Charlotte ran a hand over her hair, her mouth slightly parted. "This is...I can't believe I thought I could do this without you."

"Char, hon, you absolutely could've. I just want to help give you a leg up."

She eyed her watch and sighed. "This could take hours. We only have a few before they're back and we get ready for dinner. What if I can't get this all done by then?"

"I know." This time I frowned. "Why are you worried?"

"Can we...could we meet again tomorrow about it?" Her mouth twisted in concern. Her eyes dimmed. "I can watch Gwen in payment! Or, uh, find something—"

"Whoa, hey." This time I placed my hand on hers. Her

soft skin contrasted with my rough, dry hand. "I offered to help you, and I don't do anything half-assed. We can meet as often as it takes."

"Are you sure? I'm needy and have so many questions. You might get annoyed, and if we're trying to be friends—"

"You never annoy me," I almost growled.

"That is not true." Her eyes twinkled this time. "I recall a moment when you were twenty-one when you told me to stop talking."

I knew exactly what she referenced. My face heated. "I had brought my girlfriend back from college, and you wouldn't shut up about all the times I was an idiot."

"Oh, I know." A smug, sexy smile flittered across her face. "Just saying, I do have the ability to annoy you. It's important to acknowledge when I'm right."

"God, you're annoying," I teased.

She granted me another smile. "I've missed you, Hayden. I enjoyed being a part of your and Christian's circle. I'm glad we ended up here together this weekend."

Her words felt like a blanket wrapping around me and providing me warmth. She missed me. I missed her. Her accusations earlier were true. I did push her away, and I've lived with that regret for years. She might never know the real reasons for it, and I thought...maybe...somehow that we'd have a chance to talk about it.

"Me too," I said. It could be the two drinks, the fire, or the way she stared at me, but my face tingled with heat. This moment seemed bigger than just us reconnecting, like whatever happened this weekend would change everything.

I might've been grumpy about driving hours away from my parents and daughter, but at least one good thing would come of this. Char and I were learning to be friends again. Even being around her just a short time reminded me of all the reasons I adored her, and if I could hide my attraction and not be an ass, we would be okay.

I just had to stop staring at her lips, wondering if they still tasted the same.

CHAPTER NINE

CHARLOTTE

Son of a nutcracker. There might be an issue with being too competitive. Penny handed us sheets of paper explaining the rules, but she held up her finger first.

"I downloaded the app for our team. It has the instructions for us for the Lost Days of Christmas games." Penny studied her phone with an intense expression on her face. "I split us into teams for different tasks based on our skills. For the first round, Charlotte and Hayden need to head to the lobby for wrapping and drink-making challenges. The rest of us will head to Tinsel Town for the scavenger hunt portion to solve riddles and meet up with you in thirty minutes."

"Shouldn't we all be together?" I asked, confused why there were two challenges at the same time. It had nothing to do with being alone with Hayden, but more about wanting to be near my brother and Penny to do whatever I could to help. They bickered a little at dinner. Nothing major like what Hayden and I overheard, but enough to make Hayden and me share a glance.

Penny rolled her eyes. "You hate the teams. I can adjust it?"

"Pen, no." I pulled her into a hug, feeling awful that I stressed her out for a second. I wanted to do the opposite of that! "I've never done anything like this, so I was curious. Hayden and I will totally be fine."

"My sis is just concerned that she and Hayden won't beat us." Christian smirked.

"Not true. We'll kick all your asses," I fired back, forgetting our mission to help save the wedding. Hayden cleared his throat, signaling me to stop. By some grace of a Christmas angel, I shut up.

"The app breaks down each competition with points, right, baby?" Christian slung his arm around Penny. She leaned into him, which was a great sign.

"Yes. Then, after the final round, the points are totaled." She frowned. "Why do you have your crazy face on?"

"I have a wager for you, Char. We need a DJ for our wedding…"

"Oh! Yes, we sure do. Great idea, babe." Penny pinched Christian's side. "I forgot how sexy being competitive was on you."

"Calm it down." Garrett pointed at them. "What's the wager?"

"If we beat Hayden and Char, then they DJ our wedding."

I shook my head. "I love you, but I refuse to DJ your wedding."

Penny grinned, a sparkle dancing in her eyes. "Mm, we'll see about that."

"Whoa, we need our side of the wager." Hayden winked. "I say they do a planned dance. Something to really embarrass them."

"Hm, we could do better, I think. Matching outfits too? That we pick out?"

Hayden nodded. "I'm in."

"Now we're talking." I clapped. "Okay, deal. It's on."

Christian narrowed his eyes at me but kept his arm around Penny. That seemed really great, so maybe betting was bringing them closer?

"Now that that is settled, we can head to our separate portions and meet back up in thirty minutes for the final round. Don't let me down." Penny put her hands in the middle. "Let's all cheer on three. One...two...three. Go, team!"

Garrett, Christian, and Penny bundled up, since the Tinsel Town Riddles started outside. I was grateful to not do that because I had been cold since the car accident. Wrapping presents and making drinks—even with Hayden—was more my style.

"Shall we?" Hayden gestured to head toward the main lobby. He barely took a step before he stopped, frowning at his phone. "Shit."

"What is it?"

"It's my mom." He rubbed his eyebrow as he stared at his phone. "She set up an interview with her next-door neighbor's daughter, Frankie."

"An interview for...?"

"Watching Gwen." He rolled his shoulders. "She wants the interview for Monday afternoon. I just...why would she think Frankie is a good fit? I've tried finding someone, and they never work out."

"Gwen goes over there all the time, right? Frankie has probably met her. You should interview her. You can't avoid it for too much longer, Hayden."

"Look, you're right, but..." he said, closing his phone. "I want to have fun tonight and not worry about my life back home. Could we leave it alone for today?"

"You're helping me with coaching stuff, I can help talk through this." My stomach twisted. I wanted him to let me in, let me be his friend. Friends helped each other!

He cracked a knuckle before meeting my eyes, and his face softened. "I'd like that, but tomorrow."

"First thing then."

He laughed, like I had wanted him to. His shoulders relaxed, and we continued our pace toward the main lobby. It was a short five-minute walk. "You better bring your A-game, Coach. I'll avoid the wedding if I have to DJ it."

"We're both in agreement there."

He opened the door for me, ushering me in, and my mouth fell open. *Son of a snowman.*

Since we had left to head to dinner, the place had been completely transformed. Twenty tables were set up in a circle, each containing ten boxes and several rolls of wrapping paper. Christmas music blared from the speakers, and it was like a million sprigs of mistletoe had exploded from every corner.

Was Santa playing cupid this trip, because what the

mistletoe-loving heck? They were everywhere! I couldn't take a walk without encountering three of them. I'd have to dance my way across the lobby. But the snow globes! There were at least two hundred placed on end tables and shelves.

Hayden gaped at the lobby, the same wonderment crossing his face. "Holy shit."

"It's almost a Christmas porn created for people like Christian and Penny." Green and red lights were everywhere. Snowflakes hung from the ceiling. Snowmen stood in corners, some moving.

"Do you think they bring wrapping paper into the bedroom?" he teased.

"My parents were always telling him to wrap it up," I said, absolutely losing it over our joke. I cackled.

Hayden too let out a deep, delicious howl of laughter. He squeezed my shoulder—the uninjured one—and smiled. It had been a long time since I saw the full effect of a Hayden grin. My stomach flipped over ten times, and a flurry of butterflies danced in my gut, because damn, he was so handsome.

"Do I have something on my face?" He frowned. "You're staring at me weird."

"Honestly?" I scrunched my nose. "It's been a while since I've seen your real smile. Looks good on you. Happiness suits you," I said.

His eyes warmed just as our phones went off. He pulled his out of his pocket. "We're table eight." He squinted and jutted his chin toward the back.

"Getting old, eh? Need some glasses soon?" I teased as we walked over toward our station. There were two pairs of scissors, four different strands of ribbons, and two dispensers of tape. Every table seemed to have the same supplies, with a large pile of boxes sitting in the middle. We had to wrap as many as possible in the time frame. I removed my jacket and placed my hands on my hips. It was almost game time.

He grunted. "I have some, thank you very much. You wait until you're this close to thirty and talk to me."

"I'm going to need to see proof of these glasses, Hayden." I counted the tape a table over and frowned. "Wait, they have more tape than us. Not fair."

Hayden froze and noted the difference. "Unacceptable."

I counted another table with more bows than us too. "Who is in charge around here?"

"That would be me."

I spun and grinned when I recognized whom the voice belonged to. It was my buddy from earlier. This time, he was dressed fully as Buddy the Elf. Yellow tights, green jacket and hat, the whole thing. "Brendon, my man!"

"Ah, glad to see you're doing okay." Brendon smiled, his eyes dropping to my sweater. "Very festive shirt."

"Oh, this old thing?" I refused to blush. "Felt like going a little wild tonight."

"I can see." Brendon stepped closer, his minty cologne washing over me. The man smelled like a candy cane. It was wonderfully strange. "Now, was there a problem?"

"Yes." Hayden joined us, his chest touching my back. His warmth spread through my sweater, heating me up from proximity alone. What was he doing standing so close to me? We'd had a wonderful truce going on for hours. Sure, I still had a crush and got butterflies when he touched me, but I had stopped obsessing over it.

But he touched me.

I didn't hate it, if I was being honest.

"All teams should have the same number of supplies. I've found three discrepancies, which puts us at an unfair disadvantage." Hayden used his stern Daddy voice, one that shouldn't affect me in any way.

It was bossy and direct. Yet...my thighs clenched together. In my deepest, darkest fantasies, I wanted Hayden to boss me around in bed. I wanted him to walk me through everything he dreamed of, and I'd do it, without a second thought. But this wasn't that at all. This was a silly Christmas competition with Brendon the Elf in charge.

My sweater was a little too heavy. Maybe they could open a window? Or extinguish one of the million fireplaces they had going. It'd ease the growing heat in the lobby.

Brendon blinked. "You're right. They should be the same. I'll make sure we double-check."

"See that you do."

Brendon took off toward another person wearing a full Santa suit, and once he was out of view, I hit Hayden's arm. "Don't be mean to Brendon. He reports to Santa."

"Okay," he scoffed. "He was staring at your chest the whole time."

"I mean, look at it?" I faced him, sticking it out. "It's ridiculous! Of course he's going to look. That is the point!"

"You want him looking at you like that, Charlotte?"

Oh no. He'd used his deep voice again. His eyes darkened, and he clenched his jaw.

The butterflies tripled in my gut, a whole swarm of them overtaking my senses. "Him specifically? Perhaps not. But I'm single, Hayden. Sometimes a girl just wants to flirt and have fun, maybe kiss under a mistletoe. If Brendon is the guy, then who cares?"

Hayden's nostrils flared again, and his gaze dropped to my mouth.

The holiday music disappeared, and the people around us stopped existing. It was just Hayden and me, and he was looking at my lips. My body tingled like it was surrounded in Christmas lights, and a small, tiny groan escaped my mouth.

His gaze snapped to mine, his eyes dangerously wide.

"What. The fuck. Was that sound?"

Oh no.

I stared, my mind blaring the alarm. *Run.* My throat dried up. I didn't mean to let that throaty moan escape. My vision blurred as we stared at each other, his gray eyes penetrating my fickle shield. His pupils dilated as he stepped closer to me with one hand raised toward my face.

What is happening? I froze.

"Okay, folks, the competition is starting in two minutes! Make sure you're at your table. If you're not sure, download the app or ask one of us here!" Brendon yelled into the microphone, the sound penetrating whatever bubble had formed around us.

I jumped a foot in the air. Hayden sucked in a breath and moved so fast that I would've been embarrassed if my heart weren't on the verge of shutting down. He had put several feet of distance between us as he ran a hand over his face. His body language screamed *regret*, which wasn't great for my ego.

I had been doing so well, being friends with him and not letting my crush sneak through. But he broke the rule and stared at my mouth. I used all my strength to compartmentalize and get into competition mode.

Thank goodness for Brendon speaking a little too loudly into the microphone. It forced all other thoughts from my mind.

"Every table should have ten boxes, tape, scissors, and four options for wrapping paper. The first round is to wrap as many as you can in ten minutes. The more detailed the wrap, the more points. Bows and ribbons get you extra points, and neatness and creativity do as well. I'm starting 'Jingle Bells,' and when it stops, it's go time!" Brendon cheered.

"Shit. Okay. Speed and details. We can do both." I stretched my arms above my head, wiggling side to side. I wanted my arms' full abilities.

"You look ridiculous." Hayden set his jacket down on the chair like a normal person, amusement crossing his face. "Are we arm wrestling for wrapping paper?"

"Nope. We have to cut straight lines fast and use details. Are you good at cutting paper?"

"Most of Gwen's gifts are in giftbags with tissue paper. That's a no for me." He crossed his arms and eyed the materials.

I imagined this was how he looked on the field. Guilt ate at me knowing I had never seen him coach at the college level. He had just started his job there when everything went to hell, so I'd missed out on a lot of things, like how serious he looked while making a game plan. *And hot, but that doesn't matter.*

"Penny might not actually want to win this thing if she put me on this activity." He gripped the back of his neck. Then his gaze flicked to mine, his gray eyes sparkling. "I'd rather continue the conversation we were having before Bernie interrupted us."

"What?" I organized the materials by color. That felt important. Christmas colors needed to be coordinated so we used the correct ribbons and bows. Scissors sat in a nice row, and I frowned at the tape. If one of us ripped off a bunch of pieces and prepped them, that would speed things up.

"Charlotte." Hayden drew nearer to me, his warmth and scent surrounding me.

I blinked up at him, noting the heat in his eyes that wasn't there before. Wait. His words hit me again and clicked. *We were talking about the sound I accidentally made.* My face heated as questions swirled in my dumbfounded brain.

"Nothing to talk about. I had…heartburn and burped?"

Good gravy, I am the worst. I cringed and rubbed my temples, wishing I could just wrap myself in this paper and be shipped to the other side of the world. That would be preferable to lying to Hayden.

My dignity had reached a new low.

I felt more than heard Hayden's laugh as he leaned toward me. "Liar, but I'll follow your lead. Plus I refuse to be a DJ at Christian's wedding. We have a few more minutes. Let's make a plan."

Yes. We must win. Focus on the competition.

"Your head is finally in the game." I eyed the layout of our assembly line. "I'll cut while you tear up a hundred little pieces of tape. You can place them on the edge of the table, leaving a little bit hanging so I can grab it. Then once I wrap, you cut and tie ribbon. If I have time, I could curl it."

"Nah, I can curl ribbon. Can't wrap worth shit, but curling? I'm the best. I could beat Bernie at it, I guarantee it." He puffed out his chest, looking mighty proud of himself.

"Interesting flex." My lips quirked. "How do you know how to curl ribbon?"

"My mom showed me to ensure I wasn't a total failure once they move away. I might not wrap well, but I would sure as hell make Gwen pretty bows. That girl loses it at the sight of rainbow ribbons. She once kept one for a month in her bedroom." He sighed, the smile disappearing. "I'm not handling them moving away well."

Oh lord. Daddy Hayden was sweet, but the vulnerable one? The one talking about real feelings? I was a puddle of emotions. A snowman-in-the-desert type of puddle.

"Penny and I can help. I happen to be great at wrapping. It was expected of us at age three. My mom took us to classes. My friends would do fun things while Christian and I were stuck at Macy's with a bunch of older women."

Hayden laughed. "How did I not know this about you?"

"There's quite a bit you don't know about me," I said, tensing at the way my voice deepened in hidden meaning.

"Hold on to your reindeer, smell the candy canes, folks, it is about to start!" Brendon yelled into the mic so loud that the speaker distorted. "Three, two, one, go!"

I slid the scissors down the green-and-red-polka-dot wrapping paper. I aimed for an easy square to fit the smaller of the boxes. "You preparing the tape?"

"Yes, Chef."

I snorted. "Don't make me laugh with scissors! Isn't that the first rule of parenthood?"

"Not sure. Didn't read that book."

"Damn it, Hop." I chuckled again as I cut my third paper. "This is good, right? I should wrap some?"

"Yes, so I can bow them up." He glanced at the tables next to us. "They are going to town, but there is no zhuzh. We can bring that."

"How do you even know that word?"

"There's a lot about me you don't know." He repeated my words back to me, his voice dropping an octave.

Goose bumps exploded down my body. He nudged me with a proud smile on his face. "Focus, Char. You seem too distracted."

"Ugh."

I wrapped three boxes, using the pre-cut tape and smoothing down the paper in crisp angles. They looked good. Once I confirmed they were acceptable, I cut more squares. I even doubled up the paper. See, work smarter, not harder.

The music blaring over the speaker seemed louder and more techno. It was off-putting and intoxicating. My pulse matched the beat as we worked in unison. "I'm glad it's you and me doing this."

"Penny knew we'd work well together. We're coaches.

We remain calm under pressure and can compartmental-ize." Hayden worked on a tricolor bow that was gorgeous. Watching his large, calloused hands curl the delicate ribbon was an experience.

"Mm, you might be right about the coaching part, but I'm not the best compartmentalizer right now. My mind is racing."

"Oh, so is mine, Char. I have a lot of things on my mind, most of them about you. But I can focus on the task at hand—winning the overall competition while also get-ting a better score than Christian. I do it on the field all the time."

That intrigued me. The comment about me, sure, but the field. "How do you do it on the field?"

We kept working quickly together as he spoke. "Emo-tions run high. You want the best for your players but also the team. My goals don't always align with the guys. My job is to win once the game starts. How do I balance their egos, their wants and dreams, with my own? How do I deal with bullshit calls and adrenaline? What if my baby girl was sick all night and I got no sleep, but I have to show up and lead the team? I push the bullshit aside and focus on what matters in that moment. No use worrying or thinking about shit I can't fix then and there."

"I can do that most of the time, but I let emotions creep in too much."

"That comes with experience. You'll get there."

He passed me one of my paper squares, and I started on the ninth box. This wrapping paper design showed elves sledding, which made me smile. It was kinda cute. "I wish these boxes had something in them instead of just air. We could donate something to a shelter or a school."

Hayden stilled. "Damn, that's a good idea. Make sure to tell Barney that while he's staring at your *sweater*."

"Hayden." I swatted at him, curious at his jealousy. "What is it with you and that guy?"

He grunted as he bent low to tie together a bright gold-and-silver ribbon. The grunt and delicate ribbon were so opposite that it was endearing as hell. "I don't like how he looks at you."

"Because he's flirting? It's harmless, and I enjoy it. Some people might find me cute, Coach, even if that's gross to think about." It was easier to say this while focusing on a task that used my hands. I had to focus on the scissors instead of his reaction.

"Charlotte."

"What?" I kept my head down, taking my time to wrap this box a little more slowly than the others. I could feel the weight of his stare boring into me. It was almost physical. My neck broke out into goose bumps, but I refused to face him. I checked the large timer displayed on the wall, and it read three minutes. "Keep cutting ribbons, please. We have three minutes left to see how many we can finish!"

"Look at me."

"No, we don't have time." My voice was on edge, a little too high and whiney. Hayden needed to remember the goal. "Please, we can't lose!"

He placed his hand on mine, removed the scissors, and used his other one to turn my face toward him. His thumb grazed my lower lip, and his dark gray eyes were almost silver. He was so intense, so serious, as he stared me down. "You are fucking beautiful."

"Oh."

"Yeah. *Oh*." His eyes danced with amusement. "This just proves I'm great at compartmentalizing."

"Wait. What?" My mind was fuzzy. It had to be the car accident, or the drinks, or the fact that Hayden had touched my lips and said I was beautiful. The man who told me he'd never care for me or see me that way had said those words to me. My axis shifted. If he thought I was beautiful, then why not say those words three years ago?

He chuckled, the deep vibration of his laugh wrapping itself around my soul. The sound of his joy was like a huge bear hug, squeezing around you. He moved his fingers across my jaw, his nostrils flaring. "I understand I've said things that made you think I only see you as Christian's little sister. I've done a damn good job at hiding my attraction to you."

Attraction. To me. Hayden Porter attracted to Charlotte Calhoun. What in the ever-loving holiday hell? He said those words! To me! With his mouth! I was gonna stab him.

"Two-minute warning!"

I eyed the tables around us, and they had more gifts wrapped but fewer ribbons. "Hayden, we're going to lose."

"Maybe this round, but it was worth telling you you're beautiful."

Compartmentalize.

What a great time to learn to put my emotions in little gift boxes and wrap them up and store them deep in my mind. The hurt I felt at what he said that night three years ago? Wrapped up tight. The confusion I felt now? Double wrapped it. The lust and desire I had from him touching me? Yeah, I used a whole spool of ribbon to tie that one up. Winning the competition was key. Saving the wedding was our only goal.

Like an evil game master, the music became louder as time ticked down. Hayden and I worked fast, like we'd done this our whole lives. Cut, wrap, tape, ribbon, repeat. We put finishing touches on four more boxes, so we had fourteen wrapped perfectly, each with curled ribbon.

"And time is up! Drop the wrapping materials!" Brendon yelled. "We're going to have our judges come around and take score with our holiday rubric!"

"I think we might come in third. They have more presents." I frowned, chewing the inside of my cheek. As someone who grew up with the motto *If you ain't first, you're last*, this didn't sit well with me. Plus I really didn't want to DJ the wedding, but...if that meant there was a wedding, would we have to suck it up and do it anyway?

Brendon came up to our table and slid me a grin.

I returned his smile and even added a little hip pop to my stance. "How'd we do? Any inside information?"

"Dare I ask you to meet me over there and I can give you a preview?" he teased. "There's a nice-looking mistletoe waiting for us."

"I like your style, Brendon. For an elf, you're just my type." I blew him a kiss.

He caught it, laughed, and moved on to the next table.

Hayden glared at me.

"What? I told you. I like flirting. I haven't had a date in years. Wait, I sure have, but I haven't had a good one. Not one where I can laugh or be myself. If I want to make out with a guy in an elf costume, who cares? I just want to be kissed, dang it!"

His nostrils flared, and he reached toward me. "When you say things like that—"

"Alright, the next competition starts in thirty seconds, folks! We'll have the scores updated in the app, but we were running a little behind, so we're moving on to the next round. Get back to your tables and get ready!"

CHAPTER TEN

HAYDEN

I really wasn't a fan of that man-elf. Brendon continued to find the perfect fucking times to interrupt me. It was like he knew I wanted to cross a line with Charlotte and stopped me.

Wait. My parents always believed in signs—was this one? Telling me to back off? Like this wintery, holiday version was my personal hell. I wanted to ask Charlotte if I could be the person under the mistletoe but I stopped myself?

What am I doing?

We legit just agreed to be friends. That was it. I was a single dad without my shit together. I could offer a one-night stand. Charlotte was a relationship kinda gal who deserved to be someone's main priority. I couldn't offer her what she wanted, plain and simple. She was off-limits despite my attraction to her.

If I had to tattoo KEEP AWAY FROM CHARLOTTE onto my eyelids so I would not forget, that would be great. Because what the hell had gotten into me? Kissing her would be a huge mistake. Nothing could come of it, and we had already learned our lesson, and I hated not having her in my life. I'd be a damn fool to repeat it. Even if the thought of her kissing someone else made my fists clench when I couldn't stop fantasizing about her red lips and how full they were. They drew me in every time she spoke.

I had a craving for cherries all of a sudden.

"This is wild," she said, those lips pursing as she scanned the room.

Bernie and his team of elves were scattered throughout the lobby carrying large bottles of alcohol. They didn't just walk either. They jogged with jingle bells attached to their hats and socks. *Obnoxious* was too kind a word. They needed to be stopped.

"I'd never judge," Charlotte said, a cute smirk forming on her face, "but do you think they keep the socks on all the time? Like, in the bedroom?"

I snorted. "Probably. Bernie absolutely does. I'd bet Gwen's inheritance that he has a full back tattoo of Rudolph too."

She swatted me. "No. No he doesn't."

I shrugged, tilting my head. "One will never know."

Her quiet laughter made me smile. I loved the sound of her little chuckle. She leaned closer to me with her arm stretched out toward Bernie. "Looks like every table receives one large bottle, two small bottles, and a mini Santa bag. What on God's green earth are we about to do?"

"Directions, here." An elf tossed a sparkly scroll onto our table. "Don't touch it."

Written in a black font: DO NOT FLIP OVER UNTIL WE SAY GO.

Madness. I ran a hand through my hair just to rid myself of this restless energy. The high from the wrapping challenge never quite wore off. Hey, maybe that was why I wanted to kiss Charlotte. The adrenaline rush. The postgame adrenaline that I always had after a win.

See, I wasn't a total jerk. Content with my solid investigation into why I had the hots for Charlotte again, I nodded. I wasn't going to cross a line. I just needed to find a way to release this energy after the competition was all said and done. As I waited for the next round, I checked my phone and frowned at the third text from a random number. It's me. Hayden, please call me back. This is important.

Who is this? I replied.

No answer.

It almost felt like a prank, but I shoved my phone in my pocket. If it was truly important, they'd call.

"Okay, folks, this is round two," Brendon's voice crackled over the speaker. "Each of you received some mystery materials you'll use to create a holiday drink. The more festive, the better. The tastier, the better. This will challenge your senses and your quick thinking. You have ten minutes total before you present your drink to the judges in the sleigh. Wave, judges!"

Three people sat in a full-ass Santa sleigh near the front door. The women wore dresses from the early 1900s, probably, and the dude wore a top hat and a monocle. I had zero clue how that related to this holiday tomfoolery. Charlotte about buzzed with excitement.

"What do we have?" I picked up the green bottle and turned it over to find a label.

"We aren't told yet." Charlotte rubbed her two fingers together, a wrinkle between her brows. I knew that face well—she was making a plan.

"You seem intrigued."

"This place is bonkers, and that means something coming from a Calhoun." Her voice had a dreamlike quality to it, and I couldn't tell if she loved the entire thing or hated it. Or maybe she was confused, just like me.

"It's all a bit much." I set the cool green bottle down as Brendon glared at me. "What?"

"Don't touch the materials until the music starts. That's the rules." He pursed his lips, irritation written all over his face.

Big whoop. I touched a bottle. I rolled my eyes.

"Behave, Porter. He could turn the judges against us, and we need every point possible. Christian texted me a list of his favorite artists and freaking Butthole Surfers is on it. Who even is that?"

I choked on my own breath. Her brother was a pain in the ass. "Brendon needs to take his job less seriously, that's all."

Right on cue, the evil elf shouted into the microphone, interrupting me. "Okay, ready, go! Read your instructions and impress us!"

An upbeat version of "Rockin' Around the Christmas Tree" blared, startling me for a second. How were we in a family-friendly resort with club Christmas music? Was there a DJ? Did reindeer even like this music?

Focus, Hayden. I let the thought of clubbing reindeer go.

"Okay, are you good with your nose?" Charlotte asked, unscrewing the lid on the green bottle.

"Wait, what?"

"I don't know what this alcohol is." She scrunched her nose, wincing. "Something not pleasant?"

She handed it to me, our fingers brushing. I ignored the spark as I sniffed. "Brandy. For sure. My mentor took me out for drinks, and he made me try all the expensive kinds. This is definitely brandy."

"Great. Cool. Never had it." She placed her hands on her hips after setting the supplies out. Her tongue traced the outside of her mouth as she stared at the ingredients. "Cranberries? Cinnamon? Candy canes? This is so not my thing. I'm panicking, Hop."

I squeezed her shoulder in a friendly, supportive gesture. Because I was a gentleman, I also ignored how warm her skin was.

"Don't panic. We're a good team." I eyed the materials. "There's cranberries?" I shifted my weight, which made me closer to her. Ignoring the brush of her arm against mine, I pulled out a quart of cranberry juice and some cinnamon. "If we have a lime and something like triple sec, we can make a modified sidecar."

"For real? No idea what that even is, but I love the sound of your confidence."

"Yeah. Here, let me do this." I rolled up my sleeves and pointed to the knife in the bag. "Okay, is there a lemon or lime anywhere?"

Her gaze froze on my arms, her lips parting. I stared,

unsure if I had something weird on them. Sometimes I colored with Gwen and didn't realize I had marker all over me, but my forearms seemed okay. "What is it?"

"Uh, nothing." She ducked her head. "Knife, you said?"

"What just happened?"

"Hayden, drop it."

"Why are your ears red?" My lips twitched. Was she thinking something dirty? It'd be great to know I wasn't alone in my overwhelming attraction. "Do you deserve to be on the naughty list, Charlotte? What's going through that pretty head of yours?"

She ignored me. She stood a little bit too straight to be comfortable, but I appreciated her effort. I smiled, enjoying myself more and more. Charlotte was flustered about something, and I liked it.

"Lemon! Here!" she shouted ten seconds later, throwing it into the air.

"I need you to cut that." I poured the brandy into one of the shakers. They didn't have any shot glasses, so I did my best to measure two shots. I needed orange liquor, something to balance the flavor of the brandy. "Curaçao or triple sec...hm." I stepped closer to Charlotte, grabbing the other two bottles of mystery drink. Taking the lid off the clear one, I sniffed. "Think this smells orangey?"

I held it out for her. She met my gaze, and my stomach tightened from the eye contact. Charlotte had no idea what her large brown eyes did to me.

She broke the trance, closing her eyes and sniffing. "I think it's citrus enough."

"Works for me."

I poured a swig into the cup and then stirred. I licked the stirrer and frowned. Something was off. It was almost great, but why settle for average? Taking another straw, I swirled the cocktail and held it out for Charlotte. "Hm, can you try this for me?"

"My hands are sticky." She held them in the air as she leaned over and closed her mouth around the stirrer, just an inch from my fingers. Holy shit. That was hot.

"Mm. Hayden, that's delicious." Her eyes lit up like I had impressed her.

It had been so long since she looked at me like that...I wanted more of it. "Thank you."

"I never knew I liked brandy until now. Makes me feel tougher. More boss-like." She laughed at herself and eyed me with a maniacal glee. "What else do we need?"

Her energy was contagious. My goodness. I couldn't stop smiling at her.

"Would you be able to grate the lemon? I want to pour it into the glasses and rim it with a sugary lemon mix."

"Who even are you right now? I'm loving this version of you." She nudged her hip into mine, like we were the best of pals. Hayden and Charlotte. BFFs. We could wear matching bracelets and everything.

"Because I can make a drink?"

"Yes! And that you care enough about a rim. I don't know, I don't hang out with a lot of men who worry about details like that. They'd just drink from a bottle." She shrugged, a weird tinge coming through her voice. "I'm complimenting you. It's not my best delivery, but it's really cool that you pay attention to the little things. To even find someone normal to date, I spend time with guys who forget things like holding doors, or not checking your phone every five seconds. You're focused on a sugary topping. That's cool, that's what I'm saying."

"Huh." In my effort to ignore her the last three years, my brain must've just shut off at the idea of her being with other guys. Obviously, she dated. She was a fucking knockout. But she must be dating idiots, because who wouldn't hold the door or put their phone down when they were with her?

She liked that I focused on little things. It made me smile and want to continue it.

I took one of the bottles and crushed the sugar cube into smaller pieces as she grated the lemon onto a napkin. Her compliment warmed me. "Thanks, Charlotte. I know I can get caught up in my head often, so I make sure to pay attention to small things. I even keep notes in my phone—" I shut my mouth fast.

I had almost shared my secret.

"You what?" She faced me. "You keep notes on your phone?"

"Never mind." My face heated as I picked up her lemon zest. "We need to hurry."

"Hayden, you adorable man. I have so many questions. I'm not letting this go." She handed me the third glass as I swiped the lemon around the top of the glass and then dipped it into the sugar mixture for the rim. Most of it stuck, and then I poured the liquor. "I think we need to name this. Might get us some more creativity points."

"Sexy Santa Sidecar," I said, without thinking. I met her gaze, and we shared a smile. God, I loved having this moment with her, like we had our own secret inside joke together. I tore off a piece of a napkin and wrote out the drink name.

"Wait!" Charlotte dove into the bag. She pulled out marshmallows and a toothpick. "We need little snowmen in the drinks!"

"Great idea."

"One minute to bring your drinks to the judges! Once the music ends, you're done."

We finished the snowmen and placed them in the drinks. Carrying them, we walked over to the judges and set ours down next to our number without spilling. Done.

Charlotte gripped my arm and jumped up and down as we went back to our station. "This is so fun. I want more. I'm addicted to Christmas and competitions. I acknowledge that I, for sure, have a serious problem, but this is the best date night ever. I don't want it to end!"

It had to be a slip of her tongue. She didn't mean *date* as in the two of us, but I didn't bother correcting her. I smiled. I sure as hell didn't want it to end either.

CHAPTER ELEVEN

CHARLOTTE

Why am I nervous?" I chewed a hangnail as I watched the judges sip each team's drinks. They gave nothing away, which annoyed me. Like, *come on*, people. Give me a smile or a wince or a wink. Give me something!

"I'm not good at a lot of things, but making drinks is one of them." Hayden's voice came directly behind my left ear, his breath tickling my skin in a wicked, dangerous kind of way.

It was warm and unintentionally naughty. I had a lot to unpack in my We're Over Hayden mission. But the dude made it difficult! The attention to detail? The forearm porn? The deep, low chuckle? Ugh.

I only had so much strength. If he put on his glasses and volunteered reading to young children, I would die.

Clearing my throat, I found my voice and sounded totally normal and chill. "I like your confidence, big guy. Drink making is not one of my skills."

He placed both of his hands on my shoulders and squeezed. "Trust me. We'll win. I have a good feeling about tonight."

Maybe he put his hands there to distract me as the judges lifted our Sexy Santa Sidecars. It had been months since I felt this tense, this on edge, from a silly competition! They had to like our drinks. I couldn't fathom losing this competition to my brother, let alone not winning this thing for Penny.

"See?" Hayden whispered, his deep timbre a Charlotte-specific aphrodisiac. "The dude on the left widened his eyes. The woman in the middle tilted her head to the side. They are impressed."

"You can't know that," I whispered back. He leaned closer, his chest pressing into my back. This was the danger zone, baby. For two winning-obsessed people, this adrenaline was our kryptonite. I could feel his heart pound in his chest, and its erratic rhythm matched mine.

"I study people for my job, Char. I watch the pitcher for their tells. Do they grab their hat twice before a slider? Do they lean a little bit to the left before a curve? Reading people is something I do on the daily, and the judges like our drinks."

"Do you study everyone?" I asked without thinking. "Like me?"

He laughed and stepped back. The removal of his touch sent a blast of cold air over me. I missed his heat already, which was absurd. "I know what spot you prefer to sit because you're left-handed. Does that not answer your question?"

"You do." I wiggled my brows. "What else do you know? Huh?" I poked his side, charmed and curious about what he knew about me from studying me. "What am I thinking now?"

"I'm a smart enough man to know to step away from this game." He held up both hands, a huge smile on his face. "I will say it's easier on the field than real life. So calm down, tiger."

"Coward." I narrowed my eyes, teasing him. Looking back at the judges, I could see they were on group six. "Uh, I want the scores! Have you heard from the team?"

He pulled out his phone, shaking his head. "Silence. Well, Garrett texted me that he found twins he wants to flirt with, and damn it. He ditched the competition."

"No." My stomach dropped. "He can't...what if they are disqualified? What if they are arguing the entire time? Hayden, this is bad."

Hayden ran a finger over his eyebrow, releasing a long sigh. "We don't know for sure what happened. Plus the next activity is with the whole group. We can monitor it."

"And do what? If they lose this...it'll crush them."

"Okay. Any idea what the third competition is? So we can mentally prepare?"

I opened up the competition app—they had coded their own app for these games; that took some serious dedication—and groaned. "Lyric Mess Up?"

He squinted at my phone. "Does...does that say we read lyrics on a projector?" His voiced cracked on the end.

"Yeah, that gonna be a problem for you, Gramps?" I teased.

He grumbled. "I should get my glasses. Do I have time to run to the room?"

Hayden in glasses will murder me. My eyes fluttered, and I dug my nails into my palms to calm myself down. Were they thick and black? Oh my. This was the opposite of good.

"Char, can you cover me if I run back for a minute?"

I nodded, barely able to get the words out. "Y-yes. Are you sure you need them?"

"Yes. My vision's getting worse. My parents think I should do LASIK, but the thought of someone touching my eye freaks me the fuck out. Okay, I'll run to get them. You need anything? Your shoulder still doing okay?"

"I'm fine, Hayden. Go get your bifocals."

"Okay, I'm not there yet. Settle down, Char." He smirked before jogging out of the lobby. Once he disappeared from view, I gripped the table and released the longest sigh of my life.

He wore freaking glasses. Life was unfair and cruel. Was this revenge for the time in third grade where I laughed when my teacher accidentally farted? Or the time I hid from my Sunday school teacher and jumped out, scaring her so much she fell? It had to be.

I wasn't used to being around Hayden so much. He over-whelmed my senses, and I had forgotten how intoxicating he could be. My breath shuddered, and I walked toward the front doors to cool off for a minute. The judges were con-spiring, probably taking bribes.

Get a grip, Charlotte. They don't take bribes.

We don't know that, do we though?

Fuck. The wind knocked some sense into me the second

it hit my face. A cold dose of reality was exactly what I needed to settle down. I had too much going on in my head right now. Between the interview, and Penny and Christian, the competition and Hayden... *Hayden*.

Should I google *how to get over a crush* or *cheap spells to break feelings*? Might be worth it.

"Hey, you okay?"

I jumped. "Jesus, you're quiet."

"Any reason you're standing outside in freezing weather?"

I bundled my arms around my middle before glancing up at Hayden. My heart stopped. The world froze. Someone call the doctor. My skin grew two sizes too small.

The man wore dark glasses, and it was the end of me. He looked like Henry Cavill and Chris Hemsworth had a love child, and that child wore thick black glasses. I couldn't breathe. He was too sexy. Too handsome. Too *perfect*.

"What?" He adjusted the frames, frowning. He shifted his weight side to side, like he was uncomfortable. "I know they are dorky—"

"You look so hot," I blurted out. I wasn't one to have a filter on my best day, but of all the things I could say why did I say that?

His gaze snapped to mine. The air became charged. Puffs of condensation left his mouth, his gray eyes zeroing in on my mouth. "Char—"

"Hayden! Charmander!" Christian's familiar voice penetrated the moment. A wall went up on Hayden's expression, and he stepped back.

He looked at me like I was nothing more than a decoration. Something that blended into the background. I could've been a tree for all I knew. It was probably for the best, because he looked too good with those glasses.

"How'd you do? We had to run into a forest! I almost tackled this huge dude from Normal. Who lives in a town called Normal? Not me, that's who." Christian's energy was unmatched.

"That was something." Penny smiled, but it wasn't her normal cheer. Her cheeks were super red, and she looked cold.

Did they argue? Where was Garrett?

"There he is," Hayden said, almost reading my mind.

Garrett swaggered on up with a flask in one hand and a goofy smile. "Hello, teammates. I have . . . news."

"What news?" Penny asked.

Garrett took a drink before eyeing all of us. "They dropped the scores."

"And?" I probed, almost choosing violence. Garrett often chose drama for fun. "What place are we in?"

"Not first." He cringed as Penny sucked in a breath. "We're in second."

"How are we second? Who didn't perform?" Penny asked, a frown replacing her smile.

We couldn't lose this. A wedding was at stake. Hayden met my worried glance and shrugged in a *we did what we could* gesture.

"Who's in the lead? We have a few more chances for this." Christian cracked his knuckles, a sure sign of his stress. "Could we see the breakdown?"

"It's too cold out here. Let's head inside and game-plan." Hayden took charge, the air of authority in his voice sending a bolt of electricity through me.

"Good idea. I can't even feel my toes anymore. It's probably fine. I don't really use them for much." Garrett giggled at himself. "Guys, I might be drunk."

"Dude." I nudged his side as we all headed back into the lobby. The elves had cleaned everything up, probably preparing for the next round. Irritation danced along my neck. I leaned closer to Garrett, away from Penny and Christian, who stood off to the side with their arms crossed. "Why are you drunk? I need you focused to help us win."

"Because I'm at a bachelor party? Because I can?" He hiccuped and rolled his eyes at himself. "Penny kept passing me her shots 'cause she hates vodka."

Penny didn't hate vodka, but that didn't matter.

"Okay, but you could have said no. We have to win this for them." I tried not to let worry show in my voice, but Garrett wasn't getting the message.

"Nah, it's fine."

"It's not fine!" I whisper-shouted. I felt more than saw the stares of the group, and I straightened my posture, clearing my throat. Being dramatic wouldn't help the cause. "Where the hell is the next competition?"

"The ballroom." Hayden approached us, his gray gaze focused on me. He put his hand on both our shoulders and gently squeezed mine. "I don't know how I'm saying this with a straight face, but this next competition is even weirder than the others."

"Weirder?" I asked, mouth gaping.

He nodded. "Prepare yourselves and follow me."

CHAPTER TWELVE

HAYDEN

Good evening, participants. Welcome to round four of the Lost Days of Christmas. You'll note that we are almost through our games and things are heated. I placed the scoreboard on the screen for you to look at."

> *Jingle My Balls* 43 points
> *Wrap It Up!* 42 points
> *Sleigh My Name* 39 points
> *Ho Ho Homies* 37 points
> *Yule Be Sorry* 35 points
> *Sleigh What?!* 30 points

I scanned the ballroom, noting the excessive decorations as I eyed our competition. Now that teams weren't broken into two, I could study them more. Jingle My Balls and Sleigh My Name were our biggest competition at this point.

"I'm pissed we aren't in first, but those are some damn good team names." Charlotte stood next to me, her face set in fierce lines. "Don't tell him, but Bernie is starting to piss me off."

"Not into the elf anymore?"

She growled. "We might want different things in life. Plus, it'd be hard to date someone who lives at the North Pole."

I snorted, more pleased than I should be that she didn't want to date him.

"Now, round six is simple. We took two lines from a popular holiday song, put it through Google Translate twice, and displayed the lyrics. You have to guess the title of the song. You have one minute to write down your answer on the sheet at your tables." Brendon paced near the podium, looking way too smug. This man clearly enjoyed the power. "Once my team of elves collects your paper, we'll show the answers. Each answer is worth two points."

"Let's go!" someone from *Sleigh What?!* shouted.

Charlotte scoffed. "They are in last. They don't have a chance."

My lips quirked. I loved a shit talker, and Charlotte was one of the best. She leaned toward Penny and whispered something, causing Penny to laugh. They bent their heads together and snickered for a bit, and the image of them smiling warmed me. Penny laughing made me feel better.

"Y'all were worried. I am the king of lyrics. I know everything, and when I drink, my mind expands, and I'm even smarter." Garrett pointed to his chest, grinning. "You wait and see. I'm gonna be the hero."

"Not sure that's how it works, bro, but I'm glad you're here." Christian pulled him into a hug on one side, Charlotte on the other. "Both of you. Hayden, you join this hug too."

"No hugging, idiots. It's about to start!" Penny hushed us. "Pay attention."

I covered my mouth with my hand to hide my amusement. Since Gwen came along, I hadn't had a lot of game nights with these two, but it was clear their competitiveness had only grown.

"First song begins now. You have one minute!"

RATTLESNAKE, RATTLESNAKE, RATTLE-SNAKE PEBBLE.

"What the fuck is this?" Garrett mumbled.

"Come on, hero," I teased because I couldn't stop myself. "Expand your mind?"

"Rattlesnake isn't even Christmas?" Christian ran his hand over his hair, the ends sticking up making him look unhinged. "Snakes? Worms? Pen, you got anything?"

"It's clever." Charlotte smiled as she studied the projector screen in the front of the room with a half smile. "I really like this idea. It's so unique."

"Thirty seconds!" someone yelled.

"Wait." Charlotte held up her finger. "If you say it in a rhythm like *rattlesnake, rattlesnake, rattlesnake, pebble*? It sounds familiar."

"All you did was say the words! There was no rhythm!" Christian yelled. "'Jingle Bells'? 'Twelve Days of Christmas'? Maybe there's a snake in there?"

"Wait! 'Jingle Bells.' Hold on." Garrett snapped his fingers, his eyes growing to the size of ornaments. "Jingle bell, jingle bell, jingle bell rock."

"Write it down! Yes, G-thang. You sexy rock star!" Penny threw her hands in the air and shimmied. "That's totally it!"

"This game is dumb," Christian said, despite writing the answer down on our paper just as the timer went off. "If you call him sexy again, I will kill him."

"Murdering me won't make me less attractive. My obituary photo will be hot as hell." Garrett puffed out his chest. "Not just a pretty face. I know lyrics too."

I shook my head, my lips twitching just as Charlotte caught my eye. A soft smile was splayed across her lips, but it disappeared as a light pink blush crept up her neck. God, I would love to know why she blushed. Even if nothing could happen because of it, I just wanted to know. She cleared her throat and took the marker from Christian's hands. She spun it around her fingers in a fun twirl a few times before Brendon spoke again.

"Song two. Make sure you write your team name on the paper, please. You're lucky you weren't the only ones who forgot, Jingle My Balls."

"They can't even follow simple directions," Charlotte whispered. "How sad."

"You're ruthless." I nudged her. "I wouldn't want to play against you, Coach. You'd intimidate me."

She beamed. "Good. Remember that."

And if you viewed him
you would suggest it shines

all other animals
I used to laugh and insult her.
They never left poor Rodolfo…

"Rodolfo?" Christian frowned. "Insult?"

Penny chewed one of her nails as she paced, muttering to herself. If I didn't also want to win, I'd observe how everyone reacted. It was entertaining as hell.

"Oh, come the fuck on. This one is so easy! It's 'Rudolph the Red-Nosed Reindeer'!" Garrett pointed at the screen. "It's right there."

"How do you even know this?" Christian yelled. "If this was trivia, I'd kick all your asses. I know that shit. Dumb shit. Random shit. I own it. But this? Not so much."

"Stop saying you own shit. That's weird." Charlotte wrote the answer down on the paper. "Mom and Dad always said we all have our strengths. Being bad at this is just one of yours."

Garrett laughed. "God, I love your sister. Can I marry her? Char, be my wife. Make me a kept man."

She laughed instead of throwing up on the spot. I'd prefer that reaction, because it's how I felt at the mere thought of her being with Garrett. An ache formed in my chest that must have come from dinner, because what the heck?

Christian glared. "Absolutely the fuck not."

Charlotte handed the paper to one of the weird elves who sprinted from table to table, and then faced her brother. "And what if I wanted to marry him, dearest brother? G and I could just make fun of you together. We could have daily roasts of you."

"Big fan of this idea. Huge fan, actually." Garrett slung an arm around her.

"You smell like a bottle of rum."

"Like a sexy pirate then?"

"No." Charlotte laughed and shoved his arm off her. The ache dulled. Weird coincidence.

"Fine," Christian said, rolling his eyes so much he reminded me of the freshmen boys on my team, the teen-aged divas. "You can marry whomever you want, Charlotte. If a dumbass hat rack like Garrett made you happy, I'd allow it."

"But he's your friend," I blurted out without thinking.

Christian blinked a lot, moving his attention to Penny, then me, and then Garrett. "Is this a real conversation?"

"Yes." Penny laughed. "If Charlotte wanted to be with Garrett, would you stop it?"

"No. I'm not an idiot." Christian set his palms on the table and lowered his head to be eye level with Charlotte. "Hey, I thought we were messing around, but if you wanted to date Garrett, you know I'd never stop you, right? If you're happy, I'll be okay. That's all I want."

Charlotte's face softened. "I'm not interested in Garrett like that, but this is awfully sweet of you. And unexpected."

"I'm feeling things. It's weird." Christian scratched his chest. "I don't like it."

"Bro, you gotta talk more about your feelings. Not healthy to keep them bottled up." Garrett kissed the top of Charlotte's head. "No proposal today, so don't worry."

"I'll breathe easy now." She smiled, clearly more amused than annoyed.

Did he always have to be so close to her? Garrett touching her felt like a bug under my skin, itching and annoying me, and I couldn't stop it no matter what I tried.

"Next lyric is up. Sixty seconds on the clock."

> *Santa Claus has a little friend, his name is Dominic.*
> *Kicking the cutest ass you'll ever see.*
> *When Santa Claus and Dominic visit his farmers,*
> *It will be why can't deer climb the Italian hills?*

I hated being zero help on this challenge, but I grew up like a normal person and listened to Christmas music only in December. Garrett hummed with his eyes closed, swaying side to side when he snapped his fingers.

"'Dominick the Donkey.' I am the best."

"Write it down, fast, come on!" Penny yelled. "I wish we got points for speed on this round. Or having the best handwriting."

"Competitive looks sexy on you, Pen," Christian said.

My gaze immediately went to Charlotte. Her face read *This is good, right?* Christian complimenting Penny was a great sign. Christian even pulled her toward him in a hug that bordered on a little too much for public.

Charlotte's entire body relaxed as she watched them, some foreign expression on her face. It almost seemed like sadness and relief. I didn't like seeing sadness on her face at all. It made me want to fix it that second.

"Alright, folks, we're going to tabulate the scores and announce the winners in ten minutes. Use this time to hit the bar or visit the photo booth." Bernie grinned like an evil little elf. "This is going to be a close one, so we'll see how our judges are feeling. Did we mention that we're also adding bonus points?"

"What?" Penny screamed. "Bonus points for what?"

The crowd of teams booed and pounded on the table. The relief on Charlotte's face disappeared, and she swallowed hard.

"Hey," I said, nudging her arm, "remember when you were into Bernie? Do you regret that yet?"

She laughed. "I do. Thank you for the reminder."

"You hit your head this morning. It clearly caused you to make poor life choices for a minute. It's fine though. No harm was done."

"To think I was gonna find him under a mistletoe." She closed her eyes, but her words caused my stomach to drop in a horrible, roller-coaster type of way. Imagining the two of them together sent a hot bolt of jealousy through me. Christian granting Charlotte permission to date Garrett really fucked me up.

Not that I was using that as an excuse for never pursuing Charlotte, because I damn well knew I had a million excuses, but hearing Christian explicitly say that made me want to do something. What? I had no idea. I was a mess. I had no one to help with Gwen. My main source of support was leaving, and I was in no place to date. Let alone the fact that Charlotte was one of the few people who could also help with Gwen. It was too messy.

I stood not a foot from Charlotte, and the urge to touch her overwhelmed me. Her hair was one of my favorite things about her, and some had escaped around her face, and

I wanted to push it behind her ears. It'd be too intimate, but damn. Today reminded me of why I struggled around her years ago. She was easy to be around.

"Hey, let's go. The other team is done with the photo booth. I want one of all of us in the most ridiculous get-ups we can create." Penny pointed toward the corner that was set up like a snow globe. She and Christian ran over to get the next spot in line, but whoa. The decorations were insane. People could walk into this snow globe for the photos, and holy Christmas bonanza. The props went beyond the normal booths I'd seen at weddings.

We could dress in a full reindeer onesie. Or a full Grinch. Or a blow-up gingerbread man.

"Why?" Garrett swayed to the left a bit and shook his head. "Why would anyone want to put those on after another human? It is disgusting."

"Because Penny wants us to." Charlotte narrowed her eyes at him. "We're gonna do it for Penny and Christian."

"No. I'm not...look, I am a germaphobe. You might not assume that about me, but I will gag. You can't make me." He pointed toward the bar. "I'm going—"

Charlotte grabbed his hand and yanked him toward her. The movement caused him to almost crash into her, but their chests touched. The jealous feeling from earlier returned full force at the sight of them inches away. I had the urge to...hoist Charlotte up over my shoulder and take her away from here.

"You will do the photo booth. This isn't up for discussion, Garrett." Charlotte spoke in a direct tone.

"Hot," Garrett said, mirroring my own reaction.

"Stop." Charlotte rolled her eyes and dragged him toward the corner. Their hands were still intertwined. Sure, he was drunk and needed babysitting right now. Especially if Penny wanted this photo and he resisted it. But shit, how much longer could I fight my attraction to Charlotte?

What were my reasons for not kissing her again?

My phone buzzed on cue, like the universe reminding me of my issues. It was a random number.

> Hi Hayden. It's Frankie. I hope your parents told you that they gave me your number and asked me to get in touch. I'm excited to meet you and talk about watching Gwen. I know your mom set up Monday, but my professor switched my classes so could we meet Sunday instead? I can work around your schedule.

Classes? Was she in college? Part of me thought she'd be too young, too inexperienced, but class schedules maybe meant more flexibility.

> *Hayden:* No problem. Let's do 4:00 pm.

Sunday night would be the last Sunday dinner at my parents' house before they moved. Sure, they'd be back for Christmas weekend and the wedding, but that was only for two days. They had performances the next two weeks and practice. New Year's was a work night for bands.

We all prepared for the photo, and Charlotte actually got into a costume. There was a little dressing booth off to the side, and she ducked in. I put on a green top hat and green overalls, along with a cane. I had no idea if I was a Christmas version of the Monopoly man, but Penny had a vision for this photo, and I obeyed.

I waited for her to come out. When she did, I sucked in a breath. She was dressed in full elf gear—a sexy elf too—with red-and-white tights, a red sweater thing that hugged her body, and a hat and fake ears. She even wore pointed shoes and did a heel click.

As I watched her spin around and smile, reality hit me. It wouldn't be fair to her, or to myself, to start something I couldn't finish. I swallowed down a ball of regret and made sure my costume was in order.

Christian was Santa, obviously, and Penny his Mrs. Claus. She positioned the five of us so they were in the center, Garrett was on the ground as a reindeer—which, hell yeah, that was funny—but it put me together with Charlotte. Her familiar and comforting vanilla scent surrounded me as I neared her.

"Could you imagine how much fun Gwen would have here?" Charlotte asked. "She would be the cutest little snowflake. Or the snowman princess. I don't know, but I keep thinking about her. She would have an awesome time."

Fuck. This woman was incredible. How could I not want to be with her when she mentioned my daughter with genuine care?

"Yeah." My voice cracked, and I adjusted the green polka-dot bow tie. Maybe I needed distance from Charlotte to get my head on right. Three years of distance had helped, but one day together had put me right back where I was.

"Okay, folks, three, two, one, smile!"

Flashes blasted us. The elf working the photo booth pressed it again, and Penny immediately ran toward the computer. "Oh my God, Christian, babe, we need to print this out and hang it at our house."

He rested his chin on top of her head, wrapping his arms around her. That was another great sign. "Yes. Hell yes. This is perfection. Look at G...and Hayden...God, this is golden. Could be wedding favors for everyone who comes."

"We can put them on T-shirts and hand them out."

"I'm taking this as a good sign," Charlotte whispered right next to my ear, her breath hitting my neck. "Talking about wedding favors means they want a wedding."

She was so close to me. Too damn close. Her body heat surrounded me, and it was like every muscle went on red alert. I focused on Bernie, who held a clipboard and bossed two other elves around.

"Don't you think?"

I nodded, clearing my throat. I couldn't ignore her or not speak. We'd just gotten to a solid place again, and it wasn't fair to her to shut down. I forced myself to say, "Great sign."

"I need to get out of these clothes." She laughed at herself.

Heat flooded me. Charlotte meant the costume. I knew she meant the costume. But with her wit and care for Gwen and how good she smelled and thinking about kissing her... when was the last time I was this messed up? High school?

I followed her lead, removing the costume and laughing when Garrett fell over twice in his reindeer outfit. It was good for his ego to look that ridiculous.

"Alright, everyone, we have the winners. Please return to your tables, and when the song ends, we will showcase them on the board. Thank you all so much for playing our games. This is our Super Bowl here that we prepare for all year. This year has been one of the best. You have about two minutes to get back."

"I feel like we could create games like this, babe." Christian rubbed Penny's shoulders. "We could even start a neighborhood competition for kids to play too."

"Yeah." Penny wore a dreamy smile, her eyes dazed as she glanced at Christian. "That would be the best, and we could have your dad dress up as Santa at the end."

I snuck a glance at Charlotte, who smiled at them, her cheeks a little pink. She was so beautiful that it wasn't even fair. Scrubbing a hand over my face, I hoped that'd knock sense into me. I could get through the announcement and then sneak off toward my room. Penny and Christian didn't have any plans for the rest of the night besides "fun," and getting an uninterrupted, full night's sleep seemed real fun to me.

"Why am I nervous? I totally am." Charlotte jumped up and down, her hair flopping on her shoulders with the movement. Her eyes sparkled. "I think we won."

"We better win," Penny said. "We need this."

"Let It Snow" started fading out, the crowd going silent as the presentation slide updated. "Wrap It Up! You are in first place, congrats!"

We won.

I'd won a lot of games in my life, but nothing compared

to this—balloons fell from the ceiling. Loud music blared. Air horns blasted. There weren't even that many people in the room, yet it was so damn loud.

"We fucking won!"

"Hell yes!"

Christian swung Penny around. Garrett fist-pumped the air and twirled with a stupid grin on his face. That left Charlotte...

She jumped on me. "We did it, Hayden! We won!"

She wrapped her legs around me and hugged me tight, her cheek pressing against mine as she squeezed me. I felt like an overheated laptop that had stopped functioning. My motherboard failed. All I could feel was her soft hair tickling my face.

She pulled back and grinned so wide that it stretched across her whole face. "I could almost kiss you right now."

I stared at Charlotte's lips, the tug on my lower gut urging me to close the distance, to taste her again after all these years. My nostrils flared, and I bent closer to her. I could do it. Kiss her right here. I could calm this fire inside me. Her mouth parted, and she sucked in a breath when she realized I wanted to kiss her too. I leaned in just as Garrett, Penny, and Christian all threw their arms around us in a group hug.

They jumped and cheered, chanting and being general idiots. The movement changed Charlotte's face, and she withdrew from whatever moment we just had. I fought the urge to yank her toward me as she slid down my body, even though I knew it was for the best.

She joined her brother in jumping and cheering, but her smile dimmed. I knew her real smiles, and this one was performative. I wasn't sure what the hell was going to happen next, but we had to talk about this. Because if she wanted to kiss me too . . . that changed things.

CHAPTER THIRTEEN

CHARLOTTE

Have you ever almost died from regret? Not like a real death, but an ego one. Like the mortification made the thought of melting into the snow easier than accepting reality. That was how I felt knowing I not only jumped onto Hayden, but then said, *I could almost kiss you right now.*

Why? Why would those words come out of my mouth?

Plus his entire body turned to ice. Was it in horror? Was he remembering the last time we kissed and didn't speak for years? We had moments of flirtation, and sure, we'd always had that, but we had just decided to be friends again. What the hell was I doing?

Avoidance. That's what I should do.

That's what you did for three years. Worked out well, huh?

Wiping my palms on my thighs, I took a deep breath. I could face him. I'd just say I got carried away with the win or the relief of Penny and Christian acting more like themselves. Yeah. That made sense. Content with my plan, I felt more confident facing the group.

Penny and Christian accepted the money prize, waving their hands like they were in a homecoming parade. I filmed the entire thing, obviously, and couldn't stop chuckling. They were absolute weirdos, but at least they were on track with the wedding.

"I hate to bring this up now, but we should talk about it," Hayden said, his deep voice coming way too close to me. He stood with his hands in his pockets, his glasses perched on his nose, and damn. Just damn.

Have you ever slipped on ice? That sudden loss of balance where you swerve left then right, and you aren't sure if you'll make it? That was the same feeling I had, where prickles of unease zigzagged from my spine to my feet. I was falling. He wanted to talk about what I said. "It was an accident."

"We beat—wait, what?"

"No, you go. What?"

Just when I thought I couldn't be worse, I surprised myself. I crossed my arms to put up a barrier of protection against those glasses. They had superpowers or something. "What do we need to talk about, Hop?" My tone came out a bit too icy. (Ha, which was fair because his comment felt like me crashing through ice.)

He frowned for a beat, confusion swirling in his gray eyes. He opened his mouth but then closed it as he studied me. He must've been okay with what he saw, because he smiled. "I think this'll make you happy to know, but I downloaded the app and checked the scores for the first competitions."

"Okay." I didn't track his line of thought.

His smile shifted to a very Grinch-like playfulness as he tilted his head to the side. "Char. We beat them."

"We beat everyone?"

"No. Well, yes, but we placed higher than Penny, Garrett, and your brother." He beamed at this point. "Guess who has to do a dance tomorrow for us? Coordinated and filmed?"

It was slow, but the words finally made sense, and my smile also turned Grinch-like. "Hell yes. We don't have to DJ!"

"Exactly." His joy was contagious. "This might be my favorite moment of my life, you know, minus having Gwen."

"Obviously. That's hard to top." My own laughter eased the mortification and tension that lingered. Some of it remained, but not all of it. I could use this, latch onto the fact that those competitive a-holes would have to dance for us.

Something niggled the back of my mind, like a small scratch. It made me pause. "Wait, Hayden."

"Hm?" He stepped closer. "What's wrong?"

"Nothing's wrong, but…come here." I grabbed his elbow and guided us away from Garrett, Penny, and Christian. Hayden stared at my fingers on his arm, and I dropped them. "I know we won overall, and they do seem back to normal, right?"

He nodded.

"I don't…I don't want to cause stress to them. What if they really need a DJ and not having one is part of their arguing? We could volunteer, to make sure the wedding happens?"

"You're killing me, Char." He groaned and stared up at the ceiling. "How selfish is it for me to not care about that right now? We won and they lost, and those are facts. I want to enjoy that."

"Even at the cost of not having a wedding?" I whispered, even though we were far away from them. "Trust me, I also want to see them dance and blackmail them for the rest of my life, but we can't…maybe it'd be…" I paused, nervous to finish the sentence.

How silly of me. My face heated, and I rubbed my fingers together, hoping the worries escaped with the motion.

"Maybe it'd be what?" he asked, his voice kind.

"A nice way for us to hang out again." My stupid voice cracked at the words *hang out*. "If you want. You know. There's no…We could also make them separately on a shared playlist. That would be easier."

Be more awkward. Please try. Reach a new personal record.

"Charlotte." He released a soft chuckle and tugged the end of my sweater in such a sweet, intimate move that my head spun.

I stared up at him, the rest of the room disappearing. He had the ability to do that. When he focused on me, it made me feel important, like I was the only thing that mattered. My heart thudded so hard against my ribs that it was a shock he couldn't hear it. His thumb brushed against the bare skin of my stomach, and I sucked in a breath.

"I'd love to hang out with you and make playlists. Sure, I'm not a fan of being the bigger person when I could make your idiot brother do a dance routine, but it's the right choice."

"So we vow to not tell them that we won?" I asked. His

finger remained on my hip, moving left and right in small circles. How was that tiny little movement the most erotic thing I had ever felt? I couldn't catch my breath.

"Correct."

"Penny will know though." I swallowed, swaying a little toward him. "She'll check and be pissed they lost. She's honest to a fault."

"True." He twisted his lips as he glanced over my shoulder. "We could…hm."

I turned to see what the rest of the group was doing, and the motion caused me to put distance between us. But his grip on my hip tightened, almost like he didn't want to stop touching me. I didn't know what to do with this information, but that sensation of falling through ice increased. "Uh," I muttered, unsure where my ability to speak full sentences went. I was an educated woman! I was a chatterbox, yet no words would come out.

He seemed so normal and unfazed. No erratic breathing or inability to speak. Just confident and sexy Hayden. Maybe I should poke his hip and see how he liked it? No. That was the wrong choice.

"What we could do," he said, his lips curving up on one side in a smirk, "is create the playlist tonight and tomorrow at brunch, and we make a big deal about it. Like how selfish and amazing we are to do this even though we won."

"Oh, I like that. They won't enjoy knowing we have something over them."

"Nope. That'll annoy Christian for months."

"Yes!" I grinned, forgetting about his touch. "And we aren't working against the wedding either. So we come across as heroes, we still won and get bragging rights, and we save the wedding. That's a real turkey."

"Um, I'm sorry? A real turkey?"

"Oh." I snorted. "Right, this is a newer Calhoun expression my dear father started as a joke, and I unfortunately adopted it. Kind of like how my dad texts *neat* in all caps every other day."

"I've received my fair share of *neat*s from your dad in my lifetime. You're going to have to explain the turkey comment though."

"In bowling, when you get three strikes, you got a turkey. Whenever three good things happen, it's a real turkey."

"Calhouns are so strange. Wonderful, but strange."

"It's our family mission and vision. *Be wonderful, be strange.*"

He chuckled, the deep rich laugh hitting me right in the chest like an arrow. Between his glasses, the sound of his laugher, and the way his sweater fit him, he was a real turkey.

"Incoming." He released his grip on me, his face almost falling in disappointment. Huh. That was…wonderful and strange to see.

"Look at the prize basket!"

Ah. That's what he meant. Penny arrived carrying a huge basketful of crap. Christmas crap.

"Babe, you shouldn't be carrying that." Christian yanked it out of her hands.

"And why shouldn't I be carrying this?" she said through clenched teeth.

My brother's jaw tensed, irritation flaring behind his eyes. "Because you are to be my wife, and I take care of you."

"Caveman doesn't suit you." Penny yanked the basket right out of his hands. "Let's look through this. Oh my gosh, I am so excited!"

While winning the competition had made them act more normal, there still was evident strain. It assured me that Hayden and I had made the right choice in deciding to create the playlist. I wanted to ease any burden from them so the wedding would go on as planned. Even if that meant spending more time with Hayden alone.

"Babe, you are strong and beautiful and my favorite, but set the basket down at a table so we can go through it." Christian's tone didn't match the words, but it worked.

Penny marched over to a table and set the basket down hard. "There."

"Can you guys either go...I don't know, screw this tension out? You're killing my buzz." Garrett pulled open the ribbon and pulled out a holiday mug. "Nice. I love a mug. Dibs. I call *dibs*."

"He's right." Christian eyed the basket. "I will be taking my fiancée and this basket to our room. We can go through the prizes tomorrow."

"Oh, will you?" Penny asked.

Christian grinned before picking her up and hoisting her over his shoulder. "We'll see you at brunch in the morning."

"Christian!" Penny yelled, but she smiled. But her tone shifted really fast. "Put me down."

"Nope." He smacked her butt before grabbing the basket. She laughed, and just like that, they walked down the hall, her squeals echoing back toward us. She seemed happy with the turn of events, and that's all I cared about.

To repeat Hayden's words, they were wonderful but strange.

"I wanted that mug." Garrett stared after them with a sad look. "It was really nice."

"G, you can get your mug tomorrow."

He shrugged and stared at us with mischief. "What's our wolf pack gonna do? Wanna play a game, drink at a bar? They might think they won't see us until morning, but I have a surprise for them."

"What does that mean?" Hayden demanded.

Garrett shrugged, looking way too proud. I didn't like it one bit. "Oh, nothing."

"Dude, what did you do?" I asked, pointing a finger at his chest. "Tell me right now."

"You'll see." He wiggled his eyebrows. "Let's say it's a fun little gift for them."

"You don't understand," I argued, annoyed that Garrett was being so nonchalant about it. "We can't do anything to ruin this weekend or wedding. If you pulled a prank, it could upset them."

"Char, I love you, babe, but if they can't handle this joke, then they are doomed." He yawned and had the audacity to look surprised. "How am I more tired than you both? I'm way more fun."

"They can't handle any more stress than the wedding itself. Can you please tell me what you did? I don't want to ruin this for them."

"It won't, okay? I promise. I think my hangover is starting now. God, is this what it means to be thirty? Not a fan.

Four out of ten stars so far. I might go to bed so we can go wild tomorrow." He clapped Hayden on the shoulder and pulled me in for a hug. "Don't worry so much, Char."

"Please don't ruin this." I debated telling him what we knew, but Hayden shook his head slightly, almost in warning. I trusted Garrett but wasn't sure what he would do if I shared my concerns. "What can I do to get the prank out of you?"

"If I was on top of my game, I'd say marry me, but I just need sleep. It'll be fine. Plus it'd be too late to cancel anyway. I already paid for her. Anyway, night, y'all. Don't have too much fun." He kissed the top of my head before marching away.

"I really don't like him sometimes."

"He said *her*. Paid for *her*. He ordered a stripper. Fuck." Hayden took off his glasses and ran a finger over his eyebrow before meeting my gaze. His intense gray eyes, the same color of snow under moonlight, narrowed. "We have to stop this."

CHAPTER FOURTEEN

HAYDEN

I had to hand it to Charlotte. She charmed her way into finding out what room Christian and Penny were in. They had been given a suite on the third floor at the very end of the hall. Of course, it wasn't a convenient location near the lobby, where we could hang out on chairs and wait for what...some woman to arrive?

"I am not judging. I would never. However, I have no idea what we're looking for. We can't just ask every woman who is on this floor what they are doing." Charlotte chewed on a hangnail on her thumb, her attention darting down the third-floor hallway and to the elevator. It was 10:00 p.m., so most guests were heading in for the night.

"Can we ask if they are going to room 300 or not?" I slid down the wall, resting my arms across my knees. There was a break between rooms right in the middle, where the ice and vending machines were plugged in. The little nook was perfect for sleuthing but not exactly comfortable. "Why are we friends with Garrett? I need reminding."

Charlotte joined me in leaning against the wall. She left six inches between us, which was for the best, but I wanted her against me. My fingers still buzzed from touching her skin. It might've crossed a line, but my finger almost did it involuntarily, and then I couldn't stop. She was so soft and warm. *So mine*, my brain finished. Even if it wasn't true, it felt that way.

"He's a good human most of the time. It's the fifteen percent rascal in him that gets in the way." She leaned her head against the wall and yawned. "I'm also tired. The igloo seems like ten years ago."

"Ten years ago, you had braces and made Christian and me watch and score your dances with what was her name… Delsey, that's right." I smiled at the memory. "Which was totally normal for a fourteen-year-old. Asking me for beer was not."

"What's the point of having an older sibling if they don't sneak you the good stuff? Delsey and I got into some trouble after Christian and you went to college." She released a small chuckle, almost like a sigh. "It's strange and cool that we have so many memories together."

"Yeah." I cleared my throat, her words feeling heavier than face value. "So, about Garrett. Can we ice him out of the group?"

"Nah. He's generally harmless. Plus he's gonna meet someone one day, and they are gonna kick his ass. I need to stick around until I see that happen." Charlotte stretched her legs out and groaned. "If we don't do something, I'm going to fall asleep. Should I go grab my laptop so we can work on the wedding playlist for our DJ debut?"

"Great idea. I can keep an eye out."

"I feel like you'd be better at trying to stop a stripper than me? She'd be nicer to you. Just smile at her and be kind about it." Charlotte stood, and I tried, and failed, not to stare at her glutes and the way her jeans hugged her thighs. They were made for her strong body, and her thighs were a foot from my face. "Be right back."

"I'll be here."

I used the few minutes of alone time to text my mom. She was a night owl and confirmed that Gwen went down without a fight. My baby girl's latest thing was to stay up until ten, asking no less than one hundred questions a night.

Can I have a pool party?

Can I have a bubble machine?

Does Santa poop?

Endless questions. I needed to start writing them down and creating a book to embarrass her when she got older. A buddy of mine suggested starting an email to write a message to send to her once she's a teenager. Is that when kids needed emails nowadays? I didn't know. I did know I wasn't going to let her create a dumbass email address like I did.

blingdaddy83@outlook.com

That shit followed me around for years.

The elevator pinged, and I bolted up, my pulse racing as I prepared to say something. Stopping a stripper in an effort to save a wedding wasn't something I had ever done before.

This was new territory. Should I say please and thank you? Fuck. I scrubbed a hand over my face as soft laughter hit me.

Charlotte had returned.

"I take back what I said. You shouldn't be the one to stop her." She grinned like we shared an inside joke. "You look torn between constipation and murder."

"I do not," I replied hotly. "You're teasing me."

"No." Her grin grew as she ran a finger over my forehead. "Your face is so damn serious. There's a reason you're a good coach that has something to do with your character and all that, blah blah, but you also look scary as hell."

"I'm not scary."

"Hop, you have a very intimidating stance and face when you don't smile. Either wear the glasses because you look good"—her voice dropped lower—"or smile." She held up her laptop and cringed. "We can see if there are already solid playlists to steal and edit?"

"I like your thinking."

She sat back down next to me, crisscrossing her legs so her knee touched my thigh. She logged in, and I admired the stickers all over her device. It was such a Char move to have stickers of *Schitt's Creek*, *The Office*, and *Abbott Elementary*. She also had a *What We Do in the Shadows* sticker right in the center. I had zero clue what that even was, and I had the urge to ask her a thousand questions. I wanted to learn about this version of Charlotte.

Once she fired up Spotify, she pulled a hair tie off her wrist and put her hair up. There was nothing inherently sexy about the gesture, but a few curls escaped, and her bare neck was exposed. She would always be sexy to me. End of story.

"Okay, I found a playlist called Christmas Wedding Reception. It has the classics. Ella Fitzgerald and Louis Armstrong with 'Cheek to Cheek' and 'O Tannenbaum.' But I don't... These are perfect for background music."

"Hm. Christian and Penny don't strike me as *background* people." Christian self-described as a maniac and an epic dancer. The one year I went clubbing with him, he would be on the floor for hours. "As much as I wish we could copy another one, they will want people on the dance floor."

"I agree with you. We need some 'Last Christmas' and 'All I Want for Christmas Is You.' Hell, Christian learned dances from NSYNC when they were big. He'd never admit it, but he'd blast NSYNC's 'Merry Christmas, Happy Holidays' without shame." She hummed and snapped her fingers. "We need a DJ name. It'd help inspire me. Rowdy Rudolph? Simpin' Santas? DJ Mistletoe?"

"Mistletoe Mixmaster," I said, quite proud of myself. "That can also be the title of the playlist. Titles matter."

"Oh, I love it." She smiled as she started a new playlist and typed in our title. "I'm gonna email the link to you so you can add to it too. Okay, best Christmas dancing songs?" she said.

I typed the question into Google. "Here's a starting point."

- "All I Want for Christmas Is You" —Mariah Carey
- "Last Christmas" —Wham!
- "Rockin' Around the Christmas Tree" —Brenda Lee

- "Feliz Navidad" —José Feliciano
- "Jingle Bell Rock" —Bobby Helms
- "Santa Claus Is Coming to Town" —Bruce Springsteen
- "Christmas (Baby Please Come Home)" —Darlene Love
- "It's the Most Wonderful Time of the Year" —Andy Williams
- "Step Into Christmas" —Elton John
- "Wonderful Christmastime" —Paul McCartney
- "Jingle Bells" —James Lord Pierpont (various renditions)
- "Let It Snow! Let It Snow! Let It Snow!" —Dean Martin

I tilted my phone toward her, but she leaned closer toward me to see. The movement put her face even closer to mine. I could see the two freckles on her cheek, the mole right beneath her eye, and the bruise.

Shit. Maybe it was the dim hallway light, but the bruise on her forehead was a deep purple now. "Char," I hissed. Using my other hand, I traced the bruise. "This looks pretty bad."

She winced but nodded. "It throbs."

I let my touch linger on her skin, gently outlining the bruise, and without meaning to, I continued the movement down her jaw. Her skin was so soft, and I loved how she let out a little hum and closed her eyes. She leaned into my touch, sighing in what I assumed was contentment as I stared at her lips.

My whole body tensed with desire. Attraction and lust weren't common for me. I didn't date, and it had been months since I'd been with a woman, but fuck, Charlotte was beautiful. Continuing my gentle caress of her face, I traced my thumb over her bottom lip and fought the urge to groan. Her mouth was so plump.

"Hey." *Jesus.* My voice had come out all raspy and deep. I tilted her chin up to look at me, and she took her time opening her eyes. When she did, I was done for. Her large brown eyes and lush black lashes stole my thoughts. The words I had planned to say disappeared. All I could think was *Kiss her.*

Her mouth parted, and the pulse at the base of her neck raced against my finger. She licked her lips and leaned closer. My skin buzzed as my stomach tripped over itself. I dipped my head. I couldn't think of a single thing I wanted more.

"Char," I whispered, our breaths intermixing with only an inch between us. I needed her to say yes to this. To grant me permission. To be aware that this kiss would change the status quo of everything.

Ding.

Charlotte jumped back so hard that she smacked the back of her head on the wall. "Shit!" She set her laptop down and rubbed her head. "That hurt."

Fuck. I ran a finger over my eyebrow, my body feeling a thousand pounds. Did she need to jump that far away with that much effort? "You alright?" I asked, my voice giving away my frustration. We were so close to kissing.

Stupid elevator.

"Hayden," she whispered, hitting me in the side. Her tone had shifted. It was serious. "This has to be her."

A beautiful woman with long brown hair and a red trench coat strutted from the elevator with an intense expression. She meant business. She scanned the hallway, nodding at an exit before she spotted us. A candy cane swung from her fingers.

She narrowed her gaze on us.

"Hi," Charlotte said, standing. "Any chance you're heading to room 300?"

"Maybe," the woman said, her voice sultry. She pursed her lips and stared down the hall, toward room 300. "But if I were, why do you ask?"

"We're here to stop you. If we have to beg, we will." Charlotte smiled but it was awkward.

"Stop me?" She tilted her head. "Do you have something against a sing-a-gram?"

"I'm sorry. What?" Charlotte twisted her hands together, shifting her weight left and right. "A sing-a-gram? You're here to *sing*?"

"Yes." The woman laughed. "I was hired to go to room 300 and sing three carols to a Mr. and Mrs. Calhoun. I take it you are not them."

Charlotte blinked, her eyes wide as she repeated the same words. "To sing, for them? Not... wow. Okay. A sing-a-gram."

The woman looked at me, amused.

"Char, hon, we should let her carry on with her sing-a-gram. Penny and Christian would love this." I nodded toward their door. "We're leaving now. Excuse us."

"Wait. I can't believe Garrett did this. I thought you were—"

"Coming in the morning," I blurted out. Charlotte did not need to share our first thoughts about this. If I weren't already secretly in love with Charlotte, I would be now. She was horribly awkward and trying so hard not to be. It was fucking adorable, and I reached over, squeezing her shoulder.

"Some people prefer late visits. Now, excuse me, I'm going to go sing."

"Let's go, Char," I said softly, placing my hand on her back and guiding her toward the elevator. I picked up her laptop with my other hand. "Let's let her do her thing."

"A sing-a-gram." She shook her head, laughing. "I almost called her a stripper!"

I chuckled as we entered the elevator. A beautiful voice carried down the hallway, the stunning woman definitely singing as Christian and Penny stood in the doorway.

What a trip.

I pressed the button to head to our rooms. Charlotte looked up at me, the red spots returning to her cheeks. "I feel silly that we spent all night guarding against a singer. You could've been doing other fun things."

"I'm doing exactly what I want to right now, Charlotte."

"Oh."

Maybe it was the mirrors on every side, but the elevator felt small. I saw a dozen versions of Charlotte, all equally gorgeous. I met her gaze in one of the reflections and went to war with myself.

Kiss her. Don't kiss her.

Do it. Ignore the pull toward her. Deal with the consequences later.

The air felt heavy around us, the scents of cinnamon and her vanilla perfume surrounding me. We just stared, neither saying anything as we arrived on the first floor. It had been years since I had a first date, and this felt like one. The twisting of my stomach and the sweat on my palms felt so strange. My mouth dried up as we walked toward our doors at the end of the hallway.

"Uh, so," she said, her voice husky. She fidgeted with her phone as we faced each other outside her room. That's when I noticed something I hadn't before. There was a mistletoe above her door.

Kiss her. Just do it.

"Charlotte." I bent down and set her laptop on the ground before nearing her. My heart fucking pounded like I had sprinted from center field to home plate. Placing one hand on the door behind her, I cupped her face with my other. Her chest heaved, and her lips parted as her gaze moved toward my mouth. "Do you still want to be kissed under the mistletoe?"

CHAPTER FIFTEEN

CHARLOTTE

Forget feeling like I was falling through ice. This was like being on a roller coaster when you've forgotten to fasten the seat belt, so you were hanging in the air, trying to grip something to save yourself.

Hayden sucked in a breath, his eyes narrowing on my mouth. My knees almost gave out. He was so close. The man of my dreams had just asked if I wanted to be kissed. I gulped for air. I was free-falling into chaos. From the little touches all night, to my crush that never went away...my body was primed.

My stomach bottomed out. My brain left my head.

Hayden lowered his face so our lips were a breath apart. "Can I kiss you, Charlotte?"

Heat exploded between my thighs. His lips had barely touched mine when he asked the question, and yet he waited. Not quite closing the distance but not leaving enough air, so I breathed him in.

"Yes."

He moved his hand to the back of my head, digging his fingers into my hair as his lips finally met mine. Fireworks exploded at the contact. My skin felt too tight, and my head spun in wonder as Hayden kissed me softly at first. Gentle teases of his lips. Our mouths connected as he released a deep, contented sigh.

He smelled like cinnamon. Without thinking, I wrapped my arms around his broad shoulders. I let my hands explore his muscles and feel the heat radiating off him. I'd dreamed about running my fingers through his hair for years, and I took my shot. I threaded them through his thick, silky locks.

"Do that again," he demanded, breaking apart to trail kisses down my neck. "You smell so fucking good, Char. I need to taste your skin."

"Yes." I arched my back, allowing him access to my collarbone as he nipped the sensitive area there. He was just everywhere. His lips on my body, his hands on my back, yanking me closer to him. There was no part of our bodies that didn't touch, and I was heating up with a fierce need. Every time his tongue swiped against my neck, I shuddered.

"More," he grunted. "I need more of you."

In one motion, he gripped my chin and guided my mouth to his as he kissed me hard. This one was messy and fast. He peppered my lips with small kisses and then slid his tongue inside. This was unlike any other kiss I had experienced. He didn't just kiss me, he devoured me.

He groaned into my mouth, digging his other hand into my hip as I kissed him back. I sucked his lip into my mouth, biting it to give him a little sting. He tightened his grip and nudged my legs apart with his knee. He tilted my head back and took the kiss further.

My world was Hayden. How he kissed me like his life depended on it. How his warm tongue explored my mouth, yet his lips were so soft. The deep, pleasurable sounds he made in the back of his throat as he pressed his body against mine. It was all warmth and hardness.

"Perfect," he whispered.

It was like we knew we'd only have this one kiss together, so we put everything we had into it. The erratic beat of his heart pounded against my chest with the same crazy tempo as mine. His erection dug into my hip, and I rocked into him, releasing a small moan.

"That," he said, pulling back and staring down at me with wild eyes, "might be my favorite sound you've ever made."

"Yeah?" I breathed so heavily that my voice came out all huffy and throaty.

"Definitely." He grinned. His pupils were dilated, his hair stuck up in every direction, and his lips were red and swollen. He looked so damn sexy like that. "I want to see what else I can do to get you to make that sound."

Oh, sweet baby Jesus. I gulped, my skin absolutely on fire with lust. Nothing made sense anymore except him putting his mouth on me. My body burned with need.

Call me selfish, but I had never been kissed like that in my entire life. It was intoxicating and addicting, and I wanted to explore more than I needed to breathe.

"So do I," I whispered.

"Fuck yes," he said, his voice husky. He picked me up

with one hand, wrapping my legs around him. "Open the door. Let me in your room so I can show you."

I shuddered at the desperation in his voice. He sounded like how I felt—like I would die if I didn't have his hands on me. He sucked my earlobe into his mouth, the sensation so incredible that my head tipped back, and I smacked it against the door. "Shit!"

"Char." He stilled and set me on the ground. "Hey, your head. Are you okay?"

"Yeah. Just in a hurry, and your mouth is distracting me."

He studied me with so much concern on his face that my stomach swooped. His gray eyes drifted from my forehead to chin, and he ran his fingers gently over the back of my head. "Is there a bump? I shouldn't have done that. Not with—"

"Are you saying you regret this already?" I blurted out.

He dropped his hand. Something flashed across his face, but it happened so fast I couldn't decipher it. Yet again, my big, unfiltered mouth spoke without permission, and I ruined the moment. Cold already seeped into my bones at the loss of him touching me. My stomach heaved at the reality facing me. He regretted kissing me, yet again, and I was silly for thinking it was different this time. Maybe he'd leave, and I could just...melt into the floor forever. Becoming a permanent fixture at this hotel.

"Charlotte," he said, enunciating my name to the point that it was awkward, "I think you misunderstood me, and it's important we're on the same page."

"Oh, is it?" I fired back. We remained outside my hotel room, where anyone could potentially walk down the hall and see us. It was almost midnight, and it felt like my time at the ball had ended. How could I be so foolish? Kissing Hayden led to heartbreak. I freaking knew that, but he had put on those glasses and kissed all the rational thought out of me.

"Can we please go into your room and talk?"

"Just talk?" Why. Why did I say that?

His lips quirked. "To start, yeah."

Footsteps echoed down the hall, and the sound zapped an iota of common sense into me. "Okay, fine. Come on."

The lock unclicked, and I shoved the door open. Sitting on the couches near the fire was smart. It was away from the bed that seemed to shout at me to have Hayden sit there. *Sure, great idea.*

"There. We're in my room, where we can talk." I sat on the sofa and crossed one leg over the other in a dramatic fashion. The fireplace was remote-controlled, and I turned it on. Instantly, the mood was more romantic and intimate— not my goal.

I chewed the side of my lip, and my knee bounced up and down with nervous energy. Before, when his mouth was on me, I couldn't think. Now all the thoughts came back with a vengeance.

What did that kiss mean? Does he like me? What do we do now? Was it a mistake? What if he shuts me out again for three years? What if this makes my crush worse? What if I never get kissed like that again? Will I die alone?

Hayden studied me with a frown. "I wanted to talk, but it's clear you're uncomfortable. Do you want me to leave?"

"No. Yes. Wait. Maybe."

"Yeah, that answer isn't gonna work for me." He neared me, bending down onto his knees so his face was level with mine. "What's going on?"

"I'm scared." My filter stood no chance.

He reared his head back, like I had hit him. "I *scare* you?"

"No, not in the way you're thinking." I gripped his forearm in an attempt to calm the terrified look in his eyes. "You started saying something about how we shouldn't have kissed and—"

"No." He shook his head. "You stopped me before I could finish my sentence. We absolutely should've kissed. One hundred percent should've."

"Oh." A flicker of hope grew deep in my gut.

"Yeah, Charlotte." His eyes heated as he rested his hand on my knee, stilling it. "What I was trying to say is that we shouldn't have kissed against a door when you were in a car accident this morning."

My thighs clenched at the reminder. That flicker of hope grew a little more, but unfortunately my overactive mind took control over my libido. "Last time we kissed…" I cleared my throat, my eyes prickling at the onslaught of emotions. I blamed exhaustion.

Hayden sucked in a breath and took my hand in his. "Please, baby, tell me what you're thinking."

"Okay." I gulped. I nodded to myself and rolled my shoulders back. *You can do this. You are brave.* Plus I refused to kiss Hayden again without getting this out. I was caught up in the moment before, that was all. "I'm worried that you'll regret us. I know things have probably changed after that kiss, but we never truly talked about what happened three years ago. You kissed me back, Hayden, and then told me you'd never be into me and cut me out of your life. I am terrified it'll happen again."

Hayden's face paled, and his grip slid from my hand. He ran his fingers through his hair and closed his eyes. When he opened them, he looked tortured. "I assure you there was a reason that happened, and I am truly so sorry for how it made you feel. It kills me to know I hurt you."

I ran a finger over my lips, the sensation of kissing him still evident. They stung a little from his teeth, and while I wanted to do it again, we had to talk this out. "That was one of the most mortifying and worst nights of my life. I confessed I loved you, Hayden. You shoved me away like I was nothing. That's hard to forget. We just tried to be friends again after three years, and not even a day in, we kiss and mess it all up. I'm conflicted."

"You weren't nothing to me. You've never been nothing. You don't think I dream about that night and the sexy red dress you wore? You had your hair down, and the dress dipped low in the front, showing off way too much cleavage for that shitty college bar. You are unforgettable, Charlotte."

"You remember my outfit." I swallowed down the ball of emotion. That meant something.

"I told you, Char, I remember everything about you."

My eyes fluttered, and I swallowed hard.

Hayden continued, his voice softer than normal. "You pulled me into that corner, grabbed my shirt, and my God, your perfume smelled so good. Whenever I smell someone wearing something vanilla, I think of you. I wanted to lick you."

"I would've let you," I whispered. "But this doesn't add up. You turned me down. You broke my heart."

"I know." He gave me a small smile and caressed my face. His gray eyes swirled with regret and sadness. "You were drunk, Char. I didn't want to take advantage of you. On top of that, if I had let that kiss continue, it would've ruined my entire career. They had just hired me as the assistant baseball coach. Not only that, but I was also the youngest coach on staff, which was its own controversy. The other coaches were at the bar that night. If they saw me kissing a student...I could've been fired. There aren't a lot of rules, but not touching students is one of them."

"I was of age—"

"I know, Charlotte. I know, trust me. But once my brain caught up to the moment, I freaked out. I had worked my ass off to get that job. My future flashed before my eyes, and I did the only thing that made sense. Please believe me when I say I wanted you. *Want* you. My reaction had nothing to do with how I felt, or you, and everything to do with my career."

His reasoning made sense. I understood it, but it didn't take away the sting or the damage of three years ago. "Thank you for sharing that, but the words you said...they gutted me, Hayden."

His jaw flexed as he stared at me, not saying anything.

"Do you remember what you said?" I needed to know. For some reason, this mattered a lot to me. When he thought about that night, did he repeat the cruel words? Or did he block them out?

He sighed. "I said whatever I needed to push you away. Something about never falling for you or thinking of you that way."

Don't be foolish, Charlotte, you're like a kid sister to me. "When I told you I loved you, you laughed at me." My voice shook. I hated showing emotion, and I hated crying even more, but all the pent-up feelings from that night returned as soon as the high of the kiss had disappeared. "This is why I assumed you regretted kissing me again. Old wounds resurfaced."

"I wish I could take those words back and we could redo the last three years. I wish that more than anything. I'm so fucking sorry, Charlotte." His voice was firm and steady. He picked up my hand and kissed the back of it. "I knew I should've told you the truth, but a few weeks later, Simone told me I had a daughter and that derailed my life. All my focus was on my daughter and surviving being a single parent. I put every ounce of myself into being a good father, and I always told myself I'd find you once I figured my life out. I'd have told you the truth, but news flash, Char, I'm still a mess."

My eyes prickled at the weight of his words, the depth to them, the slight tremble in his voice. "Oh."

He slowly released my hand. "It's midnight. It's been a long-ass day. You should get some sleep."

On cue, I yawned.

"Come here." He hoisted me up into a bear hug. He enveloped me in his arms, his scent and warmth surrounding me. He cradled my head against his chest as he sighed.

He felt so good, and I breathed him in. I could live in this cuddle and be content forever.

He kissed my head and gave me one last squeeze. "We'll talk tomorrow, okay? We have an interview to work on, right?"

I nodded. There was so much to unpack here. I needed a week away just to digest everything that had happened. He let go and walked toward the door, stopping and turning around one last time. It was almost like he didn't want to leave.

"I don't know what tonight means, and I stand by what I said: I'm still a mess. But I'm done pretending I'm not into you and don't want to be with you. We have some things to discuss, but I'm gonna be dreaming about that kiss for a long time. Sleep tight, Charlotte."

CHAPTER SIXTEEN

HAYDEN

Who the fuck was I?

I woke up smiling and rested. It had been years since I slept this much. There were no sore muscles or exhaustion headache. There was an energy there that wasn't there yesterday, and it all had to do with Charlotte.

That five-second kiss three years ago was nothing compared to last night. All my blood traveled south as I remembered the feel of her body against me. The softness of her lips, the little moans that escaped when I nipped her skin. She was the definition of perfection, and my body buzzed with a need to feel her again. I wanted to see her hair down, her skin pressed against mine, and— *Calm down.* I didn't need to get a boner right now.

I needed to shower and surprise her with coffee. It wasn't every day I slept that damn well, and I was calling it the Charlotte Effect. There was no tossing or turning, no lying there thinking about life's meaning. I had dreamed of her lips against mine and how we could make this work between us.

There were a hundred unanswered questions, but I wanted to figure them out. The first step would be getting her coffee.

Charlotte was a fiend for caffeine. The rhyme made me smile as I threw on a hoodie and made my way toward the small café at the hotel entrance. Char preferred oat milk lattes and anything with chocolate. Literally anything. I even requested her drink kid temperature. The first time I heard her order a tea kid temperature at a Starbucks, it confused the hell out of me.

Whistling a Christmas carol, I marched toward her room. Maybe the holidays had finally gotten to me. *Or maybe it's Charlotte.*

I knocked on her door and waited. My pulse sped up at the thought of seeing her again. Would she be happy to see me? Or did we need to talk about what happened again? I'd do it if she asked. I never wanted to see her face fall in disappointment again. Knowing I put the frown on there fucking ate at me.

The door clicked, and I adjusted my stance as nerves rippled through me.

"Hi." Charlotte pushed the door open and smiled shyly at me before her gaze landed on the coffee. "Did you...did you bring me caffeine?"

I nodded, not able to fight my smile. She looked adorable. She wore an extra-long T-shirt with the softball team logo on it and red-and-white-plaid pajama pants. Sleep lines covered her face, and her long, curly hair hung in messy waves around her shoulders. Even in pj's, she made me want her. My skin heated as I thought about kissing her, and I held out the drink and food to stop myself.

"I brought you an oat milk latte and a chocolate croissant. Your favorites."

"Wow, uh, thank you." She cleared her throat and ushered me in. "I'm still in my pj's, sorry. I wasn't...I didn't know. I should go change—"

"No." I set both our drinks on the counter, along with the croissant, and took her hand, lacing our fingers together.

She stared up at me, her cheeks blushing. "What are you... doing?"

"Saying good morning the right way." I cupped her face and kissed her softly. She tasted like toothpaste, and her lips were so warm. "Mm, that's better."

I ran a hand down her back, guiding her toward the sofa where she sat last night. Then I grabbed the food and handed her a drink. Despite the fact that I wanted to spend hours kissing her and removing every piece of her clothing, we had to talk.

"You seem in a great mood." Charlotte hummed into her cup. "I don't recall you being much of a morning person. In fact, I remember you being quite a bear before nine a.m."

I grinned. "Last night was the best I've slept in years."

"Because you're away from Gwen?" she asked, tilting her head in the cutest fucking way.

"No." I sipped my plain black coffee and admired her toenails. They had snowflakes painted on them, and it was charming as hell. "I'm away from Gwen a lot during the season. That wasn't it."

"Huh." She clicked her tongue. "It's so cozy here. I also passed out, which, ha, I assumed I'd be up all night overanalyzing what happened." She laughed a bit before inhaling right over the cup. "I can't believe you knew what drink I liked. This is so kind, thank you."

"I remember everything about you," I replied, vowing to be honest moving forward. I had told her my truth last night, so there was no going backward. Only forward. Even if I didn't know what the hell that meant.

"Hayden," she said, her voice clogging with emotion, "did you order it…not as hot?"

I nodded. "You prefer kid temps so you can drink it right away."

"I can't believe you. No one does that for me." She stared out the window, a contemplative expression on her face. "Do you know all our friends' drink orders?"

"No, Char." I fought a smile as she pieced it together. She complimented me last night on how I remembered small details, and this was a perfect example.

"But you know mine."

"Yes."

She tucked her knees up to her chest, holding the croissant in one hand and her coffee in the other. She wiggled her snowflake-covered red toes before facing me. "What are we doing?"

Buzz. Buzz.

My phone vibrated, interrupting the moment. Seeing my mom's name on the screen shifted my mood. Gwen came first. "It's my girl. I gotta take this."

"Of course." She waved her hand, the red splotches returning to her cheeks. For some reason, the thought of leaving her right now seemed like the wrong decision. She asked the question I didn't know the answer to myself, and if I left her here with that thought, she could come to false conclusions.

"Do you care if I take it in here?"

"What? Oh, not at all. Please." She grinned, and I felt like a million dollars. Definitely the right call.

"Hi, sweetheart! How's Gigi and Geepaw's house?" I smiled at my daughter's toothy grin staring back at me. She hadn't quite figured out how to hold the smartphone, so it only showed half of her face.

"So fun. Last year, we watched a movie that had monsters!"

"Last night, you mean? And monsters?"

"Last year. Last year, we watched *Puss in Boots*. The monsters were good ones." She shifted the phone so now I saw up her nose.

"Gwen, baby, hold it a little farther from your face. I see your boogers."

"Boogers!" She giggled before dropping the phone. "Oops!"

"What are you and Gigi doing today?"

"Gigi is taking me to the park. Gigi is. We have yummy bread and milk, and Gigi and we're going to the park. The bird park."

My daughter and parents named the parks around their house. The bird park was the larger one with a swing set. One time, Gwen saw birds there, hence the name. The other park was swing park (even though they all had swings), and the third one was Gwen's park because my daughter thought she owned it.

It all made sense in the mind of a three-year-old, and that's what mattered.

"Are you going to wear your coat? And your gloves?" I asked. "It's cold out there."

"Yes. Gigi will tell me."

"I miss you. Are you having fun?"

"Yes. Gigi and *Puss in Boots*, and last year, we played with friends."

"I'm glad you're having fun, sweetie. I love you. I'll see you tomorrow!"

"You too, Daddy. You bring me present? A big one? Red?"

"Yup. I'll bring you a present. Can I talk to Gigi for a second?"

"No. She's pooping."

I snorted. I covered my mouth with my hand as Charlotte's eyes danced with amusement. Gwen was an absolute gem. For three years old, she spoke well but she was a hoot. My mom would die of embarrassment, which somehow made this so much better.

"I am not pooping. Gwen. We don't share that about people. We say they are in the bathroom."

"Bassroom."

"Bath."

"Bass."

"Ah, you sweet girl." My mom laughed. "You look well, Hayden. Maybe you need to actually do things for yourself more often."

"Ha, I don't know about that." I grabbed the back of my neck, not sure how I was gonna do anything if I didn't find help. That was tomorrow's problem though. "I slept seven hours."

"Holy Batman, that's… Whatever you did, do it again and again. You seriously look great."

My attention flicked to Charlotte for a beat, and she quickly pretended to study the bathroom door. It would almost be funny, if I weren't unsure about our future.

"I feel great. But hey, is Gwen still using the bathroom on her own? I know she loves when you two baby her."

"She's been doing okay. She woke me up at four to get help, which I don't mind, but she seemed independent."

"Okay, good. I can't have her regressing. And whenever I'm away, I feel like she does something like that."

"No, it's not because you're away. It's normal for her to go through ups and downs. "Hayden Orion, I swear, you need to do more stuff like this. I will fly back once a month to get your butt out of the house. I like this side of you, where you don't look twenty-eight going on eighty-seven."

"Wow, you keep me humble."

"Shut up." My mom laughed. "Now, how is Charlotte?"

Charlotte choked, coughing into her fist as my stomach dropped.

"Have you finally pulled your head out of your butt and told her you like her?"

Well, shit. Never thought my mom would be the reason I'd confess everything to Charlotte. Chewing the inside of my cheek, I debated my next move. I could admit it, deny it, or downplay it. I wasn't quite sure how I felt about everything, but I for sure regretted not leaving the room when I had the opportunity.

"It's complicated, Mom." I gripped the back of my neck, Charlotte's gaze boring into me.

"Most things in life are, hon, but this weekend is the perfect time to tell her. I'm sick of watching you pretend you aren't into her. It's been years, Hayden." She clicked her tongue, her telltale sign of disapproval. "With your dad and me leaving, I'm worried you'll let fatherhood be the excuse for not putting yourself out there."

I ran a finger over my eyebrow, a dull throb starting from stress. "Going right at me, huh?"

She shrugged. "I want a daughter-in-law when we come back next year."

"Mom," I spat out, "good God, reel it back." My neck burned as I tried to come up with an excuse to end this call. My mom wasn't someone you hung up on.

"No. I've seen the way she looks at you. You're your own obstacle in this scenario, and I've been nice for years. Do something about it. Especially this weekend, before you're totally on your own."

"Wait." I shook my head. There was a lot to unpack, but one thing stuck out the most. "How she looks at me? What do you mean?"

"Whenever you're in the room, she's always watching you with longing on her face. She also loves Gwen. Remember that weekend last year, when you were out of town with the team and we were sick? Who do you think I called to help? Charlotte. She dropped everything she was doing to bring food and medicine. Why? Because she loves Gwen. Plus she blushes whenever you touch her."

A strangled, dying cat sound came from Charlotte, and I smiled. "Oh hey, did I tell you I'm in Charlotte's room right now?"

My mom blinked three times, her mouth parting, before she laughed. "It's awfully early to be in her room, Hayden."

"Sure is."

"I'm hanging up. Tell…tell Charlotte hello for me." My mom blushed, and it felt a little validating to pull a fast one on her.

"No need. She's heard this whole conversation."

"Mm, well, we'll chat about this later. Bye."

I hung up and set my phone face down before turning toward Charlotte. Her eyes were the size of saucers as she gripped her coffee cup like a lifeline. I opened my mouth to say something, but nothing came out. I tried again before she burst out laughing.

"I'm so uncomfortable," she chuckled. "I don't even know what to do."

"This had junior high levels of embarrassment." I joined her laughter and relaxed into the chair. "My palms are actually sweating."

She snorted and reached for my hand. I opened it, and she trailed a finger over it. "Hayden, what the heck."

"Told you." I wiped the moisture on my hoodie before facing her again. "Now that you've had some coffee and food, I think we should talk about us."

CHAPTER SEVENTEEN

CHARLOTTE

Hayden liked me. His mom said so. That felt important. Also Hayden had told me he wished he could take back that night three years ago. He kissed me hard and brought me my favorite coffee, without even asking my order. That gesture meant a lot to me.

"So, we kissed last night," I said, the same squawking sound coming out. "And your mom thinks you like me."

Hayden's lips twitched. "I do like you."

"Cool. Cool. Great." I stood and wished I wore something sexy or at least better than plaid pajamas. I wasn't even wearing a bra, and we were about to have quite possibly the most important conversation of my life. No one had prepared me for this situation. "You like me."

"I always have, Char. I know that's hard to believe after what I said, but it's true. My mom also said something that's pretty relevant. I'd never use being a single parent as a reason not to date, but I want to be someone who can give you what you need. Time, attention, dedication, all of the things you deserve. With a demanding job and a daughter who I'd drop everything for, I'm not at a place to be a good partner in any capacity. I can't offer weekends away or date nights unless I find a babysitter. I don't even have someone lined up to help with the season." Hayden held up his hands and sighed as they dropped in defeat. "You have no idea how much I want this with you, but I don't know if I'll be what you need."

I twisted my fingers together, the sensation grounding me in the moment. A blip of irritation formed in my gut, growing and doubling in size. "Have you thought about asking me what I need?"

He licked his lips, his eyes widening as his hands hung in the air.

"You're right. What do you need?"

"I don't need weekends away or date nights or all this attention that takes you away from Gwen." My throat tightened with emotion. Attempting to be together wouldn't be easy for Hayden and me. Our lives were so intertwined that everything was complicated. That meant we had to be careful. "I want to spend time with you, and I want you to be honest with me. That's it." My voice broke a little at the end, the tension in the room surrounding me.

It wasn't a bad tension, but it was thick and evident. Whatever we decided in this hotel room would determine our future or lack thereof. "Do you—" I started, unable to finish. I couldn't put my pride on the line. It had hurt too much last time.

I wouldn't survive this if I asked to be with him only for him to turn me down yet again. Even if his reasons were valid. I totally understood them. I played with the end of my shirt, focusing on the landscape through the window. "You have to take the leap, Hayden. Not me."

He breathed deeply, the sound of his stress causing me to look at him. He frowned and ran a hand over his jaw a few times before nodding. "That's fair."

"What do you want then?" I let my hands fall, standing to my full height as his gaze moved from head to toe. This was me. Pajamas and bedhead and no makeup. "What are we going to do? Pretend we didn't kiss? Continue being friends? It'll be hard, but if that's what you want, I'll find a way to do it."

"No." He pinched his nose. "I can't pretend it didn't happen. I want this."

"And what is *this*?" I pointed to him and then myself.

"I want to be with you." His tone shifted to Coach Hayden, where his words were firm and left no room for misunderstanding.

The command in them had me standing up straighter. I liked this Hayden.

"I want us to be together. I don't know what that means. Fuck." He ran a hand through his hair before closing the distance between us. He looped one arm around my waist, the other pulling gently on my hair to tilt my head back. "God, you're gorgeous."

My knees almost buckled at his words. Hayden said the words I had dreamed about hearing my entire life. I smiled so hard that my face hurt.

"I love your smile." He touched my dimple with his finger before trailing his hand toward my waist. He stared at me with hooded eyes. "I've thought about being with you for half my life, but I'm nervous as shit."

"Me too," I whispered. My limbs tingled, and my heart pounded against my ribs. Every nerve ending was in tune to this moment. The way he smelled like coffee and aftershave, the softness of his grip on my hair, the possessive way his fingers dug into my hip. I felt protected and safe while also hot and ready to climb him like a tree.

"We could mess everything up, but what if we don't?" He ran his nose against mine. "We work in a field where .300 of success gets people into the Hall of Fame. I'll take those odds with you."

Then he kissed me again. He wasn't gentle this time either. No probing or teasing. He slid his tongue into my mouth and groaned like he'd been waiting years for it. I gripped his hoodie as he kissed me deeper.

Kissing Hayden was my favorite thing ever. I decided then and there that I never wanted to stop. He didn't just kiss with his mouth. He put his whole body into it.

"Fuck, your mouth is trouble."

"Yeah?" I arched a brow, absolutely giddy and over-whelmed by him. "What are you gonna do about it?"

Heat flashed in his eyes before he used one arm to hoist me up and toss me on the bed. I wasn't a petite or fragile woman. I had more muscles than average and was thick and curvy. But he tossed me like it was no big deal, and holy cow, it was sexy. He licked the corner of his lip before he played with the strings of my pajamas. "You are so damn hot right now."

"I'm in plaid pajamas."

"Yes." His nostrils flared as he massaged my calves. "Doesn't matter. Everything you wear is sexy, Charlotte. You are my own personal aphrodisiac."

I gulped. "That's . . . unrealistic."

He shook his head as he ran his hand up my knee, over my thighs. "These make me think of waking up with you and how that'll feel. Or wondering if you wear anything underneath them. Or how it'd feel to slide up next to you and take this off. That's what I think when I see you in them."

"Oh."

He winked before dipping a finger into the waistband and sucking in a breath. "No panties?"

I shook my head as my entire body heated. He looked at me like he wanted to eat me for a snack. No one had looked at me with this much heat and care. Not one other person. Even if .300 were okay odds, it was gonna be easy to become obsessed with Hayden. He had never stared at me like this, and I already wanted more.

What turned him on? What did he like? Was he as aggressive in the bedroom as he was on the field, or gentler like he was as a dad? I needed to learn the answers to these things immediately. "Hayden," I whispered as he slid a hand over my waist, under my sleep shirt. I moaned as his calloused fingers teased circles beneath my belly button. It wasn't even that naughty a touch, but my body was in hyperdrive.

"Char." He let out a frustrated groan, one that didn't sound like pleasure. He fisted my shirt as he repositioned himself to sit at my side.

The absence of his touch cooled me, and I shivered. *He's pulling away.* Fear clawed at my throat. He had changed his mind. I couldn't even look at him as he spoke.

"We should go slow."

"Hm? Slow what?" I willed my heart to settle down and my stomach to stop clenching in dread.

"I don't know what this is yet, so I don't want to compromise anything by going too far." He released my shirt and rubbed my calves, almost like he couldn't stop touching me as he stopped whatever this was.

"So if it doesn't work out, we can say we at least didn't sleep together?" *Come on, filter, where are you?*

He tensed. "No. I just—" He ran his finger over his eyebrow like I'd seen him do a hundred times before. "I don't want to hurt you, and no matter what choice I make, there's a chance I will."

"You're trying to be a martyr then." He was trying to do the right thing, even if it felt like the opposite. "It sounds like you're in your head too much."

He nodded as he gazed at me. His gray eyes swirled with lust and longing. I realized that maybe he was right. I had my own insecurities to deal with too. "You're right. Going slow might be a good idea for us. I need to figure out some of my own things too."

"I'm glad you agree with me, but now we have a new problem." He pushed up from the bed and paced near the fire. With his hands on his hips, the hoodie stretched across his chest, and the glasses, I was completely gone. My feelings sure as hell weren't slowing down.

"Which is?" I asked.

"What does *slow* mean? Because I'm fucking struggling not to touch you right now."

I blushed. "We can touch? Slowly?"

A buzzing sound interrupted our moment, and I glanced at the clock. *Dang it.* "Brunch is in twenty minutes."

Hayden stared at the ceiling before saying, "What are the chances we skip it?"

"And deal with Christian and Penny? Absolutely not. I need to change before we head down there." I jumped up from the bed and dug into my suitcase for a chunky red sweater that had a snowman and gingerbread man hugging. It fit me well and was cheery. A double win. I also grabbed my red bra and underwear.

"I've been thinking about your bra and panties a whole lot, Charlotte." Hayden neared me, his nostrils flaring as he reached out and ran his fingers over the fabric. "I want to see it on you. Is that slow?"

"You want to watch me dress?" I asked, my voice a whisper.

He nodded. "Please?"

Oof. My thighs clenched at his low voice. I had never been shy about undressing, but I wasn't one to feel super-confident strutting around naked. Statistically, we had both seen naked people often with the amount of time we spent in locker rooms. This wasn't a big deal.

Yet. The way he stared at me like he couldn't breathe without me. His lips parted, like I was the sexiest thing he had ever seen. It was intoxicating to know I could do this to him. He watched as I laid my clothes on the bed. My pulse freaking skyrocketed as nerves rooted my feet to the ground. I could do this. I wanted to do this, to push him.

I lifted the edge of my sleep shirt and tossed it onto the floor. Hayden sucked in a breath. Meeting his gaze, I took my time putting the bra on. My nipples tightened with need and from the cold, and Hayden turned to a statue. His chest heaved, and he fisted his hands at his sides. But his face. My goodness. He seemed transfixed with me, and it was the sexiest feeling I had ever had.

"Christ, Char." His voice cracked, like he was on the edge.

I did the hook and adjusted the straps. This bra made my tits look great, and Hayden seemed to appreciate it a whole lot. "Still think slow is the right choice?" I teased.

"Fuck if I know. You're stunning."

He didn't blink. Not once. I slid my pajama pants down, and my breath caught in my throat at Hayden's growl. "Come here."

I didn't think about disobeying.

He slid his hands up and down my sides, his thumbs teasing my nipples as he kissed the center of my chest. "I have never wanted anyone the way I want you. I need you to know that and believe it. Tell me you understand."

I nodded, my eyes prickling from the overwhelming emotions. He covered one breast with his mouth, sucking the fabric into his mouth as I squirmed from the pleasure. Without thinking, I ran my fingers over his hair, and he groaned.

He cupped my breasts and buried his face between them

before he jumped back, almost like he was struck by lightning. "Fuck, I'm sorry."

"Sorry?"

He faced the window. "I told you I was going to go slow, then watched you undress and wanted to devour you. I'm being an ass."

I quickly put on my jeans and slid the sweater on. "You're not being an ass, I think we're both struggling a bit. It's hard not acting on this attraction."

"Yeah." He faced me, a half smile on his face. "Maybe we just... do what feels right."

"It felt right with you touching me."

His tongue darted out on his bottom lip, and his eyes flared. He closed the distance between us and placed a quick, sweet kiss on me. "I need a few minutes before I can head to brunch with you, but this conversation isn't over, okay? We'll figure it out before we leave tomorrow."

I nodded. I added hoop earrings while Hayden stared out the window, his stance still rigid. Living in the moment wasn't something I did well, but I really needed to. *Figuring this out* before heading back to reality felt heavy, because what if we didn't? What if we gave in to our attraction after years of fighting it and nothing came of it?

CHAPTER EIGHTEEN

HAYDEN

It had been years since I felt like I couldn't control my libido. Charlotte had woken up a part of me that had been dormant. Watching her dress had been the sexiest thing I had ever seen. Thinking about it had me adjusting myself under the table. It took more effort than it should to focus on the conversation at hand.

"What did you think of your late-night visitor?" Garrett asked as he downed half his mimosa. He was a loud eater, and I had no idea how his parents didn't make him eat outside.

"Yes. Candy sang three songs for us." Penny grinned. "It was so weird and wonderful. She also handed us candy canes and curtsied."

"It was so cool. Such a unique present, thanks, man." Christian held out a fist, and Garrett bumped it.

"Not gonna lie, Hayden and I thought she was a stripper and stood guard."

"Why the hell would I hire a stripper? Come on, Char." Garrett playfully bumped into her.

She narrowed her eyes. "Because you're *you* and a general pain in the ass."

"I second that," I said.

"I'm sorry, what?" Penny hit the table, her laughter so loud that other tables glanced over at us. "You stood guard? What were you gonna do? Stop her?"

"I don't know! It was awkward, and this conversation is done." Charlotte snorted and met my eyes for a beat. She smiled, a slight blush to her cheeks before she focused on Penny. "Do you have an agenda for us today?"

"Obviously." Penny pulled out green sheets of paper. "Free time until early afternoon. We're gonna ski for a bit. Then Christian and I have a couple's massage."

"I could call Candy back, see if she could follow us around all day and sing?"

Everyone laughed at Garrett.

"We can meet in the lobby for a drink around four? There's a dinner and karaoke tonight, then four different holiday movies in each section of the ballroom. I originally planned a drinking game for the movies, but we can't—"

"We can still make it a drinking game, babe." Christian gave her a look, and she nodded. "We have a list of items that make us drink depending on what movie we pick."

"*Home Alone, Christmas Vacation, Elf,* and *A Christmas Story.* Hm, I vote *Christmas Vacation,* right?" Garrett clicked his tongue. "That's the best."

"Or *Home Alone*." Charlotte laughed. "These lists are insane. *Drink when Marv speaks Angrish*. This is awesome."

"There is an ugly sweater contest tonight too. The more original, the better. There is a team gift card for a prize, and I do plan to win." Penny puffed her chest and took her time meeting all our gazes.

She truly was the perfect match for Christian. She was a holiday hooligan in the best, kindest way.

Brunch went on for another hour, everyone rehashing the competitions from last night. We all stood just as Charlotte grabbed my forearm, stopping me. Heat spread through my body from her touch. It was like the entire hour of distraction was for nothing. Images of her flashed through my mind, and I wanted to kiss her.

"There's something we need to tell you," Charlotte said to the group.

Wait. What? We didn't talk about this. She couldn't tell them before I even knew what we were doing. I tensed and pulled from her grip. I had to stop her without hurting her feelings. Shit. My mind spiraled, and nothing came out before she said, "Hayden and I scored higher than your team. There was a bet on the table, but as a kind gesture from our hearts, we made a playlist for the DJ at the wedding even though we shouldn't have. I want it noted that we are better people than you."

Garrett cackled. "Holy shit, you devious little monster. I love you, Charmander."

Charlotte winked at him, which I didn't love. Penny and Christian stared at her, then me, their expressions reflecting matching dread. They were so damn competitive that this was the most offensive thing we could've done.

Even though we had good intentions about helping with their wedding. I mean, they seemed so much better this morning. They were touchy and happy.

"I hate you." Christian narrowed his eyes at his sister. "This . . . this has to be one of the best moments of your life."

"Oh. It is. Top five, easily." She smirked and leaned to hug both her brother and Penny. "Have fun skiing. Love you!"

Penny, Christian, and Garrett took off to ski, leaving Charlotte and me to ourselves. She spun to me, a twinkle in her eye. "I love one-upping my brother. Does that make me immature? You know what, don't answer. It feels too good."

"You're an evil little elf." I found myself smiling too. With a quick glance toward the hallway, the others were gone, and I pulled her toward me. "I'm into it though."

"Evil elves?" She scrunched her nose and smiled. I let myself stare at her two freckles under her eyes. I never let myself look too closely, and now I could.

"No. You." I tipped her chin and kissed her. I couldn't get over how good it felt. She sighed into me, like the kiss meant as much to her as it did to me. "I'm into you."

"That will never get old. So what shall we do?" She wiggled her eyebrows and leaned into me. Hints of vanilla and evergreen filled the air. I ran a finger over her jawline, honestly obsessed with just touching her skin.

I wanted to take her back to one of our hotel rooms, but that sure as hell wasn't going slow. I owed it to her to be mature and find time for us to learn more about each other outside of the bedroom. That would happen, for sure. But not yet.

"I think we should work on your interview."

Her shoulders slumped, and her entire body tensed. "Right, the interview."

"Are you not looking forward to the opportunity?" I studied her. She blinked a lot and shifted her weight side to side.

"What do you mean? Of course I'm excited, but nervous too." She crossed her arms and stepped away from me. A sure sign of defensiveness.

"When I mentioned the interview, your entire body changed. Do you not want to talk about it? We don't have to, if you explain what's going through your pretty head."

"I do want to talk about it. It's just…" She tightened her eyes to slits. Her hands flailed in the air, and her mouth twisted into a thousand expressions that I couldn't stop watching.

I knew Char in so many ways, but the thought of learning everything about her excited me. She spoke fast when she was nervous and used her hands when she was passionate. I'd seen her have whole conversations with her hands wild in the air, and I loved it. This insecurity coming from her was new, and it didn't sit right with me. She wasn't insecure about anything.

She had a heart of gold, would improve anyone's life she entered, and truly believed in building up people. It was a no-brainer that she was right for the job. She just had to believe it, and she didn't right now. I could help with that.

She struggled, and I took her hand in mine, interrupting her. "Okay, before you answer, we're going to do an activity. Let me grab some paper and a table."

"You're using your coaching voice on me. Not sure if I've told you this before, I like this version of you, Coach Porter."

"Then be a good girl and let me help you," I fired back, enjoying the way her eyes lit up. This new level of banter was top tier. Big fan of this stage of our relationship. "There, go sit at that booth near the fire."

"Say please."

This time my body lit up. I liked hearing the command in her voice. "Please, Char, go have a seat so I can help explain to you why you're the whole fucking package. Now, stop sassing me. It's distracting."

She grinned and almost had a skip in her step as she moved toward a booth. I found a pen and pad of paper near the host stand, and I snatched them. I placed them on the table and tapped my finger on them. "What do you have so far?"

"Meaning...my résumé? I already applied."

"Great. I meant plans. Practice plans, program goals, merch ideas. I've worked with a lot of high school coaches, and they always need fundraising. How are you gonna bring in more funds for the softball program? What makes you different than Chad?"

She shrugged, the same defeated look crossing her face. That was just unacceptable.

"Charlotte, honey, here's what you're going to do. Write down ten things about yourself that are amazing. We all get impostor syndrome from time to time, but I refuse to let you live in this headspace. The Char I know wouldn't back down from a challenge before it even happened, and that's what your body language tells me."

"It's not that I'm backing down before the interview." She spoke with more fire than before, which made me happy.

She spun the ring on her middle finger around and around. "I'll go and do my best, but I know Chad will get the job. He and the athletic director are friends. They go to happy hour together and make it very clear that I'm not in the 'cool circle' of coaches." She pushed her hair behind her ears, her jaw set in a hard line. "I'm naive to think I have a real chance, because I know how this ends."

My blood boiled at the resignation in her voice. "You can read the future? When did that happen?"

"You know what I mean." She rolled her eyes.

"No, Charlotte, I don't." I shoved the piece of paper at her and handed her the pen. "You're going to write down ten things about yourself and show why you deserve this. Is the AD the only one on the panel? I don't give a shit about Chad and him being friends. It's about the sport and the program and—most importantly—the athletes. Write the list down."

She sucked in a breath, and I softened my voice, aware that I had let my annoyance drip into my tone. "I refuse to hear you talk about yourself like you're not deserving of everything. If I'm around, my woman isn't accepting defeat until the decision is made."

Her face relaxed, and neither one of us mentioned the fact

that I said *my woman* like a twenty-first-century caveman. It was how I felt though.

"What if I can't come up with ten things?"

"Write. The. List."

She wet her lips before finally taking the damn pen to the paper. She twirled it around her fingers once, twice, and then a third time, but she hadn't written a single thing. That was fine. If she wanted to have a test of patience, I'd win.

I had a three-year-old gremlin at home. I practiced patience all day, every day. I survived potty training with a strong-willed child. I was the king of patience.

"Are you sure this is helpful? Can we work on my presentation or something?"

"No. You're not getting out of this."

"You're making me rethink this whole being together thing. I forgot how...bossy you could be."

"You didn't forget a damn thing. You're just stubborn as hell, and if you need help, I'll make the list for you." I yanked the pen out of her hands and wrote in all caps CHARLOTTE BEATS CHAD LIST.

> SMART AS HELL
> COMPETITIVE TO THE POINT IT'S SEXY
> BEST PLAYLIST MAKER
> THE BEST TEAMMATE ANYONE COULD
> ASK FOR

"Hayden," she said, interrupting me. "You think I'm smart?"

"Of course I do." I scoffed. "You're strategic and forward-thinking about everything. I remember how you'd set a calendar reminder for Christian and me to help us remember our parents' birthdays and anniversaries, along with their favorite places to eat. People don't do that, Charlotte. It's detailed. Important. You inspired me to keep a list about those I care about so I never have to ask them what they want for a gift."

"Really?" She leaned onto the table, her eyes dancing with glee. "I inspired you?"

"Fuck, why do you look so surprised? You're extraordinary." I laughed and ran a hand over my face. "You told me once you carried an EpiPen everywhere with you because one of your teammates was extremely allergic to bees and she was forgetful. You make playlists for people as your love language. I still listen to—"

"Rainy Daze and Weird Vibes?" she answered, her voice soft. "The one I made for you seven years ago, back when Nina broke up with you?"

"Yes. That one. You knew all my favorite artists and helped pull me out of that slump." I wished I could dive into her mind to unpack why she didn't realize she had everything going for her. "You're fucking incredible. Own it and stop this insecure shit."

"Wow, Coach Porter. Do you motivate all your players this way?"

"By telling them the truth? Always."

"With this much profanity?"

"Finish the activity."

Charlotte grinned, her nose scrunching, and it was adorable. Despite being direct and a little forceful with my words, it worked. She filled out the rest of the paper with her very neat handwriting, and pride filled me.

I loved this part of being a coach. Helping others find their value and be proud of who they were fulfilled me in a deep way. Becoming a father had also formed a huge need to build confidence. I wanted Gwen to think, believe, and know she could do anything.

"I'm not one to talk about myself, but this feels...good." She clicked her tongue. "I'm not sharing my list until you do one too though. It seems only fair."

My gut twisted. My evil elf was turning my words against me. "I'm not interviewing for a job though. I know what I can do."

"You know why you're awesome? Tell me then, Coach."

"This is about you, Charlotte." I covered her hand with mine, gliding my thumb over her wrist. "You go in and make it the hardest, most contentious decision that interview panel has ever made. You make them sweat choosing Chad, because I tell you what, they will notice you."

"What if I do all that and it still doesn't happen?"

"Then you keep doing the work that matters to you, and another opportunity will open up. When you give your heart and soul to something, it rewards you. It'll give back to you, Char. You're meant to coach and shape the minds of student athletes. I know that as much as I know Gwen will change the world. Let me believe in you when you don't believe in yourself."

She sniffled and sat back against the booth, her gaze moving toward the window. Moisture filled her eyes, and my chest felt like someone jabbed me. *You made her cry, idiot.*

"Char—"

"I kinda want to throw myself at you and kiss your face for saying all that."

"Then do it."

She slid out of the booth and fell onto me, her familiar scent and warmth surrounding me as she wrapped her arms around me in a hug. "Thank you," she said, her muffled voice blocked by my shirt.

I cupped the back of her head, closing my eyes and holding her. "You're welcome. That's my job, baby, to build you up. You gotta let me."

Soft kisses covered my neck and then my jaw. Each touch of her lips on my skin sent a flurry of emotions through me. Need, want, desperation, worry, *love.* I loved this woman. Avoiding her hadn't dulled the feelings, and being around her again reminded me. She was an addiction that I got full access to this weekend, but what happened when our time ended here?

I kissed her temple as she slid off my lap and onto the booth next to me. I liked her here, right by me. Our thighs touched, and I didn't have to pretend I didn't notice. Leaning into her, I felt drunk on her. I forgot about all my worries and focused on the feel of her muscles against mine, the softness of her pants.

"Go get your laptop, and I'll write down some practice interview questions we can go over. We can set a timer if that helps you. One hour. Then we stop."

"And then we can go back to the hotel room?" She arched a brow, her cheeks reddening. "Because I need to be honest, Hayden. I want to have my way with you right now."

I snorted into my fist. "Oh, you have no idea how little self-control I have this second. So, please, Char, get your damn laptop so we can work on this."

She grinned wide and sprinted out of the booth. The hour would be dedicated to her interview, but it would also give me time to figure out what the hell I was gonna do. Charlotte had rooted herself under my skin. I refused to cross any more lines with her until we agreed on the future.

I just had to figure out what the hell the future meant to me.

CHAPTER NINETEEN

CHARLOTTE

One hour turned into three, which turned into an early dinner at one of the resort's cafés. Scratch papers were spread all over the surface, along with two plates of fries and sandwiches. We deserved a drink after the first draft of the interview plan, and two empty beer glasses sat next to two new ones. Of course, this place dyed their drinks red and green. It wasn't every day I had a red beer.

"How are you feeling about everything?" Hayden wore his glasses because we stared at my screen so much, and every single time I glanced at him, I wanted to kick my feet and squeal. He was so hot it didn't make sense.

Sitting made me stir-crazy, so I paced to the right of the table as I took in his question. I actually felt good. "I've never felt more prepared for anything. I know my plan to stand out and make it about the student athletes and the program. Comparing myself to Chad isn't conducive, and you helped me remember that I am pretty awesome."

"Yes, you are." He sucked in one side of his cheek as he

scanned the papers. A wrinkle formed on his forehead as he picked up one sheet, set it down, and repeated the process. "Where is the mock-up of the scoreboard redesign? I liked the way you drew it with the potential sponsorships on it."

The red ink popped out, and I pulled it from the pile. "Here."

"You able to digitize this?" His right knee bounced up and down as he took a sip of the green beer. "I think if you can print this out in a 3D rendering with the monetary opportunities with it, you'd be impossible to beat."

"I'll work on it. My friend is a designer and owes me a favor."

Hayden organized all the materials into a nice pile as he said, "Char, hon, I honestly don't know how they won't hire you. I want to hire you for our team with these ideas, and let me make this clear."

I didn't respond, and he wrapped his fingers around my wrist, drawing my attention. I met his eyes. "I'm listening, Coach."

"These were your ideas. All I did was help guide you on the best presentation format because I've lived through this before. The plan? You. The vision? All yours. Own this shit."

"You're quite the motivational speaker." I blushed at the way he stared at me, so intense and serious. "I'm definitely feeling more confident about this whole thing. Gwen is lucky to have you as her dad."

"I've been low a few times in my life, and loving and believing in yourself is the hardest hurdle. Once you've mastered that, everything will work out." He smiled, but the expression was distant, almost pained. "My mom was the best at that. She's been so good at teaching Gwen self-worth. I'm good with it on the field with the guys, where I can be more direct and crasser. I want to be there for Gwen too but I'm not...my approach isn't the best. If I had more time, I'd read more books on how to be that for Gwen."

"Being direct isn't bad."

"Yeah, but I'm worried I'm not always going to be the parent she needs. My dad kicked my ass when I needed it, and my mom was there to pick up the pieces and make me better. I needed both parts, and I can't play both roles. I can be tough, but Gwen feels so much, and I swear, if I even raise my voice, she cries." He scrubbed his hands over his face, the glasses rising up onto the top of his head. He placed them on the table and looked so conflicted that I wanted to curl up in his lap and reassure him.

"Being three years old is all about big feelings and learning about the world around them. Didn't you just tell me not to compare myself to Chad? Why are you comparing your situation to others'? It's not a competition."

Screw it. I moved next to him onto the bench and ran my hand over his upper back. He tensed for a beat before he leaned into me. "Do you think the fact that your parents are moving away for a year has you doubting yourself?"

"I'm gonna need another beer if we're going to touch that comment." He barked out a laugh. "Okay, can we go back to your interview prep? I prefer that, rather than where this conversation is heading."

"Ah, don't like when the tables have turned, huh?"

"Nope. I'm great at helping with others' problems, just not my own. Super healthy, I know." He leaned back into the booth, his hands shoved in the pocket of his hoodie. He tilted his head to look at me, his gray eyes swirling with mischief. "Any chance I can distract you so we don't talk about this? I have some naughty ideas I think you'd approve of."

"Not a chance." I poked his side, a rush of heat making me clench. Naughty ideas? That sounded amazing, but this weight he carried around since becoming a solo parent had only grown in size. I couldn't fathom the stress he had, having an adorable person depend on you for everything, but not talking about it would make it worse. "Hey," I said softly.

"Hm?"

"You really helped me with this interview. I appreciate it so much. But if you and I are going to... explore whatever this is, I want it to be reciprocal. Let me help you, and if I can't, I can listen. You don't need to carry all this yourself." I ran a hand over his shoulder and arm, squeezing his wrist. He was so warm and thick. Mm.

He groaned and pinched his nose. "I don't trust people easily, let alone with my girl, so the thought of finding someone to help watch her causes me so much stress, it paralyzes me. The three I've interviewed were all busts. Too immature, not CPR trained, was on her phone the entire time. I want someone who pushes Gwen but keeps her in line and is kind. I'm supposed to travel with my assistant coaches in the next few weeks for some showcases down south, and now I'm not sure I can go."

"Okay." I ran my finger up and down on the table, tracing an invisible alphabet to do something with my adrenaline. "Are you open to ideas here? Or just wanting to be grumpy?"

"I'm not grumpy." His gaze flashed to me. "I'm disgruntled. There is a difference, Char."

I snorted. "You're cute, and you're wrong."

"I like it when you sass me. It's always been one of my favorite things about you." He grinned and leaned forward. His lips brushed against mine before he said, "I also like the fact that I can kiss you now."

"Yeah, big fan of that." I gripped his chin and kissed him back. It was soft, quick, and gentle, like we'd been doing this for years. My skin prickled with awareness, and heat spread to my thighs, but I pushed his chest with my other hand. "Could you take Gwen with you when you go away? Hire someone to travel with you where she'd be near you. It's only for one year, right? I think there are nannies who do that."

"Huh." He worked his jaw left and right, his eyebrows a hard line. "I'd feel better about it if she was closer to me. I didn't...how do you find one?"

"There is this thing called Google. We go there and type in—"

"Such a smart-ass." He laughed, the deep, reassuring sound rumbling in his chest. "I could see how this neighbor's daughter works out for the short term, the random late nights in town. Then take my time for the traveling nanny. I could ask—"

"Wait!" I smacked my forehead. "My best teacher friend

used to nanny and knows a few still working. Worst case, she knows the company and can set up a call for you."

"That'd be...damn." Hayden's face turned serious, his eyes burning into me. "Thank you. That's a great idea, and I'd be really appreciative."

"I didn't even get to the best part yet either. This is where I really look like a hero too." I clicked my tongue, drawing it out. "I made a spreadsheet for after the holidays, where my parents, Christian and Penny, and I all watch her. We love that girl, Hayden, so it's not a chore, nor is it a burden. We can handle January for you, so that gives you four weeks to find the right person before the season starts in February. I already asked them, and it's scheduled."

"How..." he started, then stopped and swallowed. He seemed torn up instead of the joy I had anticipated.

A lead weight formed in my gut, the sensation of sinking pulling me down. He hated the idea. I shouldn't have done it. He was the father, not me. I overstepped! I panicked. "I-I shouldn't—"

"Charlotte. Let's go to your room." He nudged me to leave my side of the booth, and I jumped out of there so fast.

His tone was off, and he wouldn't look at me. My insides were an absolute mess, clenching and twisting. I might've overstepped, but I thought he needed help. Would he want to break this off, whatever it was?

He grabbed my laptop and the papers, and jutted his chin toward the hallway. "Walk to your room, please."

He'd said *please*. That was a good sign. His body language was stiff and awkward though. Tense shoulders and his jaw flexing every few seconds. The walk to my room took only a minute, and my hands trembled when I unlocked the door. This unsettled, spiraling sensation was horrible. "I can—"

The second the door clicked shut, Hayden set my laptop and papers on the dresser, and he hoisted me up onto the bathroom counter.

"Fuck." He groaned into my neck and then slid his hands up the back of my shirt. He dug his fingers into my skin as he whispered, "You're amazing."

"Amazing?" My mind spun. I thought he was upset with me. "What's...you were mad."

"No." He kissed right beneath my ear and hummed against me, the deep growl sending a bolt of lightning between my thighs. "Overcome with want. I can't tell you how much your gesture meant to me. It's too...I want to show you. If you'll let me."

He pulled back, his gray eyes heating as he stared at me. He moved his hands to the front of my shirt, dancing along my rib cage as I shuddered. "Please."

I nodded.

His relief was immediate. He lifted the hem of my sweater, taking his time removing it as he held eye contact. There was something so hot about the confidence emanating from him as he stared at me. He wasn't afraid of connecting, and that was a huge turn-on.

He set the sweater to the side, his hands running up and down my body as he teased my nipples with his thumbs.

"Oh," I moaned. I arched my back, the sensation from just his fingers overheating me.

"There you go with that sound again." His eyes flashed

with heat as he pulled the red cups down enough to expose the tips. He kneeled so his face was at the same level as my breasts, and he cupped both of them. "What else makes you do that? Will my mouth?"

I couldn't even speak seeing him kneeling before me. He licked one pebbled tip, smiling up at me as I bucked off the counter. "Hayden," I begged. For what? I had no idea. Just more of this, of him.

"Mm, I like hearing you say my name this way." He flicked the other nipple, not in any rush to take my damn bra off. He blew on each one, the sensation causing them to tighten. Goose bumps exploded down my body, and he chuckled as I squirmed.

My pulse raced as heat overwhelmed my body. Every part of me was attuned to him, and it consumed me. He licked the corner of his lip as he trailed one finger over the waistband of my jeans, dipping into it. His eyes flared. "Your skin is so soft."

He kissed right below my belly before trailing his mouth up my stomach and between my breasts. Only then did he undo my bra. He watched with a slack jaw as he slid one strap off and then the other. I trembled as he sucked in a breath again.

"You are stunning." He kissed my mouth as his hands found my breasts again, his fingers making small circles around my nipples.

The teasing sensation had me on the edge of the counter. Rational thought stopped working. "Skin," I blurted out. I grabbed his sweatshirt and tugged it. "I need this off. I want to feel you."

"This is about you, baby." He grinned as I struggled with his hoodie. "I want to make you feel good. Will you let me?"

Who was this man? Would I let him? I'd let him do anything he wanted if he would just touch me. "Okay, but you can do that shirtless."

He laughed. "Your attitude is so fucking hot." He whipped the sweatshirt off and tossed it to the side, returning to his position on the floor before I could admire him. "Your turn now. Pants are coming off."

From this angle, his broad shoulders were sculpted. Each muscle was thick and hard, created from years spent training. I ran my fingers over them, pounding with the need to lick him. "You're perfect," I said, my voice all husky.

He stopped running his hands over my waist and smiled. "That's my line."

He undid my jeans and shimmied them down my legs, leaving me in just my red underwear. He struggled with the pants, almost like he was as turned on as I was, and basic human functions were off the table. He carried it off better than me though.

The red fabric was soaked. Before I had time to feel embarrassed, he licked his lips and said, "Spread your thighs for me."

"Oh." I panted. I did as he said. My arousal was right there for both of us to see. "Like this?"

"Yes. You good girl." He ran a hand over his jaw, his gaze zeroing in on my pussy. "Look how wet you are for me."

I squirmed as he lifted one thigh onto his shoulder and then my other. He kissed the sensitive skin by my knee, licking all the way up. My clit pounded with an aggressive, animalistic need. If he didn't touch me there, I wouldn't survive. His shoulders were too far out of reach, and I clutched the bare counter for something to ground myself. "Hayden, please," I begged.

"I've fantasized about you for years. I'm taking my time making you come."

"Oh God." I dropped my head back. My eyes fell shut as he oh so slowly slid my underwear to the side.

He breathed on me, and I bucked.

"So sensitive." He slid a finger over me, spreading me wider. "So wet."

"Hayden." I trembled. "More."

"I've always wondered," he said before thrusting his finger into me.

A combination of a moan and desperate cry escaped me. His finger felt so good. "Wondered what?"

"How you would taste." Then he flattened his tongue against me. Stars exploded around my eyes. My heart stuttered—like it had forgotten how to work. My veins filled with ecstasy, and my muscles clenched with the most pleasurable, explosive feeling.

I came alive under his touch.

He sucked my clit into his mouth before finding the perfect rhythm of thrusting and swirling, and my God, he was the oral king. I'd never come from oral before, but I was only seconds away. He growled against me, the deep vibration causing another sensation over my nerves, and oh my lanta.

"I'm gonna—"

"Come on my tongue."

"Shit!" I arched my back as the orgasm rammed into me all at once from every direction. My legs shook uncontrollably around his head, but Hayden held on to me. He coached me right through it.

"Ride my face, baby.

"You scream so good.

"You taste like heaven."

I cried out, hard, as he sucked my clit into his mouth, drawing a few more seconds of pure bliss. My chest heaved as I fell back onto the counter, completely spent. My legs were noodles. He kissed my inner thighs with a tender gaze.

Hayden winked and said, "Big fan of your panties."

"That's what..." I laughed, breathless. "You had your tongue on my pussy, and that's what you say."

"Mm." His eyes flashed.

He slid my underwear back into place before massaging my calves. "I love your muscles. Have I ever told you that?"

I shook my head, absolutely melting at the feeling of his large hands on my legs. I'd dreamed of Hayden saying things like this to me. His bare chest glistened with sweat, and I needed to touch him. "I-I need to touch you."

"This is about you, Char." He cupped my face and kissed me softly. "To thank you for doing something so kind and thoughtful. I'd never have asked for help out of fear of being a burden."

"You and Gwen are not a burden," I fired back.

"I know that now." He smiled. "Maybe we are good for each other after all."

My heart skipped a beat. We should talk, but he was shirtless and standing right in front of me. "Hayden." I ran my fingers down his warm chest, stopping at the waistband of his jeans.

He sucked in a breath.

"Please," I whispered. His words held the weight of our unsaid things, and if we were communicating with soft touches, it was only fair we both got a turn.

He closed his eyes and took a heavy breath, his grip on my thighs tightening. When he met my gaze, his gray eyes were almost charcoal. His voice was raspy and laced with frustration when he said, "I want this so fucking bad, baby, but we need to talk first."

CHAPTER TWENTY

HAYDEN

Was there an award for being the best version of myself? I wanted a ten-foot-tall trophy for the amount of strength it took to step back from Charlotte. My dream woman. Her body still shook from her orgasm, and her gorgeous, wide eyes were satisfied. Yet her posture straightened at my words, and something like fear flashed across her face.

My cock strained against my jeans, the almost feral need to touch her again about taking over every sense. But we still hadn't talked about this. "Here, wear my sweatshirt."

She pressed her lips together as I grabbed my hoodie and gently put it on her. It left her hair in a mess, and I grinned. "I like you in my clothes."

She flashed a quick smile. "I like you without yours."

Chuckling, I held out a hand and helped her off the counter. Her long, bare legs were such a tease, and while I was proud of myself for showing such restraint, my libido was not pleased. She paused and stared at me. "Where should we sit since you want to talk instead of letting my tongue explore your body?"

Fuck, that was a hot picture. "That mouth is gonna get you in trouble."

"Maybe that's my plan." She crossed her arms and dug her toes into the carpet. "I'm not gonna lie, I'm turned on and cold and feeling weird about you denying me. It's bringing me back to…before, even though you've made it clear that's not the case." She shivered and flipped the switch for the automatic fireplace.

I rubbed her shoulders and pulled her against me. Her familiar and enticing smell assured me that somehow, even with my life being crazy, we could make this work. I kissed the side of her neck, and she molded into me. "We have decades of knowing each other, and with that comes a lot of emotions we'll have to work through. I want us to be certain and on the same page before we go too far. Trust me on this: all I want to do is explore your body and learn everything about you."

"Same page then," she whispered. "What page are you on?"

"I want to explore this with you. I want to see where this goes." I sighed, pulling her closer. "My life is complicated, messy, and I can't just think of myself. God, if it was just me, there'd be no question about this, Char."

She swallowed hard. "What does *explore* mean to you?"

"That's a great question." I laughed, grateful that she hadn't pulled away or said no yet. She could. She *should*. It would be painful to let her go, but if she didn't want me and all that came with my life, she should walk away. "I can't really do date nights."

Hearing myself say it out loud caused my chest to ache. I had to get a better balance of my life. Disappointment wedged itself into my ribs, making each breath hurt a little. "We could see what happens?"

"Hm."

Hm? What the hell did *hm* mean?

"I need more than that, Char." I spun her around to read her facial expressions. She was an open book and often narrated her stream of thoughts. She was uncharacteristically quiet. "Baby, I want to be with you. I want to try."

"Like, exclusively?"

"Abso-fucking-lutely." I reared my head back. "That's not even a question."

She scrunched her nose in a smile. "So we date."

"Without real dates," I clarified.

"I happen to enjoy movie nights in, and game nights, or cooking dinner with you." She exhaled, her shoulder relaxing as she placed a hand on my chest. "If *real dates* are going out to fancy restaurants or wine tastings or weekends away, sure, they are nice, but I don't need those. My love language is sharing life together. Grocery shopping dates, watching a movie at home, walks to the park...those sound perfect to me."

Fuck, she was perfect. I closed my eyes as my mind turned on its axis. How did I stay away from this beautiful, wonderful human all these years? "When you say stuff like that, it makes me think this could really work between us."

"Why couldn't it? If we want this, then we make it work." She tilted her head. "I'm going to use your words against you, Hop. You guided me to focus on all the reasons I would bring value to the coaching position, not all the things I lacked. You need to do the same with us. Think about all the reasons we could work instead of all the reasons it might not."

She was right. It was my own fear holding me back. I could practically feel the truth wrapped around me, keeping me from admitting it and diving into something I wanted. Could this implode? Sure as shit could. Would it drastically affect my life? Yup. The fear of getting hurt loosened, and the other elephant in the room jumped front and center. Two elephants, actually.

Gwen and Christian.

"Gwen—"

"Nothing changes with her. Even if you crushed my heart into a million pieces, I will always be there for her," Charlotte said, her bossy teaching voice coming out. "I will follow your lead on what to tell her, but I will not change how I love that little girl. If that is a concern, then you can toss that out the window."

"But what if—"

"You hurt me three years ago, and I still was a part of her life, right?" She placed both hands on my bare chest now, her nails digging into my skin. "I'm not going to beg for a chance with you, but do *not* use your daughter as a reason for us not to try."

"Your attitude is kinda hot," I mumbled.

She laughed and moved her hands to cup my face. "You've mentioned it a few times. Glad you approve."

My hands easily found her waist. "Okay, since you've left no room to discuss my daughter, there is one more thing we need to discuss."

"I'm on birth control if you don't have a condom."

I choked. "Jesus, Charlotte."

She laughed, and I fucking loved that sound.

"What? I didn't know if that was the other big topic that you seem to be intent on discussing."

"No. I have a fucking condom." I snorted and rested my forehead against hers. "You're ridiculous, and I love it. We need to talk about Christian."

"Mood killer."

"I know. I'm sorry. But what...how...do we tell him?" I asked, hesitant to speak the entire truth. There wasn't a normal way to say, *Oh hey, can we not tell him because, if it doesn't work out, I still want my best friend?* Did that mean I didn't think we'd make it? Or that I assumed we'd fail?

"Oof, that is a good question."

I tensed. She agreed with me? I didn't like that.

She pulled back and played with one of the strings on my sweatshirt and clicked her tongue. "I agree with you though. We shouldn't tell him or Penny. With the argument we heard, I don't want anything getting in the way. If we stole their thunder in any way, I'd feel terrible."

"Right." I sighed, relief flooding through me. That made more sense than my own inner fears. A part of me felt shitty for thinking such a selfish thought, but I'd have to deal with that on my own. "After the wedding, we can tell them."

"Deal." Charlotte grinned and wiggled her eyebrows at me. "Does that mean I get to touch you now?"

I laughed again. I'd laughed more with her the last day and a half than I had in months. It felt good. "We need to meet them."

"Hayden." She rolled her eyes. "I don't enjoy you being the mature one today. It's annoying, to be honest with you. Fine. Let's be mature. Get out of my room then."

She laughed while she said the words, but her comment from earlier had stayed with me, about hurting her three years ago and taking some time to heal that wound. "Hey, you know I'd rather stay in here with you, right? I don't... I've fantasized about you for years, and it's gonna kill me to go act normal for a few hours."

"Oh, I understand your reasons." Her tone was laced with sarcasm that made me pause.

"Sounds like you might be mad about it?" I asked, watching her slide on jeans and toss my hoodie onto the bed. She put on her bra way too fast and faced me with hands on her hips.

"Nope. Not mad in the slightest."

"There feels like a *but* in there somewhere."

She smirked, her entire face full of mischief. "I'm just gonna have fun tormenting you tonight since you're hell-bent on not getting naked with me."

"If you flirt with Garrett or that fucking elf..."

She snorted. "Ha, not that kind of torment. We might be a secret for a few weeks, but when I'm with someone, I am with *them*. Just you. I'll find other ways, Porter. Now, do you have an ugly sweater?"

I wanted to dive into her comment more, but she seemed playful, so I let it go. I shook my head. "Must've missed that memo from Penny."

"Unacceptable and Grinch-like of you." She pulled out a booger-green sweater with things taped to it.

"What is that?"

She cackled. "I printed a ton of horrible pictures of Christian before he grew into his looks. My mom obviously helped with this." She put it on and modeled for me. "Here, we have the time he shoved Lincoln Logs up his nose and got them stuck. This one is him covered in dirt when he made us all treat him like a dog for a week."

"This is brilliant." I laughed, admiring all the photos of my best friend. "I'm jealous I didn't think of it. I only have a boring red sweater that I actually think is nice."

"Hm, that won't do. Let me think." She faced the mirror and braided her hair along her forehead. It went to the side, and then she tied it back into a pony. As a single dad to a daughter, I wanted to learn how to do that, while I also admired how pretty it made her look.

She caught my gaze in the mirror and snapped her fingers. "Oh, I have it. I have the best idea. We're gonna call it the Suite Spectacle!"

"I'm not tracking, but I admire your enthusiasm."

"First off, go put a shirt on. It's not fair for you to be shirtless around me when I can't touch you. Second, get a sweater you're alright destroying."

"You can touch me—"

"Shh. Go." She pointed at the wall between our rooms.

"Yes, ma'am."

There was a skip in my step as I went into my room to grab a sweater. I put on a navy-blue one on the off chance I stained another shirt. With living with a toddler, I'd always spill on my white shirts. Chuckling to myself, I left my glasses on the side of my bed and replaced the hoodie with the blue sweater.

My phone buzzed with a text from the same number that had called and left no voicemails. **Can we please talk Hayden?**

At some point, I'd need to figure out who the hell this was, but not today. Not when I had this time with Charlotte.

Even in the short time of staying at the ski resort, not being around Charlotte had me antsy. It was like we were in our own little bubble here, and the illusion would fade when we were apart. It was insecurity, I knew, but I was already halfway addicted to her. Could I handle not seeing her for days, or weeks, at a time? Or only talking to her on the phone?

It'd be better than the last three years.

That was true. But Charlotte was a forever type of girl. When I pictured us being together, she always ended up as my wife, which was crazy. I needed to slow my roll and not scare her away, because if she didn't want that, then fuck. *Stop.*

She told me to focus on all the ways it could work, not all the ways it wouldn't. I owed her that much.

I returned to her room to find her lips bright red and big-ass Christmas tree earrings hanging from her ears.

Christian's face covered the trees, but her pillow lips looked incredible. What a weird thing to feel while staring at photos of Christian. "You look great."

"Thank you." She beamed. "Now, sit here. I have the plan."

"You're reminding me of that time you *planned* a whole scavenger hunt when we were kids. Who ended up with a broken arm in the emergency room? Me. I did."

She waved her hand in the air. "That was your own damn fault for climbing a tree! The riddle was clearly in our attic. Not the tree. Now, this is nothing like that. We're going to use all the paper we can find in one of our hotel rooms to make snowflakes. Then we're cutting them and stapling them to your shirt."

"That is . . ." I shook my head. "Ridiculous."

"Yes, but just think what you could do with that gift card. Twenty-five dollars to the resort store will be epic. It'll feel so good to bring Gwen back a free gift."

"She has enough—"

"Winning feels good, no cap. Now stop arguing with me and sit down."

"Have I told you that I like your mouth?"

"Yes. But I refuse to let your charm distract me from this plan. It's all formed in my head, and it's gonna be great."

She worked fast, cutting out weirdly shaped snowflakes. She stapled them to my sweater, totaling fifteen in all. Some were from the notepad on the desk. Some were from the free holiday magazine they gave us and, of course, two were from toilet paper. "All created from hotel room resources. The creativity! The execution! We nailed it."

"You are my perfect competitive freak." I pulled her toward me, our ugly sweaters clashing with pins and staples. "Thank you. I'm not sure I'll win, but I look damn good."

"Yes, you do." She weaved her arms around my neck, and I rested mine just above her ass.

I'd always wanted to hold her like this, and a contented, almost-too-good-to-be-true sigh escaped. I kissed her. I'd never get over the fact that I could kiss her now. She nipped my bottom lip, sliding her tongue against it before she pulled back. I gripped her tighter, wanting to deepen the kiss, but she shook her head. "No, you made it clear: no tomfoolery. You can look, but you can't touch."

"But you're sexy," I grumbled. "I want to touch you."

She licked her lips and walked toward the door. "Come on, Hop. We now have to behave for the next four hours and pretend not to like each other. Let the tormenting begin."

CHAPTER TWENTY-ONE

CHARLOTTE

Garrett, take off your jacket now." Penny bossed us around before the ugly sweater contest started.

"I love a forward woman." He winked and undid his jacket.

She ignored his comment, but she eyed his very ugly, very inappropriate holiday sweater. "Is that...two humping reindeer?"

"Yes." Garrett beamed. "I read the team requirements, and I am wearing red and green, this is homemade, and I'd consider it cozy. Wouldn't you, Char? Want to cuddle me to prove it?"

I snorted. "Nah."

Hayden caught my gaze and playfully rolled his eyes.

Penny snapped and moved her attention to Hayden. "You're next, show me your sweater."

Hayden's gaze landed on me, his gray eyes warming with amusement before he unbuttoned his coat. "I followed the rules, Penny."

"Good boy." She nodded at his blue sweater with snow-flakes. "It'll do, but it's not great."

Penny turned to me. "Yours, Charlotte. Tell me you did something good."

Everyone stared at me.

I opened my coat like I was flashing them and squeezed my eyes shut. "Read it and weep."

"Oh my God." Penny cheered before clapping her hands. "I love it!"

"Jesus." Christian groaned. "For real? For real, Char-char Binks?"

"Can I get really close to the photos, just to inspect them. Maybe the one right there?" Garrett asked, his voice closer to me. He bent down to stare at the photo near my boob.

"No." Hayden's voice cut through. "Great sweater, Char-lotte. Funny."

"Thank you very much." I redid my jacket, the embar-rassment sliding away. Yes, my sweater was booger green and covered in embarrassing photos of my brother. My handiwork was excellent and Christian covered his face in shame. The photos were all of him and they were epic.

Penny cleared her throat before saying, "Thank you all for following directions. Now let's try and win."

*   *   *   *

We didn't win the ugly sweater contest, but Garrett did come in fourth. I wanted to annoy Christian, which— mission freaking accomplished. I swayed to the beat as a group of sorority girls sang "Santa Baby." They were off beat but so confident and fun that I couldn't stop myself from moving.

I also could've been on cloud nine with everything happening with Hayden. It was almost hard to believe that we were doing this. He and I. It felt easy and impossible at the same time. Our chemistry was off the charts, and we understood each other in such a meaningful way that it was like we spent the last decade studying the other person. I knew his weaknesses; he knew mine. He acted like having Gwen would make it harder to date when, in fact, I loved her so much. She wouldn't be an inconvenience to me. Ever.

"It's our turn! Let's go!" Penny threw her arms in the air and waved her hands toward all of us. "We're singing!"

"No, thank you." Hayden shook his head. "I don't sing."

"Come on, what would it take?" Christian had been feeling the drinks the last hour and pulled Hayden into a half hug. "How much?"

"My heart to stop beating, probably." Hayden met my gaze and smirked.

"Dramatic, bro." Garrett grabbed my hand and spun me in a fast circle. "You better come up there and belt it out with me, Calhoun."

"Oh, I'll belt with you." I laughed as I almost knocked into a couple next to us. Hayden gripped my belt loop and stilled me, his hands pressing on my back and stomach. He gave me a gentle pat before releasing me.

I was a hot mess of horniness around him. His intentions were so pure and kind, wanting to talk, but I was walking on a tightrope. Every touch from him lit me up. We might know everything about each other outside of the bedroom, but inside? I couldn't wait to explore. I shuddered just thinking about him on his knees in front of me. Hottest moment of my life.

"Enough stalling, come on!" Penny dragged Garrett and me to the stage. My brother already had the mic in hand as "You're a Mean One, Mr. Grinch," came on. Christian had recently become obsessed with the newer version of the Grinch, the hip-hop song. It was short but it was so much fun, and the upbeat thuds started as Christian and Penny rapped.

I was more of a backup singer and dancer, never the center of attention. My brother and Penny sang and entertained the crowd while Garrett and I laughed and clapped along. My attention kept returning to Hayden, who stood in his ridiculous outfit, a smile on his lips and his gaze never wavering from me. A flutter of nerves hit me, wondering if we were moving too fast. I already loved the guy, and now sex and dating were involved. I was gonna fall even faster and harder, almost to the point of no return, but how could I not? He was my dream man.

The song came to an end, and the next hour flew by. People got drunker, except Penny kept her tune somehow. I was feeling the peppermint drink Hayden bought me, but my mind was on going back to the room. I wanted Hayden where I didn't have to keep my hands to myself. He stood next to me, body heat radiating from him as he leaned down and whispered, "How much longer do we have to stay?"

"Ha, you read my mind."

He ran his fingers under the back of my sweater, the rough pads trailing along my spine. "I regret keeping this secret already."

"It's the right thing to do." I wanted to close my eyes and lean into him, let his deep voice wash over me. "What's our excuse to head back?"

"Make something up. Anything. I'm getting impatient. Watching you dance all night? And letting Garrett talk to you?"

"Mm, my plan worked then." I faced him and stared at his mouth.

He breathed deeper as his fingers dug into my waist. "Fuck, I want to kiss you."

I leaned close enough to feel his breath on my face. His lips parted, and his muscles tensed, almost like he was bracing for me. Then, before my lips met his, I darted right. "We should still talk first, right?"

"My evil little elf."

I winked and made my way to Penny and Christian. "Hey, guys, I'm heading in. Can I buy you a shot before I leave?"

"I'm okay. Thank you though!" Penny pulled me into a hug. "This has been the best weekend ever. Thank you for coming. Thank you for being you. Thank you for being the best sister-in-law ever."

My grin matched hers. This was such a good sign that things were okay. She squeezed me hard before Christian joined. We now were in an awkward sandwich, and I was right in the middle. My heart swelled with joy being between them and the thing with Hayden. It all felt so right, I about burst. "Love you maniacs."

"You too. See you in the morning before we go back to regular life. Ugh." My brother swayed to the side.

I laughed as I walked away, glancing over my shoulder at Hayden, who stood with his hands in his pockets. Winking, I strutted back toward my hotel room with the hope he'd show up soon. I didn't care what he said, just that he was as desperate as I was for this to happen.

He didn't take long. I barely got into my room with my shoes off before a knock sounded on the door.

"Charlotte, I swear to—"

"Hi." I swung it open, smiling at the man of my dreams looking at me like I was a snack. He didn't say another word before he kicked the door shut and picked me up. I wrapped my legs around him, kissed his neck, and squealed when he tossed me on the bed.

"Naked. I need you naked." He tugged his sweater off, along with his shoes and socks, and then had his pants down before I even removed my shirt.

"How the hell did you strip that fast?" I laughed as I threw my shirt on the floor; the bra followed. He gently shoved my hands out of the way, and he slid my jeans and underwear down my body.

"I'm motivated and desperate. Lethal combination."

He stood in front of me, chest gleaming as I ran a finger down him. He trembled as I touched him. He was so thick and strong, and a light dusting of hair greeted me.

"I've wanted to lick you," I whispered, moving toward the edge of the bed to get a closer look at him. He always felt off-limits. "Can I?"

"Then do it." His voice was hoarse, gravelly. "Put that wicked tongue on me."

"Then be a good boy and sit on the bed."

His nostrils flared as he switched spots with me. He wore only black boxer shorts, and I was totally naked. Despite just crossing a line with him, I felt more comfortable in my skin than I ever had before. He made me feel and believe I was sexy.

I grinned up at him and leaned forward, dragging my tongue over his pecs. He tasted salty. His muscles tensed, like he was seconds away from bursting. I liked this. He always seemed so unattainable, so far out of reach, the fact that I had him right in front of me had me feeling sorta high.

I never tried drugs because I was focused on sports, but man, this rush...I understood it. I could live in this head-space and die happy. "Hayden," I moaned, flattening my tongue along his collarbone.

I bit his neck, and he shuddered. It made me feel drunk. Powerful. In charge. I made this gorgeous, perfect man tremble? "I like making you weak in the knees for me."

He chuckled, the sound deep and glorious as he ran his hand down my bare back. He dug in his fingers just above my ass. The pressure caused me to fall into him, and I used the contact to feel his hard muscles, defined from hours in the gym. Sharp angles, grit, and toughness. Hayden worked for everything in his life, his toned body included.

"Turn around," I demanded, my eyes already fluttering from his touch on my back.

"What?" He lifted his head, his eyes clouded with lust.

"I've fantasized about you like this for years. I want my look."

His lips twitched. "Years?"

"Yes." I had no shame. His tongue had been inside me, so we were past the point of embarrassment. "Strip and turn."

He swallowed and stared at me hard as he pushed his boxers down. "Tell me what else you fantasized about then."

I whimpered. I couldn't tell what way was up or down, what day it was, what month, year, or state I was in. He slid the last piece of clothing off, standing completely naked in front of me. His cock stood on end, thick and perfect.

I hadn't been with many guys, but Hayden's dick was glorious. I couldn't even speak. I had to touch him. Feel his length, how hard he was. Would he lean into my touch? Would his cock grow heavy? I fisted him, and he barked out a cuss. "You like this?"

"You have no idea."

I pumped him, licking my lips as I forgot my original plan to taste him from head to toe. Instead, I lowered myself and took him in my mouth. I didn't want to miss my chance to have Hayden come undone.

"Holy shit, baby." He cradled my head, stumbling back a step. "Your mouth is killing me."

"Mm," I hummed, taking him as deep as I could. His salty taste and intoxicating smell overwhelmed me. Each sound he made was a bolt of lust to my gut.

He jolted. His muscles tensed. He dug his fingers into my hair, growling deep in his chest. "Fuck. *Fuck*." His grip tightened, and he stopped me. "No, I'm not coming in your mouth."

"Why?" I asked, on my knees as I stared up at him. The way he looked at me…it gave me shivers. "I thought you wanted to fulfill my fantasies."

"Me coming in your mouth is *your* fantasy?" he asked, his eyes pure black and sexy. "Jesus, Char."

I nodded, and his eyes fluttered, like he couldn't hold out. I was pure lust and power as I took him again, cupping his balls in one hand. He muttered things, but they were unintelligible. I couldn't make out a single thing as he groaned and thrust into my mouth.

He was close. His thick thighs tightened, and I used my free hand to grab his delicious ass. His glutes were magnificent, meaty, and *ugh*. I groaned with him filling my mouth, and that sent him off.

"Christ, Charlotte!" he said, staring down at me as he released himself. He never broke eye contact. His face was the definition of wild abandon. His eyes were wide and dark, and sweat pooled on his forehead.

I swallowed and grinned. "Wow."

"Kiss me." He pulled me up, slamming his mouth against mine. "You are so damn sexy."

I giggled. Me. I was very much not a giggler. I would never forget this night. The deep tone of his voice and hooded eyes that were... Yeah, I'd be reliving this forever.

Hayden gripped the back of my head, gently tugging my hair so I was forced to look up at him. He kissed down my jaw, sucking my skin before meeting my gaze. "You," he said, his voice breaking. "Incredible. Fucking incredible."

Those simple words had me feeling all types of ways. Moisture pooled between my thighs from seeing him fall apart, but the tender look in his eyes wasn't just sexual. There was something more there. "So are you," I whispered back, my heart suddenly in my throat.

Closing his eyes, he kissed my forehead, then my nose, and then my mouth. "Everything feels so right with you," he said. He lay on his side, staring at me as he smiled. "Can I please stay in here with you tonight?"

"Sleep in bed with me?"

He nodded, his eyes intense. It was clear my answer mattered to him a lot. My heart thudded so hard against my ribs.

"If you want. I'm happy to go back to my room too if you're not comfortable. I just—" He cleared his throat. "Want to spend all night learning little things about you. Like this birthmark behind your ear? Fucking adorable."

Why did my eyes prickle at this? Blinking away any evidence of tears, I nodded.

"Use your words, Charlotte. You owe me that."

"Yes, I'd love if you could spend the night with me."

His answering smile made my stomach swoop. The way he looked at me had my insides kicking and screaming, and yeah, I loved how he looked at me.

He looks at me like he loves me.

I shook the thought away, because that was crazy. We couldn't love each other already... right?

CHAPTER TWENTY-TWO

HAYDEN

I trailed a finger over the shell of her ear, down her neck and over the swell of her breasts. Charlotte shivered, and her brown eyes widened when I sucked her earlobe into my mouth. "I will never get over how good you smell, how you taste right here."

She gasped at the sensation and gripped the edge of the bed. "Hayden."

I loved seeing her hands form fists, like she couldn't contain the pleasure she felt. I wanted her feeling everything I gave her. "I want to mark you, everywhere. That's not usually my thing, but you make me feel...unhinged."

I pushed up onto my elbows and slowly circled one nipple with my tongue. Using my fingers, I teased the other one until it was a stiff point. Then I moved my tongue across her chest to suck the other breast. Each time I swirled my tongue, she bucked off the bed. I bit down just enough to get a reaction to see if she liked it. She did.

Charlotte groaned, the sound almost like a growl. I did that to her. I almost made her growl. My skin buzzed.

"Do that again."

"Yes, ma'am. I love hearing you be wild. Let loose, baby. Show me what you like."

"Your mouth on my nipples."

"Mm, yeah." I repeated the process a few times before moving up her neck. I put my thumb at the base of her throat, her pulse beating against me.

"You taste so fucking good," I said, dragging my tongue over her mouth. She did the half-groan, half-growl sound again before I dragged my hands all over her body. I wanted to touch her everywhere, all at once. Her smooth, warm skin, her strong, thick muscles, the dip of her hips and the curve of her ass. I never wanted anyone more in my life.

Despite me coming earlier, I was ready to go. My cock throbbed with the need to be inside her. To finally know what Charlotte Calhoun felt like. "You're perfect," I said, kissing her jaw again because I could.

"Hayden, this is amazing." She ran her hands over my chest, then shoulders, and then back. Her brown eyes seemed darker with lust as she kneaded my skin. "I love how you take such good care of yourself."

I shuddered.

"You have such dedication and work so hard." She dragged her tongue up over my collarbone, mirroring what I had done earlier. Then she sucked the skin lightly before grinding her hips into me. "You're beautiful."

I sucked in a breath, completely undone by this woman. She nipped and sucked, groaned and made her feelings apparent. I loved this unfiltered, sexy side of her. She clawed at me as we made out, naked and rolling around. "God, Char."

At some point, I had rolled onto my back, and Charlotte straddled me. Looking up at her with her hair hanging down around her shoulders, her lips swollen and red, her eyes hooded with lust was the sexiest thing I had ever seen.

Her thighs clenched around me. "Yes, baby."

"I can't get enough of you." She rocked her hips, grinding against my cock, and a blast of heat went through me. She made no move to slide me inside her, which I desperately needed, but each brush of her skin against mine got me hotter. "I love seeing you like this under me."

"Feeling's mutual." I flashed a smile. "I really fucking love seeing you on top of me." I kissed her mouth again, hard. She sucked my tongue, and our teeth clashed together.

"Damn, Hayden. More."

That's all I thought. *More.* More tongue, more touching, more skin.

My cock throbbed harder than it had in my entire life, and I would absolutely die if I didn't slide into her. I ran a hand down her stomach, teasing her clit before sliding one finger into her. I added another, and her breathing got heavier. "I want to make sure you're nice and ready for me."

"Yes," she moaned. Her eyes were closed. "Oh, I like your fingers."

I curled them at the ends and took my time. She was tight as hell, so damn warm, and I couldn't imagine someone more perfect. Her sexy sounds, the feel of her body...I'd never tire of this. "Are you sure you want this?"

She opened her eyes, emotion swirling in them as she cupped my face. "Yes. I want you so badly, Hayden."

Fuck, her voice was all husky and deep. I kissed her to stop myself from confessing all these feelings, threatening to spill. Sex had never been like this before, where each movement was with care and love. We barely had figured shit out; I didn't need to complicate it. But I could show her how I felt.

Without breaking our kiss, I reached over and grabbed a condom I had brought earlier and slid it on. I lay on my back and lifted her onto me. I cupped the back of her head with one hand, the other rubbing small circles on her hips. "Take your time."

She shuddered. "Your cock is big, Hayden."

"Set the pace, baby."

She exhaled and lowered herself onto my cock, and *fuck me*. She was wet and tight. My vision blurred with how good it felt to have her grind on me. She went slow at first, letting my cock fill her. She dug her nails into my chest, her perfect tits bouncing as she picked up her rhythm.

Despite the inferno going on inside me, I smiled up at her. "You look good riding my cock like that."

Even after all we'd done, I could make her blush. I loved knowing I could get that reaction from her. The pink was gorgeous, and I wanted to lick her skin again.

"You're so pretty when you blush, baby." I tweaked her pebbled nipple. "I love how strong you are. I feel your thick thighs every time you grind on me. And your arms, mm, they are sexy." I trailed my fingers over her biceps as her sweat glistened. She grinded faster, taking me deeper into her.

"You feel…this is…" She stopped, closing her eyes as she let out a sexy groan. "I might…come."

"You will." I reached down toward her clit and spread her enough to rub my thumb right over her swollen nerves. She bucked and dug her nails harder into me. Her grip stung, and there'd definitely be a mark. Good. I wanted her marks on me. I wanted everything she gave me.

"Hayden, yes." She rocked harder and faster, her sounds getting louder as her orgasm neared. "Yes, yes, I'm coming."

"Look at me, baby," I demanded, not caring if it was too bossy. I wanted to watch her face as she came on my cock. I swore I forgot to breathe. Her eyebrows came down, and her lips parted into a perfect little O. Lust and something like love flashed in her eyes as she came hard.

Charlotte thrashed and screamed my name as she fell apart. It was hot as fuck. I held on to her hip, thrusting up deeper.

"Oh my God." She sniffed and wiped her eyes, and Charlotte returned. "That was incredible."

I stilled, worry clawing at me. "Why are you crying then?"

"Hayden, sweetie," she said, laughing. She bent down and kissed me. "That was the best orgasm I have ever had. The crying was involuntary. Like, I had so many emotions, they came out through tears."

"Are you sure?"

"Yes. I promise, you beautiful man." She gave me a

massive smile before she rolled onto her back. "Thank you for letting me take my time. Now, I want you to fuck me."

I chuckled. "That, I can do."

I hovered over her, caged her face between my arms, and kissed her slowly, gently caressing her neck as I thrust into her hard. "Fuck yes."

"I want you wild and all mine," Charlotte said, her voice stronger.

"Yes, ma'am." I could sure as hell do that. Running my hands down her legs, I lifted them onto my shoulders as I thrust into her again and again. Each time I stretched her out, she cried out my name, and it was my own aphrodisiac. Charlotte's voice was so sexy.

"You. Feel. So. Fucking. Good." I fucked her deep and hard. Her back arched off the bed as I slid into her, and she clawed at my back to hold on. Her breaths came out in pants, the glorious pressure making it difficult. Pleasure tingled along my thighs and cock, building and building as I continued to grind into her.

Brown hair spilled onto the pillow. Sweat pooled between our bodies. We smelled like vanilla and sex, and I licked up her chest, neck, and face. Words weren't possible at this point. Pure lust. Pure desire.

"Hayden," she begged. "More."

I lifted her hips up, pushing one of her legs over my shoulder as I slowed down. I reached between us and pinched her clit.

"Oh shit," Charlotte gasped.

"I need you to come again, baby. I need to feel you clench around me." My orgasm was right there, and it took all my effort not to go early. I refused out of pure stubbornness to come before she did again. My fingers were on her clit, my hand on her ass. I dragged my teeth over her neck, and when I bit, she orgasmed.

"YES!"

"Ride it out, baby."

"Yes, Hayden. Yes!"

Nothing made sense anymore. Just Charlotte. Just the sounds she made falling apart with me. My chest ached as I watched her, completely mesmerized by her. She slammed her head against the pillow as she cried out and I lost it. She was my everything.

I fucked her hard as she held on, encouraging me and gripping me like I mattered to her. My orgasm hit me suddenly, and *holy shit*. Pleasure so strong, so powerful, knocked the wind out of me as I came. Wave after wave of ecstasy took hold of me. My ears roared, and my pulse spiked. My chest heaved. I removed the condom and tied it off before tossing it in the trash next to the bed. Then I fell onto the mattress. I needed a minute to recover. Damn.

"Wow," I mumbled, wishing I had something profound to say after sharing that with her. "Come here."

I pulled Charlotte against me, tucking her so she rested her head on my shoulder with her arm across my body. Unreal. I sighed, a small laugh escaping. "That was insane."

"You growled like a bear." Charlotte laughed softly and ran her fingers over my chest.

"I did not." I snorted. "Okay, I might've. Sex has never been like that. I lost control there."

Her touch moved toward my jaw and eyebrows. Something soft pressed against my shoulder. She kissed me. "I enjoy seeing you not in control. You're always so...focused. On Gwen, baseball, life. I love being able to push you to the edge."

"You love driving me crazy, you mean." I squeezed her. "I need like an hour or so."

"For what?"

"Until I'm ready for you again."

"Hayden Porter," she said, laughing, "you're joking."

"No." I really wasn't. I ran a hand down her back, and over her bare ass, kneading it. "I told you, I'm spending the entire night getting to know every part of your body, and I've always had a thing for your ass."

She hissed when I dug my fingers into the dimples above her glutes. I massaged her for a few seconds before stopping. She yawned. "That felt good."

"You need sleep, baby." I kissed her forehead before turning off the lamp. "We'll have time in the morning."

Charlotte sighed, the contented sound filling me with hope. We could make this work. It'd be tough, but how could I walk away after experiencing this with her? There was no way.

Instead of sleeping, I spent the next hour holding her in my arms and coming up with a game plan. Creating plays was the most important part of my job. I just needed to do the same thing with the girl I'd always had a crush on.

CHAPTER TWENTY-THREE

CHARLOTTE

Morning."

A deep, raspy voice woke me, and butterflies assaulted my stomach as I cracked an eye open to find Hayden sitting on the edge of my bed. He wore a hoodie and jeans, his usual style, and a huge smile.

"Hi." I covered the bottom half of my face with the sheet because *hello, morning breath.* Have you ever smelled yours right when you wake up? Horrible.

Hayden looked adorable and happy, and he held a cup of coffee in his hands.

"Is that for me?"

"Yes." He tugged the sheet down and leaned forward, kissing my mouth with a smirk. "I kept you up pretty late."

"No need to brag," I teased.

He chuckled and ran a hand over my hair. "I've always wondered if you'd have crazy bedhead. You do, and I love it."

"Stop with the compliments." I brushed his hand away and pushed up, keeping the sheet around my chest. There was no awkwardness with him, and I had thought there would be. This was almost easy. I didn't want to jinx it, so I shoved the thought away. "Thank you for the coffee."

"Of course." He patted my calf through the sheet as he sighed. "I don't want to leave this place, but I miss my baby girl."

My heart about burst. "I'm sure she's so excited to see you."

"Char," he said, his tone serious, "I can't tell you how amazing this weekend was. Being with you..." He sighed and ran a finger over his eyebrow. "I'm willing to do anything to make it work, but it's going to be difficult for me to find balance."

My throat tightened at the hard expression on his face. "I know, Hayden."

"Fuck, I'm messing this up. You look worried." He set his coffee on the side table and scooted closer to me. "I had this all planned out in my head, but then you looked gorgeous and sleepy, and it caused my thoughts to jumble."

I blushed.

"I think I'm pre-apologizing for anything that happens the next few weeks. I'm going to mess up or Gwen is going to make us change plans. I've never dated since becoming her dad, so I don't know the playbook." He ran a hand over my neck, bare shoulder, and arm. "I'm going to upset you as I navigate through this, so trust me on this. Never doubt how I feel about you. If my life was simpler, we'd be together already."

My face heated as I almost said the words that had been rooted in my soul for years. *I love you.* It was way too soon, but that didn't make it less true. "Gwen is a part of you. I can handle a little *not simple* in my life. You're worth it. So is she okay?"

He blinked before swallowing hard. His gaze shifted toward the lamp, a torn expression on his face. "My parents say goodbye to us today before moving tomorrow."

My stomach bottomed out. I knew this was happening, but it had to be hard. I couldn't even imagine not seeing my parents once a week, and I didn't have a child. "I'm so sorry."

"Would you like to come over for dinner with us?"

His tone was off, like he was nervous or something. His jaw flexed as he stared at me with longing and worry. Even his shoulders were stiffer than usual.

"I'd love to."

His posture relaxed, and any ounce of tension disappeared.

"Were you afraid I'd say no?" I sat up higher, setting my mug down so I could touch him. It still blew me away that I could touch him now. Behind closed doors, sure, but for so many years I had to restrain myself.

"Maybe, a little. It'd be with Gwen and my parents." He relaxed into my touch when I ran my hands over his chest and shoulders.

"Nothing has changed for me, Hop. I love your family. Plus I want to be there for you. Tonight will be hard. Let me take care of you."

"You're fucking perfect." He pulled me into his lap, kissing me hard.

"Hayden, morning breath—"

"I don't give a shit." He wrapped my hair around his fist and tugged so my head tipped back. He kissed my neck and nipped under my ear. "I'm obsessed with you."

"Feeling is mutual."

Chuckling, he pulled back and stared down at me with so much love that my heart stuttered. "I already told Christian I was driving you back to get your car. They are at the café waiting on Garrett and you to say goodbye."

"It's barely eight. Why are they up?"

"It's your brother, not mine. You explain what's wrong with him."

I yawned and rested my forehead on Hayden's chest. "Can I just cuddle you for a little bit more?"

He laughed and tugged me toward his chest. "I knew I'd like morning Char. You're nothing like your brother."

We remained like that for a few minutes before I finally got up. It took more effort than I cared for. Wincing, I bent down to grab my underwear.

"Hey, you alright?" Hayden saw freaking everything.

"I'm a little sore." I blushed. We had sex three times last night, exploring positions I had never done. It was the best night of my life. "Worth it, so don't feel bad at all."

"I'll start a warm shower for you. Grab what you need from your bag, and I'll take everything to the car." He frowned. "I'm sorry I wasn't more gentle."

"No, shut your mouth." I pointed a finger at his chest. "None of that. You were perfect. I loved every second of it and am honestly trying to figure out how to get you naked again."

His lips quirked up. "If you want to stay over tonight, Gwen is down by eight. I'll go slower this time."

I shivered. "Deal."

It wasn't a hair wash day, so I showered and was dressed within fifteen minutes. Instead of my normal skin-care routine, I applied a layer of mascara and called it a day. Another pro of being with Hayden? He had seen every side of me. Bedhead, no makeup, wounded, sick one time. There was no shielding him or worrying if I exposed too much. It was liberating.

I tied my hair up into a messy bun. Hayden was at the door before I could even open it, and my stomach swooped. He wore his glasses again, and seriously, they were dangerous. "Hi," I whispered.

"I hope you never stop blushing around me." He licked his lips before sliding his fingers under the hem of my sweater. "You look gorgeous."

"Thank you."

"You know, I was thinking," he said, letting go of my sweater as I stepped into the hall. There was a distance between us now, but we knew we had to act that way for a few weeks.

I hated it though.

"Hm?" I probed.

"There are moments this feels like a first date with you. Then there are others where this seems like we've been together for years. It's strange, but in a good way."

"I know exactly what you mean." I beamed at him as we headed toward the café. This version of Hayden communicated a lot. It wasn't like before, or with the other guys I had tried dating, where getting an answer out of them felt like pulling teeth. Hayden said what he felt, and the impact on me was astronomical.

"Let's say goodbyes fast. I'm not a fan of acting like we aren't together."

"You can survive ten minutes, Hop," I teased.

"Barely."

I winked, and he narrowed his eyes. Riling him up would always be a favorite. Penny, Christian, and Garrett all sat at a table with to-go cups. Garrett and Christian looked hungover, but Penny glowed. "Damn, girl, how did you not get hit this morning?"

"Water. It's all about hydration." She smiled and shared a look with Christian. "My dear fiancé went a little wild with the shots."

"Might've. I did." Christian groaned into his cup. "Coffee isn't helping yet."

"Food. I need grease. Taco Bell. That's what I need," Garrett said, tapping his knuckles on the table. "It's my go-to hangover cure. You want in, Charmander?"

"I'm good. Hayden's driving me back, so we're gonna head out. He wants to see Gwen."

"Thanks for taking care of my sister," Christian said, holding out a fist. Hayden hit it. "Thanks to all of you for coming this weekend. This means so much to us. We're getting married in two weeks. I can't believe it's finally here."

Penny leaned her head onto his shoulder. "I'm gonna be a Calhoun."

Any worry from overhearing their argument left. Penny radiated happiness, and the two of them looked back to

normal. Hayden met my gaze for a beat and smiled. He had
noticed too then. The wedding was on, and we might never
know why they were arguing.

"I get to call you *sister* in a week. That's pretty dope."

She squealed and jumped from the chair to hug me. "I
love you, thank you so much again."

"Love you too, Penny." I laughed as I got a mouthful of
her hair. Christian hugged me next and squeezed me so hard
that I pinched his side. "Don't kill me."

"When Penny and I have kids, I want them to be close
like us."

"Dude," I said, pulling back to stare at him, "that was the
nicest thing you've ever said to me. Are you still drunk?"

He laughed, but a serious look remained in his eyes.

"Ready, Char?" Hayden tugged on my elbow, his fingers
rubbing along my sweater.

"Yup." I pointed at my brother. "Too emotional."

He gave me a sheepish grin. "No such thing. Drive safe,
okay?"

I hugged Garrett, and then Hayden and I made the walk
toward his truck. It was wild that, only two days ago, I
dreaded being alone with him. Now that's all I wanted. Life
was weird.

The two-hour drive felt like five minutes. He alternated
between keeping his hand on my thigh or on the wheel
when the road was covered in potholes. Thanks, Illinois
roads. We talked about the new conditioning coach and
how she was breaking a standard of female coaches at the
baseball level. We spoke about his parents moving for a year
and how he hoped to take Gwen out there to see them play

in the band. We talked about my classes and students and if I'd ever want to explore being an athletic director.

We made plans. Date nights (with Gwen, obviously) but then plans for when she went to bed. I was a giggling buffoon at this point. Dating Hayden was a dream.

"If you didn't have to work tomorrow, I'd say you should just come back to my house now." He sighed as he parked in front of the tow place. My Mazda sat there, unharmed, and a weird pang formed in my chest.

I didn't want to leave him, but he needed time with his daughter. "I'll be over soon enough. What time would you like me?"

"Now."

I snorted. "Go be with your daughter. I need to throw in some laundry. Then I'll head over, okay? Want me to grab anything on the way?"

"I have everything we need. Just bring an overnight bag."

I undid my seat belt. Leaning over, I grabbed his chin and kissed him. He tasted like gum, and he groaned when I nipped his bottom lip. "How had we gone this long without kissing all the time?"

"No fucking idea, but I'm annoyed at Past Me right now."

With one last kiss, I slid out of his truck. Of course, he got out and walked me toward my car and waited for me to get in and drive away before he hopped back into his. He was such a caretaker, and damn if it didn't make me love him even more.

Maybe the hour or two of space would be good for us. Help me scale it back, because I was definitely captivated with Hayden. Loving him most of my life had been easy; falling for him would be like breathing. The few people who knew what happened three years ago, my work besties, would be shocked at the turn of events.

Is this foolish?

When I was around Hayden, I could feel how much he cared for me. It was in the way he touched me, and held my gaze, and put his hand at the small of my back. When we were apart though, like now, doubt crept in.

No. I had to take a leap of faith. He told me to never doubt how he felt, even if things became weird. I had to believe him, or this would never work.

My small home was located about twenty minutes from Hayden's, and I quickly threw in some laundry, wiped the counters, and fidgeted.

He had asked me to spend the night. It seemed so simple while we were at the resort, where we could hide from reality. Going to his house, with his parents and daughter, that felt more real. I tossed a work outfit, pajamas, and toiletries into an actual duffel bag. Hayden would be proud. I had no idea what to do. Did I wait a few hours? Go now?

I might've been freaking out. Slightly. A flurry of chaotic butterflies twisted in my gut. There were a few presents left to be wrapped in my room, but I preferred having a glass of wine and making an event of it. Plus I was too distracted.

My phone buzzed, saving me from making a choice when Hayden Porter's name popped up. "Hi," I said, my voice shaking a little bit. "How are you?"

Soft laugher carried through the phone. "I can picture you blushing right now."

"Am not." *I most definitely am.*

"You definitely are." He sighed, and I wanted to bottle up the cuteness. He sounded happy. "I wanted to make sure you weren't... how do I say this? Freaking out?"

"Am I that obvious?"

"It's not just you. As soon as I said hi to Gwen and chatted with my parents, I had all these damn questions going on, and I'm a simple guy. You have millions of questions on the daily, so I wanted to make sure you weren't about to change your mind on me."

"Ha. I was standing here debating when it would be cool to come over. Is now too desperate? Is an hour from now better?"

"Char, any second you could be here, I want you. Don't wait an hour because you think it's what I want. Do what you need first, but I'd love for you to be here. We're watching *Elf* in a bit, and I'm making popcorn."

"That sounds nice." My smile came easier. "This is gonna take some getting used to, isn't it?"

"No way around it. I don't think we've spoken on the phone for more than a few sentences in years. I like your phone voice. Might be fun to call you on away trips."

I snorted. "Okay, already asking for phone sex, and we've been dating twenty-four hours."

"You miss the shots you don't take."

I rolled my eyes. "I'll leave here in five minutes. Thank you, Hayden. I needed the encouragement."

"You're welcome." His voice went all deep, like he truly meant the words. "Gwen is excited to see you."

I could almost hear the smile in his voice. "I'm excited to see her. I have something for her too, if it's alright?"

"Char, baby," he said, his voice gravelly and low. "It just makes me love you more when you dote on my daughter. Get your ass over here. Safely, of course."

My heart skipped a beat. *Love you more.* Each thud was a reminder that I had it bad for Hayden. The fact that he knew to call me was incredible. Maybe everything happened for a reason. Maybe we went through the last three years to get to the point we were now. It filled me with hope, and I just had to cling to it whenever worry crept in.

CHAPTER TWENTY-FOUR

HAYDEN

My parents had been out of town seven days already, and I was doing fine. I missed them, and Gwen missed them a ton, but I wasn't flailing around with my head cut off. Charlotte was a huge factor in that. I knew that. But maybe I needed to prove to myself that I could do this. Foolish, probably, but despite one major throw-up incident and having to cancel one night with Charlotte, we'd been okay.

"I can't believe we have to pretend we aren't together." Charlotte's voice came over the speaker in my truck. Gwen and I were on our way to the annual Calhoun Week Before Christmas potluck. This year's landed on a Sunday. So did the wedding, one week away.

Charlotte spent almost every night at my house, sneaking over after Gwen went to bed, and sneaking out before she woke up. I didn't want Gwen to be confused about Charlotte yet—she was just Aunt Lotte to my daughter. Whenever I thought about explaining what Charlotte meant to me, my chest tightened, and I froze.

I loved Charlotte, but I wasn't ready to bring Gwen into it yet.

I sighed. "I know. Why did we agree to this again?"

"My brother," she groaned. "Is it silly that I missed you last night?"

That ache in my chest loosened. She didn't spend the night last night. Christian, and now Penny, and Charlotte always spent the night at the Calhouns' watching holiday movies. It was another Calhoun tradition. I'd also been invited, but this year Gwen needed some stability at home with my parents leaving.

"I missed you too." I smiled and made the turn into their neighborhood. I didn't want to think about it too hard, but Charlotte had slipped into my life with such ease that I don't know how I had lived without her before. Her laughter filled my house at night, and I awoke with a smile all week. Were we moving too fast? Probably. But I knew what I wanted, and it was her. "Any crazy Calhoun traditions that I don't know about after dinner?"

"Mm, we might go look at lights, but that's it. Why?"

"Because I want you to myself. I have a feeling today is going to be a struggle." A few cars already lined the side of the street, Charlotte's familiar Mazda right in front of the house. I parked right behind her. If she brought a change of clothes with her, I could just follow her back to my house. "I just got here."

"Yeah, I'm watching you from the window. I'm annoying myself with how excited I am to see you."

I glanced into the house, not seeing her in any windows. Then I looked upstairs, her old room, and she stood with her hand raised. She wore a red-and-green sweater that hugged her curves, and her hair was down in soft waves. "God, you look beautiful."

"You can't even see me from the truck," she said, but I could hear the smile in her voice.

"Are we there? Is Uncle C there?" Gwen screamed from the back. She hadn't glanced up from her electronic game the entire ride, but now she was ready. "And Mama C?"

"Yes, honey. We'll get you unbuckled, and you can go see everyone." My baby girl squealed and clapped her hands. She'd been doing better after having a short, twelve-hour flu. It was disgusting, but Charlotte had been super helpful. She did laundry and ran to get food while I was on cleanup and cuddle duty.

There was a moment when Charlotte saw me wearing rubber gloves and smelling like vomit, but she smiled at me and shrugged. She was completely unfazed and so willing to help out that I instantly thought about building a life with her. She was such a teammate, and fuck, I wanted to keep her forever.

"No heated looks today, alright? I'm not sure I can be chill." Charlotte moved from the window. "See you inside, handsome."

She hung up, and now I had a big-ass smile on my face. I loved knowing Charlotte struggled as much as I did. One of her concerns from three years ago was that there was a power imbalance of feelings. There wasn't this time. We were both in this.

After undoing my seat belt and grabbing a bag of presents, I undid Gwen's buckle. The front door opened.

"Uncle C, Uncle C!" Gwen sprinted from my truck toward the front door, jumping onto Christian before he could set his drink down.

This damn kid had no fear.

"Hi, girlie." Christian kissed the top of her head and hoisted her on his hip. "You look older. Are you five?"

"No! Three!" She held up her fingers. "I'm three!"

"Are you seven?"

"No! Three, Uncle C! Three!"

"Is this a new jacket? I like it. I also love your hair."

"My daddy did it." She beamed at me, making my heart do the stutter thing it did every time I saw her happy.

Gwen might get sick and ruin plans, keep me up at night and fight me at every turn, but this three-year-old tyrant was the best part of my life. Shaking my head, I clapped Christian on the back. "Still trying to be her favorite?"

"Already am."

"I'm not so sure about that," I said, just as Gwen spotted Charlotte. The only other person on the planet who made my heart swell.

"Auntie Lotte!"

"Gwyneth Paltrow!" Charlotte yanked her from her brother's hands and snuggled her. It didn't matter that we'd seen her two days ago, she seemed genuinely happy to hug my daughter. "How's my favorite girl?"

"So good. I built a dinosaur today with blocks, and it was tall. I named him Dino!"

"You clever, clever girl." Charlotte winked at me before walking deeper into her parents' house. This place was a second home to me after spending so much time here growing up.

The familiar scents of cinnamon and laundry mixed with firewood greeted me. Christian mumbled something about a football game, but I didn't respond. Charlotte handed my girl over to her mom and dad, who spoiled her rotten with hugs and little presents.

My chest tightened, like someone had increased the pressure in my lungs. How did Gwen get this fucking lucky, to have all these people in her life?

The Calhouns were the best type of people, and nerves fluttered at the thought of being openly with Charlotte. They always treated me well, but would they be okay with me dating their daughter? Being Christian's childhood best friend was vastly different from dating Charlotte. What if... no. I stopped my thoughts from straying.

Shit. Was it hot in here? I fanned my jacket over my chest, getting some fresh air in there.

"Hayden, son, it's been too long." Father Christmas himself, or Mr. Calhoun, approached me with a bear hug. The man grew his beard out after Halloween every year so he looked like Santa by the time the holidays rolled around. His signature green-and-red sweater was paired with overalls and black boots.

He was a damn hoot.

"Great to see you, sir." I hugged him back. "Thanks for sending over the doll bed for Gwen. She's going to love it."

"Of course. She's our granddaughter at this point." He rolled his eyes. "My wife promised to buy three outfits for her dolls, but guess how many she bought. Twelve."

I smiled. "Thank you, she shouldn't have."

"The day I try and stop my wife from doing anything, let alone stop spoiling your daughter, is the day my marriage will suffer. I won't do it. I know my limits. Find me later to play some Ping-Pong. Christian thinks he's good, but I need some real competition."

"Of course."

He left me to tend to the fire, patting his potbelly with pride. Calhoun get-togethers were famous for their smoked meats and desserts, and my mouth watered even thinking about it. Where were my girls?

I found them in the kitchen. Charlotte was helping Gwen put on a cute apron as they stood at the counter with Mrs. Calhoun. There was an assembly line for decorating cookies already. Charlotte booped Gwen on the nose with flour, and that ache in my chest grew. It seemed almost foolish that I had stayed away for three years when Charlotte fit in with my life so well. I scratched my chest, clearing my throat to ease the uncomfortable lump.

"Char, hon, you tell Hayden here about your interview?" her mom said.

"Yeah, we had a chance to talk about it last weekend at the resort." She smiled at me, a small blush creeping up her cheeks. I knew what that blush meant, and I winked. "We're going to hit the booster angle and all the ways I'm connected to the community."

"That's a genius idea! He's been such a good coach at the college level. I bet you have so many ideas, don't you, Coach Porter?" Her mom beamed at me just like she had the last decade. Mrs. Calhoun took anyone into her home and poured love into them.

What would she think about Charlotte and me being together? The ache intensified. If she or Charlotte's dad didn't approve, that would gut me. Suddenly, I wished I had worn something nicer. Like a polo and slacks instead of jeans and a sweatshirt. I was probably too sloppy.

"I might've asked some hard questions, but the ideas were all Charlotte's. She's ready. They won't know what hit them at that interview."

Charlotte pointed the icing utensil at me. "You helped me a lot, actually. While everyone else was skiing, we worked on a plan for a program and a way to reach out to boosters. I feel so much more prepared." She sighed, and a flash of worry crossed her face before she smiled again. "It's a long shot going against Chad, so I'm going into that interview with the goal of making it the most difficult choice they have ever made in their lives."

"I didn't raise no quitter. Not my girl." Her dad jutted his chin at her and nodded. "You're gonna kick butt and make Chad regret ever being a butt to you."

"My friends have butts," Gwen chimed in, her cute little voice making everyone laugh. "I touch them sometimes."

"Gwen, we don't touch others' butts. That's in the no-touch zone, remember?" I said, pinching between my brows. "We talked about what no-touch zones are."

"I know. But it's fun."

"She's not wrong." Christian glanced up from his game, clearly proud of himself for his remark. That earned him a middle finger from me.

This family. I laughed into my hands, grateful for and amused at being a part of this wonderful madness. Throw in the Christmas decorations in every corner, and this place was straight out of a reality TV show. There was a curated playlist of Mrs. Calhoun's favorite holiday songs, and no one—not even Santa himself—could adjust the playlist.

Last year, I had parked my ass on the couch and waited for people to approach me. They'd fawn all over Gwen, and I'd laugh and never let my gaze move too far from her. This time? I took it all in. It felt different knowing I was with Charlotte. She and Gwen danced to the song, Gwen laughing loudly as Charlotte spun her in a circle.

My lips tugged into a smile. Charlotte was coming back home with us. I could be patient until then.

"Need a beer, my dude?" Christian put an arm around my shoulders and shook me. Despite me being slightly older, he acted like the older sibling in our relationship.

I shoved him away. "Sure." A cold drink sounded nice, especially when Charlotte kept looking at me and blushing.

"Oh! Drinks!" Mrs. Calhoun set a bowl of dough down and clapped her hands. "Penny, honey, I bought all the supplies for this peppermint shot thing. My friend Beatrice has been going on about it, and I want to make her jealous. Could we all do one and take a photo?"

"Oh." Penny stilled as she was midstep toward the hallway. Her already large eyes widened as she quickly glanced at Christian. There was a plea in her expression, and my skin prickled.

She looked worried. Why?

"I'll make them with you, Mom." Christian smiled, but it was tight, not quite meeting his eyes. "You show me where the ingredients are, I'll make the best damn drink you've ever had. And we can take some great photos to post to make your friends weep with envy."

Mrs. Calhoun grinned. "That's my boy!"

"Competitive in everything. I'm so proud." Mr. Calhoun lifted his mug of beer from the recliner. "To winners!"

Everyone repeated the words, but Charlotte frowned. Her attention shifted from me toward the hallway where Penny moved to, clearly saying, *Go follow her.*

I nodded at Gwen, to which Charlotte patted my daughter's head. If I weren't a little concerned about Penny, then I would've smiled at the fact that Char and I were communicating with looks. It felt so familiar and comfortable.

But Penny acted out of character, and I wanted to check on her. I jogged up the stairs and searched Christian's old room, then Charlotte's. Both empty. Then a horrible, animal-like sound came from the bathroom. Shit.

I tapped the bathroom door. "Penny, it's Hayden. Can I come in?"

"No."

Another retching sound. My stomach soured. I wasn't a big fan of throwing up. Who the hell was?

"Okay, I'm coming in to make sure you're alright."

"Hayden—"

She got sick again.

Before going in, I jogged back to Christian's room and snatched a bottle of water left on his side table. I pushed in the door, and my heart clenched for my friend. She sat on the ledge of the tub and held her head in her hands. Her skin was pale, and her chest heaving.

"Hon, what do you need?" I crouched and went into help mode. I ignored the smell of puke and assessed her. "Water? Doctor? Soda?"

"This can't be normal." She sniffed and glanced up at me with tears welling. "I can't stop throwing up. It started Monday and every morning and afternoon, sometimes middle of the night. It's constant, Hayden."

That sounded like...

"Penny." I took her hand and held it. "Are you pregnant?"

She nodded as her face crumpled. "I'm so happy. So fucking happy but I'm miserable and I'm only eight weeks. How am I gonna survive thirty-two of these?"

So much made sense now. It all clicked together. My first thought was *Oh, I need to tell Charlotte*, but I stopped. This was Penny's news to share, hopefully with Christian already. "Look at me, please."

She did as tears streamed down her cheeks. "I can't be like this on my wedding day. I can't... We weren't supposed to get pregnant this fast."

I rubbed her hands because they were so cold and clammy. "There is no right or wrong time to start a family. Take it from me, I'm a prime example of how surprises can turn out to be the best thing in the world."

She snorted. "We weren't going to tell anyone until after the wedding."

"Then don't."

"I can't...hide this, if I'm sick," she mumbled. "This is so embarrassing."

"Why? Because I'm holding your hand in a bathroom while you throw up? Penny, we've done way weirder and more embarrassing shit together in our decade of friendship. This is why you have friends: to help you when you're a little down. You and Christian volunteered to watch my daughter so I could do my job. That wasn't a burden, right?"

She shook her head.

"Then please don't worry about me. Your secret is safe with me. It's your and Christian's news. Now, I have some thoughts on the matter, but I'm not going to give out unsolicited advice."

She rolled her eyes. "Since when has that stopped you?"

Chuckling, I released her hand and grabbed a towel. I wet it and placed it on the back of her neck. "I learned with Gwen that leaning on the people you love and trust the most is the best thing you can do for yourself. I guarantee, if you tell the people downstairs, they will do anything you ask to keep it secret, to make sure you're okay on your wedding day. I'll help in any way I can, but the Calhouns are pretty fucking special people."

Something flashed in her eyes, and a little color crept into her face. "Hop, are you finally admitting you're interested in Charlotte?"

I coughed, caught off guard. "This is about you."

"No, no way." She grinned.

I was glad she had regained color in her face, but this new line of conversation was off the table. "Hey, I'm not keeping anything from you to hurt you. If anything, we agreed to not mention a damn thing until after the wedding because we don't want to take a single ounce of attention from you and Christian. Please let this one go."

She nodded. "I like how there was a lot of the use of *we*. That means you are a team."

"Well, I really like the fact that I'm gonna be an uncle soon."

Her eyes welled up again, and she threw herself at me. "I'm gonna be a mom. Holy shit."

I squeezed her back just as the bathroom door opened. Christian walked in, his brows set in worry.

"Pen, are you okay? What do you need? I brought soda and crackers."

My best friend hoisted her from my arms and cradled her against his chest. The sight of the two of them had me instantly thinking about Charlotte. *Oof*. Keeping this from her would be hard, but it wasn't my secret to tell.

"Thanks for helping her." Christian met my gaze over Penny's shoulder, his expression serious. "I'm assuming—"

"I figured it out? Yeah." I grinned, hope bursting in my gut. "I'm gonna be a fucking uncle."

Christian's facade broke and he smiled. "And I'm gonna be a fucking dad."

"Okay, enough, you two." Penny slid off Christian and wiped under her eyes. "I'm ready."

"You sure?" Christian placed a hand on her stomach. "We can go home. I'll find an excuse."

"No, I'm ready to tell them downstairs. I'm sorry for

making you keep this secret. I know you wanted to tell everyone at the resort, but you had been talking about that trip for weeks, and I figured it would've changed the whole vibe."

"Baby, I'm sorry I pushed you to share it," Christian said, holding her hand. "I'm following your lead now, it's all you."

"Ah." It clicked together. The fight Charlotte and I overheard. Penny wanted to hide the news, Christian didn't.

They both looked at me. "This is a very intimate moment for three grown-ups to be in this small bathroom, but Charlotte and I overheard you two arguing and thought you were fighting about the wedding. We worked our asses off in that competition to make you guys happy."

Penny snorted. "Oh, there was no way in hell we wouldn't get married. Glad it motivated you both though."

"Yeah." Christian pulled Penny into him. "I'll talk to Char about that. Kinda funny, if you ask me."

"I'm happy for you both. Seriously." I grinned. "Gwen is gonna be the best cousin ever."

"Dude, everyone is gonna lose their minds with excitement once they find out," Christian said, rubbing Penny's shoulder. "You want to stay up here a bit or head back down?"

"I thought I wanted a cute announcement or something, but telling everyone today feels more natural. Let's go."

Penny held Christian's hand as they returned downstairs. A part of me was jealous. I would've loved to have Gwen with someone I loved and been there for every step of the process. Visions of Charlotte being pregnant crossed my mind, and the floor about fell away from me. How could I be thinking that when it had been a damn week?

"Everyone," Penny said, her watery voice enough to have everyone stop what they were doing. Charlotte and Gwen stopped mixing frosting. Mr. Calhoun set his beer down and leaned forward. Mrs. Calhoun set her phone down.

"What is it, Pen? You feeling okay?" Mrs. Calhoun asked.

"Christian and I want to share some good news." She smiled. "I'm pregnant."

CHAPTER TWENTY-FIVE

CHARLOTTE

One perk of being around a three-year-old was that there was no room for any other thoughts. Hayden had forgotten to do laundry and meal prep for the week, so we teamed up after my parents' holiday party. I volunteered to play with Gwen because a) I got no alone time with her all day because my family passed her around spoiling her rotten and b) it was a complete distraction from the wild thoughts going around my head.

My brother was gonna be a dad. Penny, a mom. My eyes prickled with emotion even thinking about them with a little baby. I loved my niece or nephew more than words, and it was just a little nugget at this point.

"Why you cryin', Aunt Lotte?" Gwen walked up to me and hugged me. "No sad."

"I'm happy. Sometimes people have happy tears." I rubbed her back and smelled her hair. She always smelled like cookies and mischief.

"I don't cry happy tears."

"That's okay. I do. Your hugs always help me though."

"I love hugs." She snuggled deeper into me and yawned.

"You tired?"

"No. No sleep."

"Try again, princess." Hayden walked out from the kitchen with his T-shirt sleeves rolled up, glasses on, and low-hanging gray sweats.

I blinked slowly, making sure I wasn't fantasizing this. I'd done a lot of daydreaming that morning, mainly about Hayden and me, and this was straight out of it. My mouth actually watered. *Speaking of distraction . . .*

"Daddy, nooooo!" Gwen ran from me, giggling as Hayden chased her. He scooped her up into his arms. "No, Daddy!"

Hayden peppered her face with kisses, laughing his deep chuckle along with her. Despite his parents leaving, he seemed alright. It helped that Frankie worked out for short term while Hayden had already signed up to chat with the owner of the nanny service my friend had suggested.

It felt so good to be able to help him. Acts of service were not only how I felt loved, but also how I expressed it. My stomach filled with a horde of butterflies, fluttering in the wind as I watched Hayden interact with Gwen. I had never let myself look too much the last couple of years, so I wanted to soak up every ounce of them.

"We need to brush our teeth and go to bed. Say goodbye to Auntie Lotte!"

"Goodbye! Love!" Gwen blew me kisses before they disappeared down the hallway. Hayden and I had a system where she'd say bye to me, and I'd go hang in his room in case she snuck out. I'd done this almost every night this past week, and it felt natural, like I'd been here for months.

Usually, I'd play on my phone until Hayden returned, but a few minutes passed and the butterflies from earlier shifted to worry. It was a hot-air balloon in my gut, growing and filling with pressure. My interview was tomorrow. By some grace of God, I was able to not think about it all weekend, but now it came at me with full force. My pulse sped up, and I swallowed.

I can do this.

I practiced interviewing every free moment I had and knew my plan so well that I didn't need to look at it. Exhaling, I scrolled social media and stumbled upon a photo of our athletic director, Chad, and two of the football coaches at a bar watching a football game.

Sundays are for the boys! was our athletic director's description, written at eleven that morning.

Fuck. My eyes prickled again, and not from joy. They were out having drinks while I was frolicking about my parents' house. Was that even allowed? It was like the world was taunting me, telling me the job wasn't mine no matter what. I had just been starting to feel more confident about it too, and then this happened.

My notes were scattered all over Hayden's bed as I focused on breathing. Just like when I played, I had to be mentally stronger than my physical reaction to nerves. Prepare. Execute. That's all I could focus on, not Chad.

The door creaked open just as I sniffed.

"She's finally down. That girl can chat." Hayden stilled. "What happened?"

"It's stupid." I laughed, but it came out forced.

"No." He moved toward the end of his bed and sat next to me, placing his hand on my thigh. "What's going on?"

"Our athletic director is out for drinks with Chad. Well, this morning he was. I saw a post about it, and it got me in my feels." I waved a hand in the air, like that had the magic ability to withdraw all these negative, not-helpful thoughts. Sadly, it did not work.

Hayden sighed. "What would help?"

"A damn distraction." I fell onto my back, the papers falling everywhere around me and on the floor. "I'm too prepared at this point, but my mind is a racehorse right now, thinking about— Hey!"

Hayden yanked my legs toward him so I was under him. My heart leaped to my throat. His gaze swept from my hairline, over my lips and throat, to my thighs. His baggy shirt tickled my legs, and he gripped the end of it. "I like my shirt on you."

"Oh." The ball of emotions turned hot, sizzling even, as he stared at me with hunger. "I'm gonna steal it."

"Take all my clothes. Fuck," Hayden said. He almost growled as his fingers danced along my hips, teasing the waistband of my underwear. "I can't decide what I want first. Your mouth, your pussy, your skin on me."

I shuddered. *Yes*. This was what I needed. Hayden's mouth and body. "Is there a fourth option, where you get all of them?" I ran my fingers through his hair, and he closed his eyes. He leaned into my touch, and I kneaded him more.

He kissed the inside of my wrist before placing an elbow

on either side of my face. He cupped my head and stared down at me, his soft gray eyes dancing with emotion. "You know what I thought of the entire day today?"

"What's that?" I rocked forward, feeling his evident bulge grind against me.

His eyes flashed with heat, but it dimmed as he dipped low to kiss my neck. He nipped the spot under my ear and whispered, "There's nothing that could keep me away from you. That you're already under my skin."

I shuddered as his words washed over me. "Hayden."

"You don't have to say anything. This is me showing you how I feel. Watching you with your family today, with Christian and Penny's announcement, all I could think about was wanting this with you." He kissed down my chest as his hands crept up my shirt, grazing the tips of my nipples. They tightened with need as goose bumps erupted.

My stomach about dropped out from my body. From his touch, his words, him. I arched my hips as he pinched the pebbled tip. "Sit up, baby."

He eased me up and took off my shirt, leaving me in a pair of black underwear. With one hand, he tickled my collarbone with his pointer finger. "You have this mole here, and here." He trailed it down to my hip. "And here." Then to my inner left thigh. "I want to connect them all with my tongue."

"Yes." I squirmed, my body primed with want and need. My heart thudded at the expression on his face. There were moments when I realized he had stared at me like that for years, but it was behind a mask. And now? There was no mask over his face.

He did what he said and trailed his tongue from my collarbone down to my hip, then to my thigh. My entire body trembled from the warmth of his tongue and the roughness of his five-o'clock shadow. When he slid my underwear to the side and teased my folds, I about flew off the bed. "Hayden!"

"So fucking wet." His voice was rough.

I loved knowing I could make him lose control. "Skin. I need your skin on me," I panted as he thrust a pair of fingers into me. I leaned toward him, and he supported my weight with ease.

"I want your first orgasm like this," he demanded. His gray eyes were almost black. His jaw tightened as he stared at me. "Come on my hand, baby. I want to watch you come."

"But, I want you," I whined. Heat crept up from my core, my muscles tingling with need.

"You have me. You can have my cock after you come." He increased the pressure and teased my clit with his thumb. "Rock against me, go at your pace."

I did what he said and rocked against his hand. He didn't kiss me but instead watched me with parted lips. I had never felt sexier in my entire life than I did in that moment. Hayden was transfixed on my face as I chased an orgasm.

"I'm close," I groaned. Sweat dripped down my body.

"That's my good girl." He licked the corner of his lip. "You look so fucking sexy falling apart on my hand." He released a deep, lusty groan. "Fuck, Char, you're—"

"I'm coming! Yes!" Lights exploded behind my eyes as I clutched his shoulders, the orgasm absolutely numbing me from the strength of it. Waves of pleasure, so good I'd do anything to feel it again. Nothing mattered anymore except this feeling. It dimmed, and all the tension left my body. "Holy shit."

"That's one. Are you counting?"

"Should I be?"

He nodded and then slid his fingers out of me and sucked them. "Mm, yes. Next one is with my mouth."

"But—"

"Shh, baby. Let me take care of you. I can read your body better than mine, and you need this. Do you trust me?" He lowered himself onto the ground, his lips wet and his eyes sparkling.

"Of course I trust you."

"Then will you let me lick you?" He nudged my thighs apart. Then, using his fingers, he spread my pussy as he licked long and slow, right on the nerve.

My clit was already sensitive from the first orgasm, and I bounced off the bed. "Oh my God."

"Lean up onto your elbows. I want your eyes on me as I devour you." He flicked his tongue against me, his gaze staying on mine. Then he hummed.

Whoa.

I was floating at this point. The vibration of his hum along with his tongue…unreal. I did as he said, watching him pleasure me, and I had never been so turned on in my entire life. The desperate, terrifying need to keep him gripped me by the throat. "Hayden, please," I begged.

He dug his fingers into my thighs as he stroked me slowly, changing the pace to the point my orgasm exploded out of me. "*Yes!*" I couldn't be quiet. It was too much. My fingers and toes tingled from the onslaught of pleasure. It was better than anything I had ever experienced, and I held on to the blanket like it kept me from falling.

"I love how you come, so free and wild." Hayden kissed my stomach and then the center of my chest. He removed his shirt and tossed it to the side. He removed his sweats and stroked his large, wet cock. "Taste yourself on me before I fuck you."

That was the only warning I got before he kissed me. He tasted all musky and earthy, and he sucked my tongue before releasing a deep growl. "Roll over, baby. I want your ass in my hands when I enter you."

I trembled.

"Up on your knees. Yes, spread your legs." He scooted off the bed, and the familiar sound of the drawer opening and closing filled the room. Blood rushed to my ears, every sense on high alert from how good I felt.

His sheets were cool and smelled like fresh linen. My lips were swollen and wet from his kiss, and the taste of my pleasure still lingered in my mouth. My core throbbed. How did I still have energy? No idea.

"Wider." Hayden kneeled behind me, kneading my ass with his hands. "Fuck, I love your glutes. And thighs."

"This feels so good," I murmured, resting my face in his pillow. He ran a finger from the front of my slit to the back, making me rock forward. "Hayden," I warned.

"I'm gonna make you feel good, Char. I want your body so pleasured you can't even feel anything but how good we are together."

He kissed down my spine before thrusting into me. "Fuck yes, you're ready for me."

I moaned as he fucked me slowly. My skin tingled as he grabbed a pillow and placed it under my hips, pressing me down onto my stomach. The angle took him deeper, hitting me right where I needed. "Hayden, shit, you're so deep."

"You were made for me, Charlotte. Every part of you," he whispered as he quickened his pace. The new rhythm had me mewing for release, something I didn't think possible. "Yes, baby, your body needs to come again. I can feel you clenching around me. Do you like it like this?"

I nodded, but he nipped the base of my neck.

"I want to hear you say it."

"Yes, like this, please," I gasped. My voice sounded like I hadn't drunk water in weeks. "I can't believe I might… might…"

"Come for me."

I exploded. His thrusts matched my pulse, and I cried at the strength of the third orgasm. This one was just as good as the others, and it tore through me, lighting me up. My vision blurred as I held on to the sheets, vaguely aware of Hayden whispering nice things to me.

"I love the way you smell, and taste, and let go.

"I love how you trust me to fall.

"Yes, I love your sounds, Char."

I couldn't catch my breath, and once the orgasm came down, Hayden gripped my ass hard and pounded into me.

"Perfect." He thrust harder. "You're perfect… *fuck, Charlotte*." Hayden ground into me a few more times before falling onto his back next to me.

I peeked an eye open to find him staring at me, gray eyes wide and his smile wider. He still panted, and his chest heaved as he ran his pinky finger over mine. It was such a sweet, tender gesture that my eyes prickled again. The words were right there. *I love you*.

I swallowed a ball of cotton, unable to form the words out of fear. It was too soon. Yet the feeling remained as Hayden pulled me into the crook of his arms. I hugged him hard, using that as a way to communicate. "Thank you."

"You're welcome. Let's take a shower, and I'll wash your hair for you. Then we can go to sleep." He kissed the top of my head, and I fell even harder. Hayden was taking care of me, and that made me feel pretty damn incredible.

* * * *

"Eye of the Tiger" blared from my phone as I applied a light layer of mousse to my hair. With my curls, there was no point in trying to tame them. They were kinda wild. Why did I try to fit into a mold of someone else when they were best free?

Huh. Who would've thought I'd have a full-on epiphany about myself while doing my hair? Not me, but hey, I'd take it. That's what happened after my boyfriend used orgasms to get me to sleep and to relax. I woke up refreshed as heck.

"You got this. You are a badass," I said to myself in Hayden's bathroom mirror. "You will not fuck this up. You will not sweat through your shirt. You faced D1 pitchers and played on TV. This is a dumb interview with a man named Peter Peroni."

Self-talk could be helpful. Wearing my fitted maroon blouse—our school color—and a pencil skirt, I looked good. Professional and good.

Chad always wore wrinkled khakis and a frat polo. Frats were fine, nothing against them. I just hated Chad and the boys' club at school. *Especially if they were already friends.*

It didn't matter. I'd own this and walk away proud. Hayden was getting Gwen ready in her room and asked me to sneak out like I had the past week, but this morning, there was a Post-it note on the front door.

WIN OR LOSE, YOU DID THE DAMN THING. YOU GOT THIS, CHAR. I KNOW IT.

—*HOP*

I kept that note in my bag for luck.

I drove to the building eerily calm. I parked. I grabbed my folders. I applied my favorite lip balm and walked inside just like any other day. I was fifteen minutes early because a) any earlier would be weird, and b) any later would be unacceptable.

My phone buzzed, probably good luck texts from everyone. I ignored them. This was about me now. Only I could do this.

"Good morning, Ms. Calhoun."

"Hi, Tracy," I said to the athletic secretary. She ran the entire school, and we all knew it. Well, her boss and Chad didn't, but shocker. "How are you today?"

"Great. Can't complain." She smiled. "They are ready for you in the conference room if you want to head in there."

"Sure will."

I can do this. I will do this.

Keeping my head up high, I walked in and found Peter; our principal, Brett; the athletic director of the junior high next door; and one of our PE teachers, named Adam. He was also in the photo yesterday. All men, all friends. Noted.

"Morning, gentlemen." I passed out the folders and shook all their hands. Adam smirked. "Anyone else joining the interview today?"

"Nope. I figured us four would be good enough. We have two candidates, so we don't imagine it'll take too long." Peter rose, his lips pinched tight as he stared at the folder's contents. "What are these?"

"Plans for the softball program, how I would work with boosters, how I'd partner with parents and the community. My team vision and goals on developing student athletes because, while softball is important, being a good student has more value. I played D1 softball, sir, and I have a lot of good ideas. In fact, I'd bet I have incredible ones, and I came ready to play today."

Peter swallowed loudly, and Adam shifted in his seat.

But the junior high athletic director beamed at me. "I'm Mitch Birmingham, AD and AP at the junior high. I can't wait to hear your ideas. This town needs a little shake-up, don't you think, boys?"

Silence.

I sat down in my chair, all nerves gone. It was clear three of them had made up their minds before I even spoke, but instead of getting angry, I went into game mode. I was a fierce competitor, and today was no different.

"Now we'll get started. Tell us about your experience and why you think you'd, uh, be a good fit for this program…"

CHAPTER TWENTY-SIX

HAYDEN

It was noon before I got antsy enough to text Charlotte. I tried to be patient, but I was dying to know how it went.

Hayden: I need an update. Please. How did it go?

No response yet from her, but there was a missed call from the same random number I hadn't heard from in a few days.

I rubbed my eyebrow, irritation dancing along my spine. I was already on edge about Charlotte. Thankfully, my phone buzzed, and relief filled me.

Charlotte: Hi! So sorry. I've been bombarded with students. It went well. Best I could've done. I don't have a good feeling about the outcome, but I have no regrets. I left feeling proud.

Hayden: That's all you can do. I'm proud of you.

Charlotte: Thank you! They said they'd let me know tonight so any chance we can get together so I can...not drink alone?

Hayden: I've always been a fan of being the underdog so don't count yourself out yet. And you'll be proud of ME. Frankie is watching Gwen tonight for a few hours so I can come over. I want to be there, no matter what happens. Do you know what time?

Charlotte: You're the best. I know it's hard for you to trust Frankie like this, so thank you for doing this for me. And my guess is five.

Hayden: I'll be there.

There. That felt better. Charlotte had told me once that, some days, she could go hours without looking at her phone because it was an endless stream of students. She was easy to be around and talk to, so I had no doubt students flocked to her. That was why she hadn't texted. I relaxed and shoved my phone in my pocket.

Today was an easy day, everyone settling down before the holiday break. Then things would pick up. I had a tour scheduled with a potential recruit, and then I was gonna work out with some of the guys before heading to pick up Gwen. Man, my nerves were fried thinking about Charlotte. I wanted this for her so damn much, even though I knew it would be a long shot.

I'd suffered heartbreak two times in my life, and it sucked. First, when I realized I'd never be promoted from the minors and quit to pursue coaching, and then when Gwen's mom decided not to be in Gwen's life. I knew that pit in your stomach, the disappointment that could seep into all areas of your life.

I'd be there for Charlotte. I'd make sure to help her no matter what happened with the interview. My phone rang again with the random number I'd been seeing the last two weeks. I ignored it and focused on my job, hoping it'd make the time go by faster so I could see Charlotte.

Was I acting like a giddy fucking teenager again? Yes. And did I care? Not at all. I loved her, and once we got past this wedding, we could be open about it. Flashes of summer vacations, of us helping Christian and Penny navigate parenthood, of us getting married all crossed my mind. I could almost hear my mom telling me to slow down because I didn't do anything half speed. I was all in from the start, and Charlotte was no different. Maybe I'd get her flowers to show her how much I cared? Yeah. I'd get her favorite flowers before going over there tonight. That seemed like a good plan.

*   *   *   *

The other assistant coaches chuckled at me as I ran out of the office. Rosa, the newest addition, gave me so much shit, but there was a kindness about it. I never shared anything about my personal life, and now they all knew about Charlotte. I didn't know life could be like this…happy. I loved my daughter and career and the life we had, but I rarely did anything for just me, and Charlotte was all mine. I picked up flowers, then Gwen, and we made our way home. Frankie was due to arrive in twenty minutes, so I had plenty of time to get Gwen washed up and ready for dinner. I was killing this whole dating-and-dad thing.

"Daddy, do dinosaurs poop?"

I snorted, chopping up some apples. "Yes. All creatures go to the bathroom."

"I don't think so. Dinos make sparkle dust. That's what I actually think."

"Sparkle dust it is." God, this girl. She puffed out her chest and went back to building a house out of magnets. The doorbell rang, and I grabbed a towel to dry my hands as I went to let Frankie in.

When I had interviewed her, she agreed to my terms of texting me every thirty minutes. She had an older brother who had two young kids whom she watched all the time and who was also a hover parent. She could call me a hovering helicopter parent, and I'd be just fine. "Hey, Frankie," I said, opening the front door with a smile. "Dinner is almost—"

I stopped.

Simone stood at my doorstep.

"Hi, Hayden."

That voice. The tone, that light lilt to the second syllable of my name...hearing it was like a gunshot to the chest.

"Simone." I swallowed, panic clawing up my throat. Why the fuck was she outside my house, where my daughter was? "Why the fuck are you here?"

"I tried calling and texting you a few times. You ignored me." She crossed her arms over her chest, her face tightening into a scowl. "This wouldn't be a surprise if you had answered."

Gwen could see her mom. The one who left her. I glared at Simone, an anger so fierce that I barked, "Leave. Leave right now."

"No. I've tried calling and texting for weeks! I really need to speak with you. It's important. It's about our daughter." Her voice wobbled on the edge of tears. That sound used to upset me, when I wanted to please her. Now fury replaced sympathy.

Our daughter. The words made me recoil. How dare she?

"By surprising me? At my house? With *my* daughter?" My voice rose, and I gripped the edge of the door tighter. "No. *No.*"

"Hayden, if you avoid me, I'm going to keep showing up."

The worst-case scenarios flooded my mind, each worse than the last. What if she wanted to take Gwen away from me? What if she tried to fight for full custody?

"What do you want?"

I glanced inside, where Gwen sat at the table, still playing, unaware of everything. My heart thudded, and my senses went into fight-or-flight mode. Frankie would be here soon. I could get Gwen comfortable with her, and then I could hear Simone out. Yeah.

"I want another shot at being a family with you."

I shook my head before I could form a word. A family? No fucking way. I vowed to never prevent Gwen from having a relationship with her mom if Simone ever changed her mind. Gwen deserved to know her mom, even if it made me nervous. But a family? No.

"You're going to get back in your car and stay out of sight. Gwen is trying out a babysitter tonight, and once I get her set up, then I will meet you down at the park." I jutted my chin toward the playground fifty yards away. "You will never show up to my house again. I will answer your calls, but my house is off-limits."

She nodded, but the light left her eyes. "You're being so cruel."

"No, I'm not. You're barging into my life, into Gwen's, without a single thought about us. You're only thinking about yourself, which is typical. So let me be a father, and I'll talk to you in a bit."

I went inside and shut the door. Holy shit.

"Daddy! Look at my house! Look!" Gwen cheered and wiggled her hand at me. "Come see!"

It took the strength of a legion of men, but I forced a smile. "That looks amazing, baby girl. You're so creative."

"I'm good."

"Yes, you are." I pulled her into me, smelling her fruity shampoo and trying not to break. She deserved the best, and if that meant hearing Simone out, I'd do it. "Frankie is gonna be here soon. Are you excited?"

"Yes!" She wiggled her hips. "We're gonna play dinos!"

Frankie arrived, and I held it together as best I could. I wanted to call my parents and beg them to come back—but what could they do? This was a conversation for Simone and me. I was Gwen's father. I could do this.

I sweat as I made the short walk toward the park. A white sedan was parked off to the side, and I knocked on the window. It was cold out, but I wasn't getting in the car with her.

She got out and leaned against the side, her features showcasing Gwen's best. Gwen had gotten her face shape, her eye shape, her hair, and cute nose. Simone was a short-term fling, not someone I ever would've had a relationship with. But when she showed up with Gwen, we tried to make it work but she lasted a week. She stayed at my house for a week, hating every second. I could see it on her face, in her eyes, and yeah, she was miserable. That Saturday morning, she made me a single parent.

That felt like a lifetime ago.

"Why are you here?" I barked out.

She pursed her lips, staring at the ground before the facade dropped. Her shoulders slumped, and when she met my gaze, her eyes glistened. "I'm not happy. I thought I wanted to live in Europe free to find acting jobs, but it didn't work." She gulped and stared out onto the playground.

"So you tried, and now you want to be a mom?" I gritted out. I didn't want to be cruel, I really didn't, but she abandoned my sweet girl. Me. The idea of a family. She missed out on a million wonderful moments, and I wasn't sure I could forgive her for that. I swore that I could hear Charlotte's voice in my head though, willing me to calm down.

This is Gwen's mom, Hop. This is bigger than you.

I cleared my throat and forced a smile. "This is a shock to me, Simone. I hadn't heard from you in years, and you show up without warning. At my house. It's a lot to take in." I moved toward a bench and sat down a few feet from her.

She swallowed, hard. "I'm not here to mess up her life. I just want to try again."

"And you thought showing up at my house, with Gwen there, was the right choice?"

"I tried calling!" She sniffed and wiped her eyes. "Look, I'm living with my parents in town, and you might see me around."

"Wait." I blinked. "Your parents live here in town?"

They had never once expressed interest in meeting Gwen. Instead of anger, a deep, painful sadness ached in my chest. They missed out on knowing Gwen, seeing her smile and play in the rain and show off her new dance moves. Even thinking about missing those moments made me ill.

"They just learned about her." She barely spoke above a whisper.

"What?" I almost shouted. There was no way she could mean that. "You...Simone. You never told your parents they are grandparents."

"Yeah, until last week." She paled. "They— Look, you can judge me all you want—"

"I'm not judging, Simone." Okay, maybe a little bit. I ran a finger over my brow, willing myself to stay calm. "This is so fucked up."

"I know, Hayden. On my list of fuckups, this is at the top." She covered her face with her hands, her shoulders slumping. "They are furious at me for keeping it from them, shaming me for leaving her, for all of it. They said I need to grow up and take responsibility, and if I'm going to do that, I want to do that with you. You're the best dad, Hayden. Our daughter deserves a chance at having a family. We had some good memories in our short time together. I just wasn't ready."

A flicker of what-if went through me. If Simone would've said this anytime from the day Gwen became mine until the resort, I would've tried. I owed it to Gwen to try to have a relationship with her mom. I dreamed of her coming back that first year. But now? I was in love with Charlotte.

"Christ." I pinched the bridge of my nose, the galloping of my heart against my ribs so painful that it might bruise. So many words crossed my mind, none of them kind or helpful. Despite Simone keeping her pregnancy from me and choosing not to be a part of our lives, she was Gwen's mom. She had kept her safe while pregnant and knew that she wasn't the right parent for her. That took courage, even if I didn't understand it. "Are you asking me what to do? You don't get to waltz into my house and get to enter the family you left. It doesn't work that way."

She looked at me with so much sadness swirling in her eyes. "Then what should I do? Are you saying we don't have a chance?"

"You and Gwen? I'd never stop that, but I don't trust you—"

"No, you and me. Do we have a chance?"

"No."

"Then what's the point?" She groaned into her hands.

"The point is we have a fucking daughter who should be the top priority here, Simone. Not you. Not me. That's what you're still not getting. We can co-parent, if you want that path and are willing to do the work."

"I don't know if I do, okay? I don't know if this is what I want or if I'm being pushed this way. It sucks!" She stood up and paced, tears on her face now. "I don't know how long I'm gonna be here."

"Then what do you want from me? How does Gwen fit into this?" I softened my voice not to scare Simone, because I was a big dude. My voice also had a bark to it when I was pissed. Like now. "Look, I can't help you until you figure your shit out."

"Maybe I hoped you'd tell me to get lost or that you'd never let me see Gwen. Then I'd run."

"You wanted someone else to make the decision, but that's not going to happen. Only you can figure out what you need. I will never be a couple with you, but I'd let you in Gwen's life because she deserves to know you." I exhaled and rubbed my hands together to warm my fingers. The adrenaline crashed, and now a bone-deep cold made me shiver.

"I thought you'd be meaner, make this conversation easier to leave."

"I'm having a lot of thoughts I'm not sharing, but you're not a cruel person. Selfish, yes, but not cruel." The brief time we were together, a few weeks, she was wild and fun. No-strings-attached hooking up, no feelings or expectations. It was a great time pre-fatherhood. She was kind to everyone we interacted with. Immature, sure. A hot mess? Also yes. But cruel? No.

I still couldn't believe she was here. I hadn't heard a word from her since she left.

She stared up at the moon and sighed. "Can I give your number to my parents? They want to meet Gwen. Maybe they could call?"

"To start, yes."

Fuck, this was going to be messy. Gwen would have grandparents but no mom on that side? But what about the Calhouns? Or Charlotte? My stomach cramped. Was this something Charlotte and I could navigate a week into being together?

Fuuuuck. This timing couldn't be worse.

"I'm sorry, by the way. For springing this on you, for complicating the beautiful life you've built for Gwen. I still don't know if I want to be a mom or be a part of her life yet, which isn't fair to you at all."

"It's not fair to our daughter. I'll be fine regardless." That sharp tone returned at how selfish she was being. My phone buzzed in my pocket, but I ignored it. I'd call whoever it was back. I pressed the side to silence it and continued, "Look, I'm not sure us talking in circles is helpful. Give my number to your parents, and I'll work with them on meeting Gwen. I won't ignore your calls next time, but call me, don't show up."

"Okay, yeah." She wiped her eyes. "Thank you for being kind about this."

"Don't give me a reason not to." I met her gaze. "The only thing I will not budge on is you or your parents meeting Gwen without my permission and me being there. That is unforgivable to me. I'll work with you in any way, but you ignore my wishes, things will be more difficult."

She nodded, a hurt look flashing across her face. "I would never—"

"You showed up at *my house*. Gwen is the light of my fucking life, and I'm not willing to take any chances with you or your family." I stood and ran my hands over my chest and stomach, the thudding of my heart causing my entire body to vibrate.

"I understand."

"We'll talk soon then."

I shoved my hands in my pockets and walked back to my front porch, absolutely torn up about what had happened. Could the mother's parents have any rights to the child if the father was in the picture? Did they have any chance of taking Gwen from me? Or did Simone? I wanted to triple check everything to protect my daughter. I didn't trust Simone at all, and the flutter of worry expanded through my entire body. So I did what any grown man would do in this moment. I called my parents. They'd know what to do. Even thousands of miles away, they'd talk me off this cliff.

CHAPTER TWENTY-SEVEN

CHARLOTTE

Even though I had mentally prepped for this exact moment, seeing the email in my inbox caused a visceral reaction. Sweat pooled on my lower back, my breath caught in my throat, and it felt like I had slipped on black ice.

Peter's name stared at me. Taunting me. *Open it. Read me.* My stomach twisted into a pretzel, and not one of the big, soft ones. It was a tight, hard pretzel covered in salt. Why?

Oh, because Hayden was thirty minutes late. I tried texting him, and nada. Nothing. Tried calling too, because I was getting worried. Ten more minutes went by, when my phone buzzed.

> **Hayden:** I'm so sorry I can't come tonight. I
> promise I'll explain soon.

Cool. Great. My secret boyfriend backed out of a date without an explanation the night after my interview. That wasn't a good feeling. Neither was the fact that Chad saw me in the hall after school and smirked at me. He and his buddy strutted through the halls, whistling as they passed my classroom. Their rooms were located in another wing, so there was no reason they should be near me other than to taunt me. They oozed confidence, like they were privy to information I didn't know. My stomachache began then and had only worsened.

Hayden and I had planned to do this together, and his absence hurt. I was alone in my apartment.

He'd explain *soon*. What did that even mean? I analyzed every part of the text. No emoji. No hint at what was happening, but it had to be about Gwen. That was the only thing that made sense. Last night was special for me. Hayden taking care of me when I needed it…I had never felt so loved. I woke up with him surrounding me this morning. What happened within the last fourteen hours for that feeling to shift?

I wanted to respect his text. He wouldn't do this unless something really did come up. I trusted him, but old insecurities snuck in. He changed his mind. He wanted to go back to being friends. He didn't want to deal with telling Christian. I wasn't a good fit with Gwen.

My eyes prickled. I had to trust him or we'd never work. Hell, two weeks ago, I never would've thought to have Hayden be with me when I found out if I got the job or not.

You can do this. Put your big-girl underwear on.

"Oof, this is anticlimactic. It's a damn email!" I just had to click.

I clicked.

> Subject: Re: the softball head coach position
>
> Charlotte,
>
> Thanks for interviewing for the Head Softball Coach position. Unfortunately, we didn't choose you as our top candidate. Thank you for your consideration, and we hope there is another fit for you elsewhere.
>
> Peter

No.

The sensation of falling increased and spiraled. An utter feeling of loss came at me from all sides. A sob escaped me as I breathed in deeply. I knew the chances were low, but after preparing so hard for it, I had started to believe I had a chance.

We didn't choose you as our top candidate.

Heartbreaking. It was like someone ripped out a vital part of me and let it drag along the ground. I sniffed, and my nose clogged because the emotions were pouring out of me.

How could I go to work tomorrow? How could I face everyone and tell them I didn't get it? An icy numbness spread through me. I had failed. I poured my heart into this and didn't come out on top.

I crumpled into a ball and wished Hayden were here. He'd know what to do. He'd use his kind, stern voice and soothe me, guiding me on the next steps. He knew this could happen tonight and had left me alone. Why?

His absence felt like another form of betrayal. Despite his text, I felt I was owed more than that. Especially tonight, of all nights. He might have the best reason in the world, but practically ghosting me was not fine.

It was only 6:00 p.m., and Gwen wouldn't be down yet, but still I heard nothing from him. Did I even send him a text?

Fuck. I needed someone. I didn't want to be alone in my sad thoughts, and I did what I should've done the second I saw the email. I sent an SOS to our group text from the weekend trip. Hayden was on the thread, and he'd either see it, or not.

Charlotte: Hey, I didn't get the job.

Penny: Oh, baby girl. I'm sorry. It's their loss.

Christian: FUCK CHAD. Where does he live?

Garrett: Vodka or cookies?

Garrett: Or both?

Garrett: How sad are we talking? Like, get bangs and reinvent yourself sad or sob until you're dry?

Penny: How is that helpful? What is wrong with you?

Christian: We don't have enough time to dive into Garrett's issues right now. Let's focus on Chad.

I snorted but it came out all ugly. This sucked. My world tilted on its axis, and the person who I thought would comfort me wasn't there. Hayden had encouraged me to go for it, that I could get this and prove everyone wrong. He boosted me up so much that I believed in myself.

And now I felt as deflated as a day-old birthday balloon.

My phone buzzed a minute later, and hope burst into me like a bolt of lightning. *Hayden!*

Nope. My brother.

> **Christian:** You know your worth but when you forget for a little bit, it's our job to remind you. You'll be okay. You'll get through this Char.

My eyes stung even more because I had forgotten to take off my makeup. Looking like a sad, drowned raccoon, I had a full-on pity party. My mind jumped from one dramatic conclusion to the next. I should quit teaching at that school. It was a sign I shouldn't coach. I should pull back my feelings for Hayden because they weren't reciprocated. This was my usual cycle of despair before I yanked myself out of it.

This wasn't my first moment with defeat, yet it hit differently and cut me deeply. This was the moment people talked about when someone wise would say, *You're in the middle of the storm, no way through it but through it.* Or *You need the storm to find out who you are.*

I didn't want the storm! I worked my ass off to run that program, and I knew the girls. I wanted it more than Chad did and dang, this sucked.

Ugh. When did this sorrow shift from not getting the coaching job to maybe losing Hayden?

Stop. I wouldn't make assumptions until I knew for sure. I put on my saddest playlist and got ready for bed, ready to cry myself to sleep. My heart broke, thinking about how differently this night could've gone. If Hayden were here, he could kiss away the tears or distract me from the sorrow. Yet he wasn't.

* * * *

My face hurt as I prepared for work the next morning. Crying had made me puffy. I didn't fall asleep until past midnight, so dark circles matched the puffiness. It wasn't my best look. Did I pair my black pants to match the tone? Or because I was in mourning of my hopes and dreams? I didn't own much black, but I could debut the jumpsuit I had bought for a holiday party. Yeah, I'd wear all dark today to match my soul.

Shame clogged every breath, followed by disappointment. No one really prepared you for the day after you're heartbroken. There were no guides on how to act. I couldn't be normal, but it wasn't fair to my students to not show up with only three days left until holiday break. I applied a layer of mascara and sighed, just as my phone buzzed.

Hayden.

His name popped up, and my stomach somersaulted. "Hayden, hi," I answered, breathless.

"Hey, can you come outside for a minute?" His voice was scratchy, like he just woke up.

"You're here?" I eyed the hallway that led to my front door. "Where's Gwen?"

"She's in the car. Bring a coat. It's freezing."

"You guys can come inside if it's easier."

"No, she's asleep. I don't want to wake her."

I quickly checked my reflection, a flutter of concern edging its way down my chest. Why didn't he ask to come inside? Gwen could absolutely come into my place, so having me go outside in the cold wasn't a good sign. The balloon of worry expanded in my lungs as I put on a coat. It didn't make sense to worry until I had a reason. He could be in a rush.

It's Hayden. We were good now. I had no reason to freak out. I twisted the handle, held my breath, and stared into my boyfriend's eyes.

Instead of the smolder or intensity I usually saw, it was bleak, defeated. I didn't recognize him, and my stomach bottomed out.

He opened his mouth, shut it, and then said, "This isn't going to work anymore."

CHAPTER TWENTY-EIGHT

HAYDEN

The words left my mouth more harshly than I had intended. They spilled out, and I couldn't take them back. My plan went to shit within two seconds, all from seeing Charlotte's face twisted in despair. I clenched my fists in my coat pockets, digging my fingers into my palms to prevent myself from touching her.

"I mean—" I had fumbled this entire speech. "We should take a step back for a bit."

That had some resemblance to my original plan, where I explained that I loved her but needed some time to figure out Simone and what happened next. Charlotte didn't need to be a part of that complicated mess. Hell, I abandoned her last night, and the guilt of hurting her was almost too much for me. I didn't have a choice. My dad called his buddy, a lawyer, who came over in the evening to discuss all the options. While I wasn't going to go after Simone in court, I wanted to be prepared in case *she* went that direction.

Before Simone, I was confident I could handle putting Gwen first and dating Charlotte. Now though? I could only handle Gwen and Simone. I ran a hand over my face, my gut twisting.

"Wh-what?" she stuttered. She blinked slowly.

"Look, Char, I lo—will always care for you. Nothing will change that. Some things happened, and I need to handle them. I can't be with you while I'm navigating it." Pain exploded behind my chest, sharp points of pressure stabbing my heart. The back of my throat throbbed with an ache.

Is this the right decision? a small voice in the back of my head piped up, but I shut it down. It didn't matter if it was right, it's what needed to happen. Hell, I was terrified to drop Gwen off with Frankie that morning, even though Simone would never know to find her there. This situation deserved all my time and attention.

"I don't understand." Charlotte wrapped her arms around her middle, her bottom lip trembling. "What happened? What changed from the other night where we . . ."

She struggled, and seeing her cry caused a crack in my heart. The urge to comfort her had me take a step forward, but I stopped myself from touching her. "Baby, I'm sorry."

"Did I . . . do something?" she whispered.

"No. It's not you at all." The ache in my throat intensified. "It's all me."

"Is this fixable?" She wiped away a tear, staring at me with hopelessness. "Whatever you said that came up, can I help with it?"

"No, this isn't something you can help with," I said, my tone sharper than I meant. Charlotte was so good and kind, of course she'd want to help. I had to end this conversation. The longer it went on, the more likely I'd change my mind and pull her into me and beg forgiveness. "Simone showed up at my house yesterday, wanting to—"

"Holy shit!" Charlotte gasped. "She didn't see Gwen, did she?"

"No—"

"What does she want? What did you do?" Charlotte's hands came out to squeeze my forearms. Her eyes went wide, her mouth parted as she asked, "Are *you* okay? This has to be so tough for you."

I broke up with her a minute ago, and she was worried about me. I stepped back, her hands falling from my arms. "I met with a lawyer last evening, working through all the angles to protect Gwen. Simone needs to figure out what her plan is before I decide anything."

She nodded, a resigned look crossing her face. "Hayden, is that why you're putting distance between us? This isn't a deal-breaker for me. I don't know anything about the law, but I can be there for you. You'll need—"

"No." I shook my head, the pain in my chest worsening. A dodgeball-size lump sat behind my tongue. "I don't need you around this."

I had to get the fuck out of here. This gutted me, and I had no strength around her. But I owed her a huge apology. Apologizing when you fucked up was miserable. When it was an accident, it was easier, but this was intentional. I knew what yesterday meant to her, but I chose to focus on Gwen. I could've called Charlotte to explain, but I was such a mess last night on top of feeling so bad about not being there that it was easier to avoid it.

"I want you to know, I am so damn sorry you didn't get the job. We should've been together last night, and I left you to handle it alone. That's a perfect example of why I need to step back. I'll continue hurting you, so it's best to remove myself from the situation."

She hung her head, a heartbreaking sob escaping her. The helpless, horrible sound had my eyes stinging.

Walk away and get in the car and leave.

"You know," she said, sniffing, "you're right. I want someone who is willing to fight through the hard times. You're running. I would happily stand by you and Gwen as you deal with Simone, but you're not giving me the choice. You ignored me last night because it was hard? You didn't want to . . . deal with me being sad? Yeah, maybe *distance* is good, Hayden."

She even finger quoted the word *distance*.

My feet grew roots, holding me firmly in front of her doorstep. Her words were like swords piercing me. She was right. All her words, correct.

Tears rolled down her cheeks as she opened the door. "This heartbreak is worse than not getting the job. I guess I could thank you for lessening the disappointment. Good-bye, Hayden."

She shut the door. The lock clicked. We were done. I wanted distance, with the foolish hope that once Simone decided whether she was staying or going, I'd beg for

Charlotte's forgiveness, but her words made it more final. Fuck.

Compartmentalize. I told Charlotte how important it was on the field, and I had to do it now to survive. I boxed up the ache from missing Charlotte and focused on Simone and Gwen.

Simone told me she'd call me today at 8:00 a.m., and that left me an hour to drop Gwen off with Frankie.

"Daddy, why was Lotte sad?" Gwen asked, the second I got into the car.

Damn kid asked the hard questions. "Because she didn't get something she wanted really bad."

"I don't get things I want too. Maybe I can hug her?"

My poor heart. "Yes, baby, next time you see her, you can give her a hug."

Shit. Despite tucking Charlotte into the back part of my mind, her family jumped to the front. Oh my God. She'd tell them what happened, and they'll be pissed at me. I scratched my chest, about to panic, when my phone buzzed.

Charlotte: Make sure you tell Christian and
Penny. They can help you navigate this.

My facade cracked. My perfect woman would hide her pain to ensure my *friends* still spoke to me. It didn't seem fair. I didn't deserve her, and this only proved it. It didn't matter how much I loved her or pictured my life with her in a few years. I had hurt her, and I wasn't sure it was forgivable.

* * * *

If I thought time had slowed during those first few months after Simone left, it was nothing compared to the five days leading up to the wedding. My ulcers had ulcers.

"You okay, hon?" My mom's comforting voice helped ease the tension. She called as she and my dad packed for a short trip here for the wedding. They were arriving later this afternoon and I was so excited to see them. I missed them.

I took Gwen to an indoor playground hoping I could tire her out. Tonight was the rehearsal dinner, and while Gwen was invited, she often behaved better when tired. It was a trick I learned early on, that when Gwen used all her energy physically, she had less attitude to talk back and wreak havoc.

She jumped from a large mat into a pit of foam screaming, "Cowabunga!" over and over. She was happy.

That made one of us.

"Great, yeah," I said. My jaw clenched as the ache worsened in my core, numbing me to feelings of happiness.

When Gwen smiled, the ache lessened. When Gwen told me she loved me or that I was her best friend besides dinosaurs, I smiled too. But the list of things that broke through my exterior was limited.

The unanswered texts from Christian, Penny, and Garrett didn't help either. Were they yelling at me, calling me an asshole?

Of course not. They were *worried about me* because Charlotte told them to help me. That *I was going through a really stressful time.*

And Charlotte sent me one text that read I'm thinking about you and Gwen, hope things are okay.

It would've been better if she hated me and yelled at me. I deserved that. I didn't want this...support and loyalty. Running a hand through my hair, I pulled on the ends, welcoming the sting.

"Hayden Orion. I'm about sick of your shit."

I sat up straighter. "Mom."

"Don't *mom* me in that tone. You are a grown-ass man wallowing in your pathetic pity party for one, and I'm done."

Swallowing, I adjusted the phone to stop watching Gwen to face her. Hard lines had formed around her mouth, and her narrowed eyes left no room for misunderstanding. She was pissed at me.

"You don't understand."

"Cute. We're playing this game? Tell me what I don't understand."

"Mom," I said, taken aback, "what is this? I thought you were on my side."

"First, what *side*? Who is at war? You and Simone? There is no war there. The woman left Gwen and maybe wants to meet her, which you get to decide when and where. You get to decide if or when she meets her birth grandparents, and let me tell you, being a grandma is the best thing I've ever done. So those people are going to dote on her left and right. So who are we *against* exactly? Because the way I see it, you're fighting against your own happiness and winning."

"I'm great at winning."

"My God. I'm gonna smack you upside the head regardless of if your daughter sees." She pushed her graying hair out of her face, huffing more than I had ever seen. "You know what your problem is?"

I laughed. "Enlighten me."

"You're so afraid of finding true happiness, you sabotage yourself any chance you get. This thing with Charlotte—"

"Stop." Just hearing her name caused my entire body to tense. "This is what's best."

"Says who? Did *she* say that?"

"I know it."

"Because you speak for her? Is this how you're going to raise your daughter, that her voice and opinion don't matter because some man makes the decision for her? Charlotte just went through it with the coaching job, and you're doing it to her too."

"That's not true." I narrowed my eyes, her accusation pissing me off.

"How is it different?" She narrowed her gaze, fire behind her familiar eyes. "Did that athletic director not tell her he thought she didn't want the job enough? He spoke for her. And now you. You think this is better without consulting her."

"What can I offer her? An endless saga of Simone coming in and out of our lives without reason? Cancelled date nights because my daughter will always come first?"

"You're assuming a lot of things, Hayden, and I just... don't know what your dad and I did wrong for you to view yourself this poorly." She stepped back, placing a hand on her heart. She played the guilt card well. "You're worth every risk. Every potential heartbreak. Every possibility. Charlotte knows this. She always has. She built you up, even when you were teenagers. You deserve to find love and have a partner who makes you better."

"So what am I supposed to do then? I broke her heart. I heard her sob, Mom. It's too late. I ruined it." I pressed the palms of my hands into my eyes, pushing until white spots danced behind them. An ember of hope blossomed. What if...*no*. "I made up my mind, Mom. I'm sticking with it. Charlotte won't take me back."

"Oh, there you go again, speaking for someone else." She scoffed. "My job as your mom is to be there for you in any capacity, and I always will, whether I am there or in Arizona. I am your biggest supporter for the rest of my life, and I don't take this responsibility lightly. That means calling you out when you're being a total idiot. Right now? You're being an idiot, and I didn't raise a fool. Figure your stuff out and fix this, because I cannot take any more mopey Hayden. I'm sick of him."

I snorted. "Feels like you've been waiting for this speech for a little bit."

"I practiced with your dad last night."

"You did great. Very effective. Eight out of ten for sure." I stared up at the ceiling, the flickering fluorescent lights and faint smell of cleaner grounding me. Never thought I'd have an epiphany in a jungle gym FaceTiming my mom and surrounded by ten other toddlers.

Or get handed my ass by my mom.

"I love you. You're a good man. I wish you viewed yourself how others do, but that's an issue only you can fix." She sighed before smiling at me. "Now you have a chance at the rehearsal dinner tonight. Use it."

Tension worked its way around my neck, the ever-present ache throbbing. "Christian—"

"Wants you happy. Wants Charlotte happy. Stop finding excuses."

CHAPTER TWENTY-NINE

CHARLOTTE

My brother was getting married, and I was sneaking swigs of vodka in the closet of the rehearsal dinner restaurant. We were not the same. Did I enjoy being like this? No. Was I proud? Absolutely not.

Yet I couldn't stop the sting in my eyes or the pit in my stomach. Both annoyed me. If only I could box my feelings up and store them on a shelf, deep in the back, where I could ignore them. I wished I could ignore the hit-by-a-truck feeling or the kinda-wanna-cry-at-everything urge that I'd been plagued with since Tuesday.

I sure as heck didn't plan on ending the fall semester with a professional broken heart and a real one. I glanced up at the ceiling, blinking away the onslaught of tears threatening to fall.

No. Today was about joy, damn it. I was joyful!

The rehearsal dinner was set to start in thirty minutes, and I'd have to see Hayden.

It'd been five days since he wanted to *take a step back*. Who even said that?

The pain refused to leave, taking root and growing larger by the hour. After having numerous happy hours with my friends, it wasn't clear why this hurt so much. Obviously, I loved him. I had for years, so this wasn't exactly new. But now that I had felt what it could've been between us, it gave me a snapshot of the life I wanted, and then he yanked it away out of fear.

Fear was the only explanation. He'd stared at me like I was his world and touched me like he loved me. But love wasn't enough. I've seen enough movies and read enough books to know being in love or caring about someone wasn't sufficient to have a happy ever after. The hardest part of heartbreak is the potential.

My horribly messy feelings were like pasta, all intertwined and stuck together where one end joined with a beginning. Was I heartbroken about the job? Yes.

But Hayden was worse.

What if we made it work and were so happy?

What if Gwen was happy to have me in her life?

What if I made him happy and helped him carry his burdens?

None of it mattered, and shutting down the lingering emotions seemed impossible. Sniffing, I took another drink of the vodka Sprite and smoothed down my dark green dress.

We had rented out the hotel restaurant, and they had decked it out with wreaths and lights. It reminded me of the resort and all the memories that came with that. I breathed in the smell of pine trees and a fireplace and straightened my shoulders.

Did Penny and Christian require all family and the wedding party to wear red and green? Sure did. I looked like a fancy Christmas tree, while my mom wore an elegant red dress that matched my dad's tux. We were utterly, without shame, ridiculous. I had it better than Garrett though. He was assigned to dress up as Santa, beard and wig and all. His obnoxious *ho ho ho*s could be heard across the entire restaurant, but I had to hand it to him. He played the part well.

Old Me would've eaten this up. The gingerbread men on the tables, the cutout snowflakes dangling with twinkle lights from the ceiling. The place looked magical.

My phone buzzed with a familiar area code. It was Christmas Eve, so the timing was a little strange, but I answered. "This is Charlotte."

"Hi, Charlotte. I apologize for the call on a holiday, but I figured this would be a great gift," a professional yet friendly male voice said.

"Love the positivity, but who is this?"

The man cackled. "It's Mitch, the junior high athletic director."

"Oh, hi, Mitch." My stomach swooped in the horrible, missed-a-step-and-almost-fell-to-your-death kind of way. I slammed the drink down on the floor, like he could see me right now. "Uh, what can I do for you?"

"Be the softball coach at the junior high. Start the program for us. Create a dynasty of young players. We host clinics every summer for young players, but we have no oversight. It's parents running it, and it's a mess. You impressed the hell out of me at your interview, and Peter... well, he's missing out. I couldn't be sure we had the opening yet, but I found out today. Be our coach. Let's make the best softball program in central Illinois."

"You want me...to be your coach?" I asked, breathless.

"Yes. If you're still interested."

"Yes! Yes!" I screamed, the joy overtaking me to the point that I jumped into the air. "I would love to do this with you, Mitch. Ah! Thank you. I could...yes. We could start a summer camp for the girls and have the older girls run it, and—"

He laughed. "This is why I wanted to hire you. You have the passion and vision to build something long term. I saw your plan and how you can certainly do this successfully. I want to build something special for our young female students, and you're the person to partner with on this."

"Thank you, Mitch." I closed my eyes, smiling like a total goober in the closet of a restaurant. "I won't let you down."

"I know, Charlotte. Now, sorry to interrupt your family time."

"Oh, it's nothing, I'm not— We're good. This is better."

He laughed. "Holidays with the family overwhelming?"

"Something like that."

"Merry Christmas, Charlotte. I'll email you after break with the official offer, and you can stop by to talk."

"Merry Christmas!" I replied, spinning in a circle and fist pumping the air. He hung up, and I let out a squeal as butterflies fluttered in my gut with anticipation. *I'm going to be a coach.*

I impressed him. *Me.* I would get to grow a program. He wanted to partner with me.

A horrible combination of a laugh-snort left my mouth as I squeezed my hands together. This was amazing. This was what I wanted. This was...perfect. I had to tell my family!

Bolting from the closet, I ran smack-dab into Garrett's large frame.

"What the heck are you doing in there?" He rested a hand on my shoulder, balancing me.

"Why aren't you at your post, Santa?" I fired back, the adrenaline causing my voice to come out way too loud and fast.

"Sometimes, Santas have to use the restroom. Don't tell anyone though." He winked before studying me. His white beard tilted to the side as he arched a brow. "What's up? You have this...look on your face."

"Garrett." I jumped up and down and held his hand. "The junior high athletic director, the one on the interview panel, called me. He wants me at the junior high location. He wants to hire me as their softball coach!"

"No fucking way!" Garrett said, beaming. "This is great news, Char. Ah!"

"Right?"

He pulled me into a bear hug, walking backward toward the tables. "I need to use the bathroom and get back before Penny or Christian yells at me, but you need to tell everyone. I'm so happy for you, Char. You deserve this."

"Tell us what?" Christian appeared out of nowhere. His burgundy suit complemented Penny's dark green dress, and she too slid her arm into his as she frowned at me.

"What's going on? Why is Santa not at his post?"

"Bathroom," I said, a little breathless. "But I just got a call and..."

"And what?" Christian jumped in, impatient as always. "Are you alright?"

"The junior high athletic director wants me to take over the youth softball league and coach at the junior high level. He wants me to create the program!"

A chorus of *hell yeah*s echoed in the entrance to the restaurant. The noise caused my mom to pop her head into the foyer. "What are we celebrating?"

"Charlotte was offered a coaching job at the junior high. Impressed the AD there so much, he wanted her for the role," Penny responded for me.

"That's my girl. See, everything happens for a reason." My mom yanked me into a hug before hollering for my dad. "Come over here, hon. You gotta hear this news."

It was a cuddle puddle. Hugs and congrats and back pats and squeezes. My eyes watered again, some combination of happiness and gratitude for this bunch. They were my rocks, through good and bad, and I was so dang grateful for them.

Sniffing, I squeezed my parents tight before pulling back. "Okay, I can't become a full mess."

"You're not a total mess, Char." Penny grabbed my hand. "I'm taking her to the bathroom to clean her up."

"That implies I'm a mess," I joked.

"You have raccoon eyes." Christian smiled at me, pride beaming from his face. "You're a beautiful trash panda."

"Don't call your sister a trash panda, Christian Michael," my mom scolded him like we were kids again.

Rolling her eyes, Penny guided me toward the ladies' room, when my skin tingled in a very different type of way. Awareness. The thud of my heart grew louder and louder, racing in my ears as I sucked in a breath.

Hayden walked into the restaurant wearing his glasses, and his gaze landed right on me. I was not prepared for the impact of seeing him. I knew he'd be here tonight. Of course he would be. He was Christian's best man. The pang in my chest ached.

He wore an emerald-green sweater over a collared shirt, and his posture was relaxed. *How unfair.*

His lips curved up in a slight smile as he stared at me.

My stomach flip-flopped.

How dare he seem happy and smile at me?

Penny pulled, forcing me to go to the right as I ducked my head. I wasn't ready to talk to him yet. I wasn't sure if I ever would be but definitely not with raccoon eyes.

"Girl." Penny closed the bathroom door. "I've been patient. I've been kind. I'm sick of it. Tell me what's going on with Hayden."

I laughed as I grabbed a tissue to wipe under my eyes. "What do you mean?"

"Bull-freaking-shit." She hopped onto the counter despite the sign that read NO SITTING ON COUNTERTOP. "Hayden told me there was something last weekend when I was barfing my brains out in the bathroom. Do not lie to me, Charlotte Renee. He seemed so smitten and happy?"

"Hayden ended it." My throat tightened. I sniffed, and Penny ran a hand over my back.

"Why? It's clear to everyone you love each other. You've kinda danced around it for years, and we all thought, *Maybe next year.*"

"Sure. We might, but he ended it." I wiped under my other eye, removing evidence of the eyeliner gone wild. "With Gwen's mom coming back into the picture, he wanted to take a step back because it's complicated. I offered to support him in any way, but I can't force him to be with me, you know? He made his choice. I have to deal with my heart on my own."

"Hm." She frowned. "Pregnant brides can get away with crime, yeah?"

I snorted. "Probably, but please, I just want to survive tonight and get through the wedding."

"*Survive* my wedding? No. No ma'am. This will be the event of a lifetime. You will have fun and drink for me since I have this boring lemon water instead."

"You feeling okay though?"

"I'm having the best night of my life. Do not worry about me. You focus on having fun, because we're going to talk about this the rest of our lives."

"Yeah, no pressure." I snorted. I smoothed my outfit down and adjusted my hair. I looked okay. A little sad, but I was working on that. I could channel all my energy into preparing for the summer youth program and starting at the junior high next fall.

"Look at me, sis."

Her words warmed me. She would officially be my sister-in-law, but she always felt like more than that.

"Men can be idiots. They mean well, but it takes them longer to do things. We love them for it, but Hayden is having a dumbass moment. I can feel it in my bones."

"Could be true, but he broke my heart." I glanced at the ground. "He's always pushed me away, then drew me back in. I don't know if I can survive that again."

Penny hugged me hard, her arms digging into my back to the point that I winced. I couldn't break the hug though. She was intense and got what she wanted.

"We're going back out there, and I'm getting you a drink. I need your speech to be incredible tonight."

"It is. Don't worry." I laughed at the wild look in her eye. "Hey, please don't tell Christian. I kept this from him intentionally because I don't want him being angry at Hayden. Hayden needs his best friend right now."

"You're too good for this world, babe. Too damn good." Penny held the door open and ushered me through. She smacked my butt and said, "Only smiles around him. Make him weep."

I laughed and had to admit that she made me feel a little bit better. Penny was awesome and loved everyone with her whole heart.

Guests trickled in the main door as jazzy, instrumental Christmas songs played on the speaker. If Hayden approached me, I could handle it.

But first, I needed a peppermint drink, which meant stopping at the bar pronto. The bartender was helping another guest, some older woman that I didn't know, before approaching me. I ordered something minty.

"Could you make two of those, please?" a familiar, deep voice said behind me.

Goose bumps broke out over my skin. *Hayden.*

My dress felt too tight, and my mouth dried up. What would I say to him? Talk about the weather? *Oh, it's so cold outside, does your chest hurt every time you breathe?* Sure. Super normal.

He clearly was doing fine, where I was a mess.

"Charlotte."

He used his sexy, slow drawl. I bit the inside of my cheek before facing him. He leaned one elbow on the bar, his other hand resting at his side. He smelled so damn good, and those glasses were making my knees weak.

I arched a brow. "Hey."

"You look beautiful." His gaze roamed up and down my body. "Incredible, actually."

"Thanks." I provided a tight-lipped smile, proud of myself for holding it together. "You look fine too."

"Fine?" His lips quirked. "Stop, you're being too kind."

I hated that he was funny and teasing. I hated that he looked at me with warmth in his eyes. I gripped the bar and took a breath. "What do you want?"

"Baby, don't—"

"Don't you dare *baby* me." I glared at him as I whispered. "You broke my heart. The pieces aren't back together."

"Could we talk? Just for a moment? Please?"

He looked upset, but that didn't matter. *Stay strong, Charlotte.*

"No. You had all week to call me. I want to get through tonight without crying, Hayden. That's it." My eyes watered, and my voice shook. "I'm always going to care about you and Gwen, and I'm still planning on watching her in January until you find a nanny. Just...I need more time before we talk."

He blinked and swallowed hard. "I'm sorry, Charlotte."

"Here's your drink!" The bartender slid my drink toward me, and then one toward Hayden.

I took it and ran from him. I didn't care if I was being a coward. He couldn't say *baby* to me like that anymore or tell me I looked incredible. And what the heck was this timing? He couldn't do this...any other possible time?

"Aunt Lotte! Aunt Lotte! Look at my dress!"

Gwen. My heart clenched. I loved that girl with everything, and here she was, wearing a wild Christmas dress with every color imaginable as she ran right toward me. She wrapped her arms around my legs, and I crouched down to pick her up. "Hi, girlie."

"I miss you. I want to play again." She stared up at me. Her chubby cheeks and little gap between her teeth were just too cute.

"I miss you too, sweetie." I kissed the top of her head, my chest aching so hard I wanted to throw up. "I love your dress."

"Thank you. Gigi got it for me."

"Your Gigi is a smart woman." I bopped her nose before setting her down. I refused to let her suffer any of the effects from her dad and me, even if it killed me.

"Sit with us! Sit with me and Daddy. Please? We can talk about school."

"Ah, well, honey—"

"Christian put us at the same table." Hayden clenched his jaw as he ran a finger over his eyebrow.

He's nervous. Good.

"Okay." I nodded. "That's great news, Gwen. I can sit by you!" *And try not to have a breakdown. Yay for me!*

"My daddy is sad. Are you sad?"

Your daddy did this to us.

"I'm happy I get to see you tonight." I tickled her side and avoided staring at her father. His gaze was a constant weight. "Want to play I spy?"

"Yes. Yes. I go first?" She skipped toward the table.

I followed her. Hayden followed me.

A warm, soft touch landed on my lower back, and I froze. Hayden had touched me.

"Please, could I have five minutes tonight? I need to talk with you." He leaned forward so his breath tickled my neck. I was pretty sure he got that close intentionally.

He ran his nose against my ear. Yeah. That was intentional. He smelled me.

My eye twitched. "Hayden, stop."

"I miss you. I messed up. I fucked up." His voice lacked his usual confidence. "I'm here to plead my case."

"Case for what? Forgiveness?" I whispered.

"To getting you back."

I faced him, our mouths not even a foot apart. Hope and anger twisted together, unraveling as each fought for dominance. Did I dream of this? Yes. Did I want this? Yes. Could I forgive him? Ye—maybe.

His lips parted, his eyes staring so deeply at me, like he tried to find my soul, as he gently ran his fingers over my hand. "I love—"

"Aunt Lotte! Look!" Gwen pulled on my dress, forcing me to glance at her. The distraction saved me from whatever Hayden was going to say.

He *loved* what? Baseball? His daughter? Being unhappy? Me?

No. No. No. He wouldn't have done what he did if he loved me. People didn't do that.

Dinner would be served in a few minutes, but my stomach ached with turmoil. How could I eat when I was having a full-on quarter-life crisis? One just didn't digest normally with all their insides raging.

"Santa is here!" Gwen squealed. The girl spun in a circle four times before I righted her.

"Hey, don't make yourself dizzy, baby girl. You want to go say hi to him before we eat?"

"Yes, please. Daddy, can we? Please?"

"Of course." Hayden held out his hand, smiling the warm, fuzzy grin I loved. It was the softening of his features and the utter happiness on his face that had made me fall for him.

Becoming a father had changed him for the better. Some people found themselves with parenthood, and Hayden was one of them.

He guided Gwen up to Santa right next to the main entrance of the restaurant. Garrett winked at me when I caught his eye, and I smiled. He patted his knee, and Gwen jumped onto him, her mouth moving a mile a minute as she discussed everything she wanted. I'd heard the extensive list...before I stopped going over there.

She wanted a bubble machine. A water machine. Marshmallows. A sleepover. A pool party. The Grinch. And a Lego set. I wondered how Hayden managed to handle all of that. What even was a water machine? Smiling, I sat down. I counted the poinsettias in the center of the table instead of watching Gwen and Hayden. His laughter carried toward me, same with Gwen's. Hearing them happy made me happy, even if it was at the cost of my pain.

I took a sip of my drink and said to heck with it. Hayden wanted me back. I could hold on to my hurt or hear what he had to say.

Who are you kidding? You'll forgive him. Just like last time.

His phone buzzed on the table, an unknown number popping up. I silenced it. It went off again, this time with his mom's name. It happened again, and without overthinking it, I answered. "This is Hayden's phone."

"Charlotte?" his mom's warm voice said. "I'm so glad you answered, honey. He's been a mess without you. Please forgive his temporary blip of idiothood."

My eyes prickled, and I smiled. "I'm weighing my options."

"Excellent. Make him sweat a bit. He deserves it."

I snorted. I had always loved his mom. "I don't know what's going to happen. We haven't really talked, but I saw you called twice, and I didn't want you to worry. He's with Santa so Gwen can sit on his lap."

"That makes sense for the Calhouns to have a Santa at the rehearsal dinner."

"My thoughts too."

"Could you tell him to call me when he can? Nothing worrying, but we're stuck in an airport and won't get in until way later."

"I'll tell him as soon as he gets back."

"Thanks, hon. Hopefully, I'll see you soon."

She hung up, and I meant to set his phone down. I really did. I wasn't the spying kind or nosy in other people's business. Yet…my contact name was left opened. And with it was my cell, both personal and work emails, and notes.

Lines and lines of notes about me.

Left-handed—give her outside of the booth
Cries at rom-coms
Ghirardelli hot chocolate is her favorite. Marshmallows.
Loses her mind when "Get Low" comes on
Favorite singer is Taylor Swift
Dream vacation: Italy
Pepperoni when from local spot, pineapple at chains
Will stop and stare at clouds. Loves weather stuff.
Has a secret talent of baking for those she cares about.
Chocolate when sad, wine when upset
Likes to wear colorful socks. They never match.
Is the worst organizer.
Is the queen of GIFs and memes.
Birthday: March. Loves personal presents. NO GIFT
    CARDS.

Dogs over cats.
Does the worm when challenged.
Eyes light up when she talks about those she loves.

With my heart in my throat, I swiped away and went to my brother's contact. I had to know if this was everyone or just me. My pulse raced, my fingertips weighing ten pounds due to adrenaline. I needed this to be just me. I needed it so badly. You didn't keep a list like this if you didn't truly love someone. I clicked on Christian, and my eyes darted to the notes section.

June birthday.
Corona.

That was it.

Hayden knew me, had paid attention for years, and wanted me back.

I just had to decide what to do about it.

CHAPTER THIRTY

HAYDEN

Charlotte's cheeks were rosy. I loved when she blushed. She was so expressive all the time, but that blush gave her away even more.

"Santa, I was really good this year. Super good." Gwen leaned against Santa's shoulder, her eyes wide. "I think I get a lot of presents."

"Oh, do you now?" Garrett said, his voice booming. "What would you like?"

"Mmmm, I think a fruit tree."

"What type of fruit?"

"Broccoli. And corn, please."

Garrett met my gaze, his lips twitching. "Okay, yeah, a broccoli and corn tree. What else would you like?"

Cool, thanks, Garrett. How the hell was I supposed to get a broccoli and corn tree? On Christmas Eve?

"I think a big bubble machine. Like, super big. With lots of bubbles so I can play with my friend Frankie, and

Aubriella, and Jameson, and Ruby. Can we eat your cookies, Santa?"

"You sure can, and a bubble machine sounds like so much fun!"

Gwen giggled and threw her arms around his neck. "Thank you, Santa. Love you."

"Love you too, Gwen. Thanks for being such a good girl this year."

She slid off his lap with stars in her eyes. I nodded at Garrett, impressed at his performance. The guy was a walking contradiction, but he was great with kids, especially mine.

"Oh! Cake! I want some!" Gwen beelined for the dessert table.

"No, hon." I picked up Gwen before she bulldozed her way into getting some. She was cute and manipulative. One little *please* and anyone would crumble.

"Dinner first. Then yummies."

"I want yummy now."

"I hear you, but dinner is first." I set her on the chair next to Charlotte. Penny, Christian, and their parents were also at the table, but they were still walking around and mingling with guests. So it was the three of us.

I ran a hand through my hair, unsure how to proceed. I knew two things. The first—I loved Charlotte and wanted a life with her. The second—I fucked up making the wrong decision and pushing her away. My choice had her questioning point one though, so I had to make that right.

How did I do that when she wouldn't even look at me? She stared at the tablecloth, her fingers twisting together as regret clawed at my chest. I had to find something to say to ease this tension. It was the worst. I missed our easy banter, the way she made me laugh at her jokes. Not being on speaking terms was more painful than everything. "So, are you ready for your speech?"

"Yes." She flicked her gaze toward me but then away. Her brother walked up, a ridiculously happy smile on his face. Char nodded. "Hey, Christian."

"Hey, Char, Porter. My girl Gwennie." He bent down and held out his knuckles. She bumped them right away. Standing, he jutted his chin toward his sister. "Did Char tell you the news?"

"What news?" I said too fast. The tension from earlier doubled, and I gripped the table for support. Every worst-case scenario popped in my head. She was moving across the world...She brought a date...She...

"I was offered the head softball position for the junior high today." She smiled, tracing her finger over the tablecloth as she met my gaze. Pride swirled in her eyes.

"Char," I said, my mouth parting. I wanted to yank her into my arms and hug her, kiss her senseless, and tell her how fucking proud I was. The silence went on a beat too long, and both she and Christian stared at me funny. "That's so awesome. Congrats."

"Yeah. I couldn't believe it. Mitch said I impressed him during the interview, so he wanted to hire me to run the summer program and really influence young girls in the community. It might not be the high school level, but still, this is amazing."

"I am so proud of you." My voice dropped low as I envisioned helping her. I could go over practice plans with her. I could keep stats for her during the season, if she wanted. But all of that only made sense if she'd forgive me. That sobered up my derailing thoughts.

"We all are." Penny joined our table as she narrowed her eyes at me. Shit. She knew that I had let Charlotte down. Then she said, "Char deserves the world for how wonderful she is. Don't you agree, Hayden?"

"Penny," Char whispered, her face blushing again.

I waited for her gaze to meet mine. Her blush spread to her neck, and she twisted her lips together. I spoke slowly and intentionally. "I am proud of you, but you should feel proud of yourself. You impressed the AD so much that you got an offer for a job you never applied for. This is huge, and I am so happy for you and that community. It might be different than what you planned originally, but you earned this."

"Thanks, Hayden. I do feel really proud. Thanks again for your help." She grinned, but it didn't last long before she leaned toward Penny. I felt Christian staring at me, and when I glanced at him, he jutted his chin toward the bar.

I frowned.

"I want my best man for a drink. Come on. The ladies will watch Gwen."

"Of course we will," Penny said, more curt than normal. That meant one thing—Christian knew. Penny told him. He was going to tell me to stay the hell away from Charlotte.

My throat ached with emotion. This wasn't how I had envisioned this conversation. I wanted to wait until we could tell him together, and he could see how happy I made her.

Christian dug his fingers into my shoulder. Yup. He knew.

"Do we need to head outside for this?" I asked, resigned to my fate.

"What? No? It's cold as shit. I want a drink."

He ordered two shots of tequila. We did them, and then he sighed. "I love you, man."

"Yeah, uh, you too." My neck burned.

"No. I love you. Feelings are weird for you, I get it. But this is a kind of love that stays forever. No matter what. You feel me?"

I didn't respond.

He cackled. "I'm marrying my best friend, and my closest friends are here. I'm about to become a father. I couldn't be happier. But what I don't understand is why you think you deserve to suffer."

Frowning, I shifted my weight. "I still don't get it."

"Charlotte. I'm not an idiot. I love you clowns so much, but I'm sick of seeing you two dance around the reality. If it's me that's holding you back, then I've been a shit friend. I never gave you any indication you weren't good enough for Charlotte. You're the best man I know. You work harder than anyone. You get knocked down and rise up stronger. You raised a baby, by yourself, and she is one of the best things in our life. That takes courage very few people have. You're one of the youngest assistant coaches at the university level, and you've helped transform their program in just three years. Do I need to list more reasons why you're incredible?"

I shook my head, overcome with emotion. I couldn't speak. My palms were sweating, and the urge to vomit hit me hard. This was the last thing I had expected.

"I respect you, admire you, and am proud to be your friend. Even if you and Charlotte don't work it out, nothing will change. Sure, I might not invite you both over at the same time, but this is an intervention. Figure your shit out and fix my sister's heart. I know you hurt her."

"Simone showed up," I blurted out. "She might want to be a mom again, and I panicked. I pushed Charlotte away out of fear. I made decisions for her, that she would be better off without me and my baggage."

"Simone? Dude. Why the hell did you not tell me?"

"Your wedding. We didn't...Char and I...we were together since the resort. Officially. She didn't want to tell you until after the wedding. She was adamant about not stealing an ounce of your or Penny's thunder." I swallowed. "Please don't be mad at her. She did what she thought was best. Be pissed at me."

"Did she know about Simone?"

"Yes."

"She never told me."

"Because she was trying to protect me." I pinched my nose. "I love her, Christian. I do. I want her to be my wife. I want her to be Gwen's stepmom, and I want more kids with her, if she wants them. I'm just not sure I'm who she needs."

"All my sister needs is someone who accepts her for her. Someone who brings her joy and makes her laugh, and you're annoyingly funny with her. She wants support and someone she can depend on. She needs someone to build her up. Most of all, she wants to be loved." Christian's eyes sparkled. "You do that for her now. She's a lifer though. Loyal as hell. She's a Calhoun."

"I wasn't there when she didn't get the job," I said softly. "Her worst moment, and I couldn't make it. That's not forgivable."

"Says who? Your daughter's mother shows up after three years, potentially threatening the safety of your family? Yeah. That's understandable. Sure, you could've communicated better, but learn from this. Trust her to love you back. That's your issue. You're too afraid to let her return your feelings." He clapped my shoulder again, smiling. "Here comes the threatening part."

"Okay." I gulped, exhaling long and slow. "I knew this was coming."

"Dude." He laughed. "I meant... you have until the photos tomorrow to figure this out. I don't want my forever pictures of my wedding to be ruined because my sister is sad. Fix it. You have a day."

He winked before strutting off. Penny stared at us and tilted her head, the two of them communicating without words. They were in on this. The thought almost made me smile.

I ran a hand over my face, analyzing his words. Christian gave me his blessing and then some. He wasn't holding us back. It was me. I stared at Charlotte, my heart swelling with how much I loved her. She had her arm around Gwen, the two of them coloring on a paper napkin. My baby girl rested her head on Charlotte and looked up with a huge grin.

Charlotte hugged her, and when she glanced up, her gaze found mine. It was like a lightning bolt ricocheting through my body. One side of her mouth quirked up in a shy smile, and her blush traveled down her neck.

I made her blush.

I smiled back, feeling lighter than I had in a good while. We'd be okay. I'd work hard for it, that was for damn sure. Like I told my guys all the time, you put in the work if you want something bad enough.

I was done using my own insecurities as excuses. I was going to fight. For her, for us, for Gwen.

I knew just what to do.

*   *   *   *

"Good evening, everyone," I said into the microphone. Christian and Penny had requested speeches from Charlotte and me tonight instead of at the wedding. It was untraditional and on brand for them, but I was glad because this was my chance. About thirty people stared back at me in various forms of smiles.

But I focused on one face in particular. My woman.

"Love has a way of bringing out the best in us, some ways more conventional than others. For Penny and Christian, it's a new level of holiday cheer that borders on unhinged." The crowd chuckled like I meant them to.

"While we're all dressed in green and red and we have Santa here, we can agree that the future Mr. and Mrs. Calhoun are extra. And it's my favorite part about them. They match each other's extra. Christian is competitive and rowdy, while Penny will stop at nothing to win and is resourceful. He might have a louder voice, but she'd find a megaphone. Christian loves hard and aggressively, words of affirmation are his love language. He makes me a better man to talk about my feelings. Penny's love language is acts of service. She would do anything for anyone at any time. She taught me how to put others first, that giving yourself to someone else means trusting them and opening yourself up. For you to be a part of this couple's lives is a blessing." My eyes prickled, and I stared right at Charlotte.

"When I think about love, and family, and marriage, I think of supporting each other through hard times. I think about laughing at mundane things. I once watched these two laugh so hard they cried over an inside joke that made no sense. I think about the time Penny got a flat tire in a rainstorm, and Christian left a baseball game to help her. I think about the time Christian needed surgery, and Penny never missed an appointment. She also made him a bracelet to hold on to because she knew how much surgery freaked him out."

I cleared my throat. "We all deserve the love that Christian and Penny have. We deserve to be swept off our feet, to know what it's like to be accepted for who we are, flaws and all. Because look, Christian has flaws. He laughs way too loud. Likes dumb movies." Everyone chuckled. "Wears horrible sweaters that are kind of offensive. Yet Penny loves him anyway."

"Yeah, I do!" she shouted. She rested her head on his shoulder and beamed at me.

"Now, I need to be honest here as I talk about the people I love most in the world." *Shit*. Nerves got me bad. My voice came out scratchy and throaty. This was my moment. "I have another Calhoun I need to talk about because, you see...I'm not just Christian's best man. I'm also a man who is in love with the woman sitting next to him. His sister."

The room buzzed, or maybe it was my mind. I could be blacking out. There had been few times I was this nervous, to the point my brain wasn't getting oxygen. I inhaled, forcing myself to swallow, because oh my God. What if she hated this? What if she's embarrassed? I didn't know if she thought public proposals were cute or horrific. I never asked. It wasn't on my list.

Everyone stared at me. All thirty of them. And Garrett. My throat closed up. Oh no no no. The tequila shot was about to come up.

"Keep talking. I'm listening!" Charlotte cupped her hands around her mouth and shouted. "Tell me how amazing I am."

She was perfect. She knew I had frozen and helped bring me back.

Everyone laughed, and Christian nodded at me, giving me his approval. I glanced at Penny and found her smiling like a fool. The unspoken *you can do this* had me standing taller.

"My world changed when I met Charlotte. Her contagious smile, her infectious laughter, and her genuine kindness captivated me. She still finds shapes in the clouds and makes everyone around her better people. Our timing hasn't lined up, but after some much-needed advice from my best friend, I realized we have to make our own timing. Christian and Penny taught me that. You fight for the life you want, especially if it's hard. So, Charlotte. This is me fighting for you. I won't stop. Gwen and I love you, want you in our lives, and I will use my adorable daughter to get you to forgive me."

She smiled.

"I'm sorry for being afraid. I'm sorry for not trusting us. I want this to be us next year. I don't care if you want to wear gingerbread costumes or dress up as wreaths or shatter snow globes as a party trick. I'll do whatever you want, as long as you'll have me back."

People sniffed.

Charlotte's eyes glistened as she blew out a long breath. I'd only felt this stress two other times. The state championship final where I was up to bat before the final out and the day Gwen showed up.

Christian leaned over and whispered something in her ear. She laughed. Then she stood, the sound of the chair scraping on the tile floor. It was like the whole room held its breath, everyone on pins and needles.

She ran her teeth over her bottom lip as she approached me, her pulse visibly racing at the base of her neck. I had tunnel vision. It was just her. Her smile, her eyes, her hair, the little sway of her hips, and the slight dimple on her left side. I gulped.

"How convenient there's mistletoe here." She jutted her chin toward the ceiling. "Think we should kiss?"

"Get over here."

I tossed the mic to her uncle and yanked my woman against me and kissed her.

And she sure as hell kissed me back.

CHAPTER THIRTY-ONE

CHARLOTTE

"You are stunning," I said, my voice cracking. Penny stood before me. Her wedding dress was perfect, and my eyes stung. "You are absolutely gorgeous."

She sniffed and fanned her hands over her eyes. "I can't believe I'm marrying him. It's happening. We're doing this."

"You are." I held her hands and squeezed. "You deserve the world, Pen. You're it for each other. You got this."

Her jaw trembled. "I'm insanely nervous even though it's just Christian. He's seen me at my best and worst, so it's silly I'm shaking."

"This is a huge day, so be nervous. Have your feelings and let them flow. Christian is going to be a blubbering mess."

"No." She laughed, sniffing. "He'll hold it together while I'll be a hot mess."

"I assure you, he won't. He's going to see you, this dress and veil, and lose his mind. And you'd be a beautiful mess." I nodded, like that point would make her understand. "Now, are you ready? Your dad is outside the door."

She took another breath. "Yes."

This was her moment, and I wouldn't take a second from her, but my own nerves were going off like fireworks. Hayden and I didn't get to talk last night, not with all the wedding events, his parents' flight delays, and Penny's pre-wedding plans with me. We left last night with the promise to talk after the wedding.

That meant...he hadn't seen me since we had kissed goodbye. Now we'd walk down the aisle together, arm in arm. This was like prom on steroids. No, more than that. I gulped, doing my best to be strong for Penny. We held hands as I opened the door, squeezing one last time before letting go. "She's all yours."

"God." Penny's dad choked up, bringing his fist to his mouth. "Honey."

"Dad, stop." Penny's voice cracked too.

"Look at you."

"No. We're gonna lose it." Penny laughed.

I veered away from them, letting them have their father-daughter time. My mind wandered, briefly dreaming about what my wedding day would look like. Would I do the same holiday theme? Or something more subtle? I smiled, picturing Hayden wearing a Santa suit and Gwen in a Christmas tree costume.

She'd be the cutest, best flower girl ever.

I shook my head, scolding myself for daydreaming. Hayden and I hadn't even talked yet, and here I was, planning our wedding. The entrance to the main sanctuary came into view, and Hayden stood there, staring right at me. He wore a dark gray tux that brought out his eyes and *holy shit*. Wait—could I think that cuss word in a church?

"Charlotte." He pressed his lips together as his jaw clenched. "You are stunning."

"Thank you." My face prickled from his attention.

He stalked toward me, his long, confident strides so flipping attractive that I swallowed. I missed him so badly. My stomach ached with longing, and even though I knew we both wanted to be together, our conversation would still be painful.

"Baby," he said, his voice cracking as he cupped my face, "look at you. How am I . . ." He stopped, shaking his head as he stared deep into my eyes. "I love you."

"I love you too." I leaned into his hand, my stomach doing back handsprings and somersaults and cartwheels all at the same time. It was an Olympic performance at this point. "It would be remiss to not say how gorgeous you look too."

"No." He snorted. "I don't care about me. You are . . . I won't be able to look away from you. I need you to know—"

"You ready?" Penny said, joining us in the foyer.

Hayden sucked in a breath as his gaze landed on her. "Penny, you are beautiful."

"Thanks, Porter." She smiled wide, all traces of her nerves gone. "Now, I know you two have to figure your shit out, but I want to go get hitched."

"AKA, move your ass down the aisle," her dad said.

We all laughed, and Hayden held out his arm. "Ready?"

"Let's do this."

I looped my arm around his and took a deep breath. A different type of nerves took root. What if I tripped? Or ran into someone?

"I got you," he whispered. "I won't let you fall."

"Can you read my mind?"

"Sometimes? Yes. I know every expression on your face. I know when you're nervous or scared, or when you're happy and excited. You do this eyebrow and lip thing when you're anxious, like right now, and I know you hate wearing heels."

He knows me.

He loves me.

I was dizzy with my feelings for him, however messy they were. I squeezed his bicep. "Wanna know a secret?"

"Yes."

We were at the doors. The wedding march began. Our instructions were to wait ten seconds and then open the door.

Ten.

Nine.

"I was picturing *our* wedding," I whispered.

Eight. Seven. Six.

"And how I want small. Intimate. And Gwen to be a part of it."

Five. Four. Three.

Hayden gulped, his throat bobbing as he stared down at me with hope and longing in his eyes.

Two.

One.

I winked at him before pushing the doors open. I had flustered him—which was still one of my favorite pastimes. His grip on my arm tightened, and I ignored his stare. We had to walk down this aisle without causing a scene, and that took all my focus.

Hayden led us down the aisle, his calm and confident presence the push I needed to get through this. Once I saw Christian standing at the end, I teared up.

He smiled at us as we slowly walked toward him, but his eyes watered. His hands shook. I knew it. He was gonna lose it when he saw Penny.

Hayden stopped at the front of the church, shaking hands with Christian and kissing me on the cheek before we went our separate ways. I stood on Penny's side, he on Christian's.

Then it was Penny's time.

She beamed as she made her entrance, and my tears leaked over. Christian choked and released the sweetest squeak before a full-on cry escaped.

Penny's hold broke too.

They were two weirdos so in love that they bawled in front of everyone, and collective sounds of sniffles carried throughout the church.

I glanced at Hayden, who stared right back at me. Almost like he had been waiting for me to turn his way. Garrett stood next to him, but I couldn't look away from my man.

Next year. You and me, he mouthed.

My heart swelled, but I couldn't make it too easy. I shrugged.

His eyes flared with amusement.

Christian met Penny and her dad, shaking his hand before reaching for her. They complemented each other and had a beautiful, quiet moment, just the two of them. Sure, we all watched them, but the absolute love and tenderness in their expressions was riveting.

They settled in their position at the altar, and the rest of the wedding flew by for us in attendance. They did traditional vows despite how goofy they were because they "couldn't handle the pressure."

I couldn't blame them. They were crying and laughing and sniffing like crazy. Hayden caught my gaze every so often, and each time, the same bolt of lightning went through me.

He's so beautiful.

Once the pastor said they were officially Mr. and Mrs. Calhoun, the room erupted. They bulldozed down the aisle as Hayden and I followed. People hugged, cheered, and cried.

It was a blur of joy and feelings, and I floated. I was so happy for Penny and Christian, overcome with so much happiness. My parents hugged me and then Hayden. My aunts all lined up too, but Hayden never released his grip on my hand.

Gwen burst through the crowd toward us, hugging our legs before Hayden picked her up. "Hey, sweetie, I'm going to have Gigi take you to dinner, okay? Daddy needs to help Charlotte with something for a little while."

"Okay! Gigi said she has a puzzle for me."

"How fun!" I said, leaning over to kiss her. "You look beautiful."

"You're beautiful, Aunt Lotte!"

"Char, can you give me five minutes? Then, can we talk?"

"Sure."

He parted the crowd as he moved toward his parents, his large frame automatically clearing a path for him. I wanted to be alone with him, to talk about his notes on his phone and what happened between us. I needed an update on Simone and us.

Plus we had an hour before we were due at dinner.

It took less than two minutes before he was back, a determined look on his face. "Let's go."

"Oh, nice manners."

"No time for manners." He weaved us through the crowd and down the stairs. Penny and Christian didn't want the traditional send-off. They didn't want staged photos besides the two of them. They wanted candid reception photos instead. That meant we had some alone time.

"Where are we— Did you get us a limo?"

"Yes." He scanned the parking lot before sighing. "There it is."

"A limo? For you and me?" I tore my attention from the crowd to the parking lot.

"Yes." He faced me, his expression softening. "I wanted to make sure we had a little time just you and me tonight, so I rented it for us. Figured it'd be nice to not worry about driving."

"That is nice."

"Plus, I'd like to kiss you after we have this overdue

conversation. I'd prefer to do that without all our noisy friends and family watching."

I gulped, a little breathless. "Okay then."

Snow covered the ground, and I slid on my heels. "Shit."

"I got you."

Hayden swooped me into his arms, tucking me tight against his chest as he walked toward the limo. Instead of protesting, I cuddled against him and breathed him in. His spicy cologne filled my nose, and man, he smelled so good. We had a lot to discuss, but I wasn't nervous anymore. I ran my nose along his neck, and he shuddered.

"Careful, Char. I don't want to drop you, and I need to focus."

I chuckled. "Sorry. I've just…missed you."

His muscles tensed at my words. "You have no idea how much I missed you too. Almost to the limo."

He took a couple more steps before carefully setting me down. He ran his hands from my shoulders to my hips, his nostrils flaring. "There really aren't words for how beautiful you look in this dress."

My face heated. "Thank you."

He opened the door and gestured for me to get in. I slid in and sighed as the warm air greeted me. A bottle of champagne sat to the right and a bouquet of flowers next to it.

He shut the door and tapped the window. "Can you drive for thirty minutes and shut the partition?"

"You got it, boss."

The window made a mechanical noise, and after ten seconds, it closed, leaving us alone. My pulse raced at the base

of my neck, the urge to demand answers from him conflict-
ing with the desire to kiss him.

He slid over to me, on his knees as he cupped my face.
His gray eyes filled with worry as he swallowed. "I know
we need to talk, but can I kiss you?"

I nodded.

He didn't wait a second before closing the distance
between us. He kissed me softly, like I was precious to him.
He ran his fingers into my hair as he explored my mouth
with his tongue. This kiss felt different. Felt more...felt...
like he loved me. I pulled him closer to me, wanting to feel
his heartbeat against mine, but he stilled. He kissed down
my jaw, over my neck, and to my shoulder before pulling
back.

His gaze was heated as he sighed. "I want to keep going,
but we know our chemistry isn't the issue at all."

"No. It's not." I cleared my throat and ran a thumb over
my lip. "I do love your mouth on me though."

He smiled. "Trust me, baby. I love how you taste. I love
everything about you."

I laughed. "Well, that's just unrealistic."

"No." He kissed my wrist, closing his eyes for a second.
"I do, Char. But mostly, I love how you give your love to
everyone around you."

I trembled. His words were laced with passion, and he
kept kissing me everywhere. My wrist, my arm, my fingers.
"Hayden—"

"I broke your trust, and I'm going to do everything to
earn it back. I know it'll take some time, but I swear to

you." He gulped. "But only if you want this. I hurt you, and if you can't forgive me, I understand."

I ran a hand through his hair, waiting for him to meet my eyes. "You hurt me, yes. But I've spent most of my life in love with you. Of course I want this, you, Gwen, but you have to work on communication with me. That's nonnegotiable."

His jaw clenched but he nodded. Owning his mistakes like the man he was. "I'm so terribly sorry for hurting you, for putting us through this last week. For not being there the day you didn't get the job. I—"

"Simone came back after three years, Hayden. I'm not upset about you not being there that night. That pales in comparison to everything else. If you were somehow thinking those were comparable—me not getting a coaching job and the sudden appearance of your daughter's birth mother? They absolutely aren't."

He blinked. "Are you sure?"

"Yes."

"Huh." He ran a hand over his face and stared out the window before meeting my gaze. "I thought...So missing that night is forgivable?"

"I'm already over that. What I'm upset about is you being afraid to work through this with me. That you'd rather do everything alone than let me be with you." I cupped his face this time, and he leaned into my hand. "I want you. All of you. The messy parts and the hard parts. Gwen, Simone, your parents, her parents, your highs and your lows."

"You're fucking incredible." He closed his eyes and sighed. "Simone still has no plan. She finally told her parents she had a kid. They never knew."

"What?" I jerked back.

"Yup. She just told them about Gwen last week. I haven't spoken with them, but we texted a few times, and we're going to meet tomorrow at the park."

"Hayden." I swallowed the ball of emotion in my throat. "That's incredible."

He pinched his nose as his voice came out husky. "Gwen deserves to know them and have a relationship with them."

"Of course she does, but that doesn't mean it won't be hard." I slid onto the floor with him and hugged him. "So even if Simone bolts again, they could want to stay in Gwen's life?"

He nodded as he dropped his head onto my shoulder. "I told Simone she needs to see a therapist before I'd let her start to see Gwen. She is debating if she wants to. Does that make me a shitty person?"

"No." I rubbed his back. "That means you're a good father."

"Hey." He pulled back and met my eyes. "Will you be with me when I call them tomorrow?"

"Oh my God, of course I will, Hayden." My eyes prickled. This was a huge step for him. Not only trusting me to be there on the call, but for him to open up to Simone's mom and dad. "You're amazing. Seriously. This is so brave of you." I kissed his face once, twice, three times. "I think you should hear my list now."

"List for what?"

"I saw the list you have under my name. You've secretly kept those notes on me. You don't do that unless you care for someone." I grinned and cupped his face. "You love me."

"Shit." His face reddened, and he gripped the back of my neck. "I mean, I do love you, but that list goes back a long time. I should've deleted it or something."

"Hayden Orion Porter. I'm glad you didn't. Now shh so I can tell you my list to show you that I love you and that I'm all in, okay?"

"Okay." His lips quirked, and he stared at me with that half smile that I loved. "I'm listening."

"Your favorite ice cream is mint chocolate chip. And cookie dough if you're having a crap day. Best holiday movie is *Die Hard*, and favorite movie is *Remember the Titans*. You hold doors open for people, always are the last one to order if we're in a group. You remember birthdays and always get gifts that aren't gift cards. You're so thoughtful and such a good son." I sniffed. "You model what being a good human is for your daughter so much it makes me cry thinking about how lucky she is. You gave my brother confidence to love himself when no one else his age did." My lip trembled. "You're such a good dad that you're doing something that is so hard. It's easy to push people away, it's tougher to let them in. And you're letting in the parents of the daughter who left your baby. That is…only special people would do that, Hayden, and that's you. You have the biggest heart, and I'm lucky I get to take care of it."

"Char." His voice was watery. "We can't go into this crying."

"I've already cried ten times today. Weddings are emotional." I laughed, cried, sniffed, and snorted. A real sexy combo. Hayden pulled me close, hugging me so there was no room between us. "I love you and want this. All of it. Let's do this for real. No secrets. No making choices for the other. I think we'll be happy."

"More than happy," he said against my temple and then my lips. "I need to kiss you, touch you. Can I spend the next fifteen minutes showing you how much I love you, please?"

"If it involves you getting out of this tux, then yes." I wiggled my brows, earning another chuckle from him. "I want to hear that laugh every day, Hayden."

"I love you. Then, now, always."

"Then, now, always," I repeated, finally feeling content. We'd have ups and downs, but for the first time, I knew we were meant to be together. And damn, that felt good.

CHAPTER THIRTY-TWO

HAYDEN

My stomach churned, and my palms were clammy, slick with nervous sweat as I shoved them in my pockets. Today was the day. Gwen was going to meet her grandparents—Sarah and Phillip Barringer. Simone had opted out, which was probably for the best.

We exchanged five text messages, had one phone call, and agreed to meet at one of Gwen's favorite parks. Anderson Park was located about ten minutes from our house. It was a safe location, one she knew well, which mattered. She knew she was meeting her grandparents, but that meant she had a lot of other questions to ask.

So will I ever get to meet my mom? When? Will I call her Mom? My best friend Paxton has two moms. They are nice. I have two Gigis then.

Will they like me? Do they like dinosaurs?

Explaining the complex reality to a three-year-old was hard as hell.

"Breathe, Hayden." Charlotte ran her hand up and down my back. It was a rare mild day in December, with a high of fifty. Gwen wore her bright pink coat and no hat as she ran around chasing birds. "She'll be okay."

"I know Gwen will." I swallowed. "I can't help but feel this overwhelming, heart-wrenching fear of someone hurting her. Or disappointing her. Or wanting to be in her life but then leaving it. I wish I could ensure no one would hurt her for the rest of her life."

"That's all valid. I don't want that for Gwen either." She reached for my forearm, pulling my hand from my pocket and interlocking our fingers. Her palm pressed against mine, her hand soft and warm, and then she kissed the back of it. "But that is unfortunately life. We can't control who or what happens, but you can be Gwen's rock. We all can be. She has a tight circle around her, always there to lift her up if she's sad. Sarah and Phillip might want to be a part of her life, or they might not. She deserves the chance to know them though."

Hearing those words, I immediately recalled the way their voices cracked on the phone, the way they cried when they asked questions about their granddaughter... They were already in love with her, and they had only seen the photo I sent. "They want to be in her life. I can tell. They sounded so pleased when I agreed to meet in person."

"Look at you, defending them already." She laughed softly just as Gwen screamed with glee as she stomped in a puddle.

"Footprints, Daddy! Watch!" She ran onto the sidewalk,

slamming her feet down and laughing at the marks she had left. "I have big feet."

"Yes, you do, Gwennie." Charlotte bent down and ruffled her hair. "You are so cute. Could you be any cuter? Any more creative and wilder?"

"Nope. I'm perfect. That's what my daddy says." My daughter beamed with her toothy smile.

I snorted.

"I love your self-confidence, missy. It's super important to be proud of yourself."

Gwen spun in a circle, just as a car door shut. I glanced toward the parking lot as a man and woman walked toward us. Instantly, I knew it was them. My skin prickled with nerves, and my heart thudded. Sarah had the same dark hair that Gwen did, her eyes brown, and the same chin.

Gwen didn't resemble my mom at all, so it was cool to see the resemblance immediately.

"Hey," Charlotte said to me, "I'm going to take her to the swings. I love you. You can do this. Just find my hand if you need it, okay?"

I swallowed and then nodded.

Charlotte picked up Gwen and spun her around, the sounds of their combined laughter echoing off the sidewalk. My girls ran to the red swings, where Gwen dove onto one, gripping the chains as she tried swinging herself. Charlotte made a big scene, pretending not to be able to push her because Gwen was so big.

I waited. This was more tense than any game I had ever played. Even though I knew they would be safe, it was my instinct, my need, to protect my daughter. Most baggage came from Simone, that I knew, but as Sarah and Phillip approached, I tried my hardest to put myself in their shoes. They had missed out on so much already. This had to be just as hard for them.

"Hi, Hayden." Sarah greeted me with a shy smile. "It's so nice to meet you in person."

"You too." I shook her hand and then her husband's. "Both of you. Thank you for agreeing to meet here where Gwen loves to play."

"Phillip Barringer. And that little girl is our..." He trailed off, his voice cracking. "Granddaughter."

"That's her. Gwen Sarah Porter."

Sarah gasped. "That's her middle name?"

I nodded. "Simone might not have told you about her, but she obviously cared for you enough to include you in your granddaughter's name."

Sarah sniffed, and Phillip put his arm around her. "I can't believe we didn't know. I hope you believe us. We never would've missed out on...Look at her. She is beautiful."

Gwen squealed as Charlotte pretended to get hit with the swing. Gwen was into play kicking right now, and this was no different. Charlotte flailed her arms, her brown curly hair going in every direction as she played with my daughter.

"She's the best thing that's ever happened to me. You might've missed some moments, but you'll get all the new ones," I said, watching as their eyes filled with moisture.

"You want to go meet your grandparents?" Charlotte said, her voice carrying over the park with the breeze. "They look super nice. Hey, what should we call them? Gigi and Gee-paw are taken, so you gotta come up with supercool names."

"Oh yes!" Gwen clapped and waved. "They are here! For me! Do you think they'll like me?"

"Honey, they are going to love you." Charlotte got onto her knees and brushed my daughter's hair behind her ears. I loved how she always met Gwen at eye level, speaking kindly to her and never making her feel small.

"Who is that with her?" Sarah asked softly. "She's so good with her."

"My future fiancée, Charlotte."

Sarah smiled. "I'm so happy you have someone, and someone who clearly loves Gwen. I hope you know, Hayden, that Phillip and I want to be a part of Gwen's life for the long haul. I know it'll take some time to trust us, but we'll be here. We aren't going away. You've clearly done an awesome job with her. She's lucky to have you."

I nodded, the emotions swelling in the back of my throat. "Thank you for saying that."

"Are you my grandma?" Gwen walked right up to Sarah, her nose scrunching as she grabbed Charlotte's hand. "Lotte said I have to come up with a name for you. I have a Gigi already."

Sarah crouched down, mud getting on the hem of her pants, but she didn't seem to care. "I am your grandma, and this is your grandpa. We can go by many names. Grandma Sarah, Grandpa Phillip..."

"Sarah. My middle name is Sarah." Gwen grinned, her slight shyness disappearing. "Gwen Sarah Porter."

"I know! You have a wonderful name."

"Thanks, Grandma." Gwen tugged Charlotte's hand down as she attempted to whisper. "Can I play with them?"

We all heard, and Phillip chuckled. He lowered himself too. "Your dad told us you love the swings. Could you show us how high you like to go?"

"Yes!" Gwen let go of Charlotte's hand and held it out to Phillip. "Come watch! Watch me!"

"She called me Grandma." Sarah's eyes watered as she shared a look with Phillip. Gwen just had a gift of bringing people together, and my chest swelled with pride. My daughter was fearless and kind.

"Yes, come on, Grandma. My Gigi takes forever too sometimes." Gwen held out her other hand to Sarah, who took it.

"It's nice to meet you, Charlotte." Sarah smiled at her and then focused on Gwen.

The three of them walked toward the swings, leaving Charlotte standing next to me. I put my arm around her, holding her close and breathing in her comforting perfume. "Thank you for being here."

"Hayden, there is nowhere I'd rather be than with you and Gwen. Look at how happy she is!" Charlotte rested her head on my shoulder, squeezing around my middle. "Sarah and Phillip look smitten with her. I mean, can you blame them? Gwen is the cutest thing in the world."

"I like them." My voice came out gruff, but I didn't care. Charlotte was my person, the one I could show feelings to and express what I felt without judgment. Since falling in love with her and being open about it, things just fell into place, like my life needed her in it to make sense.

"They seem so genuine," Charlotte said.

I sighed, content watching Simone's parents play with my daughter. It was strange. Simone had called me yesterday and thanked me for letting her parents meet her, which was silly. Simone still didn't get it. I'd never keep people out of Gwen's life who wanted to be in it. I just had to trust them, and I didn't trust Simone.

She'd either want to stay or not, and with Charlotte by my side, I wasn't worried about it anymore. I wouldn't pressure Simone, and the day she opted in, I'd work out a plan with her.

"We should invite them over for dinner next weekend. Christian and Penny will be there, and I think it'll make Sarah and Phillip happy to see Gwen being loved by everyone. I can make those appetizers you like, and Gwen can show off all her stuff. Wait, that's at your house though. If you're not ready for them to come to your place, I can host!"

"You're amazing." I kissed the top of her head. "That sounds like a great idea, and I think my house is fine. I wish you lived with us already."

"Hayden." She swatted my chest, her smile widening. "It's been like five seconds. We'll get there."

"I'm selfish and want you around all the time." It was true. My attraction and love for her only deepened, and while I hated every time she wasn't at home, I respected her space. Our house just felt different without her there. Gwen missed her; I missed her. She had somehow ingrained herself into our damn souls within a few weeks, and wouldn't it be easier for us to just live together?

"Is it because you want my closet? You can have it."

She rolled her eyes, her lips quirking up. "I plan to, even if I don't live there."

"Fuck, I love you." I wanted to kiss her, but it didn't seem appropriate with Sarah and Phillip just a few yards away. Phillip pushed Gwen on the swing while Sarah stood to the side, cheering her on.

"I love you too." Charlotte gave me *that* look, the one she reserved just for me that made me feel a million feet tall and like I could do anything in the world. Her eyes widened, and her cheeks reddened, and her gaze swirled with love and pride. My heart always skipped a beat when she stared at me like that, and I twisted my pinky around hers.

One day, she'd be my wife. One day, she'd move in with us. And maybe, one day, we'd give Gwen some siblings to love on.

"Don't cry, Grandma! Swings are fun." Gwen stood in the mulch with her face twisted with worry. "Why you sad?"

Sarah sniffed and kneeled, her watery smile visible even from where we stood. "I'm so happy to meet you, sometimes joy makes me cry."

"My daddy gives me hugs when I cry. Do you need one?"

Sarah's voice shook when she said, "I'd love one."

Gwen launched herself into Sarah's arms, and fuck. My eyes prickled with tears too, as my baby girl had already given Sarah her heart. Sarah cradled my daughter's head, her eyes closed as she squeezed her back, and I just knew. I knew they were good people.

"This was the right move. It might be hard and weird feeling, but it's the right choice, and I admire your strength.

You're a good father, Hayden." Charlotte squeezed my pinky before letting go.

Gwen asked everyone to play tag, and Phillip was the first to chase her. Sarah, Charlotte, Phillip, and I let a three-year-old boss us around, but man, she was a cute, little bossy thing. She laughed harder than I had heard in a while, and after twenty minutes of it, my smile grew.

Family was such a strange word. Some of it was by blood, by birth. Like Gwen and me. And Sarah and Phillip. But other times, it was the Calhouns, choosing to be a part of Gwen's life. It was funny how a month ago, I had been stressed about my parents leaving and how Gwen was going to do, and look at her now. Surrounded by people who loved her.

I meant what I told Sarah and Phillip—Charlotte was my future wife, and seeing her now, with the parents of my ex? Laughing and encouraging me? She was an angel. She was the perfect woman for me, and I was gonna spend the rest of my life showing her how much I loved her.

I just had to plan the right time to propose...

CHAPTER THIRTY-THREE

HAYDEN

Ten months later...

Three things were evident since Christian and Penny's wedding. The first—I needed therapy if I had any hope of being a good long-term partner. Despite having phenomenal parents and a kick-ass support system of friends, there were parts of myself I had to work on. Navigating this new path with Simone's parents in the picture was a lot to handle. Charlotte helped but that wasn't her role. I had to deal with this on my own.

It sucked. Not gonna lie. I hated opening up and revealing vulnerable parts of myself. But I learned that wedding night that I wanted to commit to Charlotte, and it wouldn't be fair to her if I didn't work on myself too. She supported me the whole way and encouraged me on days when it seemed like too much.

The second thing was that I never had to make a permanent decision about Simone. She agreed to go to therapy before attempting to meet Gwen, but a few weeks in, she took off to Europe with friends to find herself again. I had refused to convince her to be in Gwen's life. Gwen would want to learn about her birth mom someday, and Sarah and Phillip could help her.

Her parents had been a pleasant surprise though. Charlotte and I had monthly dinners with them, and things were going well. Gwen thought they were awesome, and that's all that mattered.

The third thing was making Charlotte my wife. I wanted her to be my partner more than I could breathe. I wanted to see my ring—the one I held in my hand right now—on her finger and her in a wedding dress. I wanted Gwen and me to wait for her down the aisle as we asked her to be our family. She owned half my closet already, and Gwen was so used to seeing her in the morning that there would be no change once Charlotte actually moved in and accepted my proposal.

Had I asked her to move in a million times? Yes.

To marry me? Also, yes.

But those were when we were naked or laughing. Charlotte said she wanted the whole production, and she deserved it. She taught me how to love openly and how being vulnerable was a gift, not a burden.

She was perfect for me. That sentence was still true to this day. She brought me out of my shell and loved me so much that I didn't know it was possible to be this happy.

On days I could get away in time, I'd often volunteer to run the scoreboard for her junior high team. I loved the sounds of the game and getting to watch her coach. She lit up on the field, her whole personality shining as girls surrounded her. Did this town expect her to take their eighth-grade softball team to the state finals? No.

Did Charlotte think she could do it? Absolutely.

At today's game, it was the bottom of the seventh. Her team was up one run, and the opposing team had a runner on third. Our pitcher, Mack, was exhausted, but she was still throwing well. Charlotte signaled something from the dugout, and Mack nodded.

If they won this game, they were in the championship.

"You got it, Mack," I shouted from the press box. It was a nice setup because it was shared with the high school. Their sound system was top-notch, something I was going to use to my advantage as soon as they won this game.

Because they needed a win, or I wouldn't propose. Something about the right timing and all.

Mom: Has she won yet?

Christian: HAVE YOU DONE IT

Penny: Who cares if they lose, just propose I'm sick of keeping this secret.

Garrett: Don't do it if they lose, that's not a great idea

Christian: Hard agree, pen. They need the W

Dad: She'll say yes! I know it!

Garrett: Look at this onesie I bought Graham?

Garrett sent a photo that read just escaped nine months locked up for baby Graham. Penny and Christian had made me an uncle to the cutest baby boy. Gwen was obsessed with him too. Kept asking for a new baby for herself, which made me think of Charlotte.

I knew she'd say yes. She showed me every day she chose me and wanted a life together. But our timing was everything, and there was no time like the present.

I tensed as Mack threw the third and final strike, abandoning the runner on third and securing the win. Coach Calhoun was going to the championship. The balloon of pride almost had me welling up. She had a vision and brought it to life her first year.

Oh. The best part? Chad had a terrible first year at the high school level and had the audacity to ask her to help and be his assistant coach. He asked her yesterday, right in the middle of middle school playoffs. She rightfully told him to piss off until this season was done.

I voted for turning it down. Charlotte was on the fence. He didn't deserve her, but I'd let her make her own decision there. I was her cheerleader no matter what she did. I always would be.

Now it was my game time.

I tapped the mic, the loud thud echoing through the speakers. "Congrats on the win, Bulldogs!"

Everyone cheered, and Charlotte looked up at me with the goofiest smile on her face. That was my woman.

"Now, I have a very important question for Coach Calhoun. Can you go look at home plate for me?"

She tilted her head, holding a hand over her forehead to shield the sun. *What?* she mouthed.

"You heard me. Go home."

She smirked, like she knew what I was doing. Good. Let her enjoy this. She deserved all the attention and love. The girls all waited with huge smiles as she jogged toward home plate. I had paid the umpire to do this, because there was no way I could sneak onto the field unnoticed, so he had placed the key ring there for me as soon as no one was paying attention.

"Please move in with me, with Gwen. I love you and want you in our home. That is a key to our house with a key chain from Gwen and me."

Charlotte held it in her hands, her slight headshake telling me she was surprised. Gwen picked a pretty purple beaded one with softballs on the end, and I chose a snowball with the year. She was balling it up as a coach, and I wanted to be cheesy for her.

"I need an answer. Breathe if it's yes."

Everyone laughed. But I waited.

She looked up at the press box and rolled her eyes. "Fine."

"You hear that, folks? I poured out my soul, and she said *fine*. Better than a no, I guess." I paused for the crowd to react. "For this next activity, could you please go look on the center of the diamond, Coach Calhoun?"

She sighed, like she was annoyed with my antics, but I was ready. I was more than ready. The same umpire made it look like he was clearing the pitching mound, but he had set the ring on the center of it. A little risky, but worth it.

She stilled once she realized what it was.

"Will you marry me?" I asked into the mic.

She picked it up and stared at it before glancing up at the press box. She shouted something but I couldn't quite make it out. *Please be a yes, please be a yes.*

"Was that a yes?"

The crowd hollered now. I opened the window. "Ask me to my face!" she yelled, cupping her hands around her mouth.

Oh. Of course.

I jogged down the stairs, through the door, and over to the third base dugout fence as everyone cheered. The cool October air hit my skin as I approached Charlotte. She looked fierce, confident, and beautiful. A sparkle danced in her eyes, like this amused her.

My gut settled. I had chosen this proposal because I knew she'd enjoy it. And just like that, seeing her smile at me as I neared her, my nerves disappeared. The last ten months had been the best of my life. Laughter came easy, and talking about feelings wasn't painful.

I even maybe kinda sorta was proud of myself.

"Charlotte," I said, fighting a smile. The field smelled like dirt and popcorn, and the wind whipped her hair around from her ponytail. I gently pushed some wild hair behind her ear, my heart racing. "I want you to be my wife. Will you please marry me?"

She glanced at the ground, arching a brow.

"Ah, of course." I laughed now. My stubborn-as-hell woman wanted the whole on-the-knee thing. I crouched and took the ring she held in her hands. From this angle, the nerves returned, but they were the healthy kind. We'd talk about this moment forever, telling our friends and family and future kids. I'd do whatever she wanted, as long as she said yes.

"I like when you look up at me," she whispered, her eyes glistening. "If you know what I mean."

"I know what you mean." I shook my head, snorting. I spent a lot of time on my knees around her. "Now, I'm going to ask this one more time, and you're going to say yes and put me out of my misery. Charlotte Calhoun, will you please marry me?"

"Yes. I think I will."

I took her left hand, slid the ring on her finger, and pulled her in for a kiss. The crowd cheered, and the girls all swarmed us, clapping and squealing. Charlotte giggled against my mouth, her hands trembling as she gripped the collar of my jacket.

"Does this match your dream proposal?"

"This is better." She nuzzled me. "So much better. Marrying you is the dream come true, Hayden. I can't wait to love you forever."

Charlotte might've won the game, but I was the real winner here. She had taught me to believe those words.

She would love me and push me and help me grow. Not that it was a competition, but I was coming out on top with the real prize. I got to be with this woman, and I'd never let her forget how much she meant to me. That was a promise.

ACKNOWLEDGMENTS

I can't start this acknowledgment section without mentioning Rachel! There are three very special Rachels in my life who just make writing so much more fun.

Having people who tell you when your stuff is good, and when it's bad, is hard. Rachel Rumble, you wonderful human being. Thank you for being my friend. I've loved how our friendship has grown the last few years, and this story wouldn't have happened without you. Truly. Hugs hugs hugs hugs hugs. (Are you uncomfortable yet?)

I still can't believe a Twitter hashtag brought us together, but Rachel Reiss, you are the GOAT of tearing my manuscript apart. Thank you for letting me email you in all caps panicking or using only symbols as a reaction. Having writing friends makes this life so much better, and I am so grateful for you. I love reading your words and am already salivating for another story of yours.

A huge thanks and hug to Rachel Gross, who always celebrates this part of my life with me. It's not every day you get to talk about writing romance at your day job, but you've never made me feel anything but amazing by supporting me. You've helped me understand, and believe, that you can be a badass at work and be a badass mom. It's not an either/or situation, and that has been a game changer for me.

Mikaela Brown and Avery Keelan, thank you SO much for always being available for me to slide into your DMs for a rant or question. I'm so glad the world brought us together.

The team at Forever is one of the best. I'm very grateful to work with them and be a part of the Forever family. Dana and Estelle—adore you both! A huge thanks to Alex Logan, my editor, for working through this story with me. This story was hard. Not gonna lie. I've never had to revise, edit, change, delete, rewrite, cry, drink wine, repeat so much on a story before. This book challenged me, and I'll always be grateful for your patience and nudging. I am obsessed with Char, Hayden, and Gwen now, and this story wouldn't be what it is without you.

Haley W., Brandon G., Joe W., Luke A., Sarah P., Tom H., Mike S. . . . thanks for letting me share this part of my life at work. It means so much to me that you are all so supportive. I'm super lucky. Just stay on my good side so your names don't become the villains'. I'm not beneath doing that.

I'll always be grateful to Cathie Armstrong and Jessica Faust for listening and for answering questions and helping me navigate this publishing world. It can seem so scary, but when you have the right partner, it makes all the difference.

Finally, I can't write these acknowledgments without talking about my husband. This is a love story to you as a father to our kiddos. Navigating this whole parenting thing (#teamnosleep) is wild, but watching you love our family is one of the best things ever. Every interaction Hayden has with Gwen is just some variation of you with our kids. Funnily enough, those scenes with Gwen? Easiest parts to write. Thank you for letting me hide in the other room to write this story (twice). Thank you for helping me when I wanted to toss my computer outside. And thank you for pushing me when I'm stuck.

Thanks to you, dear reader. I hope you enjoyed Char and Hayden's (and Gwen's) story. It has a special place in my heart, so thank you so much for reading. I wouldn't be able to write these stories without you.

ABOUT THE AUTHOR

Jaqueline Snowe lives in Arizona, where the "dry heat" really isn't that bad. She prefers drinking coffee all hours of the day and snacking on anything that has peanut butter or chocolate. She is the mother to two fur-babies who don't realize they aren't humans and a mom to the sweetest son and daughter. She is an avid reader and writer of romances and tends to write about athletes. Her husband works for an MLB team (not a player, lol) so she knows more about baseball than any human ever should.